Skeleton Crew Press
www.cosmicfs.com

CAMBIO

The illustrations were made with Blender and finished off with Pixelmator.

Edited by Miss Doris Low

First edition 2012

10 9 8 7 6 5 4 3 2 1

ISBN no. 9780615688992

AUTHOR'S NOTE

The following story is a work of fiction. Some of the major characters although made up, are named after my friends; some here, some now on the other side. My use of their names are in a tribute to them.

Most of this story takes place in a town called Rota in the province of Cadiz, in southern Spain. If you ever get a tingle to see a beautiful place in Spain, this is truly a great place to go.

CAMBIO

Dear Michaela,

I hope you enjoy the story. Eventually, I'll get "Wickeder" finished too!

Love,

Nick

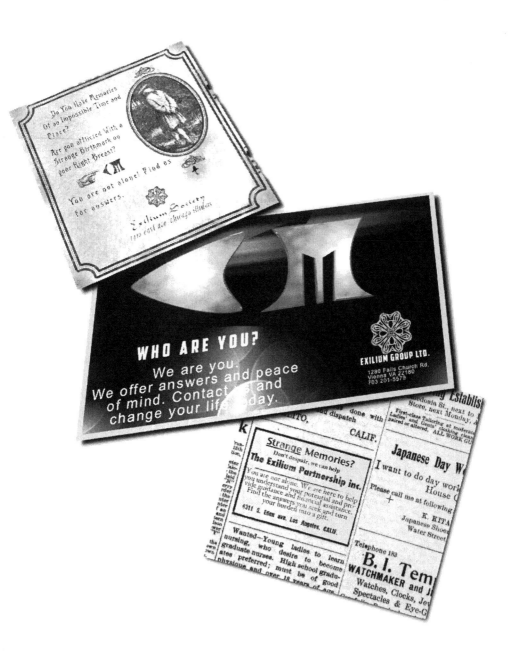

Do You Have Memories Of an Impossible Time and Place?

Are you afflicted With a Strange Birthmark on your Right Breast?

You are not alone! Find us for answers.

Exilium Society
110 east ave chicago illinois

WHO ARE YOU?
We are you.
We offer answers and peace of mind. Contact us and change your life today.

EXILIUM GROUP LTD.
1280 Falls Church Rd.
Vienna VA 22180
703 201-5579

Strange Memories?
Don't despair, we can help
The Exilium Partnership inc.
You are not alone. We are here to help you understand your potential and provide guidance and financial assistance. Find the answers you seek and turn your burden into a gift.
6311 S. Ellen ave. Los Angeles, CALIF.

Wanted—Young ladies to learn nursing, who desire to become graduate nurses. High school graduates preferred; must be of good physique and over 18 years of age.

Japanese Day W
I want to do day work
House C

Please call me at following

K. KITA
Japanese Shoes
Water Street

Telephone 183
B. I. Tem
WATCHMAKER and J
Watches, Clocks, Je
Spectacles & Eye-G

```
RTTUZYUW RUEKFOS0565 0172249-SSSS-RUQYSDG.
ZNR SSSSS
Z 172249Z JAN 87
FM FOSIF ROTA SP
TO RUEALGX/JOINT STAFF WASHINGTON DC
RHDLCNE/CINCUSNAVEUR LONDON UK//N2//N22
RUSNNOA/USCINCEUR VAIHINGEN GE
RUFTAKA/CDR USAINTELCTRE HEIDELBERG GE
RUFRQJQ/COMSIXTHFLT
RHEHAAA/WHITE HOUSE SITUATION ROOM
INFO RUFGAID/USEUCOM AIDES VAIHINGEN GE
RUEAIJU/NPIC
RUETIAA/DIRNSA
RUEHC/DEPT OF STATE//FOR INR
RUEKJCS/DIA WASHINGTON DC
REUNAAA/CNO WASHINGTON DC
RUCNFB/FEDERAL BUREAU OF INVESTIGATION
HQ USAFE RAMSTEIN AB GE//IN
USCINCCENT INTELCN MACDILL AFB FL//CCJ2-JIW/CCJ2
Z 172249Z JAN 87
BT
A. FOSIF ROTA SP 131201Z JAN 87
B. FOSIF ROTA SP 171632Z JAN 87
S E C R E T
MSGID/SPOT/FOSIF/04/JAN
SUBJ: NAVSTA ROTA SP OVERRUN
1. (S) COMPANY F MARINES REPORTED BEING OVERRUN IN THEIR ESTABLISHED
POSITIONS AT APPROX 2300Z BY UNKNOWN ASSAILANTS FROM OUTSIDE THE
NAVSTA PRIMARY GATE. CURRENT CASUALTIES APPEAR TO BE LOCAL GUARDIA
CIVIL, SPANISH POLICE, COMPANY F SECURITY FORCES (USMC) AND ELEMENTS
OF SEAL TEAM TWO.
2. (S) AS PER REFS A/B, THE ASSAILANTS APPEAR TO BE NON-HUMAN ATT.
ATTEMPTS TO DRIVE AWAY WITH WARNING SHOTS UNSUCCESSFUL UPON FIRST
CONTACT AND NUMBERS APPEAR TO BE IN THE SEVERAL HUNDREDS.
3. (S) FIGHTING APPEARS TO BE CONTAINED AT THE MAIN GATE AND
FOSIF/NAVCOMSTA BUILDINGS 533 AND 8 RESPECTIVELY CONTINUE TO BE
PROTECTED BY REMAINING COMPANY F SECURITY. BASE HOUSING IS BEING
EVACUATED AT THIS TIME AND ALL AMCITS MOVED TO THE FLIGHTLINE OF
VR22 SQUADRON FOR IMMEDIATE EVAC.
4. (S) REQUEST ASSISTANCE BY RAPID RESPONSE FORCES AND EMERGENCY
MEDICAL ASSISTANCE/EVAC FOR CASUALTIES.
5. (U) POC: LT R VERHOEF FOSIF IWO PHONE: 00 34 956 82 2217/2218
BT
#0565
ENDAT
DECL: OADR
```

NNNN

CONTENTS

CONTENTS cont.

Chapter One:
Service to the Emperor

216 B.C., Xianyang, East Asia

The Emperor's city had stood as a beacon, illuminating the rest of the world as a magnificent jewel-- glowing with art, ideas and natural beauty. At the time, this single city had the highest concentration of science and discovery within its high walls. During the span of a single year, the city became engulfed in worry, desperation and growing panic. The parks and villages that were once bathed in the music of birdsong now stood stark and hollow. The birds were the first to feel the advancing darkness and had fled, leaving mankind to fend for themselves. Fountains that entertained the eye with lively cascades of water, now stood dry, silent and slowly refilling with dust. The channels of water had been diverted and filled countless barrels that stood at the ready inside the fortress. The jewel ceased to shine and instead took on the shakiness and pallor of a starving, overworked horse that life's beatings had brought to the edge of an almost welcome death.

Concentric walls and courtyards surrounded the Emperor's inner fortress. Just inside the fourth courtyard, stood a tall man outside an enormous black door. The door was over twenty feet high, made of ironwood and thicker than the girth of three men. The man waiting outside was a foreigner, but dressed himself in the clothes of an upper-caste member of the Emperor's society. Between the man and the door stood a tight row of foot soldiers, expressionless and wearing full battle armor with their swords partially drawn-- no more and no less than the width of a man's thumb from the scabbard. A red sash adorned their waists as a mark of the Emperor's trust—each had proven their skill and honor in battle.

The foreigner's name was Danhieras and for his precious time being wasted, was beside himself in fury. Although his eyes flitted over the helmets of the warriors in front of him and around the thick, black door, he saw neither—he simmered in his anger to have been pulled from his important work at the whim of a mere human. The advancing darkness occupied his only thoughts for the past year—at first he limited his sleep to five hours per day. Now, he would only sleep three —it tended to make him irritable and his tirades were boundless.

He had waited for twenty minutes to get through the previous door as the Emperor's Chamberlains acted out their individual roles, announcing in established hierarchy the visitors that are granted trust to pass to the inner chamber of the fortress. He had little patience for oriental culture and language—most here could not even pronounce his name, instead calling him "magician" or "astrologer". He was neither of these. He existed long before the enlightenment of man, trapped in a human form and incarcerated in this world.

Someone rapped twice on the inside of the door and the guards sheathed their swords and stepped aside. The creaking of pulleys and meshing of wooden cogs preceded the door's opening, revealing the wrinkled, sneering face of Hsu. Hsu was one of eight chief Chamberlains, trusted to screen all visitors to the inner chamber. He wore the traditional black robe as all Chamberlains wore, the better to remain unseen and not to disturb the view of the Emperor. Due to his senior position, his sleeves enjoyed a contrasting gold stripe that circled the cuff. "To your knees, dog."

Danhieras' eyes narrowed and he clenched his fists. "I prostate myself to no one," said the foreigner, holding up the wood calling token bearing the painted mark of Emperor Shi Huangdi. "Not even to *your* master. Now step aside or I'll tell him of your insults to his honored guest."

Hsu's sneer dropped to a scowl. "No one enters here," said Hsu, pointing the tip of his rattan staff at Danhieras' face. "...without first passing my scrutiny. Now remove your clothes so that I do not mistakenly identify you as a lowly assassin!"

Danhieras had heard enough of Hsu's sarcasm to last this and many more lifetimes. "I said step aside, Hsu. I don't have time to waste."

Hsu struck the floor with the cane. "Very well! If you refuse to be tested as an assassin, you will be treated as one! Guards! Do not allow this criminal to pass or leave!" The door slid shut and the guards shuffled back in their original positions, halfway drawing their swords.

"Hsu!" shouted Danhieras, "Open this damned door you rat-faced degenerate!"

The guards that usually stare straight ahead now watched the raving foreigner with nervous concern.

He could hear the retreating clack of Hsu's cane striking against the floor. "Enough!" growled Danhieras, pulling his loose sleeves up around his elbows. He outstretched his right arm and slowly unfolded his palm towards the floor. After clearing his throat he began a low hum while concentrating on the space between his hand and the stone floor. When his low hum began to resonate, he broke into strange words. The thick wood beams overhead began to creak and pop, causing dust motes to cascade downwards. The guards stirred while watching the foreigner speak to the floor—strange stories circulated about the man who could produce flame at will but not get burnt.

His voice rose until a spot in the floor began to glow. The glow increased in brightness and began to flash with the intensity of lightning. "Goodbye boys!" He let his arm fall to his side and stepped forward. A brilliant flash of lightning crashed and the foreigner was gone. The stink of sulfur hung in the air and the ears of the guards rang from the terrible thunderclap. None dared move—their job was to prevent anyone uninvited from accessing the door. To leave it unprotected meant execution.

Emperor Shi Huangdi sat on his low chair, dressed in his battle uniform, as he has done since rumors of the approaching black hordes began to reach the city. He had not journeyed outside of the outer fortress walls in several months and had recently increased the number of fortress guards from two hundred to three thousand. In front of him, rested two battle-worn swords, one long and heavy, pulled from the dead fingertips of General Kwai. The second was shorter but light and balanced—it worked best with enemies close by. Next to the rack was a quiver, stuffed with arrows made so perfectly that neither arrow varied from its neighbor more than the weight of the lightest feather. The bow rested behind the emperor's chair and was tested personally by him twice per day. If the cord broke the Chamberlain responsible and his entire family would be arrested. The weapon would then be tested with a new cord by executing the unfortunate Chamberlain and in turn, each of his family members.

Twenty lower Chamberlains knelt in a semi-circle sixty paces from the Emperor and with high, nervous voices, read scrolls on current events in his lands in front of large maps hanging from the ceiling.

The emperor contemplated with unease the latest news and lifted a cup of tea to his nose and inhaled the deep fragrance lofted by the steam.

An enormous crash shot through the room, deafening the Emperor while brilliant flashes of light left bright colored spots lingering in his eyes. Danhieras stood only a few inches away from the Emperor's shaking hand. The cup lay dashed on the floor in pieces and the foreigner's slippers were damp with spilled tea. "A thousand pardons, Emperor—I thought I'd end up a bit further back." Danhieras stepped backwards while rubbing his temples and squinting.

Chamberlains scattered towards the far doors screeching and tripping over themselves in hysteria. Emperor Shi Huangdi slowly placed a hand over his galloping heart while the color gradually returned to his face. The wailing cries of his Chamberlains molded his fright into burgeoning fury since none had attempted to rush to their master's aid. Standing, he shook his head, grunting in disappointment at Danhieras. "Silence!" Boomed the emperor. "All of you-- on your faces!" The hysterical men dropped in obedience and whimpered prone on the floor. "Your weakness is a disgrace and you shall all be scourged!"

The Emperor's anger began to abate and he wiped the sweat from his brow. He looked at the perspiration on the back of his hand and shot an angry look at Danhieras. "Why do you intrude so? Are you not disgraced as well?"

Danhieras winced from the Emperor's shouts and returned a pained look. "You can thank Hsu for that. Why do you insist on calling me, just to have me wait for an hour? By then you'll have forgotten why you called me in the first place."

The Emperor stood firm with his fists on his hips. "Do not speak down to me in front of these imbeciles!"

Danhieras looked into the Emperor's angry face and began to laugh. The Emperor's fury melted and he too broke into laughter. "My head is killing me," said Danhieras, "and your yelling isn't making it any better."

"You think *my* yelling was loud magician? Wait until you hear these monkeys scream in pain!" A low wail emanated from the men on the floor.

Two sharp raps echoed on the far door. It slid open revealing Hsu, kneeling low with his forehead touching the floor. He announced in a loud, wavering voice, "Divine Emperor, I have discovered that the foreigner plots to assassinate you and your son!"

The Emperor looked curiously at Danhieras who shrugged and rocked back and forth on his heels. "And where is this assassin, servant?"

Hsu replied in a confident voice, "I have him surrounded by guards who are ready to take his head by your blessed order."

The Emperor sat down on his chair and loudly clapped his hands together. "I am truly blessed to have a Chamberlain who is more effective than my top Generals! Rise servant!"

Hsu's face rose from the floor with toothless exuberance, only to be replaced with sinking fear when he saw Danhieras, smiling back at him.

"Come forth, servant," said the Emperor, his voice dripping with honey. "I have a task that requires your special talents."

Hsu's hands shook and his face drained of color. When he attempted to get to his feet his knees buckled, keeping him floundering on the floor. "M—my lord?"

The Emperor swept his index finger over the room towards the prone chamberlains. "You are to take these weeping old women to the square and have them whipped—each of them one hundred times! When it is over, you shall have a new job—to watch over that square so that no foreign assassins will ever escape your attentive gaze!"

Hsu knelt again, sobbing. "Please! Please!"

The Emperor shot to his feet. "Guards! When the last is whipped, mount this old fool's head on a spear in the center of the square so that he may remind the others against treachery. Carry out my orders!"

Soldiers flowed through the open door and lifted Hsu and the weeping Chamberlains and bustled them out the door. When they were gone, two guards remained in the chamber and sealed the door.

The Emperor looked over at his guest and noticed that he was still in pain. "Are you going to die, magician?"

"Oh, eventually Emperor." said Danhieras, massaging the back of his neck while grimacing. "—But probably not today." He hooked a thumb at the wall behind him. "For some time I've lost my touch going through walls and my head feels like it hit all of them on the way over. It does save time but I think I'll be *walking* back to my quarters. ...If you don't mind me asking—why was I summoned here today?" Danhieras opened his left palm and produced the wooden token, now charred and crumbling.

The Emperor clucked in disapproval and walked to the large map behind his seat. It showed the still unconquered regions that he intended to unify. "News of the black hordes," he tapped the map with his finger. "This time, only three day's journey from here."

The pain in Danhieras' head began to throb. "That doesn't leave me with much time. Have you sent out riders to investigate?"

The Emperor sat back down and nodded. "Twenty of my best. I fanned them out in an attempt to count the size of their army.

Danhieras looked at the map and saw the large red circles painted on nearby towns. "Have they begun making contact with the villagers?"

The Emperor gazed at the map for a few moments lost in thought and then lowered his eyes. "My riders have found those three villages razed to the ground. There were probably no survivors, as there were no bodies to count."

"Were there signs of fighting?" Asked Danhieras.

"Hardly. These people were mere serfs—farmers and the like. None had even the weapons to put up a fight. One of the comments my rider had was particularly disturbing. Some of the surviving farm animals were bitten by something."

"Bitten?" said Danhieras. "By humans or by other animals."

"It's hard to say. He said the bite marks didn't look human, and thick black liquid ran from their wounds. Worst of all, the animals that were affected were changing, and that even the sheep began feasting on their own flock."

Chapter Two:
Frank's Monkey

1986- Rota, Cadiz Spain

Jim Smith arrived at work just after 8:00. He was from the blue-sky corn fields of Iowa and tall like the rest of the Smith clan—he stood a few inches over six feet. Originally from farmer and coal-mining stock, he was built tough but with a soft heart. He was good natured and studious—he was the first in his family to earn a university degree and was now the sole representative of the Drug Enforcement Agency at the Naval Air Station in Rota Spain. He was rubbing the sleepiness out of his eyes when Chief Simmons walked into his office with a troubled look on his face.

"Jim, can I talk to you about Norton?"

Jim sat back expecting to hear another sordid story about how Norton, a notoriously mischievous Petty Officer was caught drunk on duty.

"C'mon in Deron—what's he done now?"

Chief Simmons sat down in the chair opposite and exhaled. "He's busted up really bad in the hospital. He went out drinking, and squared up against a real animal. This guy not only gave him a hell of a beating, but made him eat broken glass."

Jim sat up straight. "Good God! Who the hell was this?"

Chief Simmons shook his head and said, "That's just it, the hard-headed dipshit isn't saying. He's just inches away from being medically discharged but he won't tell us squat. The rumor mill says it's one of the SEALs-- I'm hoping that you can find out who."

Jim sat back in his chair and drummed his fingers on his desktop. "Well, I do know their Officer in Charge-- Commander Frank Gutierrez. Since it's Wednesday, I'll be seeing him over at the *Hay Motivo* bar for lunch."

"How well do you know him—I'm just worried that these Special Forces guys will cover for each other."

Jim smiled at the inference that Frank was a lean & mean warrior. "Frank isn't a SEAL. He respects them enough, but he's more an underhanded efficiency expert that was sent out here to make something of them. I'm sure he'll deal with this appropriately."

At 12:30, Jim walked over to the small *Hay Motivo* bar. It was only open on Wednesdays, but was a great way to deal with the tension during the middle of the week. At only 600 pesetas per month, you could drink all the booze and eat all the tapas that you could hold.

As usual, Frank had gotten there earlier than Jim and was standing in the doorway holding his third beer. "Hello *Dickhead!*" he shouted grinning ear to ear.

Frank was a strange bird. He had gone bald in his early thirties and for spite, took it out on everyone else. He was jovial but loved to punch shoulders and swear. He sported a U.S.M.C. tattoo on his forearm from his first tour as a Marine. He was accepted into the Citadel and graduated, but didn't care to become a Marine officer. He was forced to serve his contracted time as a regular Navy sailor until his sea-dog skipper sent him off to Officer Candidate School. Since he's seen it all in one form or another, his bosses use him to turn troublesome commands around and make them productive. He was the Navy's enforcer. Since he knew how to read his audience, his foul language and methods rarely gotten him into trouble.

"Oh you pottymouth!" Jim sighed. "I see you you didn't come for the food!"

Frank let him in and placed his hand on the back of Jim's neck, steering him straight to the bar. Jim felt like a child in trouble, with his balding principal delivering him to detention—in this case, to help empty the bar.

During drinks, Jim politely waited after the first volley of 'Frank stories' and interrupted, "There's been a problem with one of your boys."

Frank sobered up and scrutinized Jim's face, "How bad is it?"

"One of *your* guys put one of ours in the hospital and he's a real featherweight. He's messed up-- and was even fed broken glass from a beer bottle."

Frank set his drink down and automatically retrieved his hat from his belt line. "Come back with me. I've got a feeling I know who's responsible."

As they walked out towards Frank's car, he continued, "One of my newer guys has been trying to prove his mettle towards the others and has been trying to pick fights with anyone he can. All he does is brag about his victims and from what I've been hearing, he's one cruel bastard."

When they arrived at the SEAL administrative building, they walked down the hallway to the main office. In the center, there were two desks stuck together. An older lady in civilian clothes typed away on a rust colored IBM Selectric-II typewriter. Sitting across from her was a sailor in dungarees, flipping through an electronics magazine.

The secretary was slim with short white hair and wearing turqoise earrings shaped like marijuana leaves. She looked up, grasped the lit cigarette out of her mouth and parked it onto a nearby ashtray. "*Hell.* You're back early."

"Jim, Ruth. Ruth, this is Jim. Ruth? Jim works for the DEA and will seriously bust your ass for wearing drug paraphernalia."

"We've met Frank." She noticed that Jim was looking at her earrings. "My grandson picked them out for me when he was four—thought they were pretty. I shall forever wear them with pride. Got any kids yourself Jim?"

Jim smiled. "Yes. A girl. She's six months old now."

Ruth nodded. "Children are the innocent lambs of the human race. Just don't name any of them Francis—like that prick."

Frank took that queue to head to his office. "Oh Ruth? Any calls?"

Ruth took the cigarette out of the ashtray, pulled her lungs full of nicotine and looked at him, exhaling with contempt. "Jesus. Who would intentionally call you?"

"Cute." Frank invited Jim through the double swinging doors that entered into the office. The louvered doors looked like an actual bar from the old west. Jim really liked Frank's office because it was filled with uncommon things such as ancient maps, Soviet relics and bizarre items that could only be seen in a sideshow.

On his wall, Frank had two human scalps that came from an old museum that went out of business, as well as a jar stuffed with a two-headed cat basking in formaldehyde. On the near wall were iron manacles from an old slaver ship as well as various rope decorations fabricated from sailor knots. One that took Jim's interest was the 'Monkey's Fist', a two-foot knotted rope that was held by a loop and on the other end was a three-inch iron cannonball encased in intricate knots. It was used to stop mutinies by swinging it around at anyone that gets in your way. It appeared quite old from the reddish stains on the bottom side. *Rust never sleeps*, thought Jim.

Frank sat down behind his huge, wood desk and yelled, "Boardman! Get your ass in here!"

Frank pulled out a cigarette and stuck it in his mouth.

A lanky sailor in dungarees with round spectacles walked through the doors and looked at both men. "What?"

"That's 'What *Sir*'!" Yelled Frank pointing to his cigarette. Boardman rolled his eyes and walked over to Frank's desk, and let out an audible sigh. He reached over to pick up the grenade-shaped lighter from desk, sitting only an inch away from Frank's tapping fingers.

He lit the lighter and placed it before Frank's cigarette and said in a dopey tone, "Frank, you want me to get your friend anything?"

Frank sputtered, and tore the cigarette out of his mouth, "That's *Commander* or *Sir*!" He blew a lungful of smoke into the sailor's face. "…Fuck off Boardman." The sailor shuffled out of the room shaking his head.

"What was that about?" asked Jim with a wry smile on his face.

Frank sat back displaying growing amusement, "That fucking kid—his sweet Mama, the US Navy, spent a mint to send him to specialist courses to make advanced weapons and explosives and *then* he receives a job offer from a weapons manufacturer for almost twice what I make! He was one of the few the Navy chose to provide flexibility to forward deployed SEAL teams. He has a background in electronics, physics, math *and* machining. He was sent to Smith & Wesson for three months to learn how to design firearms from scratch, Ford Aerospace to learn how to machine metals like ti-fucking-tanium and then off to Fort Bragg to learn explosives and propellants."

Jim broke in, "And so now he lights your cigarettes?"

Frank sat forward in his chair, "That prick blew up my new quonset hut by testing a new type of tracer bullet! It was going to be my new officer's lounge! Besides, he was fired by the time I arrived and by then he had his… *attitude*. He's been letting everyone know that he's getting out and stuck his shitty little offer letter in my face. Since then, I've made him *my* bitch."

"Boardman!" screeched Frank almost shaking out of his chair. Boardman walked back in, his head at an angle and a face exuding impatience with his boss. "Yes …Sir?" The *sir* was almost too late as Frank was just getting to launch out of his chair. Frank slowly reclined back, belched and said, "Go out to the the staff office and tell Petty Officer O'Neil that I want to see him."

Boardman performed a Benny Hill salute (making Frank's eyes bug out and face turn red) and said "Aye Aye!" He turned around and walked through the bar room doors just before one of Frank's topless hula dancer paperweights flew past his head.

"I really love screwing with him!" said Frank straightening his desk and shaking his head.

After ten minutes, there was a knock outside Frank's office. A large sailor wearing exercise shorts and T-shirt walked in and said, "Sir, you wanted to see me?"

Frank put on his serious, but uninterested look on his face and continued straightening his desk as he spoke, "Word on the street was that you were involved in a brawl last night."

The sailor put on a bland smile and shook his head, "No sir, just a little misunderstanding."

Frank locked his eyes on O'Neil with visible disapproval on his face, "Apparently, you messed this boy up and forced him to swallow glass. There were several witnesses that say you started the whole thing."

O'Neil smacked his lips twice and looked at the ceiling, "He could have just walked away and nothing would have happened. This sounds like sour grapes to me."

Frank got up, sticking his chest out, "You sound like you want to fight someone a bit tougher... more of a challenge perhaps — someone like me?"

The Sailor looked mildly shocked, "No sir." He said, in a measured tone. "I won't make a mistake with you because of those oak leaves. Besides, you don't know who you're dealing with."

Jim sat glued to his chair with eyes as big as saucers. O'Neil was almost a full head taller than Frank and each of his arms were larger than both of Frank's combined. Frank had a small potbelly hanging over his belt, but he was probably just half the larger man's weight. Frank was going to get killed.

Frank smiled, rubbing his hands together, "No problem O'Neil. There's no rank involved and no rules, you can do what you want to me and I won't tell. Let's take this outside and may the best man win."

O'Neil put an assured smirk on his face, did an about face and began to depart Frank's office. In a flash, Frank grabbed the Monkey's

Fist off the wall and swung it at a fierce arc towards O'Neil's neck, driving him into the door jam with such force that O'Neil tore one of the swinging doors off its hinges. Jim could only look on with horror as Frank swung the Fist again and again into O'Neil's ribs and abdomen. O'Neil was in the fetal position on the floor with his face contorted in pain—he no longer resembled a cocky warrior but of a frightened child laying in front of an advancing steam roller.

Frank stopped and shifted the Fist into his left hand. "Oh my God!" He said, in a quavering voice. "What have I done?" He held out his right hand to help pick O'Neil up off the floor and gradually helped get him back on his feet. "I'm sorry! I'm so sorry! Are you OK? Here —let's get you into this chair."

Frank immediately swung the Monkey's Fist back and slammed it between O'Neil's shoulder blades, hurling him out of the chair and headlong into Frank's huge oak desk. As O'Neil slid slowly to the floor in a stupor, Frank dropped the Monkey's Fist and began pounding his own fists into O'Neil's face, breaking his nose and swelling both of his eyes.

When it was apparent that O'Neil was no longer conscious, Frank stood up and wiped the sweat off his brow. He picked the Fist up off the floor and placed it back on the wall. The savage attack only lasted for about ten seconds, but O'Neil was turned from bully to broken wreck. Jim looked at the Monkey's Fist as it slowly rotated to a stop on the wall, fresh blood shined on the dingy cords. It finally dawned on him that it wasn't rust after all.

Frank sat back down, panting heavily and calling, "Boardman!" with a breathless shout. When Boardman walked in, his eyes bulged. "Frank! Are you all right? What in hell happened?"

Frank looked sideways at Jim with resignation on his face and said in a low, patient voice, "*Commander* or *Sir*, and yes, I'm fine. Please call the hospital and let them know that this ...*asshole* tripped and has a boo-boo. See if they can send over a corpsman and check him over."

Boardman skipped the usual bear baiting with Frank and ran out to his desk to call the hospital.

Jim still looked stunned and said, "Frank, what good will this have done? Now there's going to be two injured sailors at the hospital."

Frank looked at Jim with a raised eyebrow as he lit another cigarette. His breathing was still heavy and sported glistening droplets of sweat on his bald pate. "Trust me, 'Punkin. This guy would have gotten off anyways. Bullies usually antagonize the witnesses, so take it from me-- every bully lies. The only way to make them see the light is to feed them their same medicine." Frank brightened up, "Besides, I figure, one or two more times with my 'equalizer' and he'll be as peaceful as a lamb."

Jim was out of his chair, standing over O'Neil, making sure that he was still breathing. O'Neil let out of couple of moans and a shoeless foot trembled slightly, but he seemed alive.

"Shit, Jim! Will-you-relax?" barked Frank. "I didn't hurt him that bad. I left him in better condition that your friend at the hospital."

Jim didn't feel better from Frank's medical diagnosis—he felt relieved when a corpsman arrived and started checking O'Neil. He wiped up some of his bloody face with disposable wipes and then broke an ammonia capsule under his nose. After a few seconds, O'Neil began to stir. The corpsman gave a few concerned glances to Frank and Jim but continued to check over the first blackening phases of bruising around O'Neil's neck amongst the red weals that throbbed across his shoulders and abdomen. When O'Neil was fully awake, he was racked in pain and had trouble standing up.

"Just a misunderstanding, right O'Neil?" grunted Frank with a bright smile across his face.

"Y-yes sir." nodded O'Neil while being escorted out the door by the corpsman.

Boardman was standing outside the office watching the broken sailor walk uneasily past when Frank caught his eye, "Boardman! Get some tools and fix my fucking door!"

Jim returned to his office a little shaken. His head was buzzing with worry about the Sailor that just had his guts turned inside out by Frank and his own career since he was an accessory to the violence.

The phone next to him rang out so abruptly, that Jim almost felt his heart stop. "Um, DEA liaison office. Smith speaking", spurted Jim —glad that even in difficult moments he could pull himself to answer the phone.

"Hiya Jim!" answered back in the friendly but gruff voice on the other end. "It's me, Rip. I'm a-just reminding you that today is Wednesday and that means darts night." Jim rubbed his temple as he had completely forgot about darts.

"Aw Rip, I don't know—I've had a *real* shitty morning. Besides, this afternoon is the 5k fun-run and I'll probably just want to collapse for a week.

Rip paused on the phone for a good long second, "Well mister, I've been trying for over a year to get you into my lodge—we need good men like you and I'll be damned if I'm going to let you screw up my Wednesday nights as well! You may not realize it Jim, but some of us look forward to certain days of the week, not as an excuse to drink, but to get plastered with people that make us happy."

"Thanks." Sighed Jim, "I'll be there as usual at eight." He put down the phone and his mind crept back to Frank's office. He had seen fights before, but never where another man was beat unconscious in such a calculated way. Frank had taken apart O'Neil as easily as a fisherman cleaning his day's catch.

Chapter Three
Bob's Team

In a dry and dusty part of the same world, a boy named Cesar lay in his deathbed blurring in and out of consciousness. During better times, he was a healthy boy, with tan skin and a brilliant smile. He had wavy coal-black hair and although slim, was not at all gaunt compared to the starving street children that were abundant in Calderón, Mexico. His life was drawing to a close and would not be measured in hours or minutes, but within weak breaths.

It was a hot, humid afternoon, typical of June's waves of sweltering air that permeated his village. Although the heat was stifling, he had given up sweating as his organs began an orderly and absolute shutdown. He could hear his Mother and Grandmother wailing hoarsely next to him, although it felt like they drifted far away. He felt steady pressure building in his eyes and ears when suddenly, he felt something come loose, like he was sliding feet-first towards the end of the bed. As the room began to draw dark and all sounds waned, he saw a burst of light, which cast away of all discomfort.

He squinted into the sunlight as he stood in a park at the base of a large tree. "Crap!" He shouted. "How did I get here?"

A woman approached him under the tree, laughing at his outburst. She didn't appear like any woman he had seen before—women from his village had dark hair and skin. She was fair and didn't have the typical Indian features that were prevalent in his country. To Cesar, she appeared famous or as royalty—she didn't wear a skirt that had seen arduous work as he didn't see any patches or frayed edges. She wore a white dress that was bordered and crossed across her waist and bust with gold ribbon. Her hands were holding his and were smooth and delicate as the petals of a flower.

"Hello Cesar. I'm so happy to meet you at last." She said with a smile.

He felt a tinge of shame to have this majestic woman looking at his poor clothing, so he broke his gaze and looked down. His course, woven shirt was gone, replaced by a white and blue shirt that had no discernible thread. *It's unbelievably soft*, he thought as he felt it drift across his arms in the gentle breeze. It felt like it was spun from the fuzz of a newborn chick. His cracked, brown sandals had become soft shoes that matched the material of his shirt. The soles were thicker and made of a firmer substance that was flexible yet so light he could barely feel any resistance when lifting his feet. His trousers were white and went all the way down to his ankles.

He had never had long pants before and glanced around in all directions hoping to show his Mother and Grandmother his beautiful new clothing. He looked around and slowly realized that he was standing in the middle of a park that seemed familiar, but was nowhere in Mexico. Ordinarily, he would have been frightened to be alone in an alien environment, but he felt calm—especially with this woman nearby.

They stepped away from the tree and turned onto a sidewalk that ran through the park. Manicured grass hills rolled amongst buildings, lakes and outdoor pavilions. Cesar turned to look back at the strange tree and saw a group of people standing near where he first arrived. They were smiling and chatted amongst themselves excitedly. At once, the leaves began to rustle from a breeze and a young woman materialized in front of them. The small crowd began to cheer. The woman gazed in disbelief at the people standing around her. She ran to them and began crying. She hugged an older woman and kissed her face repeatedly.

It began to sink into Cesar's thoughts that he may have died, but the imagery of the church he visited every week yielded no familiarity--he saw no man suffering countless wounds upon a cross or melting candles dripping wax like yellow, frozen tears. He wanted to ask if he was dead, but felt that he knew that answer. With each second that he beheld his surroundings, the more he didn't mind.

"Your name is Theo isn't it?" he asked. She nodded to him as they walked towards a towering white building, stretching upwards to a massive domed roof. Two, giant pillars chaperoned the gleaming steps that lead to the massive open doors, built from dark metal which looked like bronze.

"How 'come I know your name?" asked Cesar as they both passed through the doorway.

"Bob will explain it to you," replied Theo, "He insists on greeting you first and he'll give you all the answers you need, sweetheart." As they walked, Cesar continued to observe Theo both trying to understand who she was and why he felt as if he'd known her before. He followed closely behind Theo as she opened the door marked 'C.S.B. White'.

"I am Robert White—please call me Bob." A dapper man in a grey pinstripe suit approached him in a spacious round room decorated with beautiful cherry wood, more books than he'd ever seen and strange oriental decorations here and there. Bob had an infectious grin on his face and seem delighted to be introduced to the boy. He had a gravelly yet pleasant voice, similar to the old Catholic priest that would tell stories of the old days to the children of his village. "And you, Cesar, are my new assistant." Theo stood behind Cesar with her hands on his shoulders and winked when he looked up at her.

"Sir… What happened to me?" asked Cesar.

"Well, let see…" chuckled Bob, tapping his chin in thought. "This place doesn't look like Mexico as there aren't any burros around and you're feeling much better… I've got it! You've croaked!" said Bob, snapping his fingers in triumph.

Cesar felt Theo's grip tighten slightly on his shoulders as she flashed a shocked look at the older man.

Bob noticed the look of concern evident in Cesar's face and changed to a more sympathetic tone, "Forgive me for my levity little chum, but you, like so many other children, had become sick. Much too sick to recover I'm afraid. But today is not a day for sadness! Aha! We are most certainly glad that you have finally arrived." Bob nodded towards Theo. "Theo, is going to perform a little field work and you shall be assisting me in tying up loose ends in some of our… projects."

Cesar felt like his mother and former life were a distant memory. For the first time, he realized that he lived his short life in abject poverty in a hovel of a home. They were only rich in love—his mother worked her fingers raw to provide food and his grandmother would sew her arthritic hands to numbness and her tired eyes to darkness to make their poor life slightly bearable.

As Cesar thought about his family, Bob's smile wavered just slightly. Bob pointed to a gilded picture frame on the wall in front of a large desk depicting Cesar's shared bedroom. Cesar was surprised at the scene-- it was an overhead view of his mother's bedroom. He could see himself lying in the crook of his mother's arms, almost as pale as the patched sheets covering the bed. He walked closer to the image and noticed that it was moving. It was if someone had knocked a hole in the wall and he could peer right through into his former home. He was astonished at the way he looked as his eyes were slightly open but were unfocused. He had seen himself in mirrors before but this time it was drastically different. He guessed that the same way a mounted, stuffed animal looks dissimilar from one that's alive—physically alike but with endless differences. His Grandmother sat shaking at the end of the bed crying and softly beating her fists into her lap. He had never heard her cry before.

"Unfortunately, they are not able to hear you." Said Bob, in order to pre-empt an expected reaction from Cesar. Bob approached Cesar and stood next to him, preparing himself to answer any difficult question that may result in Cesar seeing his weeping family.

"I died from enceph-enceph...alitis—from a mosquito bite?" Asked Cesar, wondering why he didn't feel the sadness of the separation of his family or how he knew the name of his fatal illness. It seemed to Cesar that the information was just there—popping into his head when it was required.

Bob tweaked his trim moustache, "Sure did, boy. Just be glad that your life albeit short, was with those two lovely ladies." Bob stood and in silence, contemplated the scene as if he was observing an art collection.

Cesar turned to Bob and asked, "Why am I here? I...I mean what am I to do here?"

Bob stole a quick glance back at Theo—his smile had shortened a bit. "All that and more will be explained shortly. But now we must say our goodbyes to Theo. Just follow me boy-- I'll show you where we need to begin." Bob had the look of a showman, the way he stood so straight but yet relaxed.

Theo gave him a slight nudge forward. "Have fun Cesar, we'll catch up later once you've seen the sights!" She winked at him again, turned her back to him, lifted her heels from the floor and rose quickly through the air, disappearing unhindered through the ornate ceiling.

Chapter Four:
Anything for Charity

The afternoon was perfect for the 5k run for charity. Jim Smith mingled in the parking lot with the other would-be runners, but refrained from conversation. He felt relieved to be participating, as the stress of being witness to another man's beating was clouding his mind.

Before the run started, an older man that Jim had known for the past year came up shaking his head with a big smile on his face. "Hello there Jimmy!" said Roger "Rip" Damhorst, a Navy retiree and head of the local Masonic lodge that called Jim that morning. "I didn't know those sorry legs could go past *walk!*"

Jim was trying to stretch his legs in a professional manner, but only looked like a clumsy flamingo trying to keep his balance. "Anything for charity. Too bad they haven't thought of of a bake sale to earn money—less strenuous for me!"

"Well, have a good run anyways." Said Rip, eyeing a slim black man sitting on top of a wall not far in the distance. "It'll be entertaining to see what you are capable of."

The race started and as usual, the lanky, young sailors were off like a shot. Jim padded along trying to set his pace—if he even had one. As he started running, he tried for the life of him to figure out how he got himself into this. The most he had ever run was five miles-- back when he was a student and even then it was very slow. There were chubby women passing him that were on the overweight sailor program.

Rip made eye contact with the slim man on the wall. He was very dark—as if direct from the heart of Africa. He was slim but well muscled. Rip nodded with his typical stern look and the man on the wall nodded back and began to breathe in a slow, controlled manner. He was trying to picture himself running in that very race—as if he was taking the place of the visibly tired and lagging, Mr. Smith.

While Jim tried to concentrate on anything other than his heart trying to chew its way out of his chest, his eyes began to glaze over slightly. He found himself beginning to lengthen his stride and his breathing became somewhat rhythmic. He almost felt detached—as if someone else was running and he was simply perched on another's shoulders. It felt almost effortless. He decided to run a bit faster—at least to catch up with the overweight ladies that passed him earlier. He found not only did he catch up to them, but felt as if his own mental resistance was holding him back. He decided to lay on the gas and reveled in the exhilaration of wind blowing through his hair and the vibration of his pounding feet. He was passing people like they were standing still and could feel that he had more power to spare. He became concerned that this was the strange onset of a stroke, but felt great—*hell, better than great*! He felt as if he was built to run forever, so he gradually began to pour on more speed. He found that instead of running his legs into a flurry, that he could increase his stride so that each would encompass double the length of his normal gait.

The finish line was only a mile away and Jim decided to go flat out and run as fast as his legs could carry him. He had caught up with the young, athletic punks that were trying in vain to be the first across the line and as he passed them he could feel the wind pulling his hair by the roots and his eyes watering. Each crash of his soles to the ground was as crisp and abrupt as an electrical discharge. He blasted across the finish line and pulled to a stop. His smile faded when he noticed the look of people that had watched him arrive. He turned around to watch the other runners approach and was stunned to see that the athletic Navy runners were still at least a football field's length from the finish line. As runners arrived, they had a look of unpleasant shock. The petty officer holding the stopwatch could not believe the time that he had recorded. He hadn't just broken the previous record, but shattered it. She was nervously trying to verify with others that he had indeed followed the entire course. Rip walked up to him and asked how he felt.

"Never better! I've never ran that well in my whole life!"

"Don't you feel it's odd?" asked Rip with an analytic frown on his face. "You aren't even short of breath."

Chapter Five:
The Fountain of Knowledge

Cesar stood rooted to the center of Bob's office, mouth agape for several seconds after Theo disappeared through the ceiling. Cesar turned to Bob for an explanation and only received Bob's rising mirth as he chuckled at his confusion. Cesar looked down at his feet and practiced raising his heels from the floor and trying in vain, to push off from the balls of his feet.

"You have plenty of time for that later." Laughed Bob as he buttoned his suit jacket. "We've other marvels of much greater magnitude to see first."

Cesar followed Bob down the hallway to a large foyer leading to a large arched door with a polished silver handle. The door had a large symbol of an eye inside a triangle carved into the center.

"Cesar, this is our first stop, so prepare yourself for something amazing." Bob opened what looked like a pocket watch, nodded, clipped it shut and returned it to his vest. Ceremoniously using a single finger, he touched the handle and the door made a soft *boom* sound, which seemed to resonate for several seconds. Bob withdrew his hand and stepped back just as the door opened.

Cesar was awestruck by the sheer size. The room was cylindrical and seemed as big as his former town. Although dark, it was breathtaking in its beauty with gigantic columns encircling the center among huge benches carved out of marble. The concave ceiling was decorated like the night sky. Given the strange things that he had seen thus far, it might well have been the universe. They both walked inside the softly lit space and Cesar noticed that in the center was a glowing blue shaft penetrating the floor to the ceiling.

The walk itself took over 15 minutes to the center. What Cesar previously believed to be a solid shaft was actually a fountain of water —except that it was glowing with brilliant light. He could feel that the fountain was knowledge and that he could at that very moment ask any question and immediately become bathed with the answer.

"We *loosely* call this the Cosmic File Server," said Bob admiring the view. "It's proper term is the *Universal Thread* and although the width of the shaft you see before you appears to be fifty feet wide, it is actually has neither size or dimension."

Cesar squinted at the display and could see individual streaks and pulsating blobs making the journey from the top of the shaft to the shaft of the carved well underneath. "Why does it look so... wide?" asked Cesar.

Bob crouched and pointed over Cesar's shoulder explaining, "You are really observing the *intensity* of the thread while magnified by an energy field that surrounds the shaft to both protect and concentrate its force. What you are seeing is the cumulative knowledge of everything in the two worlds—all things known and unknown. Animals are born with instinct—a type of programming from this place that allows them to survive within moments of being born."

Bob walked over to a large, intricately carved, marble bench and Cesar followed. After they sat for a few minutes watching, Bob continued, "Humans toil their entire lives to try to absorb as much of this knowledge as they can and even the greatest of genius will not even scratch the surface."

Cesar judged the way Bob said 'Human' as if it no longer applied to either of them. "If I'm not... human," said Cesar, "What am I now?"

Bob pretended to magically pull a coin out of Cesar's ear and said, "Human beings are a temporary incarnation of a species which slowly evolves, largely because of our intervention. We simply refer to ourselves as 'Origin', but we have had many names throughout history such as the Greek Daemons, and Judeo-Christian Angels. We are the middle entities between God and man and frequently walk among mankind both as our enlightened selves or by living one mortal life after another."

"Is that God?" asked Cesar, mesmerized by the constantly moving rush of light from ceiling to floor.

"No, but this is a part of him... his gift to all of us. We, in our current state can peruse it almost in its entirety, but there is knowledge that is inaccessible to us—mostly for good reason."

"Do you mean because of the rebellion?" asked Cesar abruptly.

Bob was surprised at how well Cesar was already absorbing facts from the fountain--- and following his conversation. "Yes... there was a betrayal many thousands of years ago. Rebels were attempting to overthrow the Creator using his own knowledge against him. God decided on exile for all of them except for the leader. This very bad apple went by the name of Rothiel."

Bob made a circle with both hands. "He was imprisoned in a big 'ole ball of stone and buried down inside the Earth for over ten thousand years. He will be released in four days time and will most probably gather his former army."

Cesar knew that despair would only come from his release, "What's going to happen?"

Bob smiled and grasped his lapels with both hands. "I'm glad you asked! Our job is to make sure this *son of a bitch* stays out of trouble!"

Bob had long since stopped talking when he realized that Cesar was drifting in and out of attention while silently perusing the fountain for answers. He felt that little Cesar was an astounding choice, although he knew the trio was planned from the start. Bob hadn't until now, felt that it would be effective.

"Bob, why am I part of this group?"

Bob straightened and scrutinized the boy's face — it almost caught him off guard thinking that he was reading his mind. Bob pursed his lips and thought for a moment before beginning, "Since consciousness constantly evolves from a youth in his or her nonage to the old in their dotage, our esteemed Creator has deemed it necessary that our group represent a mature man, a young woman and a child. In order to fully and completely observe an event you need at least these three people. Between the three, the description will be in most cases extraordinarily different, but when combined as a whole, the truest. Dear boy, there will be times that Theo or I will completely overlook something important, but you will see it clearly."

Cesar kept looking into Bob's eyes wondering what he meant — he wasn't sure that he would be helpful to them both, but hoped that he could make a difference. "Do the rebels have access to this place? I mean, I... saw that some of the exiles built the pyramids to try to communicate with or locate Rothiel, but how did they get their knowledge if they do not have our level of access to this fountain?"

Bob sat up straighter in his seat and crossed his left leg. Bob was careful with his answers and considered them for a significant amount of time. "Not really. In human form, the amount of knowledge is too great and would soon kill the poor sod who gained access."

"How did the rebellion start?" asked Cesar, crossing his leg the same way as Bob.

"In times past, there was plentiful, outward interaction between origin and the human beings living on Earth. Human beings, such as you up to a couple of hours ago, live their lives under a veil of ignorance. They begin their lives as infants with the most minimal of instructions from the fountain. As they grow, they share and compare the knowledge between themselves, which originated from this very place. Depending on the will of God himself, some information from this fountain leaches into a human being's mind in order to kick-start the human race into a new direction."

Bob held up both of his hands for emphasis, "The rebels that were exiled fell into two distinct groups: the followers of Rothiel, of which we are most certainly concerned, and those who did not follow him but were betrayed by his preaching and have fallen under the same punishment. The leader of the second group has attempted to stop Rothiel's followers since the first day of exile. Although God forbids us to have direct contact with them, we try to... arrange help as needed. "Danhieras is their current leader. He's since adopted a human name from a deceased schoolteacher named Roger Damhorst. He's the organized type; as soon as he and the others found themselves in exile, they wrote down every last aspect of their knowledge in a series of books, which they continue to use today. The exiles live normal human life spans and over generations of repeated births and deaths they begin to lose their former memories. Their compendium of books and their dedication to each other has allowed them to live in anonymity yet keep an edge over their fellow humans."

Bob took a moment to look at Cesar's eyes to see if he was still following the conversation. Cesar's eyes were still locked on his. "As to your question about the pyramids, Rothiel lost his access to the fountain but still had retained his memories. His followers knew from their past that they could build massive structures that would be able to amplify Rothiel's brainwaves underground. Once they were able to establish successful contact, they built several more in order to pinpoint the location of his cell—in the hope that they could dig his angry ass up. Once, they actually got very close, so the Creator shifted his prison to a different location. After several generations, their knowledge began to fragment and erode—forgotten really. Ultimately, his followers were unable to reconstruct, or even understand their former technology."

Cesar followed Bob with a serious look on his face. When Bob finished he asked, "How did Rothiel's group betray God?" Bob straightened the creases in his trousers and continued, "As far as Rothiel's followers are concerned, the lives of the humans on Earth were considered fleeting and folly at best. The most arrogant of origin would kill humans at will and many would attempt to convince humanity that they were their true creator and demand their loyalty to them alone."

Bob pulled out his pocket watch and flipped the cover open. He snapped it shut after gazing at the face for a mere second. "Rothiel was the most prolific of these and roamed the Earth with a 'belong to me, or die' philosophy. He spent an inordinate amount of time here gazing into the fountain, slowly trying to absorb everything about his future adversary. At the same time, he was so skilled in the art of lying, that he convinced his followers that he could successfully cast God out and take his seat."

Bob hooked a thumb at an image of Rip Damhorst floating across the reflective surface of the fountain. "For Danhieras and his men, they spurned Rothiel's offer. Their betrayal was for not taking appropriate action in alerting God. They were likewise expelled to Earth."

Chapter Six:
The John J. Kestly/George Washington Lodge No. 60/69

"Let's come to order and have everyone take their seats."
Growled Rip, whacking his gavel on the wooden base. He sat in his
thick, elegant chair leaning to one side, a combination of his gout and
his continually flaring piles. The men inside the large pre-fabricated
building began shuffling over to vacant chairs. "Where the hell is Big
Lee anyways?" Said Rip, looking around the room.

Gideon Blunt, known behind his back as *Filthy McNasty*, a
greasy, portly bloke more shaped like a penguin than that of a lawyer
that he continually pretended to be, closed the door behind Big Lee and
shouted, "All present and accounted for, Worshipful!"

Rip chewed his cigar as he watched Big Lee plod slowly over to
a chair in the corner that was markedly different from the others, both
larger than a standard chair and built from reinforced concrete.
Everyone's eyes darted between Lee and Rip for the uncomfortable
period of time it took Lee to get to his chair. The lodge-members
weren't sure if Rip was annoyed by Filthy's *Larry Fine* whining voice
or the fact that Lee appeared to be taking his time getting to his seat.

"Smith has passed the first test." Barked Rip with his trademark
scowl. "It is still premature, however, and will still require a couple
more trials before we can be certain that he is our conduit."

Filthy leaned forward in his seat fiddling with the buttons on the
front of his brown suit and remarked, "So, which one of us do you want
to give the next test?"

Rip sat back and scrutinized the eyes of the gentlemen sitting
around the sides of the lodge. Rip looked back at Filthy and said, "I've
been thinking either Ricardo or Noise."

Ricardo Kayanan was of Filipino stock with long, black hair and
a face that appeared more feline than human. He was watching Rip talk
with such unblinking concentration that Rip for a moment thought that
he was fully asleep with his eyes open or getting ready to pounce on
him. Kayanan was a quiet man, but the most dangerous that he had
ever encountered—as Rip looked at Kayanan, he felt relieved that he
was on their side. Noise was Rip's nickname for Hank, a tall, almost
seven-foot tall giant of a man with long shaggy hair and a constant
smirk on his face. Hank was louder than anyone else in the lodge. For

the thousands of years that Rip has dealt with Hank, the most difficult was to shut the man up.

As Rip both feared but knew was inevitable, Hank's booming voice erupted first. "Sooo, whaddya want?" Hank was already agitating himself off his chair and whipping his large head in all directions as if seeking consensus. "You want me to test his strength or see how he does in changing density? Hank raised his left leg and placed the sole of his cowboy boot on the armrest of his chair and rested his arm on top of his knee, content that he was the center of attention and looking like a statesman. Rip waited a second, then opened his mouth to discuss, but was immediately cut off by Hank as he shot off his second volley. "I've got an idea!" stood Hank and waving his hands wide. "I can show up at his apartment and begin by kicking the piss out of him..."

Rip tore the cigar from his mouth and clenched his teeth together in fury. He felt the first licks of flame erupting inside his mouth. "SHUT....IT!" growled Rip, trying to limit the spittle on his lip. "The last thing I'm going to do is bring all this out in the open too soon. If he's not the conduit, I don't want to bring our abilities or this organization out in the open!"

Hank stared at Rip with a blank expression on his face, his jaw slack. "I mean, if I start kicking the piss outta him, we should be--"

Rip stood up and stomped his foot several times on the floor, seething with anger. A rolling cloud of blue flame filled his mouth and he could feel a slight burning in his nostrils as the flame propelled itself upwards into his sinuses. As he bellowed in his fury, long curls of fire leapt out of his mouth and nose.

"Noise! Keep your damned mouth shut when I'm speaking! You keep interrupting me and I'll sew up your mouth shut with your goddamn intestines!"

When he finished screaming at Noise, Rip clamped his mouth shut to stave off the flames. For several seconds, small popping noises were audible as the flames would abruptly cease and then explode back to life in an instant. Rip's face was bright red and his chest was starting to hurt. He had high blood pressure since he was thirty and a malady of other health-related issues due to smoking and eating all the wrong foods. Scrapple had long been his favorite.

It didn't help that his body generated unstable explosive compounds that irritated his digestive tract. Although his nostrils didn't hurt from the quick act of rage, he could smell the vapor similar to kerosene around his lips and brought up a napkin to dab off any that may have collected outside of his mouth. As his breathing normalized, he reached to a table next to his chair where a tall glass of water formulated with electrolytes stood. As he drank the first few gulps, he could feel a welcome reaction of the water with his throat and felt tickling droplets pop out of his mouth.

The room had gone deathly quiet as all present realized how angry Rip had just become. Rip's body could generate massive amounts of explosive power but sometimes his gift could spread outside of his own control when his anger peaked.

Kayanan stood and looked at Hank, then at Rip, "Why don't you just decide what test is appropriate, who should give it and then let us know what you've decided." Kayanan's collection of butterfly-shaped blades was just visible under his leather coat.

Rip could have kissed Kayanan for being so level headed and strangled Hank for being so outspoken. Rip sat back down, wincing from the dull pain in his right foot. *Damn gout—why the hell was I stomping my bad foot?* Thought Rip as he contemplated between the two. Noise was discussing something to his partner, the 'always silent Simon'. Those two were always together, thought Rip, yet he couldn't get a peep out of Simon when he wanted one and could never shut off the incessant bitching from Noise.

Better get back to business, thought Rip. He nodded towards Gellan while rubbing the sides of his abdomen and said, "Why don't you tell the boys about this afternoon and what your observations were."

Gellan, the slim black man that tested Smith that afternoon, stood and flipped through his steno pad. "At approximately three this afternoon, Smith was taking part in a charity run. We observed him start at his natural pace and after a couple of minutes Rip gave me a signal to start. It was really easy—I just looked at him awhile and then tried to picture myself running in his place. It felt kind of strange- a gentle rushing and I felt like I was in both places—both on the wall and running in that race."

Filthy looked from Gellan to Rip and asked, "Did... he run fast like Gellan?"

Rip grinned, chuckled and said, "That boy was so out of shape that I could have beat him! About ten seconds into the race he was *flying* down that road!"

Gellan added, "Honestly, I think that if he would have went all out he could easily run just as fast as I can—maybe even faster."

"And, he wasn't even breathing hard at the end!" laughed Rip. "His average speed in the run from start to finish was 39 miles per hour! I'm fairly sure that Seth was right that Smith is the conduit. I just want to be sure. We're going to wire Seth up tomorrow and see if he can give us the location of a savant."

Hank spoke up, "Isn't Seth really, like, ill? Why don't we see if the conduit can copy Seth and maybe he can pick up the slack?"

This brought Rip's mirth to a halt. Rip's smile withered from his face and his lively eyes hooded themselves back to the look of an angry sick man.

With a patient sigh, Rip answered, "I don't know how many *more* sessions Seth can give before either passing into a coma or dying. I don't want to waste Seth's energy on a test just to weaken him further or to cause harm to Smith—we all know what it does to Seth when he plugs in. If we lose Seth now, he's no use to us as an infant. We need to make do with him for as long as possible."

Hank seemed to accept this and turned to mumble more commentary to Simon while shaking his head.

Rip turned to Big Lee and said, "Corey, have you located your son yet?"

'Big' Corey Lee was tall at six-three and was a very heavyset man with light coffee brown skin. He was slow walking and when he sat down, it was with the delicacy of a swan and the energy of an elephant.

"Naw man, I went to his 'ol haunts in Italy and all over Greece, but he's not in any of those places anymore."

Rip's eyes narrowed at Lee and said, "You've got to find him-- sooner rather than later. --Where the hell is your dog anyway?"

Big Lee rolled his eyes and said, "He's napping out front— relax, ain't no one going to steal him!" With that, there were a couple of guffaws around the room.

Rip ignored the sniggering coming from Hank and Filthy and gripped his gavel tight in his fist, "Rothiel, gets out in almost three days. You probably have an idea of what comes next, so I want as much in place before he gets lucky and wipes us all off the face of the Earth. Have you forgotten what that man may know? He most likely knows how to get rid of us permanently."

Lee rolled his eyes towards the ceiling while twirling his hand around, "Whatever man. Let's say I find my son—I ain't seen him fo' a couple hundred years and the last time? That boy killed me. Who's to say that he's going to see things our way?"

Rip pointed his finger directly at Big Lee. "Let me put it this way, you find him and tell him that he has two choices—to join us or to die by our hands. Under no circumstances will I let him join up with the others."

Lee shifted uneasily in his chair after hearing Rip's last comment. Rip regretted being so callous to Lee and realized that he had been leaning heavily on everyone lately.

"Corey." Began Rip, "If we are getting some progress tomorrow with Seth, we'll see if he can locate your son. I do not mean disrespect to your offspring but we are going to need every bit of help possible." Big Lee nodded his head and continued looking down at his feet.

"Ricardo." Rip decided, "Meet up at 'El Dardos' tonight at 9:00 for darts. I'll invite Smith along, get him shit-faced and see how he does with target practice. I want Noise to show up afterwards and test his control over density." Rip pointed a finger directly at Hank's eyes, "Don't—hurt—him. If he doesn't respond, just leave him alone—after all, I'm going to make sure he's good and drunk. Afterwards we'll all meet back at the fortress, hook up Seth and get some more answers—I want everyone there."

Chapter Seven
Filthy's Turn

At five in the afternoon, Jim Smith closed the door to his office
and headed out to pick up Elena from daycare and head home. Elena
was as usual, overjoyed to see her father when he came to pick her up.
He parked his car near Manoli's street behind Benny's Bar and popped
Elena on his shoulders. He passed by Manoli's neighbors and said
"Hola" to the ladies gossiping on the sidewalks who returned loud
praise to Elena as she beamed down to them.

Manoli's husband, Nino, sat outside in the cool air, talking with
the neighborhood kids and stood up to shake Jim's hand. Nino was the
hardest working Spaniard that Jim has ever met, slicing and moving
heavy slabs of rock to be used in making pool tables or decorative
marble trim. His hands felt like they were made of rock themselves.
Nino and Manoli lived in the center of the street where everyone
congregated. Manoli came out, shouted a big hello at both of them and
picked Elena up from Jim's arms. She ushered her into her house as she
had just prepared some *tarta* for the other children and Elena couldn't
possibly be left out.

Oscar, Manoli's oldest son came out and waved to Jim. Jim was
always startled at Oscar's appearance — he was the absolute blood and
soul image of a young Paul Newman — the same smoky blue eyes and
roman statue lips.

"Jesus!" said Jim, "That kid looks more like him every time I
see him!" He asked Nino why they chose the name Oscar, whether he
was named after a relative or friend of the same name.

"No, we couldn't agree on a name, and when Manoli woke me
up saying she was in labor, I turned to the nightstand to check the time.
Oscar was named after the brand of our bedside clock."

Jim arrived at his apartment a little *Alegre*, not quite drunk but
feeling good nonetheless. He chuckled to himself on Nino's reaction to
the events in Frank's office over a bottle of cheap wine. He looked at
the clock on the wall and had just less than two hours before he was to
meet Rip at El Dardo's. After darts, he would pick up Elena at Manoli's
house and sleep in late the next morning.

He wasn't in the house two minutes when he heard a sharp
rapping on his door. He opened the door to a portly man of medium

height with a thinning hairline. He had smiling basset hound eyes, a double chin and wore a stuffy brown suit. "Hello Mr. Smith" smiled the man. "A mutual friend of ours has asked me to come by and introduce a couple of products to you."

Jim's friendly disposition went flat. "What friend-- products?"

The man rocked back on his heels with a growing grin and said "Why life insurance Mr. Smith, what else is there?"

Jim was instantly annoyed by the man's whiny, nasal voice which sounded much too snidely for him to feel comfortable. Before Jim could tell him he wasn't interested or even more effectively, *lie* and tell him that he was insured to the gills, the man stepped into his apartment and opened his briefcase.

"Aaaand, you are under no obligation to purchase anything and you still get a free gift!"

Jim's happy buzz began its rebound transformation into a rasping headache. "Listen, Mr. uh, excuse me, but who are you?" asked Jim rubbing his temples.

"Ha ha ha! Can you believe it? I forgot to introduce myself!" Offering his handshake towards Jim. "I'm Gideon Blunt. I sell insurance and savings plans on behalf of the U.S. Serviceman's Association." Jim gripped his hand and received a clammy dead-fish handshake.

"Can I offer you a drink?" offered Jim, thumbing the direction of the kitchen. Blunt turned his face directly toward Jim's, waited for a few seconds while his smile grew into a sinister sneer and said, "Yes. I want you to go downstairs and buy me a large bottle of cold Cruzcampo."

Jim stood in the small shop located on the ground floor of his apartment building wondering how the hell he got into this. He didn't remember even walking out of his apartment, heading down the stairs or even walking into the store itself. He almost felt like a puppet as he asked the lady behind the counter for the 'large bottle of cold Cruzcampo'. After he paid for it and as the bottle was being stuffed in a paper sack, he began feeling like the biggest ass on Earth. The oncoming realization that a total stranger had the gall to order him out of his own home and purchase a bottle of beer for him was enraging him to an all-new level. He stormed back to his apartment with his anger building with each rapid step. He couldn't believe that he let a complete outsider alone in his apartment.

He shoved open the door, but didn't see Mr. Blunt anywhere. He walked into the apartment and heard noises coming from his bedroom. Jim opened the bedroom door and found Blunt, bent over, rummaging through his closet.

"What in fuck do you think you are doing?" growled Jim as Blunt's head appeared from behind the closet door.

"I want my beer in a large, clean glass, please." Said Blunt looking at the paper sack.

Jim, perplexed, found himself back in the kitchen, gently pouring the beer into his best glass with a feeling of accomplishment— almost enjoying the fact that he was being such a polite host. "What-in-hell?" said Jim when he realized what he was doing—didn't he just catch the son of a bitch snooping around in his closet? Jim slammed the beer bottle down on the counter and stormed into the living room to throw Blunt out on his ass.

Jim sat on the edge of the couch, holding Blunt's beer glass gently on a clean saucer, concentrating on keeping it as still as possible for his guest and most importantly, keeping it eye-level for him. He had a dish towel draped over his right forearm and was focusing all of his concentration into keeping the glass in perfect reach. Blunt was droning on about 'how many suckers are walking the planet' when Jim's head cleared. He placed the glass down on the table with a troubled look.

"Pick that back up, please." Said Blunt.

Jim's hand started reaching for the saucer and stopped just short of the glass. "N- no." said Jim, bringing his face up to look at Blunt's.

Jim's guest had lost his look of superiority and sat up straight in the chair. His face became stern and while bouncing his head with each syllable said, "Pick-it-up. Now!"

Jim twisted his face in anger and barked back, "Get your shit and walk out of my house this instant!"

Blunt's face went blank—as if drained of all emotion and he got up, hugged the briefcase to his chest and walked out.

Jim slammed the door behind him and went into the kitchen to dump Blunt's beer in the sink. As he stood at the sink wondering what the hell had just happened, he noticed that Blunt was still standing just outside his door, gazing out into space. Jim opened the door with a quick jerk and stood looking at the back of Blunt's neck. He didn't move a muscle. "Forget something?" said Jim angrily.

Blunt looked around and turned to face Jim with a look of shock. "Uh-, wait! I... ah, no." Blunt looked shaken, like he had seen a ghost.

"Then good evening." Said Jim with disdain in his voice as he was closing the door.

"Oh! Wait a second!" Shouted Blunt. "You forgot your free gift! Blunt was rummaging through a thick, canvas bag that he had left outside the door. "Here. This one's made of bronze and the other of iron." They were two large art-deco statues, which looked like muscular boxers. They were the shape of men, but instead of fists, they had perfect spheres, slightly larger than their heads. Both were smooth, but with pitted surfaces. They were poised as if they were each about to deliver a right cross. Each one must have weighed at least five pounds.

Jim looked perplexed to get such a large, heavy gift—especially after he had just thrown the guy out. "I don't think I should—listen pal, why don't you just give these to someone else?"

Blunt turned up his palms towards Jim. "No sir—that's your free gift as promised. I do an honest business and if at any time you require our great services, please don't hesitate to call on me." Jim watched as Blunt shuffled away carrying his briefcase. When Blunt reached the end of the hallway just before the stairs, he turned and waved back at Jim with currency in his hands. "Don't hesitate to call, Mr. Smith!"

Jim looked down and realized that he was standing on his porch, holding his wallet in front of him, waist high in both hands—spread wide open as if to catch money falling from the sky. "Oh fuck," he gasped, as he tried to remember how much money was in his wallet that morning.

He went into his house and saw the two statues standing on the center of his coffee table. Jim sat on the couch staring at them, trying to remember the missing time—what in hell just happened? Was it Nino's wine? He glanced up at the clock on the wall. He had been with Blunt for almost two hours.

Chapter Eight:
Darts Night

Rip sat at the end of the bar interrogating Filthy in the back of
El Dardo's pub. "You're certain? He was able to... impel you for a
significant period of time?"

Filthy gently scratched his thinning hairline, "One minute I was
relaxing and watching him make an ass out of himself and all of a
sudden it stopped working. I remember him getting angry, and then I
woke up, pretty much holding my dick on his front porch."

Rip sat back, pensively stroking his mustache. "Gideon, you
were only supposed to deliver the guards and leave—in a way its good
that you tested him, but I don't want him to react to so much so soon!"
Rip glared into Blunt's eyes.

Blunt ran a nervous finger around the inside of his collar.
"Honest Rip, it was just a slight check to see if I could just control him.
When he threw it back at me, it felt exactly like the symptoms that
others described to me when I force someone-- as if I was just switched
off."

Rip slapped his palms on the top of his thighs and stood, "Jim
should be on his way here, so you'd better make tracks. Grab Hank and
go out to the fortress and get things ready for tonight. Don't say
anything to anyone about your 'little test' either."

"Okay chief," Blunt mopped his forehead with a handkerchief
and walked out of the bar towards his car.

After a few minutes, Rip saw Jim walking towards the bar and
began preparing his character as 'the old retiree'. Jim walked in and
said his usual hellos to people drinking at the bar and bought a San
Miguel. He walked up to Rip and looked about for the other dart
players.

"They went to get some Chinese food," said Rip tapping on the
face of his wristwatch. They'll be back shortly."

"Sorry for being tardy Rip, but I just had the most unbelievable
day of my whole wretched life."

"You know," began Rip while unwrapping a cigar. "Any
problems you may have could be easily fixed if you join our lodge."

Jim gave an apologetic bow. "I've been meaning to set aside some time to join, but Manoli takes her father to therapy during that time for stroke rehab and I don't have another sitter."

Rip sighed. "Well we can't have little girlies in the lodge when we're paddling candidate's asses now can we? Anyways, what's bothering you, Jim?"

"Other than watching Frank G. beat the living hell out of a guy twice his size and... Oh yeah-- I almost forgot. Some bizarre guy showed up at my door wanting to sell insurance."

Rip sat forward. "His name wouldn't have been Gideon Blunt was it?"

Jim felt his stomach lurch. "You know him? Wait- you didn't send him to my house did you?"

Rip was dragging off his cigar and simultaneously waving his hand to Jim to calm down. "Naw. Unfortunately, he stopped by my house to sell some of his crap insurance to me and I believe that he may have jotted down information from my address book. You're not the only friend of mine that this guy has screwed. So what was the damage?"

Jim put his cold bottle of beer up to his temple and cursed. "I don't know, the guy was poking around the house and as far as I know, he only took some money out of my wallet."

Rip's eyes narrowed and his ears turned red.

"Do you think I ought to call the cops?" asked Jim.

Rip shook his head and said, "First of all, his insurance isn't even from a real company, so don't pay him when he comes to collect. Secondly, I'll pull your money directly from his colon the next time I see him. How much did he take?"

Jim scratched his head, "I don't know, I think I had around twenty bucks and about 15 Mil Pesetas in my wallet. I didn't notice anything missing in the house."

Rip noticed the darts team rolling into the bar and causing their typical amount of ruckus. "Looks like the boys are here." Said Rip getting to his feet. He noticed Kayanan walking in and taking a seat at the bar. "Looks like we can get busy."

Jim stood up. "I don't think I'll be playing worth a shit today—I was drinking wine earlier with Nino and I've been feeling loopy all evening." Rip wondered if his performance would have been more effective against Blunt had he not been drinking.

"Oh, did this Blunt character give you any free gifts?" asked Jim.

Rip laughed between drags and said, "If I recall, he gave me a worn, Roman-era coin sealed in a professional plastic case. When I went to have it appraised it turned out to be an old metal coat button that was flattened by a car running over it!" Jim spurt beer out of his mouth in a coughing fit.

When the darts teams were properly charged with beer, they separated into groups and began the competition. Jim began opposite Donny, a regular at the club. Jim had thrown pitifully in the first round with Donny having a clear 12-point lead. Jim went back to take a swig of his beer when he noticed Rip talking to a Filipino man sitting at the bar. The man he was talking to was keeping mostly to himself and tended to glance over at him a little too frequently.

When Rip returned the to the game, Jim asked him who he was talking to. "Him? That's Ricardo," answered Rip, "He's a nephew of a Navy buddy of mine. He came over to live here about two years ago. *Real* nice guy. Hey- you're up again." Said Rip motioning over to the board.

Jim got up, took a swig of his beer and picked up his darts. At first he thought he had picked up the wrong set, as they felt different. As he rolled them between his fingertips, he could feel each individual groove on the knurled end as if he could count the ridges instantly. He rubbed his fingers together on his right hand and they felt fine—just very sensitive. Shrugging, he walked up to the board, aimed for the correct block and let the dart fly. It flew exactly where he intended it to go and buried its nose exactly in the center of the rectangle. It all went so perfectly that it surprised him enough to spin around and yell, "Yow! Did you see that?" He received a couple of claps and jeers but this was the best thing to have happened to him all day.

He passed his second dart to his right hand and then gazed at the location of the first and for a short moment, felt something as thin as a spider's strand connecting the two darts. He drew back and let the second fly and as if by magic it joined its brother in the same spot.

Donny said with his typical redneck drawl, "Yer gett'in pretty fuck'in lucky aren't ya?"

Jim rubbed his fingers together again and took stock in the situation. He felt different—he knew it. He was certain that he could throw his remaining dart across the room and hit a gnat's ass. He felt the gentle spider silk pulling on the last dart, which was still in his left hand while staring at the board's target block. This time, he decided to test his skill by 'granny-tossing' it underhanded using his left hand into a high arc, burying it smack dab against the other two darts as if they were Siamese triplets. Jim spun around with his mouth open looking at the faces of his friends. Their looks were similar, but most were already well intoxicated and didn't rightly care. He did notice Rip giving a short 'throat slit' sign to the Filipino standing by the bar staring directly into Jim's soul.

Jim walked up to Rip and asked what he was doing. "Oh, I hate that goddamn song!" growled rip pointing to the speaker nearest him. "Frigging *Spandau Ballet*—I want Manuel to either cut it off or play something else."

After Donny threw his last round, Jim turned to Rip and said, "I want to show you something." He retrieved his darts and told Rip to pick any slot that he wanted.

Rip turned back and gave a quick glance at the bar, then turned to scrutinize the board. "Number 13. It's my lucky number."

Jim concentrated on block 13 and sent the dart flying. It glanced off the bottom of the board and spun across the floor under a table. Jim stood there wondering what had happened to the strange feeling connecting the dart to his desired destination.

"What are we supposed to be seeing?" asked Rip with a chuckling tone. Jim felt the remaining darts in his hands and realized that they felt different. Whatever gift he had, he felt that he had just lost it. He sidled up the bar figuring that if his luck ran dry at playing darts he could at least get his insides wet with beer. When he ordered another San Miguel, he noticed that Kayanan's seat was vacant and his corresponding drink stood untouched.

Jim sat and drank his last beer of the day with Rip, listening to his old sea stories and patiently hearing about his medical problems. It was nearing 11:00 in the evening and he thought it best to leave. They both walked out of the bar, and stood on the sidewalk taking in the night sky. As usual in the off-season, the streets were empty. Most of the apartment buildings were completely dark, with the *presianas* pulled down secure until the warmer holiday season. Since spring was barely here, there was a moist chill in the air, which seemed to purify their lungs from the cigarette smoke pervading El Dardo's atmosphere. Jim turned to say a deserved goodbye to Rip and noticed the Filipino that Rip named 'Kayanan' lurking near the corner of the bar, observing them both. "Thanks for the evening pal," said Jim. "You helped me forget a real shitty day."

"Don't stagger down the wrong alley on the way home!" bellowed Rip between pulls on his cigar.

Jim waved and began his walk towards Manoli's house. His head swum with tiredness and 24 hours worth of the strangest happenings, playing a zombie-like tug of war in his mind. The alcohol was also busy fighting over the steering wheel as he time and again over compensated his movements to walk in a straight line.

Rip watched in silence as Jim walked away in the distance and then spoke to Kayanan in whispered origin, filled with minute clicks and hums, "Why aren't you heading back to the fortress?"

Kayanan replied in the same fashion, "Valgiernas."

Rip spun around towards Kayanan with eyes wide and nostrils flaring. "Are you sure?"

"Completely. I smelled him when I was walking to the lighthouse."

"Did you see him?

"No, but I can tell he's not young. Odds are he's in his mid 40's."

It wasn't much of a relief to Rip—Valgiernas was deadly nonetheless. He served in the Quick Reaction Brigade alongside Kayanan prior to the exile. What Kayanan had in skill, Valgiernas had in cunning.

"Please tell me that you are armed," asked Rip.

"I only had the 'flies when I smelled him, so I ran back to the car for my struts. I haven't detected him since. He may have departed the area, but I'm willing to bet he was out looking for us."

"Kayanan, I can't get into it right now, but it's extremely important that no harm come to me at this point. Just stay close to me until I can get to Simon at the Puerto gate. He can get me back to the fortress safe."

Kayanan took off his leather jacket and handed it to Rip. Underneath, he wore a black vest holding eight butterfly-shaped polished steel blades. Attached to each side of his hips were two coils of very thin wire with weighted connectors on the ends. Across his belt were four V-shaped blades with precision eyelets designed to ride on the cable with lightning speed. Kayanan removed one of the V-Blades from the belt, connected it to the cable and looped it around his neck.

"We'll walk together," said Kayanan pointing to the streetlights. "If for any reason we get jumped, I'll take out the lights first and you curl up in a ball on the ground. Do not 'light up' and control your vapors — it screws up my nose and makes my eyes water."

Rip had already felt the cooling sensation as the chemicals evaporated on the back of his neck. "I'll do my best. I'll explain everything when we've finished with Seth."

The two men headed off briskly for the lighthouse parking lot where Kayanan's car was parked. Rip kept up with Kayanan's rapid pace while the Filipino scrutinized everything in view for signs of trouble. When they arrived at the parking lot, Kayanan motioned for Rip to stand away from the car while he inspected it. He saw something that furrowed his brow. Someone had used a finger to draw a shape on through the condensation on the driver's side window. It was a circle divided in two halves along a jagged edge.

Kayanan pointed to the design. "I think Valgiernas is reminding us that his boss gets out soon."

Kayanan made the short drive to *Puerto De Santa Maria* in just over ten minutes and pulled into the small, white-washed town of *Fuentebravia*. The car pulled up outside the local veterinarian's office and came to a halt. The buildings in the area were quaint with decorative worked iron in the windows and adorned with planters overflowing with bright flowers. Rip quickly got out, walked over to the door and knocked twice. His eyes continuously scanned the perimeter road for any signs of being trailed. Simon opened the door and wondered what had snared his attention. When he leaned out the porch to see what he was looking at, Rip pushed him back inside. "No time Simon. Open a hex to the fortress, then drive Rick's car back."

Simon mouthed an inaudible 'Why?' and Rip opened his hands in exasperation.

"Valgiernas just appeared out of nowhere."

Simon knew how dire the situation could be and he walked briskly towards the back of the waiting room. He stood facing the wall and began making a shaking noise in the back of his throat that turned into a gentle hum. The humming became more resonant and increased in intensity until at last, Simon reached out with his right palm out and held it in the air. The air near his hand began to swim like the waves of a mirage and become semi-opaque. As he hummed, he pointed with his index finger and slowly drew a large circle leaving a bright trail of pulsing light floating near the wall.

He drew several smaller concentric circles with lines connecting them, all radiating light erupting through the haze. Around the circles, he used his finger to trace out strange characters representing direction and elevation.

His eyes appeared unfocused, but he continued to draw the bright characters in thin air with his finger. When the last character was drawn, the light began to increase in intensity. Simon ceased humming and returned his palm to the small circle in the center of the glowing wheel and pushed. It shot outwards like a smoke ring and pierced a five-foot wide hole where the hex once stood. The hole was directly connected to a another room located over 19 miles distant, showing a large living room where several people were now turned and looking curiously towards the three men on the other side.

Big Lee was sitting in a massive cement chair holding his dog with an indignant look on his face. "Damn. Why the hell do I have to sit in the back of a truck and you get to travel in style?"

Rip thanked Simon while he simultaneously stooped and raised a leg to squeeze through the hole. The hole was thinner than onionskin paper and when he passed his other leg through, Kayanan dove through the hole, somersaulted on the floor and without any diminishing speed, shot back to his feet.

Simon stepped back and erased his mind of the hex. The hole disintegrated with a short 'pop' as the air equalized back to the room. He felt relieved that he was able to get them both back without any problems. Sometimes the hole was unstable and too risky to allow anyone to pass through. Other times he couldn't get the hex to display at all. He hadn't personally been able to travel through his own portals for the past few generations, but could get others through. He knelt to examine the fine layer of ash that collected on the floor and brought up a smudge to smell. He had a vague memory of why ash was produced from this phenomena but he couldn't remember it now. With declining memories as a result of each generation ending, it would be another couple of generations and this ability would also pass into the shadows.

He turned off the lights in the animal clinic after making sure the sick animals had enough water for the night and stepped outside and locked the doors. He turned in both directions along the street to see if anyone matching Valgiernas' description was about. There wasn't a soul outside during this time of night. He turned towards Kayanan's car and remembered that he forgot to get Kayanan's keys before sending him to the fortress. *Well, at least there aren't many bugs out tonight,* thought Simon as he fished out his keys and walked over to his moped.

When Jim arrived at Manoli's house, Nino was sitting outside talking to some of the other men in the neighborhood. As soon as he saw Jim turn the corner, he yelled for Manoli to bring some more of the wine.

"*No gracias!* Believe me, I can't take another drop!" said Jim, holding his head between his hands. Nino laughed at him and said he didn't want any either.

Manoli came out and admonished both to keep it quiet—Elena was fast asleep. "Why don't I bring her to your house tomorrow?"

"Suits me, I was going to try to sleep in tomorrow morning—this way it's guaranteed! ...Are you sure it's no problem?" he asked.

"*Que va.* She is just a dream. I'll bring her to your apartment at noon."

Jim said his goodbyes and attempted to display his best 'sober walk' as he departed Nino's neighborhood. All it did was give Nino and his circle of *amigos* reason to laugh at his expense.

"Do you need to use my father's cane?" shouted Nino amidst the howling of the other drunken Spaniards. Manoli stuck her head out behind the door and hissed at them again to keep the noise down.

Jim walked to the road along the beach and began his half-mile walk to his apartment. There was a slight breeze, which blew paper trash about on the sidewalks as he lightly whistled a song in his head. It was as if the entire town was dead and he was living Charlton Heston's role in *Omega Man.*

"Do you have the time?" said a man not three feet away from him. Jim jumped back shooting a hand to his heart. "Jesus! You scared the hell out of me!"

The man smiled and spoke with a german accent. "Forgive me. I was only trying to get the time."

"Oh yeah," said Jim holding his watch up at an angle while trying to get the streetlamp's reflection on the watch's face. "It's… Ah, ten minutes after one… in the morning."

The man walked closer, all the while staring pleasantly into Jim's eyes. He stopped uncomfortably close and took a deep breath into his nostrils. A look of recognition passed across his face. "Thank you. Don't let me keep you."

"G'night." Said Jim and continued walking to his apartment shaking his head. When he got to his apartment he fumbled for his keys and glanced over the balcony. For a moment, his bleary eyes focused on what he thought was a man standing on the other side of the street away from the streetlamp. He closed his eyes, rubbed them and tried to take a better look. Nothing. He still had a creepy feeling that the strange guy at the corner followed him, but now that he was home he just put it aside. *I just want to lay in bed and sleep for ten years,* thought Jim as he locked the door behind him. The two boxers were standing on his coffee table, reminding him of Blunt's visit. "Yard sale. I see stickers on you guys for a buck a piece." He shuffled to the bedroom and didn't bother getting out of his clothes. He kicked off his shoes, sat back on his bed, pulled a leg up to peel the sock off, stopped, said "Fuck it" and plopped back on his bed switching off the world with the first of many long snores.

Chapter Nine:
Playground in the Sky

Bob and Cesar spent several hours discussing the fountain and the possible outcomes on Earth with Rothiel's liberation. Bob pulled out his pocket watch glanced at the dial and snapped it back shut. "I think it's time we went. I've just been summoned by the Big Guy."

Cesar was astonished. "Do you mean God? You are going to meet him?"

Bob laughed as he stood up from the bench and smoothed his pants with his palms. Cesar did the same with his trousers, not knowing what else to do. "Of course! I'm sure you'll meet him in due time. I'm sure he just wants to hear our opinion on what we can expect." Before Cesar could ask, Bob wagged a finger in front of him. "And no, you cannot come along. I'm the leader of this team and being the most experienced, I'm the proper choice for providing him our status."

They walked out of the enormous room and closed the door behind them. Bob turned to Cesar, "Just touch the door handle—it knows who you are and will let you in." They continued down the hallway, heading outside. As they walked down the steps, Bob pointed to a large playground in the park. "Best you go play over there with the other children and I'll be back shortly." Cesar nodded and began walking over to the playground while looking back at Bob. Bob began a brisk walk towards a large temple nearby the circular building holding the fountain.

When Cesar arrived at the playground he began to get over the feeling of being alone with so many other children his age running about and playing. He stood on the edge of a lake where some children were riding in small boats shaped like birds, comical-looking dragons and fish, when a smaller boy approached him. The boy had hair so blonde that it was almost white. Other children seemed to be ignoring him.

"Could you ride in a boat with me? …You have to have two or they won't let you have a boat."

Cesar felt relieved to be in someone's company, being in such a strange place. He nodded and walked with him to the dock. "I'm Cesar —I… just got here today." He expressed, not really sure what to say.

The little boy shook his hand and said "Aaron. I've been here a long time."

"How long?"

"Dunno. But I haven't been to this park in a while."

They walked up to a boat shaped like a purple hippo looked at each other for approval and both shrugged and laughed. Cesar eagerly climbed inside and slid over so that Aaron could get in. An attendant unhitched their boat from the dock and gave a gentle push. Cesar let Aaron steer the boat using a chubby blue wheel and the boat gently lurched forward. Cesar took in the gorgeous view as their little hippo nudged forward slowly along the shore.

Both boys were enjoying themselves and laughed and whooped as they came close to other children's boats. Two girls gave them sour looks as they approached their pink flamingo boat. The fat girl with curly red hair shouted out, "Get out of our way!"

"That's Margaret," said Aaron. "She doesn't like boys too much and she throws a fit if someone else takes the flamingo or the swan boats."

After a few minutes, Aaron looked at Cesar and said "I saw you with Bob—are you his new assistant?"

Cesar smiled, "Yeah. Do you know Bob White?"

Aaron nodded and said, "Oh sure. He's very nice."

Cesar thought about what he said. "I guess so—I just met him. I still feel a little strange about everything here. I do like it here, but I'm not sure where I fit in. What do you do here?"

Aaron sat back in the boat and said, "I am just here, I guess."

After what seemed like an hour, Cesar kept scanning the park to see if he could see Bob. "We should get back," said Cesar, looking towards the shore to see if Bob was waiting. "Bob said that he would pick me up at the playground."

Aaron said, "Sure, but I wouldn't worry, his conversations with God can take a long time."

Cesar looked puzzled. "How did you know he was seeing God?"

Aaron looked back at Cesar shrugging, "His job-- who else would he be seeing?"

The boys pulled back up to the dock and the attendant tied up the boat and helped them climb up onto the platform. "Can I give you something?" asked Aaron as they walked back to the grass.

"I guess so. What is it?"

Aaron pulled out a small case the size of a wallet out of his pocket and presented it to Cesar. "It's called a Patch." Aaron held it up so Cesar could see. Its color was a soft bluish-white and was translucent. It looked like a hard plastic or glass but was very pliable. Aaron opened it, and then spun the top around to the back and the entire shape unfolded, doubling in size and was finally the size of a notebook. It was more like the cover of a book as there weren't any pages inside. The inside was filled with images and lights displaying information.

Aaron moved to Cesar's side to show him how to use it. "You can ask for a person's name and the image will appear at the top. You then say 'Call' or 'Get him' and it will contact that person — you'll be able to talk to them sort of like a telephone. If you say a topic like a person's name or a place, then say 'Information' it will show you everything known on that subject." He handed Cesar the Patch. "Give it a try."

Cesar opened the patch and at first didn't know what to say. "Bob White?"

The main page melted into several pictures of Bob, beginning with what looked like his baby picture, and other pictures advancing with age. A couple of the pictures were animated and must have been home movies. On the right hand side, were several paragraphs of information showing chronologically, important events of his life culminating with his obituary. Cesar read 'brain cancer' as the cause of death.

Aaron reached over and touched a picture of him in military uniform and said "information." The right hand side changed display to show his dates of when he was commissioned as an Ensign and listed his awards and duty stations. "See? You can find out just about anything with this and with it you can get in contact with me."

"Why are you giving this to me?" Asked Cesar. "Isn't this expensive? …What are you going to use?"

"I can always get another one. Besides, if you are working with Mr. White, this can come in real handy."

Cesar was already engrossed in the information rustling across the display. "I can't believe that you're giving this to me — it's a treasure."

Aaron laughed and said, "See you tomorrow, okay?" He waved goodbye to Cesar and ran over to a cart to get some popcorn.

Cesar couldn't wait to explore with this amazing book and sat at the base of a large willow tree. The branches hovered over him like a porous, swaying tent. The wind would rustle the vine-like branches and he could feel them tickle the tops of his shoulders as if it wanted his attention. Cesar was so engrossed with the patch that the beautiful park and all of its noise and excitement was of no consequence, only his thirst of knowledge mattered.

Bob waited in the large office checking his pocket watch. Time didn't matter here, but it did where Rothiel was. He kept checking the time and watched the counters march backwards. *Only 29 hours left and he'll be released,* thought Bob gritting his teeth. On the side of the pocket watch was a dial that he flicked with his thumb and the display turned white. Bob said, "Cesar." An image appeared showing several pictures of Cesar and Bob continued, "Location." The image changed to a profile of Cesar sitting under a tree. Bob looked closer at the picture and noticed that he was engrossed with some type of book. A patch! "Where would he have gotten... Connect me."

As Cesar was perusing information about Rip Damhorst, a small window appeared on the right corner with Bob's picture. A lyrical female voice asked, "Bob White for you. Do you wish to accept?"

Cesar was surprised at this and not sure what to do. "Uh—yes?"

Bob's picture dissolved into a video showing Bob with concerned look on his face. "Cesar, how are you doing?"

"I'm fine. Isn't this amazing?"

"Oh, you mean the patch. Yes, they are magnificent. ...By the way, where did you get yours from?"

A boy named Aaron gave me his. We were playing together in the park and he just gave it to me."

"Do you know his last name?" asked Bob, his brow tense.

"Hold on, I'll check." Cesar said, "Information. Boy. Aaron—younger than me." The right side of the book informed him that there over 192 million entries. Cesar looked at Bob's face and said, "Need another couple of seconds." And said to the patch, "Aaron—a boy here that I was speaking to just a few minutes ago. Blonde hair... about four inches shorter than I am... was sitting in a boat with me earlier."

The patch's pleasant voice repeated "Shall I find him now?"

Cesar glanced at Bob's waiting picture with a small feeling of victory seeping in. "Yes please."

The patch at once displayed 'No results match' and the voice stated "There have been zero boys named Aaron, younger than you, that you spoke with minutes ago, with blonde hair, approximately four inches shorter than you and sitting with you in a boat. Would you like to try again?"

Bob said with a tinge of impatience, "I'll discuss this with you later—God is on his way here now. Disconnect."

Bob's image went from his active speaking face to his standard greeting face from before.

"Bob? Mr. White?" asked Cesar.

"Mr. White has disconnected." Replied the patch.

"Excuse me," began Cesar to the patch. "I was sitting in a boat over in the lake earlier."

The patch displayed an image of Cesar and another boy sitting in the boat with huge smiles on their faces.

"That's him!" said Cesar. "That's the boy I was talking about! That's Aaron!"

The patch was silent for a few seconds.

"May I help you?" asked the patch.

"Yes. I want information on Aaron—the boy sitting next to me in this picture."

The patch was again silent.

"May I help you?" repeated the patch.

Cesar turned the patch in his hands wondering if it was broken. "Is there something wrong with you?" asked Cesar.

"There is nothing wrong with me—I am here to serve you Cesar."

"Tell me about Aaron then!"

"There are over 192 million entries for the name 'Aaron'. Would you like a different search?

As Bob waited outside the large door for his appointment with the creator, all he could think about was how Cesar came into possession of a patch. Few people were allowed to have one. Bob's came in the shape of an old-fashioned pocket watch and Theo had a small one that she wore as a pendant with the sun and moon etched into the face. Hers flipped open and became transparent spectacles that she could wear and only she could see the display. Bob did not like to wear glasses and preferred to dress technology with antique beauty.

Bob heard a slight chime and the door unlocked and opened to a large room. On one end stood two large chairs, carved out of white marble. They faced each other and in front of each wall stood stewards who welcomed Bob and asked him to take his seat. "May I get you a refreshment, Master White?" asked the steward nearest him. "No thank you, Phillip. I'm fine."

"Very well sir—Ah, he is here." The steward turned back to the wall and took his place. Bob always felt strange about Phillip serving him. Bob had served under him when he was a lieutenant and Phillip, a three-star admiral commanding the Pacific Fleet. At the time, the 'old man' was very kind, but captains and below were always respectful to him. Phillip was one of the last that had seen bloody duty in World War II and led the way in the midst of the cold war.

When Bob turned to the chair in front of him, God was sitting there nodding to him. Bob jumped up, "Excuse me my lord!" and began a formal bow. God pointed to the chair and said, "Have a seat Mr. White."

Bob complied immediately and afterwards the two looked at each other without speaking. Bob felt very uncomfortable with the silence. He knew that it was only a few seconds—surely less than ten, but it seemed like centuries. "You wanted to see me, lord?"

God sat in his chair, comfortably yet with poise, in a charcoal gray suit wearing a standard white shirt and a bright red paisley tie. He was holding a red and white striped box, which he offered to Bob. "Popcorn, Bob?"

"No thank you my lord, I'm fine."

"Bob. I know you quite well. I know not only that you love popcorn, but that you have been craving it all morning—why do you think that I would offer you any if you sincerely didn't want it?"

Bob's face turned red with a 'you got me' expression and took the box from God's outstretched hand. "It gives me the worst gas you know, but thank you."

"These won't, and don't mention it."

Bob popped a few kernels in his mouth and started chewing and realized that out of nervousness his throat was quite dry.

"Phillip, please bring a root beer for Mr. White."

Bob tried to interject in order to explain that it wasn't necessary. He felt embarrassed because he didn't want his distinguished former leader serving him. The dry hull from a kernel became caught on the back of his tongue and speaking was out of the question. He accepted the frosty mug from Phillip and after a refreshing swig and quick clearing of his throat croaked out a thank-you to the steward.

"Well," began God leaning back in the chair, "How's your new assistant doing?"

"Oh, very well I think." Said Bob wiping root beer froth from his lips. "He's actually quite remarkable in his drive for knowledge. He also seems very willing to start figuring out some of the problems we have ahead of us."

"Yes, the boy is exceptional in his observations." Added God. "Do you know why I picked him?"

"As you have said before, my Lord, you felt that 'the observations of a mature man, young woman and a child are much more exacting than a room filled with old wise men'."

"Yes, but I'm asking you why I chose Cesar specifically and not select one from the multitudes of children that are already here."

Bob sat for a moment trying to think of the best response. He had a glimpse of Cesar's life and found it quite dour and hemmed in sadness. He was bright and was quite an outgoing character in his little *barrio*, but that was all he noticed. He couldn't see where he was any more extraordinary than other children of his age. "I'm sorry Lord, I haven't the slightest idea."

God pointed to the wall and it displayed an overhead view of Cesar's town. "Cesar's nickname was '*El Genio*'—the Genius. Ever since he could talk he tried to unravel everything that his eyes laid upon —as if everything that he didn't understand was a mystery he had to solve. He electrocuted himself twice, was bitten by almost every creature that that I put in Mexico and once gave the best description of butterflies that my ears have ever heard."

God pointed to the wall again and the image changed to a younger Cesar who had, at four years old, ran down to the local bar to retrieve his uncle who was drunk and barely able to walk. "Notice that as he's holding his uncle's arm with both hands and attempting to guide him down the sidewalk, a large tanker truck loaded with fuel was driving through the town because the east bridge was too weak to handle the weight. Now observe,"

The truck lumbered down the dirt road towards the entrance of the town, which was once the East wall of an ancient monastery. The entry way was a large arch made out of very thick brick and adobe, crowned with a large bell. On the inside stood a tile mosaic showing an angel with golden locks with her arms spread over a depiction of the town with the arch in the center. She was the protector of the children of Calderón and rumor had it that she helped the weak and fought off evil. Old people saw her on their deathbeds and were awestruck with her beauty.

The truck slowed down prior to entering the archway and then jammed to a halt when the top of the fuel tank struck the arch. Dislodged chunks of adobe and brick rained down on the truck and the metal tank of the truck squealed as it ground to a stop. The arch held but the truck was jammed tight. The driver tried to back up, but all efforts to move in reverse were futile.

By this time, Cesar was struggling to keep his uncle on course, and nodding to the old soak who kept repeating, "You are such a good boy—please don't turn out like your damned uncle."

They stopped near the arch so that Cesar's uncle could rest a moment in the shade. Cesar saw the commotion and joined the throng of townspeople gathered around the truck. The driver was wringing his hands and had a look of horror on his face as he considered his options. People were yelling to drain off the gasoline into jugs or into a different truck, but a local policeman hollered back that it wouldn't work, as the truck's springs would shove the truck higher into the archway. People were emotionally bickering about the archway being preserved, as it had existed for over 400 years when built by the Spanish. It would be a crime to destroy something so historic to save an old gasoline truck. Some older women shrieked that the arch was sacred and that the safety of their angel protector was paramount. A few bolder men tried climbing up on top of the tank to use their body weight to bring it down far enough to get the truck out. It was no use. The springs were old and tired. Since the tank was full, the springs were already bottomed out.

At last, the policeman called for men to bring out tools such as hammers and shovels—that there was no other way. A shout rose up from the crowd to save the arch and a large group of people began attempting to physically push the truck from the front in a mad attempt to dislodge it.

Cesar walked up to the policeman who was trying to restore order and push the crowd back.

"Mister!"

"You people all have to get back! Get back!"

"Mister!"

The policeman looked down and saw Cesar pulling on his pants leg. He knew how dangerous it was for a small child in the middle of an angry mob and picked him up and waded through the crowd to deliver him to safety. "What are you doing here, Cesar? It's too dangerous here! Go home."

As he was putting him down and giving him a slight push forward, Cesar pointed back to the truck. "Why don't you just let the air out?"

The policeman had already turned around when he heard Cesar and spun his face back to him. "*What?*"

"The tires—if you let the air out of those tires the truck will get...shorter."

The policeman pushed the crowd's noise out of his mind and thought about what Cesar had said. *It might work!* He fidgeted in his pockets for his whistle and came up empty. He had thought about shooting a round from his revolver, and then remembered he was standing next to a truck filled with gasoline. He placed two fingers from each hand between his lips and blew a series of long, piercing whistles until the crowd calmed down.

"Listen to me! Listen! Do you know what this boy said! Do you know what this little *genius* said?" People were now looking at the boy with curiosity. "He said to let the air out of the tires!"

Almost one-by-one, dawning recognition of the solution swept across their faces and people started to cheer. The policeman ran over to the driver and told him to let air out of the tires little by little. One overenthusiastic youth pulled out a knife and jabbed it into one of the tires. "Oy!" Yelled the policeman. "You're going to pay for that tire!" Several had joined in to push in valves while others admonished the youth with the knife.

The archway released its grip from the truck almost instantly and the driver was able to slowly drive underneath to the other side. A large fat woman who previously was threatening to pummel the truck driver had hoisted Cesar up and planted big, wet kisses on his cheeks. Men and women around the truck and standing by the roadside shouted

"*Genio! Genio!*" Others were congratulating his uncle who stood dumbfounded at the edge of the crowd as he saw the multitude celebrate his nephew.

Cesar and his uncle continued their journey to their barrio in polite conversation. Cesar's uncle was surprised by this little boy and deeply proud of him. He had sons of his own but none that cared much about him these days. Cesar grinned from ear to ear while holding his uncle's hand His mind kept reaching back to the moment the crowd roared when he was lifted under the arch in celebration.

God turned and spoke to Bob with sadness in his eyes. "It was a difficult decision to make, you know. After that day everyone in Calderón was proud of this child. He was their little hero and people expected great things from him." God turned back to the wall and now it showed a large funeral procession passing from the church towards the arch that Cesar helped save. Cesar's uncle held the bridle of a mule hitched to an old, wooden wagon loaded with a small white coffin. The wagon was packed with wildflowers with the coffin nestled in the center. His uncle's cheeks were slick with tears and people lining the dirt road heard his husky, shuddering cries.

The procession passed from the church under Cesar's arch and out towards the desert graveyard that held so many of his ancestors.

When the image dimmed and froze to a still, God stood up and Bob followed his lead, placing the empty mug on the table in front of him.

"I gave Cesar a patch." Said God. "I know this boy's mind. I felt it when he entered the temple of the fountain. He's working things out and this connection to the fountain will help greatly."

"I understand," said Bob, nodding. "I... I had no idea about his past—other than that he was very bright for his age."

God turned to look at the image of the throngs of Calderón crying their hearts out for their loss. He had watched sadness in the faces of mothers since the beginning of time but it was rare when so many shared the same loss with such passion. "Yes. Very bright indeed."

Bob stood silent for over a minute. Being a talkative man, such long silence made him uncomfortable to his bones. "My lord? Was there anything else?"

"Yes." God turned to Bob and felt satisfied that Bob understood the rare importance of his new prodigy. "Take Cesar to meet Tieran. I want him to see one of his training sessions. One should start in less than an hour."

Chapter Ten:
Tieran, Chief Commander, Origin's Army

Bob left the temple feeling relieved after his meeting with the boss. He wasn't even reminded about his first principle: that there was to be no interaction with the exiles until the sentences were served. Bob wasn't sure if he was going to have to bend that rule or not, but he was relieved that no mention was made at this last meeting.

He approached Cesar under the willow tree and cleared his throat.

"Bob! Look at this!" Cesar jumped to his feet and showed the open patch to Bob.

Bob looked at the first page and noticed that it was displaying information on The Lodge. It showed several images, which looked more like mug shots than portraits of the men belonging to Rip Damhorst's organization.

"Yes," replied Bob, looking at the display. "Patches are very useful. I find that I spend a good part of the day consulting mine."

Cesar glanced at the pocket watch chain slung against Bob's vest.

"Yours is a watch?"

Bob fished his watch out of his pocket and showed the cover to Cesar. It had an antiqued gold finish and a Latin inscription running around the edge that said, '*Putamus Viam Semper Esse*'. Directly in the center, was a crudely carved outline of a heart. Bob flipped it open and Cesar saw what he expected, the white clock face with delicate hands pointing to Roman numerals.

Bob brought his face closer to the watch and said, "Patch." The watch face was gone in an instant and revealed an image of the fountain in the center.

"Tieran" said Bob at the device and the picture of a man in some type of high-tech armor was on display in the center with labeled, colored spheres rotating around with names such as 'bio, history, location and contact' in the centers. Bob said 'contact' and after a few seconds, a different view of the same man swam into view.

"Hi Bob. Got any new jokes?"

"I've someone to introduce to you. Are you busy?

Tieran smiled, shook his head and said, "Come on over—I was just getting ready for a practice session—if you want, you can join me in the action!"

Bob snickered, "Load up a wet paper sack—I'm on my way. Bob out."

The Patch returned back to the display showing Tieran in his armor. Bob clapped the watch shut and returned it back to his vest pocket.

"Let's go boy," said Bob turning to the sidewalk. "You are about to meet Tieran, the toughest guy in the two worlds. Just don't try to challenge him to any kind of game—you'll lose. I, on the other hand whip his ass when it comes to telling jokes."

"What does he do? Asked Cesar as they both headed across the green lawn toward the armory.

"Tieran is the Commander of the Army of Origin—designed to protect and defend the two worlds for God's will. He is also the keeper of the most fearsome weapon in existence—the Ikorsom or sword of destruction. This weapon is so powerful that the only ones that can use it are God himself and Tieran. Supposedly, nothing on Earth or the heavens can withstand it. It rarely ever gets used, but when it does, entire civilizations don't forget easily—just ask the citizens of Sodom and Gomorrah." As they walked, Bob looked at Cesar and brought up an index finger. "Very powerful stuff, so don't go asking him to see it."

Cesar's eyebrows knitted in confusion. *Sodom? Gomorrah?* He nodded while walking briskly alongside Bob, all the while perusing his patch about Ikorsom.

They arrived outside a large building with a sign between the highest columns depicting a fiery sword laying flat on an anvil. Underneath the carved emblem was the word, *Armory*. They walked inside and Bob made several pleasantries to men talking in the hallways. Two men emerged from a room dressed in some type of armor. The helmets were snug fitting and had clear faceplates. The rest of their bodies were clad in form-fitting armor that appeared flexible, since they walked with normal gaits.

Bob directed Cesar to a door with a panel outside that glowed 'Tieran' in a soft green hue. "If it's red, never open this door." Bob waited until he was sure his point was made, and then opened the door.

Cesar saw that the room was huge. There were weapons of every kind gracing two walls. On the far side of the room was a viewing area with seats behind a thick wall of glass. In the center of the room, Tieran sat on the floor cross-legged and meditating. He jumped up and walked across the room towards them.

"At last!" said Tieran holding his hand out to Cesar. "I am Tieran."

He looked oriental and of medium height. Not exactly the fearsome warrior that he thought he'd meet. The urge to consult the patch was beginning to overpower Cesar's thoughts just like the urge to cough when told to remain silent.

"So you're a soldier?" asked Cesar shaking Tieran's hand.

"Or a security guard. Either way, it's a living!"

"We'd like to watch one of your practice sessions." Said Bob, "What do you have cooked up for us today?"

Tieran bowed to Cesar and walked them both to the viewing area. "I'm going to warm up hand-to-hand with a group of bandits carrying kinetic weapons, then move on to a couple of Seeths using a double-harken and finally a fearsome, smelly beast with a variety of weapons."

Cesar noted that Tieran was encased in similar armor as the others he'd seen in the hallways. The armor seemed snug but it didn't seem cumbersome. There wasn't a hint of clumsiness when Tieran moved. He retrieved a helmet from a shelf on a wall and placed it on his head. The moment it was seated, a semi-transparent strap snaked out of the bottom and joined it's twin on the opposite side under Tieran's chin. A small black microphone was curved to his cheek. When he spoke again, his voice was amplified over the room although Cesar could not see the speakers.

"Go ahead and take a seat behind the glass. I'll explain some of the tactics as I confront each target. If you have a question, please wait until the fighting stops."

When Cesar and Bob walked behind the glass plane, a clear door slid shut behind them. They both chose the closest seats to the glass and Bob removed his suit jacket and placed it behind the back of his chair.

Tieran continued, "Fighting in our current state is largely unfair because our armor is invulnerable. For the purposes of a true training environment, I like to scope to an Earth-bound state."

In the center of the arena stood two columns supporting what looked like an empty doorway. The door was wider at the base than it was at the top and the air in between the door frames appeared to ripple like the moving surface of water.

Tieran stepped through the doorway and for an instant, the room flared orange and then back to normal. When Cesar looked back at Tieran, his armor had changed from its glossy modern state to one that appeared more arcane and now made of bronze and silver. The edges of his armor were filigreed in shining silver and where there were no seams before, the armor was connected by leather straps and buckles. Some of the exposed areas between the armor gaps were covered in what looked like metal scales. When Tieran turned towards the viewing area, Cesar noticed that his face was a little different as well, with pronounced wrinkles and evident scars around his neck and wrist.

Bob leaned over and explained, "When you 'scope' to a different state such as Earth, you become your most recent physical incarnation from before. This is what Tieran looked like when he lived on Earth—even uglier than you imagined, eh Cesar?"

"I heard that Bob," said Tieran, adjusting his helmet. "I also remember how you looked on your deathbed—like a shaved ass soaked in bleach! Tieran raised his arms so that Cesar could see the armor more completely. "In this state, my armor went from less than a pound to a full sixty!" It may look ancient, but it is still very advanced and will protect me from most harm."

"Okay, Cesar, we begin by setting up the obstacles and then the targets." Tieran walked to the center of the arena and pointed to the area just before him. "Wrecked car." A smashed up automobile materialized out of thin air in front of him.

He walked around the arena pointing and stating the objects that he wanted in view—mostly just large bits of junk, scaffolding and half-demolished brick walls.

The room now resembled an urban wasteland. When he was finished with the scenery, he walked back to the center and nodded to Bob and Cesar. "Six targets, human, ten for speed and ten for agility... hand-to-hand, master level."

A female voice abruptly cut in, "Weaponry for this simulation?"

Tieran thought for a moment, "Small arms- two with MP-5's, two with MAC-11's and two with HK-91's."

The woman's voice cut back in. "Simulation beginning. Any act of physical contact initiates sequence."

Six men dressed in tight, white shirts and black pants coalesced into view. They appeared very athletic and stood ready with evident confidence. Each had either a machine gun hanging from their shoulder or clutched in their hands.

Tieran walked in a wide circle around them looking at their positions and what particular weapon they were holding. They were of different size as well from small and wiry to tall and imposing. After about twenty seconds of sizing up the targets, Tieran bent down, grabbed a medium-sized rock, juggled it to test the weight and hurled it into the closest man's crotch. The man choked out a short scream and simultaneously bent over at the waist staggering backwards and puffed out several short breaths.

Cesar yelped in laughter, especially how unexpected it was for a guy to get socked in the balls with a rock—by 'the toughest guy in two worlds'. His laughter was caught short when the other five immediately erupted into gunfire. By the time their barrels were firing, Tieran was already behind the nearest wall, running very low. Once behind the wall, he kept his momentum going until he appeared on the other side and hurled an empty fist of air at the second gunman who over-reacted by covering his crotch with his hand and turned his body sideways to avoid what he believed to be a second onslaught from a rock. This gave Tieran time to dodge more incoming bullets from behind the hulk of the car.

Two of the gunmen ran to the back of the car hoping to catch him unprotected. When they peeked behind the car, Tieran was not to be found. The one nearest the front continued on the other side with a look of trepidation creeping across his face. The barrel of the HK-91 was pointed straight in front of his path and nervously jumping towards wherever the gunman's eyes fell. Tieran appeared from under the front of the car, which had been stacked on cement blocks and kicked the gunman's feet out from under him. His left hand latched onto the barrel of the gun and no matter how frantically the gunman tried to point it at him it would twist out of the way at the last instant. Tieran slugged him once across the face with the bottom ridge of his hand and the man buckled to the ground.

Cesar looked as carefully as possible to see if the man was dead and noticed that he was still breathing. When the gunman was knocked senseless, the weapon was instantly snatched up by Tieran's hand towards the second gunman at the rear of the car. Tieran shot a single round into each of his ankles from the bottom of the car and the second gunman collapsed on the ground screaming. Tieran was back up on his feet in a crouched position and reached into the car and yanked off the rearview mirror. He threw it towards to the rear of the car and saw through the reflection, that the second gunman was holding a gun toward Tieran's side of the car, waiting for him to appear. Tieran shot two bullets into the cement blocks holding up the rear of the derelict car, walked back to the front and gave a firm push. The car toppled backwards and slammed down on the second gunman, pinning the gun to his abdomen. He gave a loud, gutteral scream and began groaning in a futile attempt to free his arms from the hulk of the car. Tieran checked his watch. *Two down in less than thirty seconds.*

Bob leaned over and explained to Cesar that these men weren't real, "Just simulations. They can kill of course, but no matter how realistic this looks to you, there is no one in that room that can suffer or feel pain except for Tieran."

The four remaining gunmen ran to different areas for cover and began creeping towards Tieran's location. The first gunmen that was hit with the rock was not moving as quick as the other three and was massaging the area that took the first hit.

"What about him?" pointed Cesar. "He looks hurt."

Bob gave a quick snicker and said, "Just a very good simulation. As you've probably noticed by now, Tieran is quite the showman."

Tieran had come from behind the car and shot two quick bursts of machine gun fire towards the two nearest gunmen, the first dropped immediately down behind a large dumpster and the second dove behind a nearby brick wall. As he fired the last round, Tieran felt the chamber pop, indicating an empty magazine and hurled the gun with a fierce arc towards the closest man. The gun slammed down near the man while he was taking cover from the fire. When he saw that it was the gun, he jumped up and immediately took aim towards Tieran, who was running directly for him. By the time the barrel of his gun moved up over the dividing wall, Tieran was soaring over it and grasping the gunman's barrel with his left hand and at the same time grabbing the man's face with his right. His body twisted at an arc and he landed behind the gunman on his feet, holding the gun barrel firmly to the gunman's temple.

"Go ahead—pull the trigger," whispered Tieran into the gunman's ear. The gunman released his hand from the weapon slowly in an expression of giving up, and then spun his elbow towards Tieran's face. Tieran had jerked backwards enough so that the man's elbow just sailed past his face, and in one clean motion, pulled the barrel of the assault rifle over his left shoulder and struck the gunman's face with the stock. *Down to three.* By the time the stock sheared the man's jaw in two, bullets from another gunman were ripping apart bricks and mortar nearby. Tieran was already flanking the man's position, aware that MAC-11's squirted bullets like a firehose but weren't precise about doing it. In Tieran's mind, this was more dangerous. He would have to get out of the way and wait for the clip to empty before he could act. He dashed behind a higher wall with a scaffold connected to the backside and gripped the support with his free hand. By kicking his feet forward, he jackknifed up onto the floor just in time to hear the last shell leave the MAC and less than half a second later, the clip ejecting from the handgrip. He popped his head and the HK-91 over the top of the wall and sent one slug into the casing ejector cracking the top of the gun into several pieces causing the weapon to fly out of his enemy's hand. The second bullet shot the clip out of his fingers and caused him to flee towards the safety of an adjacent wall.

Tieran knew that he would only have to wait a few seconds to find the last two gunmen. From the shadows where he was standing, he knew that he was too quick for any of the remainders to get in behind him. He heard a small scratch of pavement and noticed the moving shadow of one of the gunmen crouched beside a crumbling brick wall. He jumped over the scaffold, sent two bullets into the midpoint of the wall and kicked both feet into it. The wall broke easily and collapsed on top of one of the remaining gunmen. The tumble knocked the HK from the gunman's hands and Tieran kicked it away. He squatted down next to the shocked gunman and removed a brick from his chest. He knew that this would certainly bring the last armed man into the fray and spun around sending the brick directly into the forearms of the last gunman, knocking the MAC into the man's face before spinning off into the air. The man screamed and ran at Tieran attempting to kick out at him with his boot. Tieran side-stepped and sent his own foot into the man's temple turning out his lights.

Tieran walked back to the center and said, "Clear."

The arena shimmered and was again, empty and clean of any of the former rubble, props and blood.

"Unfortunately," began Tieran, "This was just the warm-up. The last fight was meant to hide the ugliness in battle, as I did not kill any of them. I can't safely defend myself from what comes next without fighting with the best of my ability. Seeths are terrible creatures that have almost endless energy and are very, very fast. They aren't pack hunters, they just try to kill as aggressively as they can. You may want to take this time to leave as it will be very violent from here on out."

Bob watched Cesar's expression with questioning look on his face. "Cesar looked at Bob and said, "I'm fine. Don't worry about me. I'd like to watch... please?"

Tieran looked at Bob for a moment, nodded and walked over to a wall and selected two four-foot metal staffs, each topped with a crescent-shaped blade. He placed the handle ends together and rotated one half-turn until they locked. As he walked back to the center of the arena, he performed several spins of the double harken and rolled his shoulders forwards and back to loosen them up for the fight.

Tieran looked back at Cesar for several seconds, then said, "Two Seeth adults, make 'em male."

The Female voice broke in, "What stage would you prefer?"

Tieran hopped the long handle of the harken against his upturned palm, "Sexual prime... right after their must period."

Cesar already had his patch referencing the creatures known as the Seeth. Apparently it was a failed species that broke out on the jungles of South America over four thousand years ago. It was an aberration caused by genetic interference by a Rothiel devotee named Protaxsis. He was gifted in the art of genetic transformations in order to obtain desired characteristics from various living species.

The Seeth was one of the most troubling. It started out being a base of the common sloth. By mixing the genes of more fearsome animals, the Seeth was a large quadruped that was gifted with enormous claws and thick, scaly armor. It could eat and then rest for weeks, constantly converting its food to energy and storing it when needed. The fur around the head and upper body became compacted similar to the horn of the rhinoceros and provided the animal with an almost impervious shell. Lice and other vermin were constantly burrowing around the animal's irritated skin, which only made it ornery and prone to fighting with it's own kind. Whereas a Sloth is extremely slow and ungainly, the Seeth was rapid and vicious.

"Beginning simulation," said the woman's voice. "Sequence begins upon approach to three meters."

Cesar looked up from his patch and witnessed two animals, each about the size of an adult buffalo. They were grey in color with powerful hindquarters and a massive head that looked like it was encased in a large shell of matted fur. Their heads appeared more like an armored bear—except that their teeth protruded in an exaggerated fashion from the snouts. Most of their weight was forward above their chest and centered over two enormous arms. They walked on their claws, which were about twenty inches long. One of the Seeths reached back to scratch its hindquarters and extended its twin claws. The sight was hideous. As it scratched its back, it yawned and Cesar got a good look at the mass of teeth protruding from its jaws. Tieran stepped forward and touched his harken to the back of the one in mid-yawn. The reaction was explosive. It was as if the animals were previously unaware of Tieran's presence and they began roaring and swiping at him. Cesar noticed with disgust that from the moment of Tieran's first touch they began salivating long, shimmering sheets of saliva around their lower jaws and a steady stream of snot ejected from their noses with every straining growl.

Tieran had been jumping back and using his harken to test his distance from between them until they moved to either side of him.

Cesar, in sudden alarm, jumped up from his chair to shout a warning to Tieran. Bob grabbed his wrist and in a low voice told him not to say a word. Cesar remembered what Tieran said—to wait until the fight was over, but just the same he was worried that he would not survive those two attacking at the same time.

Tieran stopped walking and stood in a stance, alternating his glances between them until one of them unleashed a volley of slashes from both sets of claws. Tieran spun the harken to deflect some of the blows and his armor dodged the rest. The second Seeth used that moment to try to run down Tieran like a freight train and Tieran bucked out of the way at the last minute allowing the Seeth to crash into its twin. After a few seconds of the two Seeths swiping at each other and growling and hissing, they began silently stalking Tieran again. One of them leaped high into the air to try to catch him in his claws and Tieran ducked and rolled out of the way, unlocking the harken into two pieces. The two Seeths, emboldened by the tumble of Tieran, tried to fall upon him with rapid slashing with their claws and teeth. Tieran used the separated harken to individually deflect the blows and when he felt one of the Seeths wasn't riled enough, would slap the flat side of the blade on their midsections. To Cesar, the screams of these beasts were horrifying. He had heard pigs scream and had heard the noise of howler monkeys fighting in the trees, but none had come close to chilling his bones as these monsters.

They began to tire and rambled in a circular path around Tieran. He used his harken to slice a shallow cut into each of their haunches. The blood began smearing on the floor and one of the Seeths began sniffing the red liquid. His eyes rolled back and he sank his teeth into the bleeding cut of his brother. The second Seeth shrieked at the pain and immediately attacked the spine of the other. They were in a frenzy of blood, pain and violence that made the attacks all the more savage. Tieran stood at rest observing the scene as if he was no longer concerned that he was in any danger. He reconnected his harkens, shot forward and with two great swings, separated both of their heads, bringing the two brutal, shaggy masses to a complete stop.

"Clear!" shouted Tieran. The room again brightened and was again empty with no sign of the Seeth bodies. Tieran walked over to the observation wall and removed his helmet. His hair was sweaty and unkempt. Cesar noticed that there were rolling droplets of sweat running down the back of his neck. He was breathing slightly through parted lips and his armor rose and fell around his chest. The previous fight with the six gunmen didn't seem to faze him in the least—this altercation certainly got his blood circulating.

Tieran cleared his throat, wiped his forehead and with his voice slightly huskier than before called their attention to the last fight. "I don't know the outcome of this next fight."

Cesar looked at his confused. "You've never fought this next creature?"

Tieran shook his head and said, "I've never fought it in human form and won before. In fact, the quickest that I've been able to even disable it was nine hours using conventional, non-kinetic weapons."

"In Earth form?" asked Cesar.

Tieran nodded. "This is going to be very brutal in the least. Are you sure that you want to see this?"

Cesar nodded back. "I don't understand—why this creature?"

"Rothiel preferred this one. Before the exile, it was his favorite plaything. For the past few years I have been training in every art imaginable and I need to be able to defeat this creature in case Rothiel is able to conjure one up in the near future."

"Can't you use your sword? …I mean the sword of Ikorsom?" asked Cesar.

Tieran grinned at Bob. "Smart kid Bob!" he said with one raised eyebrow. He placed his helmet back on his head and connected the chinstrap with a sharp click. "That weapon is too dangerous for me to have right now. Rothiel tried to gain control of it during his rebellion — he was almost successful too. He's never been able to best me in a matched fight. I halfway suspect that he will unleash one of his *pets* and I want to be ready just in case."

Tieran walked to the center of the arena and rolled his head sideways to loosen his joints and spent several minutes adjusting buckles on his armor and stretching his hamstrings.

Bob took that moment to brief Cesar on Tieran's next appointment.

"It's basically a big, fat worm." Bob looked down towards Cesar's open patch and said, "Show Cesar the Jantu Worm."

The patch's display showing the Seeth dissolved into a different display showing an enormous segmented creature whose skin was a pallid white color similar to the color of an animal's intestines. Around the circumference of the creature from tip to tip was a series of rust-colored points about the size of a man's fist. The head did not appear to have eyes, but the patch stated that it has excellent day and low-light vision. The bulbous head was roughly the size of a garbage dumpster and looked very misshapen — similar to a potato. It was split down the middle from the underneath of the head to the tail and hundreds of stubby, rust-colored legs protruded out and provided the creature with mobility.

The patch's display showed the creature in action, "The Jantu worm is capable of speeds up to twenty miles per hour. When attacking, the worm extrudes spines to capture its prey, sometimes snapping them off to disable an opponent. It then feeds using it's powerful jaws."

Cesar noticed with visible disgust that the Jantu's mouth was vertical and opened up almost twice the width of the head. The jaws opened and closed in almost a scooping motion to feed its fat body.

The patch continued, "The Jantu's stomachs are external to the segmented body and covered by dense, fatty tissue used for energy storage. The outside of the Jantu is a tough membranous skin holding the fat in place."

Cesar looked up at Bob. "This thing's entire outside is his fat and stomach?"

"Stomachs," Bob nodded gravely. "It's a very simple creature really. It only destroys to eat and when it gets too fat to move around, it lives off its fat. It never stops eating."

"Can't Tieran chop it up like he did those Seeth's?" Asked Cesar.

Bob pursed his lips in a moment of thought, "Not really, no. A typical Jantu has several feet of fat to cut through and if you cut deep enough, its digestive juices will leak out and burn you quite severely. That, and the smell's revolting. The last time I saw Tieran take one of these out—successfully, that is—he disabled its forward legs and hacked through the back of its head enough to sever enough nerves so that it's spines became erratic and sluggish. He then cut his way though to the first heart—there's eight of them you know, and when the first heart had died off, so did the jaws. He was in origin form then— impervious to the acid and with indestructible armor."

"Do you think he'll try the same attack?" asked Cesar, his left leg shaking up and down in nervousness.

"This was a while back—I don't have any idea on how he'll do it, but it looks like he's going to use his wings." Said Bob pointing towards Tieran as he was picking up what appeared to be a roll of glass sheaves from the wall.

Tieran unrolled the thin glass panels from the straps and ran his fingers through the straps to straighten them. They didn't look much like wings to Cesar. They looked similar to glass panels from a graduated chandelier that stepped down to points hanging down to his ankles.

Tieran hurled the wings through the shimmering doorway and they shot out the other side with a burst of orange-bronze color and a loud crash of metal whipping the air. It kicked once, spinning back towards Tieran and ruffled noisily as he caught it by the leather straps. The straps formed an X shape joined by a circular badge in the center. Tieran pulled both sides together and slapped both circles to the middle of his chest armor. The bronze, feathered wings jerked about on the harness moving Tieran slightly about as the movement rippled up and down both sides. He stood with his legs shoulder-width apart while the wings began to whip about, flapping, rustling and spreading and falling. *They sure do make a lot of noise* thought Cesar, mesmerized by the sight of a man with wings rustling and fanning around him. The wings curved twice each in a circle, the metal sheaves and scales making a beautiful, rippling design in the light's reflection. Once he was satisfied, Tieran jumped slightly upward and the thunderous noise from the wing's full power resonated throughout the chamber as it carried him upwards. He soared in huge arcing lines across the arena and came to an abrupt landing in front of the weapons wall.

The moment the soles of his boots touched down, the wings collected themselves behind him and ceased making any noise.

He chose a medium-sized shield, which had a dull, greenish-gray color. He selected a straight, oriental-looking sword encased in a dark black scabbard and passed it over his head, attaching it to his back between the pair of wings. He chose four small axes with brown leather knotted grips and curved steel heads and laid them across the floor, separated by their neighbor by six feet. A leather strap dangled from the bottom of each axe and each were placed below the handle and slightly opened.

When satisfied with the axes, he returned to the wall and pulled down a nine-foot long, iron-headed pike with a small crossbar of metal two feet from the tip. He placed the pike ten feet behind the axes while looking at the far wall. As an afterthought, he picked the pike back up and moved it two feet further back.

When Tieran was satisfied with the placement of the room, he made one final walk to the weapons wall and selected a long sword with a blade that ran perfectly straight for three feet and ended in an oblique angle downwards like a strange hook. The point was beveled and clearly as sharp as the entire blade. With one strong movement, he grabbed the bottom of the sword handle with his right hand and took a practice swing with the sword at an invisible opponent behind him. The movement was so sudden and precise that Cesar and Bob at once bucked their heads back in an involuntary reaction.

Tieran walked to the midsection of the arena and said, "Simulation—Jantu worm."

The room's female voice again responded with a question, "Size and disposition?"

Tieran began swinging the sword in a lazy figure eight in front of him while the wings complemented his armor by arcing and curving to defend his unprotected areas.

"The same specimen at Rothiel's Circus, 9212 b.c."

The voice ended the conversation with "Beginning simulation. Sequence begins upon approach to thirty meters."

Cesar saw the opposite side of the room blur for a slight moment and then saw the fearsome Jantu worm. It looked similar to a huge, pale sleeping bag, all puffed out as if ready to explode. All over its body in broken rings were the dark, puckered circles that were slightly raised and looked like barnacles. The worm was easily the size of a bus. It looked like it was slightly curled up, with its head buried underneath the front and was not moving. Tieran was immediately on guard with his jaw set firm. He began approaching the creature slowly with his shield up covering his chest and the sword low and to the right. An illuminated yellow line ran across the floor at the centerline just a few inches in front of Tieran's right foot. He picked up his left boot and stepped directly over the line.

The worm began making a low gurgling noise and its shiny skin began to tremble slightly. Tieran stopped, banked his head slightly and took two quick visual checks on the sword and shield. Then he took one more step.

The Jantu's head shot up from below it's body and curved away from Tieran just as one of the spines on its neck erupted in a quick stabbing motion. Tieran's wings ripped into motion and yanked him towards the right in a rapid jerk, just as the spine struck the floor, shattering the tile and splintering the spine's tip. The spine was thick and brown in color with slight ridges along the length. Cesar felt as if his heart had stopped when he saw how fast the worm reacted to Tieran and how it almost speared him through. Clear fluid was sliding down the spine from its quivering orifice.

Tieran's wings flew him in a short semi-circle away from the attacking spine and brought him crouched at the ready, one wing folded back ready to take to the air and the second curved in front of Tieran's lower legs to compensate for the shield. He checked his position cautiously and re-gripped the sword's handle. The worm slowly retracted the spine into its back as the head rotated facing Tieran. There was a milky stream of fluid flowing from a vertical crevice in the front, which began to separate. The mouth slowly opened to a gap displaying hundreds of long, curved teeth that seemed to beckon towards something inside. A thick tongue snaked its way out of the mouth and began preening the outside of the head, paying particular attention to a deep pit on each side of the head.

Those must be its eyes, thought Cesar as he wiped his sweating palms on his trousers. Bob looked into his eyes with a tense expression and mouthed *are you OK?* Cesar nodded and tried to convince himself that Tieran would kill it just as easily as the other simulations.

Tieran began a low run with the shield covering just below his eyes and the sword ready to swing. As he approached ten meters, the worm again began shaking violently and sprung out two spines toward Tieran, one deflecting off the shield, which knocked him slightly sideways jarring his body with a solid blow. Tieran's wings compensated and helped push his upper body forward on its original path as Tieran swung the sword toward the worm's right eye. Two more spines erupted out ripping the shield from Tieran's left arm and hitting the tip of his left wing, sending several shards each across the floor. The right wing immediately counteracted by spinning him away from the spine and limiting the damage to the left wing. Tieran corkscrewed in a low spiral towards the right side of the room, nearest the observation room. He was rotating his left hand and wiggling his fingers from the pain of having the shield torn away.

The worm reacted by shuffling forward and spread dozens of spines toward the walls, ripping up tiles from the floor and striking against the glass panels of the room shared by Bob and Cesar. The glass wall shook from the massive blows. Bob placed an arm around Cesar's shoulder and shouted over the noise, "We are not in any danger —nothing can get through this barrier." Cesar nodded, but still recoiled as the beast continued to expel spines in its mad pursuit of its rival. As far as Cesar could tell, Tieran still had not even scratched the worm. Cesar noticed the shield was crushed on the floor with the one of the straps dangling broken amongst the rubble.

Tieran was taking a large stride towards the worm while holding one of the axes just over his shoulder. He jerked his right arm downwards, windmilling the axe towards the creature's head. The axe head buried firmly into the upper area of the mouth that left just the handle protruding. The creature didn't seem fazed, except when it opened its mouth one side did not respond as quickly. Tieran had kicked up a second axe catching it with his right hand. As he calculated the distance and path, he spun the axe around his palm by the leather strap. He released the second axe with the same clean throw as the first. The second had struck the right side in front of the eye and the creature bucked its head down, reacting at last from the sting of Tieran's weapons.

Tieran quickly shifted the sword from his left hand to his right and kicked off into the air. His wings slung him rapidly over the creature and when he flipped upside down and dove towards the creature's neck, a spine shot out and tore dead center through his left wing. The wing erupted into fragments, howling a shrill scream as the metal was torn apart. Tieran was shook sideways by the movement until the wing tore free from the worm. He rolled away from the worm falling to the ground as the right wing pumped furiously to pull him to a safe distance. The left no longer resembled a wing, but a dangling mass of ruined metal. Tieran hit the ground, rolled to his feet and slapped the center ring of his harness while readying the sword in his left hand. The harness opened and he grabbed for the strap, ran towards the worm and threw the wings towards the worm's agitated head. The wings bucked and flapped erratically in the air until they slammed against the worm's face.

The worm drove its face down and began grinding the wings into the floor with its mouth while spines randomly extended from all over, crashing into the floor in a desperate search for his opponent. Tieran slashed the worm's head from the right and dodged a spine that was headed for his faceplate. He dodged, sliced the spine in two and in the same movement, spun and delivered a fierce cut to the side of the jaw.

A spine shot out and buried itself into Tieran's right thigh, penetrating the armor on top and exploding the metal panels under his knee. Tieran stifled a scream and chopped at the spine just over his thigh, releasing him from its grip and then used the sword's top edge to cut himself free from the side of the spine buried firm into the floor. He was unable to put much pressure on the wounded leg and used his left to hop towards the remaining axes. The worm jackknifed and covered the axes with the left side of its body anticipating Tieran's next move. Tieran backed away and picked up the pike. He placed the heel of the pike on the floor and leaned his weight against it and shored up his stability by placing his left foot in a better position to hold his ground. The worm moved its head forwards and back in a serpentine motion —

Cesar didn't know if it was taunting his opponent or not, but from Tieran's body language, it looked like he was in serious pain. Blood was coursing from the bottom of Tieran's thigh and ran down his armored calf.

The worm burst forward and began to turn its head away from the pike and display it's array of spines. Tieran pointed the tip of the pike towards the worm's lower neck and buried it to the crossbar. The worm immediately struck out with its spines while Tieran drove forward with the pike under his right arm and hacked away the spines with the sword in his left hand.

The worm rolled over onto its back attempting to dislodge the pike and exposed its underside, a boiling mass of legs that looked like giant cracked mushroom stalks. Tieran jumped towards the underside of the neck in an attempt to hack at its throat. A thick spine erupted out as he lunged and caught him in the ribs tearing away his armor from his side and shoulder as another tore into his helmet splitting the helmet in two and exposing the left side of his face in a bloody mess. His battle sword was twisted out of his hand by the gnashing mandibles of its jaws while he retrieved the smaller sword from his back and hacked away the spines penetrating his ribs, stomach and collarbone.

Tieran rolled off the beast and attempted to get to his feet to gain some distance and get to the axes. He felt woozy and could tell that one of his lungs had collapsed. He looked down and saw smaller spines sticking through his shin and one running almost the length of his left forearm. He knew at that point that he was not going to make it. He reached to pick up an axe from the floor just as the beast's tongue seized him around the waist and yanked him violently backwards. The worm dragged Tieran into its mouth and began ripping him apart with a violent shaking of its head and tearing of the jaws.

Cesar and Bob were both standing with their hands on the glass. Cesar was screaming, horrified.

Bob shouted, "Clear! Clear damn you!"

The feminine voice echoed, "Simulation ended. Validated by C.S.B. Bob White."

Tieran found himself lying on the floor on his back, a shimmering puddle of blood bloomed across the surface of the floor around him. He felt as if sand was running from his body and with it, all his body's warmth and strength. Tieran tried with all of his fiber to get to his knees. When he raised his torso from the blood-soaked floor and turned to get his knees under him he hardly resembled the human form. His left arm was missing at the elbow, as was most of the skin and muscle on the left side of his head. A bloody froth came out of his shredded chest armor with every breath and he knew he had just mere seconds. When he stepped up on his left foot, he felt the room spin and used his right hand to wipe the blood from his eyes to get his bearings. He began shuffling crouched over at the waist towards the doorway at the center of the room with his right arm moving back and forward like a drunken pendulum in an effort to keep his momentum going. His mutilated right leg dragged behind him like a child dragging a useless toy. The scope's doorway was twelve paces away—in his normal condition he could have easily leaped that distance. Instead, the journey was excruciating in both the time it took to get to the door as well as the feeling that he was fading much to fast to make it. He shuffled to the doorway, leaning briefly against it to swallow and regroup his strength. He felt like a strong wind or tide was gently pulling him away from the safety of the doorway and pushed forward with one last heave, allowing his body to fall through the frame. At once, his vision was inundated with cool light and every stitch of discomfort was gone. The room brightened at once to its original luster with a renewed Tieran standing on the other side of the doorway, unmarked from the battle. He was no longer wearing armor, but a simple pull on suit used to relax and cool off after exercise.

Cesar felt relief pour over him knowing that Tieran survived the battle. The glass door of the observation room slid open and Bob and Cesar walked out to greet the restored man. Bob was wiping his forehead with a handkerchief and shaking his head. "I had no idea those damn things could be that ghastly!"

Cesar didn't know what to say—in short moment he experienced worry, bottomless fear and relief. Looking up at Tieran he felt exhausted and exhaled a soft, "Shit."

Tieran laughed and slapped Bob on his shoulder. "There was nothing to worry about. If my vital signs fail, the simulation ends and the scope will slide over my quivering remains. Good as new!"

Bob said, "I just don't know why you insist on fighting this vile thing in human form and go through the pain and suffering."

Tieran ran his right hand through the thick hair on the back of his head, "Pain is a formidable teacher. If you are sluggish and not on your toes, a quick jab of pain gets you in the correct form." He realized that they were both looking at him as if he was some kind of freak. "Don't get me wrong—I *hate* pain as much as anyone. I have to find a way to beat this thing and getting a nip here or there helps me remember what *doesn't work*."

Bob stuffed his handkerchief into his suit pocket and fished out his watch. After a quick check, he looked Tieran square in the eye. "Gotta go Tieran."

Tieran knew what was on Bob's mind and nodded. "I'll take Cesar to dinner and then back to the temple afterwards. Let me know how it went tomorrow morning."

Bob winked at Tieran and ruffled Cesar's hair. "Exciting day eh Cesar? I'll be joining up with Theo on her expedition. I'll tell you all about it tomorrow." He turned towards Tieran, gave a formal bow with a smug look on his face, answered in kind by Tieran giving him an exaggerated Arabic farewell sign by twirling his index finger from his chest to his lips and finally to his forehead.

Bob walked briskly towards the door and before going out turned and told Cesar, "Remember what I told you before we came? That's a good boy. *Adios!*"

Tieran looked at Cesar, "What was it he told you?"

Cesar waited until Bob was well into the hallway. "Oh yeah! He said you'd show me the sword of Ikorsom!"

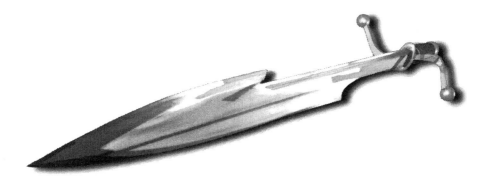

Chapter Eleven:
Ikorsom

Tieran walked towards the south end of the room and knelt to pick up the wings that turned into twisted strips of gleaming metal. He held it by the straps and examined it for a moment, then realized it was upside down and shifted it correctly in his hand. One of the spines, as fat as a thick broom handle was protruding through the center. "Remarkable how strong these worms are" said Tieran, pulling the spine free from the mass. "These wings are strong enough to withstand almost any weapon made from metal and those spines tore through them like paper."

Cesar was picking up severed pieces of metal that littered the floor. "Would it have broken your wings in your origin armor?"

"Not a chance." Said Tieran, running his palms over the plumed structure that was intact. " — Don't bother with those pieces. They will get rebuilt in just a moment." He swung the wings backwards and then tossed them underhanded through the scope's doorway making a quick flash and pop noise echo in the room. Tieran's origin wings sailed through the air as majestically as before, flapping rapidly and back towards the owner. The wings looked again like cut semitransparent glass and divided light with breathtaking beauty. The wing's motion ended the moment Tieran grasped the translucent straps in his outstretched hand. "See? Good as new."

Cesar looked down into his hands and all of the metal shards were gone, as were the pieces littering the floor.

"Rack." Said Tieran, and the wings burst again into flight and tore the air apart nosily back towards the weapons wall. They came to rest next to other items of armor and became still once more.

"That is *so* cool." Said Cesar. "Will I get to use wings like that someday?"

"You don't require them unless you are in battle — I am more than happy to train you if you like but you won't be using them as pure novelty. You have to earn the right to wear them and the training is very difficult."

Cesar was elated. "I don't mind — I'd love to become a soldier just like you!"

Tieran gave a skeptical look at Cesar, "You saw what the training sessions are like—pain is inevitable and there are no exceptions."

This made Cesar stop and think for a moment—you couldn't *exactly* die—the scope would bring you back in an instant. He also remembered what the spines did to Tieran's flesh.

"Tieran? Why didn't you pull the spines out of your body when you were fighting the worm?"

"Good question!" Began Tieran, "You seem a willing student! Bodies are mostly liquid-- water in fact. The brain and organs rely on blood pressure to circulate oxygen. If I had pulled out the spines from my body, the blood would have run out, quickly dropping the necessary pressure. I would have been incapacitated within seconds and dead from that nasty worm immediately after."

"So it's best to just leave them hanging out of you?" asked Cesar with a disgusted look on his face.

"Yup. They hurt like hell too."

Cesar cleared his mind of the thought of spines ripping through his chest and looked up at Tieran expectantly with an innocent smile on his face.

After a few moments of silence, Tieran remembered the object that Cesar was beside himself to see. Tieran sniffed. "Show *you* the sword of Ikorsom eh? I suppose there's no harm in it. You *do* however have to listen carefully to everything I say. First and foremost do not get in its way or it may go right *through* you.

"Which one is it?" asked Cesar looking at all of the swords attached to the south wall's racks.

Tieran's head came back in an expression of '*are you kidding?*' and motioned for Cesar to walk towards the south wall. "Vault?" asked Tieran.

A booming male voice toned "Passcode Commander Tieran?"

Tieran looked down at Cesar and held his index finger to his lips. "Super Nova."

The center wall began to open and slid apart slowly revealing a massive double-door. The outer door was inlaid with strange designs, which looked similar to an astronomical chart. Tieran walked over to the door and placed his palm in the center of a large circle, bent forward and whispered something that Cesar could not make out.

The door's star display changed from a dark blue background to almost pure white. A loud grunting metallic noise emanated deep within the door and then the clattering of gears and wheels announced the opening of the doors. From around the circle that Tieran touched with his hand, the entire wall began to separate. Tieran's right hand glowed with a soft blue light, radiating outward.

Cesar saw a sword resting upon the outstretched hands of a statue. The statue was clearly a warrior like Tieran, complete with stone wings that were unfurled and pointing skyward. The sword didn't look like anything special but was a strange shape. It was fairly long and the tip of the blade was curved back on itself similar to a crude fishhook. The handle had a slight downward curve as well and ended in a silver shape that Cesar could not make out. There were two guards that separated the blade from the handle and were made of gold rod, bent in the shape of a vortex with a small gold ball resting at each end. The top curved clockwise and the bottom, anti clockwise. Tieran gripped Cesar's shoulder gently and pushed him back a few feet and looked at him with a raised eyebrow. Cesar stayed where Tieran moved him, eyes locked on the sword.

Tieran said "To me." For a moment, Cesar didn't know if he was talking to him, until he heard the slight stroke of a metal's harmonic vibration and the sword released itself from the vault, rotated level and floated towards Tieran. Tieran grabbed the handle firmly and rotated the point of the sword upwards. The two guards above the handle began lengthening and counter-rotated around Tieran's forearm until it reached the elbow, protecting his flesh with a tight spring of golden metal. Tieran crooked his head towards Cesar to come forward.

Cesar stepped closer to the sword that looked old and scratched all over. When he got closer to the sword, he saw that instead of scratches, it appeared to be writing, designs and portraits all over it. Some images were large and some extremely small—some too small to see clearly.

Tieran said, "Do not touch the blade—for some, the slightest touch of its blade will utterly destroy them."

Cesar was unaware that his hands were not at his sides and felt surprised that he was about to touch the sword with an inquisitive finger.

Tieran whispered to the sword, "Thou shall not allow any harm to pass upon this child, Cesar." A shine or streak of light seemed to flow from the hilt to the tip. Cesar wasn't quite sure if he imagined it.

Tieran then lowered the sword to Cesar and the guards retreated to their original position over the handle.

"I can hold it?" asked Cesar with surprise.

"It's safe. This sword knows not to hurt you—go ahead, take it."

He held out two hands to take hold of it, guessing that he'd need the strength of both to keep it from hitting the floor. When his hands finally closed around the thick handle, he realized with a shock that the sword had no weight at all.

The guards swiftly ran around his right forearm, snaking towards his elbow. The feeling was ticklish and cool. Although his lower arm was entirely encased, it was flexible and he could bend his wrist with ease. "It's light!" remarked Cesar, marveling at the sword in his right hand. He turned away from Tieran and waved the sword around gently.

"In fact, it weighs nothing," said Tieran. "Go ahead—try to strike me with it."

Cesar looked puzzled. "You're not wearing any armor-- won't it hurt you?"

"This weapon was commanded never to harm me—the same order I gave it in your case—try it out!"

Cesar made a clumsy stabbing motion towards Tieran and immediately felt the sword's tip pull itself away from Tieran's torso.

Cesar turned it upside down to look at the pommel and saw that the silver object was a ball with a strange design carved into the center. It was two symbols, the blazing sun and shining moon both cracked in half. Upon closer inspection, the grey metal making up the blade looked like there were numerous forms of writing on it.

Tieran ran his finger down the top of the blade, "When the universe was blown into creation, this metal formed in the exact center. It *resisted* creation if you will. It is as old as time and its only will is to destroy."

A feeling of horror came over Cesar as he wondered about the multitudes of people that had fallen from this very weapon.

"This sword *is* the great destructor. Said Tieran softly. "It cannot create anything but misery and loss."

Cesar felt coldness in his stomach and wondered how many millions had died because of this relic. He handed it back towards Tieran. As if it understood that it no longer wanted to be held, the guards silently uncoiled from Cesar's arm.

Tieran realized that he probably put a damper on Cesar's curiosity and said, "How about a quick demonstration? He got a slight smile from Cesar and Tieran reached down and grasped his hand. "Stay close now. Simulation! —Twenty bull Seeths chained to the floor."

Cesar felt alarmed and looked at Tieran's face for an explanation.

"Nothing to worry about, I assure you."

The soft feminine voice echoed across the room. "Simulation begins at approach of ten meters."

The room suddenly appeared very small. Scattered across the arena were the huge beasts, all with thick metal collars around their necks connected to short chains to the floor. Cesar was frightened of them behind an impenetrable viewing wall, but to be amongst them in the open arena brought on a strong feeling of panic. He could smell their stink, hear with perfect clarity how they dragged their claws and sense their hateful gaze on his body. He grabbed Tieran's leg and kept an eye on the sword.

"Ikorsom!" yelled Tieran as he held the sword forwards. The sword began a loud trembling noise and white plasma rushed out of the blade creating a large vortex around Tieran and Cesar. A loud clap of thunder shook Cesar and to his shock, saw all of the Seeths shriek and dissolve into dust. The metal collars fell to the floor unhindered and clattered to a stop amongst the loose chains.

The room was quiet and Cesar's ears were ringing from the loud crash. He had let go of Tieran's leg and went over to look at one of the metal collars. He kicked at one and it barely moved an inch. It was so large that Tieran, Bob and himself could have easily stood through its center without touching the sides.

"You see? Its destruction is endless and absolute."

"Why can't you use it against the Jantu—or anything that Rothiel comes up with?" asked Cesar waving at the room's empty collars.

"It would destroy anything in its path. We just do not know what Rothiel plans on doing—it's possible that he could place the very

Earth in jeopardy. Everyone is better off if this sword is out of the equation."

Cesar understood. He hadn't seen much in his short life, but the past 24 hours opened his eyes to events unthinkable by anyone on Earth —Rothiel was different to the worst degree. There was a vast amount of hate burning inside him and he would probably do his worst to the Earth and Heavens—just given the opportunity.

Tieran walked over to the vault, placed the sword upon the arms of the statue and stepped backwards. "Lock in full."
The heavy vault doors began to swing shut, drowning the room in machine noise until the soft boom of the doors closed in on themselves. A quick series of soft clicks and a thunderous cracking sound ended the viewing of the most fearsome weapon known. The outer doors of the vault changed from pure white back to the star map, of deep blue with gold arcs, lines and stars.

As they both stepped back, the weapons walls began sliding back into place, covering the giant vault doors.

With the vault closed, Tieran felt relieved that it and everything around was again safe. Just opening the vault doors was a significant risk these days and made him feel vulnerable. Rothiel will be released in just hours and he felt the desire to take Ikorsom and descend on him and his followers like a hurricane. To destroy them once and for all, and save the two worlds from Rothiels inevitable wrath only made sense. He could not, however bring himself to disobey God.

Tieran caught himself and looked down at Cesar. "What would you like to eat?"

Cesar looked pensive and thought about what he had always desired but could never have. "What are the choices?"

Tieran laughed. "Whatever your heart desires."

Cesar's eyes gleamed. "McDonalds!"

Tieran and Cesar sat in the moonlit patio of the restaurant eating their meals mixed with animated discussions. Tieran was laughing at Cesar's choice of food and Cesar chided Tieran on his favorite Hong Kong selection. "I've never had McDonalds before! There was one in Calderón and it had a gigantic yellow 'M' out in front. My mother told me that we would eat there one day if we had enough money. Last year for my birthday, she brought me tamales that were wrapped in McDonalds paper and I was never so happy--- until my friend Jose told me that they don't sell tamales there. He said that she probably found the wrappers in the garbage and wrapped up her food and *lied* to me. I was so angry with him that I didn't let him try my McDonald's food and never spoke to him again. Looking back, I guess he was right, but it was the best birthday present ever."

"Your mother sounds like she loves you very much. Do you find it hard being away from her?"

Cesar's laughing eyes went soft. He sat a moment looking at his food, wiped off the burger juice from his mouth and retrieved his patch. He opened it and slid it over to Tieran. In the center was moving image of his mother and grandmother, sitting at their small patio packed full of well-wishers. Everyone was wearing their best clothes and listening to soft music from a radio. There was food and drink, but people were not celebrating. There were women nearby crying and men shaking their heads with remorse. The patio was decorated with flowers and a small picture of Cesar was sitting on a cracked wooden table near the wall.

"I watch them—my mother and grandmother when I miss them. I've seen them sad sometimes, but not like this. I wish that I could somehow tell her that I'm fine and not to be sad."

"It's a very dark time for them. I've never understood why it must be that way—it just is. Well, you know what lies behind death's door. Someday, you'll go to that big willow tree and welcome them here. They won't ever suffer like they did on Earth and you'll be a family again." Tieran felt uncomfortable not knowing the right thing to tell a child. "…Would you like to try some of my roast pork?"

He passed the patch back while Cesar whispered sadly, "Couldn't take another bite."

Cesar took a glimpse of the image and closed the patch. After moment he asked Tieran about his family.

"I'm in a different situation. I have been in service of God for several thousand years. I have had several lives on Earth and had many families and countless children. Now that there is about to be trouble on Earth, I and many others decided to remain here and stay ready."

Cesar nodded his head. He looked over at the lake and admired the shimmering reflection of the moon across the rippled water. Cattails waved back and forth in the gentle breeze.

Tieran placed his chopsticks down on the table, picked up his cup of tea and took a final drink. No matter the scenery, he couldn't bring himself to think of anything other than defeating the worm.

"Why don't we head back to the temple," said Tieran. "Bob has a room ready for you there. Why don't we meet up here tomorrow for breakfast and I'll introduce you to buns made from sweet beans?"

Cesar's smile was back and he jumped down from his chair. "Yick. Buns made from beans?"

"...And for lunch you can try fish head—it's the tastiest part!"

They both walked together on the lit path towards the temple. Where Theo first took him when he arrived. It was lit up with a soft, blue light on the outside and children were flying kites nearby that were shaped like giant fireflies that blinked on and off with green light. He couldn't have imagined a view more beautiful and again, felt sad that his family was not here to enjoy it. When they approached the temple, Cesar looked at the big Weeping Willow tree at the edge of the path. A family of a dozen or so was standing there with excited expressions on their faces. "Can I ask the fountain when my mother and grandmother will come here?"

Tieran considered what he said carefully, "I don't see why not—except that it may distract you from your job. I mean, if they are coming back in a short time, or under bad circumstances, you may not be able to push it aside."

Cesar frowned, "What do you mean, *bad circumstances*—do you mean suicide? My family would never do such a thing."

Tieran stopped and placed both hands on Cesar's shoulders, "I don't mean anything. I've seen death—in every way possible and in most instances it is very unpleasant. Your death for instance—tragic and a living hell for some. It's your decision to make, but I suggest you decide carefully."

They both passed through the doorway of the temple and continued down the long hallway. As they proceeded toward Bob White's office, Tieran stopped and pointed to the door across the hallway from Bob's. The doorplate was labeled 'C.S.B. Cesar Rivas'. Cesar looked at the huge door, "This is mine? I've never had my own room before!"

Tieran pointed to the door with his outstretched palm, inviting Cesar to open the door. Cesar grinned, stepped forward and gripped the large, bronze knob. The door opened to a large room colored in a soft yellow paint. The walls were adobe and the floor terrazzo tile. There was a bed replete with multi-colored Mexican blankets and shelves littered with dozens of toys. There was a short note laying on the bed:

Cesar,

I hope you like your new room. Theo decorated and I picked out the toys.
Don't worry- you can always redecorate later!

Bob

Cesar held the note to his chest as he looked around his room. The design, colors and even the smells reminded him of home as he thought, *I wouldn't change it for the world.* There were toys old and new, some were made of metal and some of wood. He picked up a bright red plastic robot from Japan that had a big propeller on his back and wheels under his feet like skates. It had corrugated white plastic arms that ended in rounded claws. Cesar pushed a square button on its ample belly and a string of Japanese words rang out with a tinny voice. It looked similar to a VW beetle, quite common from his hometown-- and had comical, friendly looking eyes.

Tieran was still in the doorway. "That guy is Robocon. From a 1970's TV show in Japan."

Cesar looked back at the robot. "Neat! Uh, What else does he do?"

Tieran chuckled. "That's about it. His eyes change. Some of the other big ones shoot plastic missiles and fists but Robocon is the only one that talks."

Cesar yawned and sat down on his bed opening the chest panel of his robot toy and noticed fake dials, meters and other components.

Tieran was infected by the same yawn and said, "I'll see you tomorrow for breakfast—if you need me, just use the patch."

Cesar left the robot on the bed and walked briskly back to Tieran, "Thank you for everything." He held out his diminutive hand for a shake. Tieran grabbed it and shook with a firm grip. "Don't mention it—you're a good boy, Cesar. And if you are serious about training as a soldier, you are going to have to work hard!" Tieran pumped his right arm and mock squeezed a bicep.

Cesar giggled, "I'll try hard, I promise."

Tieran stepped out of the doorway, said "Goodnight" and closed the door behind him. Cesar turned to look at his room and was equally surprised and pleased as when he first saw it. He went back to his bed, picked the robot up and sat down on the edge. He looked at the rustic nightstand and upon it saw a framed picture of his Mother and Grandmother, they were holding Cesar when he was just a year old.

Chapter Twelve:
Seth's Gift

Gellan stood by the wall of monitors watching a man straddling a moped and ringing the bell at the gate of the ranch. "Rip, Simon made it."

Rip was sitting in his favorite lounge chair, puffing billowing clouds of smoke, thinking dark thoughts about tomorrow's events. He had news to tell everyone and it would not be taken very well.

"As soon as he gets in, lets have a discussion."

Gellan pushed the actuator button opening the large gate doors for Simon and walked back to the living room. "Do you want me to round up everyone?"

Rip took the smoldering cigar out of his mouth, sat forward and placed it in a large glass ashtray on the coffee table. "Just the team—let the children sleep."

Gellan nodded, walked out of the room and went down the long hallways knocking on doors and announced the impromptu meeting.

After a few minutes, Rip heard the rasping noise of the moped outside the front door. It wound down, made a small fart noise followed by a pop and went silent. Simon entered through the main door, took off his thick, leather jacket and helmet and hung them on the nearby coat rack. He looked very cold.

Rip said, "Hell, I'm sorry Simon—we forgot to give you the keys. You okay?"

Simon just nodded and walked over to the chair nearest the fireplace and sat down. Several men began filing into the living room and taking their seats around the ample living room in one of the many couches that surrounded a large, oval coffee table.

Gellan was walking to the far end of the corridor when he saw Noise strutting towards him whistling. "Hank, have you seen Kayanan? Rip wants all of us in the living room for a meeting."

Noise stopped, scratched the top of his head and said, "I think I saw him in one of the exercise rooms. Don't worry about it—I'm going to get a beer in the cafeteria and I'll tell him on the way."

"Cool! Thanks Hank." Gellan turned and trotted back to the living room.

Kayanan stood in the middle of the exercise room swinging a thin, steel cable tipped with one of his struts in a circle waist high. He waited and then released the strut, letting it rocket up towards his target, a stout wooden peg attached to the wall 15 feet from the floor. The strut arced towards the peg and clipped it, sending the strut in tighter concentric circles around the peg until it jammed solid. By this time, Kayanan had sent up a smaller strut to join its big brother, locking it in place. Just after the second strut locked the first in place, Kayanan was hurling additional cables around the room until he had locked three pegs around the room. With each, he was able to use them for leverage and run full tilt up walls and swing himself to the opposite side of the room with complete ease. When he ran across the wall attached to the third peg, he released two sharpened steel weapons called butterflies towards his target, a wooden statue on the end of the room. The two butterflies buried themselves deep into the target, one entering the forehead and the other into the chest.

Before his momentum carried him downwards to the room's padded floor, the door crashed open and Noise stuck his head in, delivering the message like a drill sergeant screaming through a bullhorn. "Hey Flip! Laughing boy is having a meeting in the living room!"

Noise waltzed into the room, throwing Simon a beer and flopping down onto the couch in the center of the room. "Ricky's on his way!"

Rip asked, "Did someone go to the kitchen and get Big Lee? It takes him about an hour to drag his fat ass in here."

"I heard that, old bastard!" shouted big Lee coming down the hallway. "And *I* wasn't eating—Enano was!" Lee walked into the room wearing a large cotton pullover and baggy shorts. He was walking on flip-flops with soles made from car tire rubber--especially made for his weight. Behind him lumbered Enano, a fairly fat gold and white-colored corgi with short, stubby legs and a white mask of hair on his face. The dog rambled over to where big Lee was taking his usual seat, a reinforced cement chair covered with thick, sturdy cushions. Lee plopped down with a big "Ah!" and the dog looked up for a few seconds expectantly, and then lay down on the stone floor next to him.

Rip looked at the dog with disapproval, "Don't let that dog fall asleep in here or he'll have a bad dream and pop!" Corey picked his massive feet up and began massaging the dog with them. "Man, will you leave him alone! He hasn't fucked up anything in this house in a long time." The dog, as if it understood that its owner was defending it, began contentedly jabbing his tongue out of his mouth and wagged its tail, beating against the coffee table.

The table began to shudder against the onslaught and Noise piped up grabbing his beer, "Corey! He's knocking shit down again!"

Big Lee reached over, picked his dog up and laid him across his massive lap. "You wait, one day this dog will kick all of 'yo asses!"

Kayanan was last in, wearing a black tank top and loose exercise pants. He was toweling off sweat from an interrupted workout.

Rip sat himself up in his chair, said "Good. Let's get down to business." He raised himself out of his chair and walked over towards the fireplace, arranging himself in center of the group. "We all know what is going to happen tomorrow and this 'little chat' is to prepare for the next few days. I want to get your opinions of what we can expect with Rothiel's arrival and frankly, what we can do about it."

Noise, as usual, was first to open his mouth. "I think I speak for all of us when I say—when are we going to take this asshole out? We're the best prepared, we've got the best chance to be successful and we all know he's going to try to destroy us all, right?"

Rip took a long drag off his cigar and was patting the air towards Noise trying to get him to pipe down before he became further agitated. He was not about to let Noise take charge of a conversation as important as this.

With smoke pouring from Rip's mouth, he said, "Duly noted. However we need more preparation first. We don't know who is allied with him yet. I intend to be nearby when he 'hatches' and see who is there to greet him. Secondly, after he's had a couple of days to absorb his situation, I'm going to pay him a small visit…"

Noise broke in, "That's fucking stupid! His goons will kill you on sight! You know—"

Rip shot out, "Shut up Noise! He has been trapped in rock for a little over ten thousand years—he may be retarded for all we know! However, I don't feel we're that lucky and I'm sure that whatever plans he has, he'll be just as careful as we need to be. The more people that are allied to him, the more strength he'll have. See?"

Noise looked at a couple of guys nearby for visible approval, got none, and slowly took his seat mumbling to himself.

Rip continued, "Now, our session for tonight is the same as always — we are going to wire up Seth in a few minutes and see if he can find a way to revive Filo from his sleep as well as find out anything we can about Rothiel and his motives.

Kayanan cleared his throat to signal to Rip that he'd like to comment.

Rip pointed his cigar towards Kayanan and said "Go on." Kayanan took the towel off from around his neck and said, "Are you sure you want to waste time trying to get a cure for Filodraxes when Seth's so weak? I put in Seth's dextrose I.V. half an hour earlier and he looks like this will be his last session. Don't you think it will be best to use his remaining time to get a roster of Rothiel's organization or try to find the location of Big Lee's son?"

Noise and Lee both nodded their assent while Filthy stepped forward, "He doesn't look that weak to me." Filthy puffed out his chest in his typical statesman pose and gripped the lapels of his suit jacket. "—I'm betting we've got a good ten minutes before he goes tit's up. If we get a cure for Filo, it would be one of the best assets we can possibly get. Besides — technically he's *still* alive and has been that way since 1750 B.C.! I bet he can recall most everything up to the time he turned into a vegetable. I say we ask about a cure for Filo and then worry about Diano — with Filo around he could find Diano in just a day!" Filthy fell silent while something crossed his mind. His saintly smile grew into the grin a greedy child would strike on Christmas morning. "There is *one* other thing we could try... Remember when we came across a 'jack of all trades' savant? Remember how useful he was?"

This started the men muttering and shaking their heads in argument. Rip had the urge to interrupt and tell them he had already decided, but instead thought about what each man had said carefully. He tossed his cigar stub into the fireplace and walked slowly towards the wall cabinet to pour himself a cognac, muttering to himself throughout the journey. He opened the crystal decanter and picked up a clean snifter. He wondered to himself if he was banking too much on Filodraxes' help in the matter. He was even more headstrong than Rip was — at least he thought he remembered him being headstrong. His thinking was interrupted by a loud "Fuck you!" from Big Lee. Lee was looking pissed off at Filthy while the other brethren laughed. Rip looked down at the snifter and realized that he had poured so much cognac into the glass that it was almost full. He stopped, half contemplating carefully pouring most of it back into the bottle. *Screw it*. He went back to the fireplace with his full glass and placed it on the mantle—his mind was made up.

As Rip spoke, he looked at each man around the room. "Thanks for your input. We will give three minutes to try to recover Filo—no more. Seth should be able to find Corey's boy in just a minute or two and then the remainder of Seth's time I want dedicated to probing Rothiel's followers." Rip looked over at Filthy. "A savant would come in very handy—we'll play it by ear. If he answers the two questions quickly then maybe we'll get him to ask. When Seth goes, he's gone— I'm just hopeful that we can bring Filo back and get him to locate our newborn Seth as fast as possible before he gets too damaged.

Rip thought back how lucky they were this generation when they were able to locate Seth when he was just four. Doctors at a sanitarium in Massachusetts were hours away from an operation to remove an entire hemisphere of his brain in order to stop his seizures. Poor kid. The doctors didn't realize that the mere reflection of glass or the shine of their metal instruments was enough to drive Seth's mind into the Fileserver's fountain.

Since he was simply a human, he was unable to process the flow of information in a coherent manner. When his brain attempted to cope with the sheer volume and energy of the fountain, it simply hemorrhaged until he was unconscious. The damage it caused to his brain was permanent and worsened with every session.

The amount of information, unfortunately for Seth, was worth much more than his discomfort, health and ultimately, his life. Rip did not want to feel like such a cold bastard—after all, it was Seth's affliction and there was no cure other than blinding him. He has spent the majority of his life cycles in self-imposed darkness, rarely emerging in broad daylight unless he was sure that only soft light was shining on his face. Any brilliant light pulled him helplessly in the fountain.

There have been many times that the team was unable to find him in time and usually if he reached his twenties, he was so far gone mentally that he was useless to the world. Seth forever loathed the sheer pain and of the horrors that he witnessed inside, but the ecstasy of knowledge and the desire to become part of the fountain was irresistible.

The group of men including Noise nodded at Rip's announcement. It was a conglomeration of the different ideas. Most present were not looking forward to Seth's imminent torture and demise.

"Who gets to put him out when his brain flatlines?" asked Filthy. The room looked at him with concern as they in turn, remembered that several times in the past, during his last sessions, his brain would collapse. In most cases, he would continue breathing but would have seizures, one after the other. The oldest member of the group would gently smother him with a pillow from the very hospital bed on which he laid. Rip took a strong pull from the snifter just before he would announce responsibility when Kayanan spoke, "I'll take care of it. After all, I'll be attending him during the session—I'll make sure he doesn't suffer." Rip swallowed his cognac while nodding to Kayanan and felt the burning warmth of the alcohol complement his feeling of gratitude.

Rip cleared his throat, "We have one more important order of business to discuss. Noise wasn't entirely wrong when he blathered that Rothiel will kill me."

"No shit?" yelped Noise, slapping his knee with his palm and nodding his head in exaggeration.

"I'm expecting that he'll demand my allegiance when I come to visit. If I remember him well enough, he will kill me when I refuse to bow down to him. So, I'm planning on going out with a bang and take him with me if that is the case."

Kayanan sat up. "If you go alone, he may guess what you intend to do."

Rip shifted his brandy glass towards Simon and said, "That's why 'indestructo-boy' is coming with me."

The men murmured amongst themselves and most agreed that Simon was the best candidate to accompany Rip to Rothiel's stronghold. Rip added, "When I go, I am going to go really big—sky high. Who better than Simon to pick through the rubble and make sure that Rothiel is gone?" To Rip, the conversation went pretty well. He had expected Noise to rant himself foamy if he wasn't a central player in the plan. Rip swallowed the cognac in three long gulps and tossed the snifter into the fireplace.

There was some chatter amongst the men on topics presented at the meeting but the mood was somewhat somber. The thought of what laid ahead for Seth took the wind out of everyone's sails.

"Sorry to bother you," A young girl, not yet twelve years old stood at the entry of the lounge holding a clipboard that was half her size.

Rip waved her over, "What is it Trudy?"

"We have some good news." She walked up to him and handed over the large clipboard. The room was now silent and the brethren's eyes were darting from Trudy to Rip in anticipation.

Rip's eyebrows raised and he looked at the girl. "When did the call come in?

"Our 1-800 line picked up the call just after eight in the evening and was auto-forwarded to us at eight-fifteen."

Rip smiled at the girl and handed back her clipboard. "Go ahead and break the news to the boys."

Trudy turned to the room, cleared her throat and began. "Someone rang the free access phone number for the Numbers Station in Fort Myers, Florida this afternoon and passed on the following information: Name, Sharky"

"Hell yes!" yelled out Noise. "Sharky's back!" Most of the men around the lounge clapped and whistled at the news.

Trudy's smile grew even larger and she continued: "Address, 8033 Winged Foot Drive; Caucasian; Blood type, O positive; Travel plans, none; Father, State Trooper; Mother, Homemaker."

Rip was proud of his accomplishment, making Numbers Stations that spanned most of the US and half of the rest of the planet running on the a.m. spectrum at 283kHz. Morse tones were generated at 17.4Khz-- at a level that only children can hear, bearing the phone number of their local Numbers Station. When a reincarnated lodge member heard the tones, they would wait for moment when alone and phone the station. The phone number of the caller would identify exactly where the child called from and a rescue plan would kick into action. It worked perfectly.

Rip looked at the group of men. "Gideon, and ... Hank, I would like you to proceed to Florida and get Sharky back."

Gideon stood. "Uh, Rip? What about your meeting with Rothiel?"

"Don't worry—I'm not doing anything until you both get back. Make sure you do up paperwork for his birth certificate, take at least four blank passports with you and take Juani as your rent-a-wife."

93

Hank shook his head. "Do you want the regular scenario—baby snatched out of the home or do you want it done in public?"

Rip thought a moment. "Hell, if you could get them into a shopping mall, all the better. One thing though—Trudy, the recording said that the father was a State Trooper?"

Trudy nodded.

Rip said a long, breathless "Shit." He continued pouring over the possibilities in his mind. Y'know, I think it would be best for everyone if you snatched Sharky and got him on a plane back here on the same day. Law enforcement is going to comb the hell out of the area afterwards, so be *real* careful."

Rip turned back to Trudy. "Thank you dear—good work. Even Hank is pleased as he'll want to turn logistics over to him when he gets here!"

Hank blurted out, "It'll be awhile—he's not even two yet. Besides, he's the one that likes running logistics—I'm shitty at it."

Big Lee seconded, "Amen to that!"

While Hank said, "fuck you" to Corey, Rip continued with Trudy. "First thing tomorrow, get accounting to cut the tickets and tell Juani that she'll be getting on a plane in the next 48 hours to Florida."

Trudy tugged Rip's shirtsleeve. We've got another issue, Rip."

Rip's brow furrowed at her serious tone. "OK young lady— spill it."

"Well, we'd had another call-- for the international number in the papers," said Trudy. "It came in the day before from a number in Fredericksburg Virginia. The caller sounded like a black male, at least thirty years of age and said his name was Abraham Kennedy."

"Did he say any particulars or fit any known members that are unaccounted for?"

"Not really. He seemed to be distressed and said that he had memories of things that did not happen in his lifetime. He also said something very strange—if he gets drunk, he can see heaven."

Rip thought about missing brethren, especially those that had abilities that were similar to Seth's. "I'm drawing a blank." Said Rip. "This is disturbing if it's true, as I can't think of anyone but Seth that can take a glimpse into the Origin world. Do me a favor—call our East Coast operations and have Ricardo's boys investigate."

She nodded. "I'll take care of it."

Rip noticed that the mood was lifted by good news. He checked his watch for a brief period and then clapped his hands together.

"Well gentlemen, if there are no other questions, we should proceed downstairs and send off brother Seth."

The men got up from their chairs and headed off down the staircase that lead to the underground areas of the fortress. Seth was in his room on the second level. The men proceeded past his room to a space one door further down. Noise opened the door and turned on the lights. This room was called the observation room and was about half of the size of the living room. In the center of the room was a hospital bed with the head raised up in the sitting position. Nearby were trolleys loaded with instruments to track his mental activity, blood pressure and also standing at the ready, a defibrillator. On the wall facing the bed, three video cameras stood on tripods that would capture the session in film and magnetic tape. On the adjacent wall, a reel-to-reel recording system would track everything spoken over a ceiling mounted omni directional microphone and several boom mikes around the room. An up-to-date series of print encyclopedias were on a shelf on the back of the room, a typewriter and paper and several notebooks, all with the attending member's names printed on the covers. An XT microcomputer was sitting in the corner, already booted, networked via thicknet to a small compendium of searchable content from the Lodge's archives loaded on a PDP-11 server in level four.

Kayanan knocked on Seth's door and heard, "Come in, Ricardo." Before opening the door, he checked himself to make sure that there was nothing attached to him that gave off a shine. Even a ballpoint pen with a small splash of chrome was enough to set him off. He had previously removed his belt buckle and wristwatch. When he opened the door, Seth was sitting on the edge of his bed, already placing his sleep blindfold over his eyes. "Are we ready to begin?" The room was very austere—all of the lighting was diffused and the walls were covered with a dull ochre fabric. All of the furniture was wood—not one square inch of it was lacquered or painted. Books lined the walls and littered the tables of his room—it was really Seth's only journey to the outside room. None of the books had protective sleeves or even illustration pages that could be shiny in any way. On special occasions, Seth would go with the boys to a restaurant or club wearing winter ski sunglasses that were painted opaque on the insides. The side blinds would protect his peripheral vision from any stray reflected light.

Looking at Seth's somber room, the Filipino wished they had taken him out more often.

Kayanan walked over and took hold of the rack holding up Seth's dextrose I.V. bag. The entire rack had been spray painted with flat black paint and the plastic IV bottle was concealed in a burlap sack. The plastic IV tube that ran to his arm was sheathed in sewn burlap and the needle that was buried in his forearm was completely wrapped in surgical tape. The precautions must always be perfect. Seth stood up from his chair and held out his hand. Kayanan looked at the blindfolded face of his friend and saw the same pale skin, contrasting with course, black stubble that ran around his jaw and over his upper lip. "Everyone is filing into the room now." Said Kayanan as he turned and stood out in front of Seth. Kayanan positioned himself so that Seth could grab the back of his arm and he walked him out of his unadorned environment and into the observation room.

Seth could hear the rumble of the team's voices as they set the room up and could smell the antiseptic used liberally in cleaning the floors and instruments. "There's our boy!" hollered Noise somewhere off to his left. He raised his right hand in a thumbs-up and tried to smile. He lost count of all the sessions that were done here — and had died twice in this very same room. Kayanan temporarily disconnected his IV so that Seth could remove his robe. When Seth removed it, Kayanan stared at the number four in origin script that stood out upon his chest as a red welt. Kayanan hoped that in Seth's next life he would be blessed with a three. *Hell, out of all of us, he must have earned it by now* thought Kayanan. Of the Lodge members, only Rip had the numeral one on his chest. He had been that way for hundreds of years.

Kayanan's eyes dropped and noticed that Seth was already wearing the adult diaper that was to be his life's last uniform. Seth knew from vast experience that his seizures were always strong and tended to overpower his bladder. He was also aware that he would soon be passing through death's door. As a precaution, he went to the bathroom recently. He didn't want one of his brothers to be inconvenienced because he just so happened to 'shit himself'. He climbed into the bed and Kayanan reconnected the IV. When he was comfortable, Kayanan pulled his covers up and then began the long task of applying the conductive gel to Seth's head and body and attaching the many wires that would watch his body decline towards death. As he attached the electrodes, he looked over Seth's rising and falling abdomen to monitor the electro-encephalogram's diagnostic meter.

Big Lee was checking the reel-to-reel tape drive and making sure that test comments were being recorded correctly as well as tuning the sound levels on the multiple boom microphones that were around the room. A slight machine gun clatter of plastic keys shot out from the computer desk. Gellan, the fastest human in the world and the fastest typist of the group, was busy creating a new file in the computer and was standing by to type in search statements against the database. The Lodge's written archives filled several rooms and in countless languages. Unfortunately, some languages had been forgotten. Back in the 1200's, Rip demanded that all further correspondence be written in the origin language and that all generations must spend 15 years of each generation studying the scripts and speaking the language. He insisted that this language 'must remain alive'. The new computer database only held a small sliver of the archived data, but as an exercise, each generation from now on would transcribe the data into the mainframe. Rip estimated that in approximately three hundred years, with constant vigilance by the Lodge, all of the information would be entered into the database. Noise thought it was a stupid idea.

When everyone gave the thumbs up, Rip walked over to the bed and placed his hand on Seth's. "Are you ready?"

Seth's smile glimmered under the blind over his eyes, "As ready as I'll ever be."

Rip said, "Gentlemen, we as always, are honored by Seth's sacrifice and truly fortunate to have both his ability and his friendship. Let us all kneel for the benefit of prayer."

Noise grumbled, but knelt anyway. All of the team members knelt on one knee on the floor and bowed their heads.

Rip was silent for a moment, took a long breath and began, "Dear lord, we thank you for our lives, our brotherhood, abilities as well as your divine guidance. Brother Seth is to begin his journey to his next life and begin again living in this most uncertain world. Please allow us to retrieve him quickly and safely to our fold. In your name we pray. So mote it be."

The rest of the team repeated in unison, "So mote it be." Rip pushed himself back up, the gout in his feet and arthritis in his knee barking in painful yelps. Alcohol always irritated his gout and it seemed to aggravate everything else in him. After his breathing was back to normal, he leaned over to speak to Seth's ear.

"Seth? When you arrive, find out what you can about Filodraxes' condition. Specifically ask what we are missing in the formula. Then ask about Big Lee's son. Try to find out where the hell he currently lives—the moment you find out, change gears and find out who is allied with Rothiel. Try to give us the names as fast as you can."

Cesar sat on his bed playing with the red robot and asking it questions, which he knew to be pointless. "Should I? What if I don't like what I find out?" The robot said nothing. Cesar pushed the white button again, heard the clack of the switch spinning the small, plastic record and then the tinny burst of Japanese. Cesar knew that it was fruitless—he had to make the decision—whether to find out when his mother or grandmother would die and finally join him here. Either way it would occupy his mind. He resolved to find out. He left the robot lying on his bed and headed toward the inner temple.

When he arrived outside the door of the fountain, he could again feel the rush of knowledge rushing past him as if it was leaking through miniature cracks in the door. He laid his finger on the large doorknob, just as Bob did earlier that day and heard the soft boom as the door began to open for him. Cesar found himself gazing at the massive room and directly at the glowing fountain ahead of him. He began a brisk walk towards the fountain and forgot just how large the room really was. As he walked, he watched the ceiling move past him slowly, building higher and higher as he approached the center of the room. *That must be the biggest dome—anywhere!* After ten short minutes he arrived at the edge of the fountain and gazed into the flowing display. Beautiful.

He was somewhat lost in thought by the time he arrived at the edge of the fountain's pool. The muffled rushing sound and play on lights captivated him. He placed his folded arms over the thick rim of the pool that encircled the fountain, laid his head on top of his arms and laid his head sideways, taking in the fascinating display. Light from the column of energy danced across his face and feeling of the energy that seemed to gently brush his face as it passed around him.

Rip licked his dry lips in anticipation, looked around the room to make sure all parties were ready and satisfied that they were, said, "Let's begin."

Kayanan gently removed the blind from Seth's face and laid it on the table. The heart rate monitor nearest to Kayanan beeped softly and regularly. Seth had his eyes closed and slowly opened them to get adjusted to the light. Kayanan stood ready with a small, round mirror in his right hand, cupped against his leg, out of Seth's view.

Seth inserted the blue mouth protector into his dry mouth, placed both of his nervous palms on his legs and nodded towards Kayanan.

Kayanan said, "See you soon friend." He raised the mirror to Seth's face.

Seth looked at his reflection and was shocked by how wasted his features had become. His eyes were rimmed with dark circles and he looked very pale and gaunt. His reflection lasted for less than a second and was replaced with a brilliant flash of light that changed his vision to darkness with flashes of green light floating in his sight like leftovers from a flashbulb. He 'saw' the rushing of light and found his view rushing along with the current. The view became darker and he knew that in less than a second, the real pain would begin. He saw a small dot of light slowly getting larger until it exploded around him and at once he was now in the center of the fountain looking out.

The observation room was bursting with Seth's screams and Kayanan and Rip did all that they could to keep Seth from thrashing out of the bed. Rip was yelling into Seth's ear, "Seth! Concentrate! Try to block out the rest and concentrate!" The reel-to-reel tape continued to slowly spin both wheels with no added urgency, while the audio monitor needle danced and swayed to the right with every scream from Seth. Noise was watching the clock with a grim look on his face and hoped that Seth could hang on longer than he hoped. His spirits were dashed when he saw how worn Seth looked at the start of the session. *This session*, thought Noise, *will probably end prematurely.*

At once, Cesar was shocked to see the vaporous shape of a man erupt into the middle of the fountain shrieking and flailing. He appeared to be in great pain or terrified—perhaps both. Cesar looked into the man's face and recognized him as one of Rip's team—the man named Seth. Seth's hands were reaching out for any kind of purchase in a mad scramble. On impulse, Cesar leaned over the rim of the fountain and extended both of his hands into the fountain to try to save him. Cesar's fingers touched Seth's hands and immediately Seth locked eyes on him. Cesar gripped Seth's shimmering fingers and found that he could feel some type of physical presence. The moment he did, Seth stopped flailing and seemed to hold on for dear life. It wasn't skin that he could feel, but he felt almost solid pressure.

Cesar noticed that the man seemed safe and out of pain but bewildered. "Are you O.K.?" yelled Cesar over the noise of the fountain.

Seth had stopped kicking and flailing and lay on the bed sweating while his breathing began to slow. His body and soul were racked with fire and in one remarkable instant all of his pain was gone. It was as if he was hurled from a roaring fire into a cool lake. Kayanan, not sure what to do, reached over and pulled out his mouth protector.

"A boy!" gasped Seth "There's a little boy standing there!"

Rip and Kayanan were glancing at the monitors to see if he was critical. "He's not thrashing!" barked Rip. "Is he still in the fountain? He doesn't look in pain to me."

Kayanan read the erratic ink on the electro encephalogram on his side of the table, "He's still in there!"

Rip lowered his head to Seth's ear and said clearly, "Tell me what you see."

Seth looked toward the ceiling with eyes wide, "J- Just a little kid—he says his name is Cesar and that he knows me. I... can't feel anything—I think somehow he's protecting me."

Rip looked up at Kayanan with confusion. Kayanan shrugged and silently mouthed *what the hell?* Rip bent towards Seth's ear again, "Can you see the fountain?"

Seth answered back abruptly, "No—all I see is this kid's face!"

Rip stood up, his face blank. *Where the screaming shit is he if he's not in the fountain?*

Kayanan spoke up, "Ask this Cesar... if *he* can see the fountain."

After a few seconds Seth said, "He says that he can—and that I'm in the middle of it."

Rip lowered his head again and said, "Ask him if he'll help us."

Seth began nodding and asked. "He's asking me—what do we want to know?"

Rip slapped his palms together in success. "Allright--first question—how to we bring back Filodraxes?"

"Filodraxes?" asked Cesar. "Bring him back? Where is he?"

Seth's ghost-like image said, "He's been dead—or sleeping for thousands of years. He tried to defeat death with some medicine—he said that it would keep him alive indefinitely, only he fell into a coma and never came out of it."

Cesar knew from the fountain that if he let go of Seth he would be unprotected. He couldn't let go of his hands to consult his patch. "I'm going to ask the fountain!" Seth nodded to him. Cesar thought hard for a moment. *Filodraxes—I need to know more about him.*

An image of a Persian king appeared on the wall to his left and Cesar began 'remembering' things about him. *Cast out with the exiles on 9011 B.C. for betrayal of Origin. Was the former Master of the Temple and Keeper of the Fountain of Knowledge.* Cesar gasped, *He once was the master of this place?* Another wave of knowledge seeped into his mind, *In Autumn of 1750 B.C., Filodraxes, known by humans as Hammurabi, The greatest king of the Persian Empire, developed a serum that he believed would make him impervious to death. The serum has kept him alive in a comatose state, closer to death than alive. The exiles have taken care of him in hope that they may some day revive him.*

After a few moments of making sense of the knowledge that the fountain provided, Cesar looked at Seth and said, "His serum was faulty. There is a... recipe that you can give him that will revive him temporarily:"

Rip was beside himself with excitement. He could scarcely believe what his ears were hearing. At last-- a cure for Filodraxes—the greatest king of the Babylonian empire and the greatest thinker of the exiles. "--What did he say? *Temporary?* What does he mean temporary?"

Seth was already bellowing the formula for reviving the sleeping man.

"Rub his skin with the following oils: 10% oil of clove, 30% rapeseed extract, 50% olive oil and 10% unadulterated lanolin. Fill his lungs with Sulphur Hexafluoride gas, brew a mixture of strong coffee—at least 15% disintegrated coffee bean in the mixture, along with saw dust from freshly cut white ash. The wood dust must be very fresh. Mix approximately four tablespoons into one gallon of the coffee. Make sure the concoction is hot—just under boiling. Then pour it onto his ribcage, abdomen and over the neck."

Rip looked over at Kayanan with a stoic look on his face. "This is *bullshit.*"

Kayanan looked frustrated, "Something is definitely happening—Seth is just partly here—you can check the EEG results if you want."

Rip walked away from Seth's bed and over to Gellan rubbing his temples. Gellan was sitting at the computer looking at the strange formula that he had just typed. "I don't know Rip—it's strange, I'll give you that. But there's several medicinal properties that coffee is suspected of having and white ash has a very peculiar effect on reptiles."

Rip just stood there looking at Gellan with a very tired look on his face. "You don't think we're getting jacked off here?" Gellan shook his head. Rip walked back to the table. "Time for a new topic." Rip lowered his head to Seth's ear. "Seth—ask him where we can find Diano—Corey Lee's son."

Seth gripped Cesar's hands tight. "Cesar! We need to find a creature called Diano—it's Corey Lee's son."

Cesar looked up to the wall that previously held Filodraxes' picture and now saw an enormous beast about ten feet in height. It had a human's body, although covered with coarse, thick hair on the head and shoulders. The rest of his body was covered with fine hair, except where he had himself branded and scarred with different symbols and characters. The rest of his body's dimensions were normal, except for his hands that seemed exaggerated in size. The head, at first looked like that of a bull, but there was definitely the look of human expression. Two enormous horns protruded from the forehead of the beast and curved out to the sides and upwards. *Diano, Corey Lee's only son, born 21087 B.C., and champion of the circuses sponsored by Rothiel was spared death by the creator after warning the Creator of Rothiel's betrayal. Diano was strictly ordered to live "under the ground or below the sea" and never to torment mankind. Following the exile, all human-derived offspring from origin blood was slain except for Diano.* On the wall, Cesar watched scenes from past circus events. Diano tore through well-armed soldiers in a battle in the center of a large arena. He reveled in playing with wounded opponents, extending their suffering to the glee of the chanting crowd. His fighting style sickened Cesar with dread—*he enjoyed slaughtering people* thought the boy. He saw earlier in the day how Tieran fought his enemies with skill and grace, while Diano killed for the thrill of violence.

Just as Cesar desired to know where the beast dwelled, Cesar watched a map of the earth materialize. His eyes drew to an area of the world that was growing to view with a large, red circle illuminating a mountain range.

Seth again spoke, "Diano's in North Africa. He lives in a cave in Mount Gurugú, in a mountainous area called the Rif—part of the Atlas range. —Cesar says that a witch named Luisa takes care of him—she lives nearby in a city called Melilla."

Rip's eyes lit up, "Well, that sounds better!" He turned to look at Corey's jubilant face. "Your boy would definitely be living in a cave! Hey-- isn't Melilla part of Spain?"

Gellan nodded while fleet fingers flipped through his encyclopedia "Yes—it's just an hour's hop south from Malaga. Here it is! Melilla, called *Rusadir* by the Phoenicians, is one of two Spanish enclaves found in Morocco. It's just north of Nador and spans five kilometers in a finger of land called *Cabo Tres Forcas*." Gellan picked up the TourAfrica schedule and flipped to the page on Melilla. "Hmm. Since Corey's going, you'd probably have to take the boat—apparently it's an eight-hour journey."

Filthy walked up to Rip. "Are you going to ask him about the savant? It's worth a shot don't you think?"

Rip looked over at Seth. He didn't know how much time he had left—he was certainly out of pain—perhaps this Cesar kid was keeping him from harm somehow. "Yes. Let's give it a shot. Seth? Ask your friend if he can find us a savant—a real one. One that can master anything that he touches."

After a few seconds, Seth began speaking again. "Louis Plak. Age 41. He lives at 401 2nd avenue, Silver Spring, Maryland. He's a programmer for GTB, Inc."

"Kick ass!" beamed Filthy. "We need to start thinking of things for this guy to do for us."

Gellan chimed in, "I bet he can do wonders with our computer database. I've always wanted to re-do our security system too."

Rip bent down to Seth's ear. "One more my boy—just one more. Ask him the names of Rothiel's followers."

After a few seconds, Seth began, "Protaxsis—age 44."

Corey looked over at Kayanan and remarked, "Shit. It figures."

Rip barked, "Quiet! I need to hear this!"

Seth continued, "Valgiernas age 49; Hale age 34; ... Prestor age 61. Also many human followers."

Noise replied, "We could give a shit about them!"

Kayanan corrected him, "Yes, but we don't know if Protaxsis toyed with them. Remember Mycenae and Emperor Qin's battle?"

Rip broke in. "Seth looks O.K.—let's bring him home and check him for damage." He lowered his head to Seth's ear, "Seth—ask him if he's willing to help us in the future."

Seth replied, "He says he thinks so. He recommends the same time next week."

Rip swept a hand through his sweaty hairline. "Hell, that's O.K. by me. Let's bring him back Ricardo."

Kayanan whispered to Seth that he was going to inject him with a sedative and that he would be out for a while. With that, Kayanan placed the blind over Seth's face and picked up the prepared syringe from a yellow tray on the medical trolley and inserted it into the drip line of Seth's IV.

Seth, still holding Cesar's hands said, "Thank you Cesar--. I hope someday to repay this."

Cesar thought of his family. "I'll think of something for next week—I think you *can* help me Seth."

Seth's image fluttered for a moment. Seth's eyes that have been locked onto Cesar's now appeared to melt slightly. "Good—"

Cesar's hands were empty—still pushed into the fountain. He pulled them back and looked at them. He wondered for a moment if he had done anything wrong. Bob had mentioned that they had always found ways to help the exiles, but he was sure that he said that they were forbidden to communicate with them. He decided that he would not tell Bob or anyone else unless asked first.

He sat down on the stone bench seat looking at the fountain. *Today is not the right time to ask anything about my family* he thought. He picked up his patch and sat for a while perusing Seth's background as well as others such as Filopraxes, Valgiernas and a meek, older man named Louis Plak. Feeling very sleepy, he decided to go back to his room and study some more on his soft bed. No sooner did he lie down next to his robot toy, he fell to sleep, his patch glowing softly face down on his belly.

Seth snored softly on the bed as Kayanan removed the blood-pressure cuff from his arm and reconnected a fresh bag of saline solution to his IV drip. "He looks just fine, Rip."

Rip looked at Seth's face for a long moment. "How soon will we know what the damage is?"

Kayanan began disconnecting the electrodes from Seth's forehead and powered off the EEG. "Probably within the hour. I'm going to take him into X-ray to check for swelling of the brain—CAT scan to check for bleeding as well as do some blood tests—to be honest, I've never seen him in for such a long time and so coherent."

Rip looked up and nodded, "Same here." He looked away in deep thought and knitted his brows together. "I don't know what that boy did, but Seth looked like he was immune to the fountain. If his information pans out, then we have something quite extraordinary at work here—I *know* Rothiel won't have this capability." Rip looked up at the wall clock. "Witching hour. In less than 20 hours, the bad man gets released. If Seth is up to it, I'd like to bring him with us."

Kayanan stopped arranging the instruments and looked at Rip. "Why?"

Rip traced his index finger and thumb over this mustache and beard while contemplating, "—He can see the origin. At least I *think* he can. He's always seeing freaky shit that we can't see. When we go to witness his release, I'm betting there will be others observing as well. I'd like to see how many *and* see if he recognizes any of them.

Kayanan lowered the head of the bed slowly and said, "All right. *If* he's up to it. If Seth has the slightest headache, I'd rather he stay put and recuperate."

Rip smiled and nodded, "Good doctor—I agree. Just an afterthought, that's all. Great job today, by the way."

Kayanan looked down at the unused syringe bearing an adhesive label marked 'Morphine'. The syringe was almost full with the golden liquid. Just half would have been enough to send an adult into overdose. "Yes. I'm glad that things turned out the way they did."

Chapter Thirteen:
Breakfast

Cesar was dreaming about sitting in a boat, by himself in the middle of the lake. He was sitting closest to the back, no oars and no movement. A red, white and black woodpecker was near the bow, beating its beak against the floor of the boat. Cesar got up from his seat and shooed it away. "Get away from my boat!" As soon as he sat back down, the bird returned and began hammering away at the wooden floor. "Damn bird! Get out of here!"

At once, Cesar found himself, not floating in the middle of a lake, but sprawled in the middle of his bed. The soft glow of the sun was lighting up his room, welcoming him to his second day. The woodpecker struck again—this time on his door. "Oh. Uh, Come in?"

The door clicked and swung open. Tieran was holding the knob with a concerned look on his face. "What 'damned' bird?"

Cesar climbed out of bed scratching his head and stretching. "I just had a weird dream about a bird trying to sink my boat. Good morning!"

"I was heading over to the pavilion for breakfast to join Bob and Theo—I thought you'd like to come along."

Cesar jumped out of his bed and opened the doors of his closet. There were dozens of clothes hanging from a horizontal rod and four pairs of shoes resting quietly on the bottom.

"Go ahead and get suited up—I'll wait."

Cesar walked into the dressing room and pulled off his shirt from the previous day and reached for a clean shirt. He didn't know what to do with his old one, so he laid it on the floor. As soon as he pulled his new shirt over his head he looked down and noticed that the old one was gone. He looked in his closet and noticed seven shirts, folded neatly in a stack. *Only six pairs of trousers though*. He removed his pants and placed them on the floor and watched. Nothing happened. He gave them a slight nudge with his toe and the trousers remained on the floor without moving. He turned to the table and picked up the clean trousers and noticed the pants on the floor disappeared and a new pair seemed to emerge from the shelf, pushing the stack of folded trousers up slightly to make room.

"Neat!" said Cesar softly. He pulled on the trousers and buttoned them to his waist. He pulled on his socks and then the form-fitting shoes that felt very comfortable yet firm.

The two left the building and trotted towards the pavilion. Tieran saw Bob sitting under the canopy smiling and Theo standing and waving towards Cesar. "Looks like we got here last!"

Theo ran up and kissed both of Cesar's cheeks. "How was your first day? I couldn't wait to get back here to see you!"

She held Cesar's hand as the three of them walked to the pavilion. Cesar chattered on about the things he saw and what he discovered with his patch.

"Do you like your room?" asked Theo with a growing smile across her face.

"Heck yeah! I love it! I've never had such a wonderful room to myself before. Did you see all of the toys?"

Bob positively beamed. "Well, those toys *are* special. For instance, what did you think about the G.I. Joe display?"

Cesar thought back. "A G.I. what?"

"The soldier! The one with the fuzzy hair and beard! He's really rare. You didn't play with him?" Cesar shook his head trying to remember if he's seen a soldier toy. Bob tried another, "What about the Buck Rogers tin wind-ups?"

Cesar thought for a moment. "Was it a robot? I've played with a big red one named Robocon..."

Bob sat back in his chair. "Wasted. Kids just don't know what toys are fun anymore."

Tieran and Theo laughed at Bob's frustration. Bob looked at both of them. "What?"

Theo laughed loudly and tried to cover her mouth. Cesar thought she was the loveliest woman he had ever met.

"I'm sorry Bob!" Theo laughed a bit more. "Honestly! Give the boy some time—he's been here less than a day!"

Tieran grabbed a napkin off of the plate in front of him. "Who's hungry?"

Cesar's hand shot up. "I'm famished—can I have McDonald's again?

Bob looked at Tieran through hooded eyes. "Sooo. We're already polluting the poor boy are we?"

Tieran jabbed back with exaggerated flair while smoothing the wrinkles of the napkin on his lap. "Don't be sassy Bob, it's what Cesar wanted. Besides, you are most likely going to down your usual-- greasy bacon and hash browns aren't you?"

Bob laughed. "Not on your life my misguided oriental friend. I'm having scrapple and shit on a shingle. Everything a young man like me needs!" He raised his nose and sniffed. "I suppose you are going to have your usual?"

Tieran touched his fingers together. "I have simple tastes. I'm going to have rice, topped with a runny egg and soy sauce. Theo? What are you having?"

She looked at Cesar and said, "Cesar and I are both having pancakes with lots of syrup and butter. Do you want sausage too?"

Cesar sat amused in his chair watching the others bicker and taunt. "Sure. Whatever you say!"

Just seconds after Cesar finished his sentence, a man with a large tray held shoulder high arrived at their table and began placing their orders in front of them.

Bob growled at the waiter, "What took you so long?" Theo elbowed him in the ribs and Tieran and Cesar both laughed.

The waiter looked at Bob and said "Scrapple?" Bob nodded rather uncertainly. The waiter continued, "I used to work for Kraft. Did you know that this product could contain up to 50% hair?" He placed the plate in front of Bob and then went to Theo, Cesar and Tieran and gave them their plates.

Cesar couldn't believe how wonderful the aroma of the pancakes smelled. They were stacked with a dollop of butter on top that looked like a small scoop of ice cream.

Theo reached over and helped Cesar with the shiny syrup cup. "Here—pour some syrup on top of them first." Bob looked at his scrapple with mild disgust and found himself spending too much time staring at Cesar's stack.

Midway through the meal, Tieran spoke up, "So how did it go last night?"

Bob looked at Theo and said, "Pretty good. Theo has been following some of Rothiel's followers and determined that they have set up shop in an old wine warehouse in the town of Rota, Spain. It's actually a close location since Rothiel is going to get freed at a point between Jerez and Puerto Réal."

Theo added, "He'll have pier access just half a mile down the road, and the nearest airport is only 30 minutes away. He'll have to be watched carefully as he'll be able to disappear at the drop of a hat."

Tieran finished with his rice, offering some to Cesar, who politely refused pointing to his full stomach. "How many followers does he have?"

Theo took a drink from a large glass of milk. "Hmm. That's a tough question. I've counted five exiles, but there are an awful lot of human followers holed up at the warehouse. The bad part is, they have guard animals that prevent me from getting in to get an accurate count."

Tieran sat up interested. "Guard animals?"

Bob pushed his half un-eaten scrapple forward. "Peacocks-- several of them. The minute we get within 100 feet of the building they start crowing."

Cesar was sitting back in his chair positively bursting from so much food. He couldn't help but become interested in peacocks—in his village there were many roaming around the parks and gardens. "You mean real peacocks—birds? They can see us on Earth?"

Tieran answered for Bob and Theo. "They can't see us—there's nothing for them to see. They are very sensitive creatures though. It could be the slightest change in air pressure or a gentle breeze that gets diverted because of our presence and somehow they know. It spooks them—and they start howling. They are perfect guard animals because they don't sleep long or soundly. Rothiel's boys must know this and have them to warn them of intruders."

Cesar was buzzing. "You mean that whenever a peacock in my village started crowing, it might have been origin walking around?"

Bob shook his head. "No, no of course not. Just some of the time. Outdoors, everything sets the damn things off. Inside a room, only things it can't see."

Bob looked at everyone's plates. "Finished are we? Well, let's begin comparing notes. We need our table cleared, please."

At once, the same waiter entered the pavilion and began picking up plates. The waiter and Bob spent a good amount of time eyeing each other. "Not hungry, Mr. White?"

Bob removed his napkin from his lap and placed it on the table. "I had a light breakfast before I came over. By the way, it didn't *taste* like hair."

The waiter continued collecting silverware and jousting sarcasm with Bob. "The delicate taste of pig's snout and ears probably masked the subtle flavor of the animal hair. Would you like some coffee?"

Not to be outdone, Bob acted like he coolly removed a sliver of meat from his teeth with a smacking sound. "Nah. Your choices are probably too delicate for my manly constitution."

The waiter stood straight and faced Bob with a look of disapproval like that of a priest disgusted with the actions of an errant altar boy. "We have a special Sumatran blend made from beans that have passed out of the colon of a Civet. Not *manly* enough?"

Bob called his bluff with a huge grin and nod. "You're on! Sounds delicious. Just make sure you bring a pot of it, as I'm quite parched."

The waiter went off towards the scullery with the plates and emerged not three seconds later brandishing a polished silver pot and white porcelain coffee cup on a matching saucer. He carefully placed it before Bob, poured the cup and sat the pot down next to it. "Well?"

Bob looked at shiny cup holding the black liquid and his lower lip wavered. "It's still too hot—I'm going to wait a while."

The waiter gave him a skeptical look and returned to the interior of the restaurant. Theo looked at Bob with disappointment. "What are you doing? Aren't you going to drink it?"

Bob chuckled. "*Hell* no. I wouldn't let this vile..."

Everyone at the table turned to see a boy, smaller than Cesar looking at them at the edge of the pavilion. Cesar turned and saw his friend. "Aaron! Hey, have you had breakfast? --Guys, this is my friend Aaron—we played together yesterday on the boats!"

Aaron waved and said a shy "Hullo." He was looking at Bob.

Bob slid a nervous finger around the inside of his collar and tried to look pleasant. "How are you—Aaron, is it?"

Aaron said, "Fine. Are you having coffee?"

Bob sat up and looked at the cup. *How long has he been standing there?* "Why, uh, yes! I was just letting it cool off first." He picked up a spoonful of sugar and dropped it in, stirring quickly.

Cesar was turned around in his chair and looking right at Aaron. "Thanks again for the cool patch! It has really come in very handy. Are you sure you don't want it back?"

Tieran and Theo looked at each other with growing understanding. Then back to Bob. The corner of Theo's mouth started creeping towards a snicker, but she willed herself to remain calm.

Aaron kept looking right at Bob. "No—I'm fine—I'll get another one later." He turned and looked at Cesar. "Are you going to be free this afternoon to go boating again?"

Cesar looked at Bob with his eyebrows raised. "Bob? Is it OK?"

Bob felt all eyes upon him just then and it seemed the cup of coffee was screaming for attention. He raised it to his chin and smelled it. "Of course—sure! We don't have anything planned until 9:00 tonight." Aaron's expressionless eyes looked from the cup to Bob's eyes. Bob pursed, then licked his lips, took a breath and brought the cup to his mouth.

The taste was definitely coffee—but what an explosion of flavor! This by far was the best cup of coffee that he ever had walking the Earth or above. He brought the cup down and looked at the dark liquid swirl and licked his lips again. The smell and aftertaste was tremendous—it literally begged to be tried again and again.

Aaron turned to Cesar. "I'll call you on your patch at one o'clock then?" Cesar nodded and said, "Looking forward to it. I've got a lot of things I need your opinion on."

"Great!" Aaron said. He looked at everyone at the table and said a shy "It was nice meeting all of you." A chorus of "Nice to meet you too" and "Take care" came from the table and Aaron ran down the path towards the line of children waiting to get on a spinning carousel.

Theo looked at Cesar and said "What a nice friend you have there." There was a slight gleam in her eye as she said it and then looked to Tieran who nodded.

Bob was sipping out of his cup again.

Tieran sneered, "You *know* that it came out of a cat's ass, don't you?"

Bob placed the cup down on the saucer and smiled. "It is... positively delicious!"

Tieran looked at him with plain disgust on his face. "I thought you weren't going to drink it."

Bob said, "Oh, I *wasn't*. I was going to pour it in the grass and tell that waiter that it tasted like dishwater. I guess I was meant to drink it. Want some?"

Tieran and Theo both rolled their eyes. Tieran picked up the cup and sniffed it. "You know — if you like the taste, you could always go directly to the source."

Bob sat back relaxing from the contentment of the coffee and said "Can't — don't have a damned cat."

Cesar wasn't really listening — he was far too entertained watching Theo make flowers out of the other napkins.

"Back to business." Said Bob sitting up in his chair and pouring a second cup of coffee. "Rothiel gets out in twelve hours, and it appears that the exiles are very concerned about it. What have you discovered Theo?"

Theo sat up and crossed her legs. "Very peculiar things are going on with the Lodge. First, they appear to be interested in a man named Rolland Smith — everyone calls him Jim. Some of the Lodge are testing him — I witnessed one test where Gaeliin observed him during a run and this Jim Smith was able to match Gaeliin's speed."

Bob stole a look at his watch and nodded, in between sips of his coffee. "Do they refer to him in any specific way?"

Theo looked surprised. "Well, yes! They are calling him a 'conduit'. I've done some checking on Jim Smith's background too. Apparently, he catches on to things *fast*. I don't mean that he's a quick learner or that he has a knack for new things — he tends to display the abilities of others near him. When he was in high school, he tried out for various teams and was equally as good as the top players. When those players weren't at the game or ill, he played mediocre or worse."

Tieran was drumming his fingertips against the tablecloth. "Hmm. Gaeliin eh? Were there any other tests that you witnessed?"

Theo removed her patch from her necklace and opened it like a clamshell. She then held it by the hinge and sat it on top of the bridge of her nose. The moment it touched her face, the centers of each disk became transparent. It looked like she was wearing round spectacles except her eyes darted to and fro as if she was focusing on things in midair. "Yup. Just a couple of nights ago, they tested his skill at a game of darts."

Tieran's interest sparked. "Let me guess — Kainaan Toth?"

Theo nodded her head and smiled at Tieran. "Absolutely — your old buddy!"

Tieran looked over at Bob. Bob was sitting back, sipping his coffee and watching the two of them conversing. He lowered the cup, "What?"

Tieran said, "Nothing! ...Ick." He looked back at Theo. "So what was the result of the test?"

Theo began. "Well, as expected, Smith began hitting everything that he aimed at. During the second round, Danhieras told Kainaan to separate himself by 100 feet to see if Smith still had the ability and if not, depart for home."

Cesar had his patch out and said "Danhieras." His patch showed the gruff, bearded face of Rip Damhorst.

Theo continued, "Interestingly enough, I was outside watching Kainaan. He waited about ten minutes and then turned to walk to the lighthouse where his car was parked. When he walked past Oxi's Disco, he seemed to smell something and became very edgy. He reached into his jacket and pulled out two devices which he kept in each hand and ran the entire way to his car."

Tieran inquired, "What were these devices—knives?"

"Not quite—he calls them butterflies because of the shape, but they are some type of shuriken. He throws them and they fly exactly where he wants them to go. They are slightly heavier than a standard throwing star and have a notch in the side that he sometimes connects to a cable."

Bob put his cup down on the saucer and slid them both away, apparently sated. "Who or *what* made him so jumpy?"

Theo raised an eyebrow. "None other than Valgiernas. He was skulking around the taxicab parking area watching Kainaan in front of El Dardo's. He made no attempt to follow Kainaan—probably for good reason. Here's the interesting part: as soon as Smith left the bar and began walking home, Valgiernas followed *him* home."

Bob wiped his lips with his napkin saying, "We've finished." The waiter came out and picked up the pot and empty cup.

Bob slid his chair back, stood up and turned to him. "Listen, that was by far the best coffee I've ever had. Sorry that I... toyed with you like that."

The waiter bowed and said "Likewise. I learned a lesson back in the kitchen that it's unwise to tell customers about certain ingredients in food products. Please excuse my rudeness." They both shook each other's hands and grinned. The waiter looked at the others at the table with a slight bit of color in his cheeks. "Would anyone like some dessert?" The table went round with various "Couldn't eat another bite." "Too full, but thanks."

Cesar caught his gaze. "What kind of pie?"

The waiter looked surprised. "What kind would the master like?"

Cesar thought about his grandmother's sweet potato pie, cooked in an old oven perfectly, then gently lowered by her into the well behind their house to cool. "Do you have sweet potato?"

The waiter nodded and turned away. Not three seconds later did he return from the kitchen with a dessert plate holding a fat wedge of the pie. He placed it before the boy and handed him a dessert fork and napkin.

"Thank you!"

The waiter gave a slight bow, said, "Hope you enjoy." And walked back to the kitchen.

Cesar picked up the fork and dove in, not realizing that everyone at the table was watching him with interest.

With his mouth full of the delicious pie, Cesar began to weep.

Theo looked at Bob and then got up and held Cesar's head to her. "Cesar, what is wrong?"

Cesar chewed up the pie, swallowed and couldn't find his voice. He buried his tears into her dress and when he was finally able to speak, looked up. "How did they know?"

She patted his head and said, "They just do, honey. For better or worse, they just do."

Bob and Tieran chatted for a while and every few minutes looked over to see how Cesar was doing. When he finally calmed down, he went back to eating the pie. He seemed very quiet and embarrassed.

Bob felt very uneasy and fiddled with a stray spoon on the table and looked at Cesar. "You know, when I first arrived I was welcomed by my parents and grandparents—I hadn't seen them in a long time. It was a very happy occasion as you can imagine. You were brought here in your youth so it's a bit different. A—a *big* difference actually."

Bob felt a slight catch in the back of his throat and his nostrils burned slightly. "Anyways, when I first sat down here to eat for the first time, all I could think about was my darling wife and her cooking. She made the best lasagna I've ever had." Bob thought back to their second date where he ate her lasagna in her mother's kitchen, her bright red hair was pulled back in a braided ponytail and she positively shone with beauty. Bob continued with glassy eyes, "Throughout our 25-year relationship she would take her fingernail and draw a small heart through the sauce on the top." Bob's eyes began to water and his voice crack. "Well... wouldn't you know it—when my lasagna arrived..." Bob stood up, wiped the tears streaming from his face said a voiceless "excuse me" and walked to the far end of the pavilion and looked out across the lake.

Cesar looked up at Theo who was also weeping but trying to smile. "How long has he been here?"

Theo wiped away the tears and shook her head with a touch of embarrassment. "He's come and gone before many times before, but his most recent life... ended just three years ago."

"I'm sorry! Said Cesar, "It's my fault—I just missed them a lot just now—"

Theo grasped his hand and folded it in hers. "Everything is just fine. Sorrow isn't an emotion to hate but one that makes our love for distant family so special—so wonderful. Bob is remembering what it was like when he recently arrived, that's all."

Tieran had walked over to Bob and had his hand on his shoulder. Bob's face was reddened and in vain, was trying to clean up his features with the back of his hand.

Theo looked down at the dessert plate and picked up his fork. She tried a bite of Cesar's pie and her eyes widened while he watched her expression. "Mmm! Cesar this is fantastic! Who's recipe was it?"

Cesar tried to smile, but it still came out with an expression of sadness. Her question did fill him with pride for his mother and grandmother. "My grandmother—she was the greatest cook in the world. Her recipe was very old and it has always been handed down by our family." Cesar thought of her. She knew that her grandson always loved her pies and would stand in the kitchen cutting the peel from the sweet potatoes with thin lips expressing the pain in her fingers. Cesar knew that with every spike of pain that she endured making them, it was trivial to the love and pride that she had for her grandson.

Theo and Cesar took turns with the fork until they finished the wedge. At the end they were both laughing and intermittent glances toward Tieran and Bob showed that they too had gotten over the short moment of grief.

The two had sauntered back to the table with Bob midway through one of his jokes. "…and the man said, 'I don't think I could take another hot potato up my ass!'" Tieran and Bob laughed so hard that Theo was shushing them with her finger and looking around to see if some of the other patrons in the pavilion were getting annoyed.

Tieran, was now wiping tears from his eyes as he gasped for air. "That one was funnier than the British Commander roaring and crapping his pants!" Bob's face became red again from the recollection of that particular joke and began slapping Tieran's back while guffawing.

Theo decided that a couple of noisemakers were better let loose in the park. "Let's continue our merrymaking near the lake—and keep it down!" The four of them walked out of the pavilion and marveled at the afternoon sun and the cool wind that gently blew across the enormous lawns that bordered the lake. Theo and Cesar walked towards a large chestnut tree and sat down on the grass. Bob and Tieran arrived last and sat down in front of the other two. Bob pulled out a pack of cigarettes and began to light one.

Cesar looked at Bob in shock. "You can smoke here?"

"Well it ain't going to kill me if that's what you are getting at. Want one?"

Theo snapped, "Bob, don't you dare! That's why you ended up here at age 48 to begin with!"

Bob lay back on one elbow enjoying the smoke and waving the match until the flame died and smoke drew dissipating zigzags into the air. "I was just kidding. Besides, it's the only vice I've got left." He offered the pack to Tieran.

Tieran looked at the pack with a frown. "You know Bob, I'd almost rather have a cup of that nasty coffee."

Bob inhaled a deep drag of the cigarette, exhaled and again recalled the punch line of one of his recent jokes, causing him to laugh, choke then cough violently.

Tieran asked, "Which one was it, the baby elephant's trunk or the Commander?"

Bob, still coughing and laughing, "The C-Commander—man, but my father told that joke well. Ah, well. Theo? Where were we?"

Theo clipped her patch back onto the bridge of her nose. "Let's see—yes. Valgiernas followed Jim Smith to his apartment."

Bob reflected on this. "Did Valgiernas say anything to this guy?"

I couldn't really tell—I did hear a slight question about the time from Valgiernas, but after a couple of sentences, Smith walked up to his apartment. One interesting thing though, Kainaan went back to his car and retrieved an additional weapon—something that he calls a 'strut."

This raised Tieran's interest. "What does it look like?"

Theo said, "I'm not really sure. But this is what I know it has something to do with thin, strong wire, the butterflies that I mentioned before and these little guys."

She raised her right hand and the patch on her face flashed brightly for a moment and a dazzling beam of light shone from her eyes to her outstretched hand. Held out on her hand was an image of what was hanging on Kainaan's belt. It looked like a triangular piece of metal with one of the corners cut off, no bigger than a belt buckle. One side of the triangle was clearly sharpened and there was two tiny tubes running lengthwise.

Theo continued, "Kainaan went back to El Dardo's—presumably to warn Danhieras about Valgiernas and as they both made it back to the car, Kainaan had one of these strung onto the wire and one of the butterflies connected to another spool of wire. They kept to the shadows with Kainaan leading the way. Valgiernas was almost a mile away by that time but they were being cautious. I went back to find Valgiernas, but he was gone after Smith entered his apartment. I followed Danhieras and Kainaan when they left Rota and they stopped at nearby Fuentebravia, outside a veterinary clinic. Take a guess at who the vet is?"

Bob grunted, "Someone that loves animals and is probably gentle—It's gotta be either Koriet or Simon."

"Simon is correct! A blue ribbon for Bob!"

Tieran said, "He doesn't deserve a blue ribbon until he brushes those funky teeth."

Bob puffed his cigarette and said with a mystical tone, "Until you bask in the glory of the Sumatran blend, you may not speak of it's dark magic."

Cesar laughed at the way Bob sounded so pompous like a king, but he still didn't understand what was so disgusting about the coffee that Bob drank at the pavilion.

Tieran rolled onto his side and propped up his head using his elbow on the grass and his palm for a pillow. "What happened when they got to Simon's?"

Theo continued, "Well, I waited for about ten minutes to see if they were all going to leave and Simon came out alone. He locked up the office, got on a moped and proceeded towards Puerto—towards the fortress. When he departed, I entered the building and discovered it empty."

Bob blurted out, "Aha! So Simon can still hex people around!"

Theo continued, "That would appear to be the case. I checked the office thoroughly and came up empty, but next to the wall in the waiting room, I found a light layer of ash."

Cesar was lost at this point. "Hex? Do you mean Simon can send people someplace?"

Theo removed the patch from the bridge of her nose, closed it and let it hang from her necklace. "Not like you think. Remember when you first met me, I had to leave you and I went through the ceiling?" Cesar nodded.

"For origin to move to different locations, it only takes will and concentration—really not much of either. For a human, it takes much more, the knowledge of calculated mass, location in 3D space and most importantly, the ability to transfer energy of different types. The ash was merely the by-product of mass converting to energy from areas that the two must travel through. Simon, can establish a point-A to point-B portal, that when opened looks like just a hole in a wall. When you step through, you arrive at the end location by traveling just a tiny fraction of an inch."

Cesar was tapping something on the screen of his patch, his brow furrowed. "I don't get it. Rothiel's followers have the peacocks that make it hard to snoop on them. How come we don't know much about the capabilities of the Lodge?"

Bob raised his head. "Ah. Yes, that. What do you know about Seth's abilities?"

"Just that he can visualize the fountain of knowledge when his eyes see a reflection. After a while it kills him though."

"Yup. Since he has a way of seeing things that no one else can, he can also see us."

Cesar was shocked. "Even when we are invisible to them?"

Bob nodded. "He can see everything. There are some creatures that roam the Earth that are neither of our world or theirs and Seth sees every one of 'em. They are normally benign, but he picks them out immediately. If we were in his line of sight, he'd know."

Cesar thought back to Simon's ability to travel through walls. "Why didn't he travel with the other two — wouldn't it be easier?"

Bob added, "Simon was very good at this in the past — over a thousand years ago. He was able to 'zap' his buddies all over the Earth, which gave the lodge quite an edge on commerce and discovery. Once during the American Civil war, Simon had the best general store in the world. He advertised that he had literally 'everything in stock'. Anyways, a long time ago, we saw that he was having serious difficulties creating a viable portal. In the end, he had the means of opening one and keeping it open for others to cross through, but not himself — it would collapse whenever he touched the crossover horizon. Still, good for them! We had assumed that Simon lost that ability because we haven't observed it in the last 100 years."

Cesar had his patch open and was perusing the ability known to the exiles as the 'hex'. "It says here that others such as Kainaan, Danhieras and Gellan had this ability."

Tieran stood up and brushed the loose bits of lawn off of his pant legs. "The exiles forget information about their past lives over generations. Danhieras and Kainaan have amazing talents still. Gellan is so fast, that he probably didn't rely on it. None of those three have been able to hex for over 1,000 years."

Bob looked at Tieran. "You know who did have that ability and still might? Filodraxes. He was the best out of all of them — he could send entire armies through his portals."

Tieran countered, "Yeah, but he's not really in shape to demonstrate anything these days, is he?"

Theo leaned towards Cesar. "Filodraxes *was* the exiles leader. A long time ago he took some type of medicine that he thought would keep him from dying."

"And he was right!" interjected Bob. The problem is, he's just a twisted piece of leather in a coffin."

Cesar thought about Filodraxes' condition. "Why don't the exiles just kill him? Then, he would be reborn and... okay again?"

Theo stroked the hair on Cesar's head just over his left ear. "They've tried — many times in fact. Once they even cut off his head.

Nothing happened--he just kept breathing. Eventually, his head grew back on. They've tried poisoning him, burning his body—he looks a lot worse because of that, but nothing destroys him. His medicine keeps him from dying and also from living—it's quite a curse."

Cesar tried a new course. "Why haven't you tried curing him? Wouldn't it be a great help to the exiles to have their leader back?

This last comment sobered up the group. Bob looked over at Theo.

"There are some things Theo and I are unable to do—one is to have direct communication with the exiles and the most important is not to interfere directly. We are not even allowed to speak to them. If there is a cure, we cannot just leave a vial of it for them to use. They must continue their own course."

"Have you asked God?" asked Cesar, beginning to feel flustered.

Bob laughed. "Of course! You should see the volumes of ideas that have been shot down! The exiles are on Earth as punishment. They are to work things out themselves without our...direct help."

Cesar could feel the heat on his cheeks. "Bob—Rothiel isn't just interested in the exiles, but in all humans."

Bob got to his feet, gave a swipe to his jacket and gracefully put in back on. "I'm aware of that, boy. I, like you still have family in that world that I want to see protected, but I cannot cross that line."

At that moment, Cesar's patch chimed. He opened it and a soft voice said, "Aaron for you, shall I connect?" "Yes please."

Aaron's face shimmered into view smiling. "Hey Cesar—I'm over at the boats, are you coming over?"

Cesar was getting frustrated with the current conversation and with the brick wall that Bob was creating. He still looked at Bob for approval.

Bob nodded and waved a hand toward the marina, excusing him.

Cesar looked at Aaron's image and said. "I'm on my way over." The image froze and Cesar closed the patch and jammed it in his pocket and got up off the grass.

Theo got to her feet and held Cesar's hand before he turned to go. "We are your friends too. You should tell us anything that you have a problem with. There are many aspects of our work that I disagree with, but like Bob pointed out, we don't get to make up the rules." She kissed him on the cheek.

Cesar turned to go, waved and said, "I'll be back in my room before dinner." Bob, Theo and Tieran waved at the boy running toward the marina.

Theo turned to Bob with a serious expression. "Bob White! Sometimes you need to remember how old Cesar really is."

Bob looked startled by her admonition. He thought about what she said, looked at Tieran for moral support and when he received none, grunted. "I know, I know—he's just a boy—but he's a *smart* one. With all of the knowledge that he's gained in just 24 hours, I sometimes mistake his comments for that of an adult. If it makes you feel any better, I do regret being curt with him."

Theo thought about Cesar's strange friend with the almost-white, blonde hair. "Do you think that's him with Cesar?"

Bob looked in all directions, including scrutinizing the branches of the tree over his head. "...I'm almost positive. He said he gave him a patch and every time that kid looks me in the eyes I feel like I'm in for an ass whipping."

Chapter Fourteen:
Playa de la Luz

Jim awoke hearing the the screams of children playing outside, loud flamenco music played out of cheap radios and the surf gently crashing against the beach through the patio window of his apartment. Although the window was shut, Spanish construction did not evolve to the point where double-glazing or insulation was even considered. His apartment whistled with cold air in the winter and seemed to throb with sullen heat during the summer months. He raised himself up from his bed and looked at his clock. *No good. Can't see any of the numbers.* He used his finger tips to try to massage some clarity into his vision and took another look. 10:14. *Jesus.* The room was already warm with heat and the sheets around him were soaked with sweat. He swung his feet from the bed to the floor and was taken by surprise by the coolness of the terrazzo floor. He walked over to the window and pulled down on a nylon strap, raising the *presiana* shutters that covered up his window. The brightness was one last cruel slap to his hangover and when raised, he slid the patio window open to take advantage of the sea breeze to cool his apartment. No such luck. He stood in the open doorway of the patio and felt nothing—not the slightest whispers of air touch his cheek.

He wandered back inside, scratching his stomach and wandering into the kitchen. He needed a miracle and it was best served in a tall glass—Spanish style. He could never figure out why the Spanish drank their coffee in glasses—mugs seemed so much more logical. *After all, they don't drink their damned tea in a glass... or do they?* He put a small pan of water over the gas burner in his small kitchen and lit the blue flame with a match. The smells of sulphur and unburnt, butane gas gently basked in his nostrils. The smells themselves weren't unwelcome—similar to Pavlov's dogs, he knew in his brain that the precursors to smelling and more importantly, *drinking* coffee were the noxious smells used in the production of flame. Before the water began to boil, he dropped a fat teaspoonful of Nescafe into the bottom of a tall glass and generously covered with a thick layer of La Lechera condensed milk. He watched the vapor bubbles begin to collect on the bottom of the pan. *Hurry.* He wandered over to the refrigerator and poked his head inside. Just the usual items, all of which he never had the desire to create food with. *Eggplant? Why in hell did I buy this?* The bubbling of the pan pulled him back into a world that was more exciting. He could worry about food later. He poured the boiling water into the glass and it became cloudy in an instant as the hot water and the condensed milk began reuniting. He dropped in the teaspoon and began a slow stir.

He walked his creation into the living room and sat down on the sofa, turning on the TV with the remote. He continued to gently stir his concoction, not caring that his already sweating body would probably sweat considerably more once it feels hot liquid and absorbs caffeine.

The television would only pick up four channels, the worst quality was in Jerez that came in with double vision. It gave him a headache to watch, so he satisfied his hunger for boob tube viewing by watching the local Rota channel, TVE and CanalSur's public channel. He watched the news on TVE, which was nothing but sports-- round-ups showing football games and golf. *Why on earth are European sports so damned boring?* He sat back and looked out of the window at the other apartments facing his and looking outwards to the ocean. Most of them had laundry out to dry on retractable clotheslines and colorful inflatable beach gear, fading in the sunlight.

He looked back to the screen and the commentators were discussing bullfighting. *Now there's a sport!* Thought Jim. He watched as a commentator discussed the latest injury to a new bullfighter named Jesulin de Ubrique. Jim sat back watching some of the scenes leading up to the injury. "That guy, bar none, is the dumbest looking bullfighter in history!" Jesulin de Ubrique was tall, skinny and with an Adam's apple that would choke a horse. With every pass of the bull, Jesulin's face would appear just over the cape filled with intense fear. It wasn't until later on in the fight, where the bull was drained of so much blood from the Picador and was so tired from the many passes it made around the jittery bullfighter that it would refuse to charge any more. Jesulin would use this time to torment the bull by slapping it across the face with the sword or taunting it with his anorexic face.

The doorbell chimed and Jim glanced at the clock. "Crap! Manoli's probably here!" He looked down and noticed that he was only clad in his underwear briefs, yelled a loud "*Un momento!*" and ran into his bedroom to throw some clothes on. He pulled on some shorts and his favorite T-shirt, black and sporting a very colorful Green Tree Frog. He ran to the door, rotated the bolt and swung the door open.

"Hola, Hola!" sang Elena in Manoli's arms.

Jim grabbed for his daughter and kissed her on her cheek. "Hiya my little jalapeno!" Manoli was there with the whole family, all dressed for the beach.

Nino, was standing quietly, wearing dark sunglasses that hid his hangover. He noticed Jim's condition. "You too?"

Jim nodded and said, "Well, don't just stand there—come on in!"

Manoli walked in holding her younger son's hand. "*Venga Pablo!*" Pablo was only two, but because of his fetish for food and lots of it, looked at least like he was seven. He was busy stuffing a chocolate ice cream into his face and looking up at Jim.

Oscar, was quietly smiling behind his mother and wearing his usual football jersey and swim trunks. "*Hola Jaime.*" He walked in and headed to the living room to watch TV.

Nino was last to come in, removed his sunglasses and exhaled as if the pain was getting to be too much to bear.

Jim inspected his face like a concerned doctor. "Let's see... Hmm. *Moscatel* again?"

Nino nodded. "And her mother as well. Do you have any asprin?"

"*Claro*. I eat them like candy. Would you like a coffee?"

Nino put a sour look on his face and held his small belly with his right hand. "Not a good idea I think. I'm going to start with beer in about an hour and don't want to confuse what's inside."

Jim laughed and guided him to the living room to have a seat.

Nino commented on the weather. "*Joder*, is it warm. Are you coming to the beach with us?"

Jim scratched his head, tried to think of any pressing business and came up empty. "I'm free all day—what the heck—let me go change into my trunks."

"*Que chulo!*" Said Oscar, picking up one of the heavy boxer statues. "Papa—look how heavy these guys are!"

Nino was reclined on the easy chair, just with one eye open and on his son. "Don't touch those! You're going to break them!"

Jim shook his head. "Not a chance—they're both made of metal. Do you like them?"

Oscar nodded and was moving them clumsily as if they were dolls play boxing. "Of course! They are really amazing. What are they?"

"I have no idea. Go ahead and keep them — some guy that tried to sell me insurance gave those ugly things to me."

"I can have them? Are you sure?"

"Sure, but you have to carry them home."

"Cool!"

Jim wandered into the bedroom and closed the door. He whipped off his shorts and underwear and pulled on his navy blue swim trunks. *Crap. There's still sand in them. Oh well.*

He walked back out and Pablo had his refrigerator open, staring inside with the same dumbfounded expression that Jim had earlier.

"Sorry Pablo — we don't really have anything fun to eat just yet."

They all walked out of the apartment, Elena wearing her bathing suit and sun hat in Jim's arms. Jim looked at the walkway outside of his apartment and saw everything that they brought. "Jeez, you guys came prepared."

Nino picked up the two beach umbrellas and two sand chairs, Manoli picked up a cardboard box with packed food and a big canvas sack filled with toys, sun cream and a faded collapsible fan.

Pablo latched onto the bag as his mother made her way to the elevator and Oscar brought up the rear, lugging Jim's old, torn gym bag holding the heavy metal warriors.

The sun was broiling and it wasn't quite 11:00 yet. They sat on the beach just outside Jim's apartment and Nino set up the umbrellas. Oscar had abandoned his prize toys near the beach chairs and was off running up and down the beach trying to catch seabirds. Pablo sat on the sand making designs and fiddling with seashells. He didn't dare go far from the sanctity of the food box. Manoli told Nino when he finished with the umbrellas that he needed to get refreshments from the corner store.

"Why didn't you tell me when we walked past it on our way here? Woman!"

Jim got up and wiped the sand of his rear. "I'll go with ya. I'll pay since you were more than kind to watch Elena for me."

In the midst of Manoli and Nino's protestations, Jim said, "*Ni hablar!* This is my turn."

Elena played under the umbrella shared with Manoli. Jim said, "Elena—do you want ice cream?" Elena looked up at him confused, then turned back to her creation in the sand. *"Helado*—do you want helado?"

Elena squealed yelling *"-Lado! -Lado!"* This word brought crumbling down, the walls of concentration that held Pablo's interest in his sand toys. He got up and began lumbering toward Nino and Jim. He was like a small portly soldier on a crusade that mattered beyond anything else in life. Manoli tried to call him back, *"Ven aqui! Ya!"* Pablo continued marching towards Nino and Jim—the both of them laughed at his persistence. Nino picked up his big boy with a grunt. "He'll be fine," he said.

The three of them went back up the steps to his apartment building and across the courtyard to the grey, cracked sidewalk that led to the shops and restaurants that hugged the beach. The shrill cacophony of seagulls echoed between the apartment buildings, making Jim's headache throb. Just fifty yards away from Jim's apartment building was a small store called *'A Tus Zapatos'*. It meant 'To Your Shoes', but for Jim's time speaking Spanish, he still had no idea what it meant or why it was called that. They went inside and grabbed two baskets. Nino tried to select beer from the large wall refrigerators, but Pablo continued to impatiently direct him to the floor freezer holding the many varieties of ice cream.

Jim grabbed two large, bottles of iced Cola and a plastic bag containing shabby quality disposable cups. "Should we get ice?" asked Jim. Nino was half buried in the floor freezer with Pablo kicking his sides like the rider of a stubborn horse, yammering, *"-Colaaate! Colaaaate!"* Nino finally brought up two boxes of chocolate flavored bars and stuck them into the boy's wailing face. "Here! See? Now stop crying!" He dropped the bars in the basket while Pablo's chubby hands shot downward in a vain attempt to possess them. "You are not getting any until we get to the beach." Said Nino. "Jesus, stop being spoiled!" By the time they departed the store, Pablo was on his second, with slippery chocolate goo running down his double chin and belly. Jim carried the bag, hot behind Nino's heels.

Nino came to an abrupt halt, turned around and looked at Jim's face with alarm. "Let's go the other way—it's out of the sun. Jim shrugged, thinking nothing of it. When he turned to follow Nino towards the alley on the far side of the store, he heard the rasping laugh.

Before he could turn around, Nino was grabbing Jim's arm to get him to continue towards the alley. Jim turned and saw Cordón. It had been longer than a year since he last saw him, but there he sat, grinning with yellow-brown teeth and pale gums, laughing at Jim. He sat on a low wall, slowly twirling something shiny in his right hand. It looked like a straight razor.

Jim scowled and bent down to put the bag on the sidewalk, when Nino grabbed him and put his mouth close to his ear. "Now is not the time! I'd gladly help you but I can't risk having Pablo here. Jim! Stop!" Jim turned to Nino and saw that the veins in his arms bulged and his muscles were tense. His face was wild—he had never seen Nino so angry and desperate before. Jim calmed down, picked up the bag and calmly followed Nino to the alley.

"Where is my property *Yanqui?*" shouted the gypsy.

Jim wanted with increased desperation to drop everything, run back and kill him. *Nino was right*, he thought. *I can't drag anyone else into this.*

Nino was walking briskly with Pablo and when the three of them entered the alley, Nino began to run. Jim caught up holding the bags of clanking bottles and rustling plastic close to his chest. "Why are we running?"

"*No me fía*—I don't trust him—what if he's already found Elena?" Jim's legs began to pump faster until he passed Nino and got to the end of the courtyard. From the top of the stairs he saw Manoli slathering sun block cream on Elena's back.

Jim's knees were shaking and he hadn't felt such a clammy feeling of fear in a long while. "*Jesus*, Nino." said Jim, "that son of a bitch is back."

Nino stopped running and Pablo was starting to get unruly. The rapid pace made it difficult to eat the ice cream and he ended up dropping half of it back on the courtyard.

"Don't say anything to Manoli, Jim. It will make her very nervous. Did you hear what he said to you?"

Jim swallowed and turned to look back towards the store. There was no one watching. "Yeah. I'm going to kill that *pimp* if he comes near her."

Nino huffed Pablo to his free arm and then spent the rest of the short journey trying to get his circulation back in the left arm. "We have to talk. Let's drop this off and then go to the shore—I don't want to leave the children out of view."

"Sure. Hey-- Pablo's eating the paper."

Pablo stopped chewing on his ice cream sandwich and tried to spit out a wad of paper. "Yuck!" Nino pulled the mess from Pablo's mouth, threw the ball of chocolate-saliva-paper into a nearby trash bin and looked at himself with disgust. "I'm absolutely covered!"

They dropped off the boy and bags of refreshments at Manoli's umbrella and both walked to the shore. Nino was washing his hands in the water and bringing up handfuls to take care of the mess on his chest and waist. "Dios mio," said Nino. "Did he manage to get any of it into his mouth?" After the salt water washed away the ice cream Nino, picked up a small rock from the beach and chucked it across the small waves. "Any idea on what you are going to do?"

Jim had a hard time trying to think of anything besides violence. "You wouldn't happen to have a gun do you?"

Nino gave Jim an incredulous look. "What would I do with a gun? Oscar would probably find it and shoot me with it or worse—with Pablo, it would go right into his mouth!"

Jim laughed and nodded. "I guess you're right. Still… there's Frank—I'll go ask his advice."

Nino looked at Jim with a blank expression. "Frank… this same Frank that almost killed that big sailor with the monkey's ball?"

"Actually," laughed Jim. "It's called 'Monkey's Fist', and yes, he's the one."

Nino looked toward Manoli and then up around the courtyard. "Are you sure? From what you said, he didn't sound very sane to me."

Jim thought about it for a few seconds. "Really, that's his finest quality."

The gypsy sat on the short wall watching everyone with the type of arrogance and insolence that a mean-spirited dictator would have. If he saw a young girl that he thought was attractive, he'd make sucking noises with his lips and waggle his middle finger at her. An old woman gave him a dirty look when she passed by and he stood up. Although the sidewalks were packed, the people seemed oblivious to him. When he grabbed at the old lady's purse and tore it off of her shoulder, bringing her down to the sidewalk, a few stole glances, but kept from intervening. He opened the purse, saw only a few coins and threw it at her. As he went to re-take his seat, a black Citroen pulled to a stop next to him. A man wearing a black T-shirt with a bulky fanny pack sitting in front got out. He was wearing dark sunglasses and his hair was mostly gray. He walked up to the gypsy and said, "Are you called Cordón?"

Cordón shifted the brim of his large hat slightly higher and reached one hand into his back pocket and tightened it around the razor. "Who the hell are you?"

The man slapped off Cordón's hat and grabbed a fistful of dingy shirt in his left hand. "Don't try it."

Cordón grabbed the man's wrist and snarled, "Let go of me, or I swear…"

The man shoved Cordón backwards off the wall, and unzipped his fanny pack. With his right hand, he pulled out the black Glöck pistol and kept it at his side. He stepped over the wall and stomped down on Cordón's hand as he tried to unfold his razor. Cordón shrieked in pain and the large man jammed the weapon into the gypsy's gurgling mouth. "Are you hungry? Shall I make you lunch?" Cordón shook his head slightly, eyes wide with fright. He opened his lips to speak and the blackness of the gun was covered in spittle and bloodied teeth. The man reached into his fanny pack and pulled out two oval pills. He removed the gun, stuffed the pills into the Cordón's bloodied mouth and put the barrel of the gun to his forehead. "Swallow it."

Cordón shivered and he swallowed the pills.

The man with the gun used the weapon to tap his chin. Cordón opened his mouth in compliance to show that the pills were gone. The man shoved the gun back in the fanny pack and roughly picked the gypsy up from the sidewalk by his hair. He shoved him roughly towards the car. "Get in. Now!"

Cordón felt loose teeth and ragged tissue in the inside of his mouth with a grimy finger and bent down to pick up his hat. He watched the big man with distrust and defeat in his eyes, then slowly walked to the right side of the car, opened the door and got in. He kept his head as close to the side window as possible, hoping to avoid more physical abuse. He kept his hat planted on his lap with his right hand and kept his left ready to try to protect his face from impending blows.

His mouth hurt as his lips and gums began to swell. He tasted the strong copper taste of his own blood. "Who—who are you?"

The man got in and looked at him. "Valgiernas. My employer is going to want to meet you. If you even look at me the wrong way, I'll break something off. If you forget to bow to him, or speak without being asked, you'll die horribly. Did you hear everything that I have told you?

The Gypsy nodded and said with growing sadness, "*Si*—yes." He wondered what his employer wanted or even *who* he may be. As the car pulled out on the road, the gypsy finally noticed the crowd. They watched him get savaged by this man and ultimately watched him go with him as gentle as a lamb. His feeling as the car pulled past them was to make them pay. He began to cry. There was no sadness, only fear, loathing and embarrassment. Just minutes before, no one dared to look at him the wrong way—not even the local Rota police would give him a hard time. He tried to make himself sound as meek as possible, "What are you going to do with me?"

Valgiernas continued watching the road. "Keep that mouth shut."

The black Citroen continued towards the old part of town. 'El Cordón' sat helpless, fearing for his life and clutching his greasy, worn hat.

Chapter Fifteen:
The Right Tools

Frank Gutierrez sat at his kitchen table, brow knitted in concentration, his eyeglasses reflecting the pieces of a scabbard resting on the table around a gleaming, steel blade. Frank was busy test fitting the two halves of the scabbard, which he made himself out of beech wood. The scabbard would eventually be bonded together once he was assured that the blade flowed easily in and out without the slightest friction or defect. His apartment in Fuentebravia was a typical Spanish three-bedroom penthouse, with the exception that every last decoration and detail on the inside of his abode was decorated as if it was a Japanese museum. On the entry hallway was a large glass display bearing the battle armor of a Samurai capped with traditional mask and helmet. Different colored katanas graced the walls alongside scrolls and folk paintings. He could not live without couches, but they were the only western items that he owned as furniture. His door alarm buzzed. "Shit! Shit, shit shit!" Frank gently placed the scabbard back down on the counter and walked over to the intercom. He hit it with the bottom of his fist. "*What!*"

"Frank? It's me, Jim."

Frank's terse expression changed in an instant. "Oh! Punkin! What are you doing in my neck of the woods? Come on up!"

Frank pushed the entry button, looked down and remembered his dress. He rushed into the bedroom and untied his Japanese period-authentic apron-loincloth, which made him look like a slightly underfed Sumo wrestler and pulled on shorts and a *Citadel* T-shirt.

Frank heard the knock at the door, walked up and opened it with a cheery expression. "Back for more huh?"

Jim walked in and looked around. "There's no one in the back that's tied up and getting spanked?"

Frank closed the door behind him and pointed to the couch. "Tea?"

"Of course! Thanks!" Jim always liked this part of the ritual. Frank would prepare Japanese porcelain cups, dump green tea and sugar in each and then pour super-heated boiling water into them from a cylindrical bamboo ladle. There was nothing authentic about it, but the appearance made you think that it wasn't the same that Aunt Suzanne would serve. After stirring, the contents became a greenish-blackish slush. After a few minutes, the tea would drop to the bottom and you could drink. Frank always had a knack for making the best tasting tea.

"So," began Frank, "What have you been up to?"

"I have a slight problem. Do you remember that Gypsy that ran off with my girlfriend? Well, he's back, and-- ahem... Well, just that."

Frank had his poker face back on. Jim looked around to see if the Fist was hanging anywhere nearby.

"You... have *got* to be shitting me. That guy is back? Where's Elena?"

"At Manoli's. I thought it's probably best that she stay there for a couple of days until I figure out what to do. Jim shrugged. "I don't know... I've thought about a gun, but you know how you are not allowed to own one out in town..." Jim left the question open to see if Frank would disagree, reach under the sofa, yank out a chrome automatic and hand it over.

Frank smiled a devilish grin. "A *real* gun anyway. Have you thought about an air rifle?"

Jim looked at Frank confused. "I'm not going to shoot his squirrel, Frank. I want something that'll blow his head off... If, uh, I happen to need one for that."

Frank walked to the living room with the tray. "What you need is a deterrent that will do the job if you need it. You're thinking of air rifles from Sears. I bet we can set you up with one that will tear chunks out of him the size of silver dollars." He placed Jim's cup on a square ceramic tile and passed it to him. He placed his own on the table opposite.

Jim looked around the room. "Don't you think that a Japanese sword like one of these would be good enough inside the home?"

Frank's eyes and nostrils grew huge. "Don't you even think about it, *Gai-jin*! Most of these babies have already seen combat. I don't want their divine blades to taste the inferior blood of a drug-dealing gypsy!" Frank got up and indicated for Jim to follow. "Look at my latest prize. A supreme craftsman hammered this out over 300 years ago. See that stain near the hilt? My son was playing with it a while back and that's his fingerprint stain. Other than sanding it down, I can't remove it—I wanted to saw his head off with it when I discovered it."

Jim looked down at the piece of metal and imagined Frank at a yard sale in Maryland believing some biker's story hook line and sinker.

Frank expected a look of astonishment, but instead saw Jim nodding at the objects with mild boredom. His eyes narrowed. He reached out and pulled two sheets of thin paper from a brown box labeled, 'single ply paper, white, non-acidic', and placed one in each hand. He carefully picked up the blade with the sheets of paper and held it towards Jim's face. "Look at the flowing edge—it's a byproduct from the way they folded the metal over and over again. It's actually a crystalline structure."

Jim looked at the box of paper and was just about to reach over and grab a handful in order to properly satisfy his urge to hold the object that Frank was fawning over. Frank noticed Jim's eye movement and in haste, placed the blade back down on the table and covered his coveted object with a three virgin sheets of paper.

"I'm almost finished with the scabbard—it's taken me three months now. All of the wood is made from beech wood—very fine grain and no knot. Notice the handle—here is the silk cord that I will wind around stingray skin, in turn, wrapped around the wooden handle. Everything must be perfect."

Jim wanted to award Frank's showmanship with one last long glance. "Ah. Nice. What has this got to do with me, Frank?"

Frank looked at Jim with sympathy—he just did not understand. "For modern day creeps, use a modern day weapon. If you were a Japanese student, you'd practice for years with a wooden sword before you could even touch one of these."

"Frank," said Jim pointing to the kitchen table, "Do you want another fingerprint stain on your cheap knock-off?"

"Stay away! Don't even breath on it!"

Frank motioned to the cups that it was at last time to have their tea.

Jim took a seat on the beige couch and picked up his cup. He took a sip and looked about the room. "New bonsai tree?"

Frank sat down and picked up his cup. "Yup. Thing's sixty years old."

"How many times have you been to Japan?"

Frank slurped some tea, let out a great "Ahh" and placed the cup back down on the flat, coaster. "Never been."

Jim almost spilled his tea on the couch. "Ow! What? You've never even been to Japan?" He looked at all of the decorations, the painstaking work he's done on the various creations and impeccable library of books. "Look at all this shit!"

Frank looked hurt. "If you must know, moron, I've always had an interest. I've read countless books on the various topics and even took classes in kanji. I also believe... that I was Japanese in a past life."

Jim chuckled rudely. "This I've *got* to hear! What made you, Mr. *Know-it-all*, believe that you were once Japanese?"

Frank sat back with an air of dignity. "Simply that I've always admired their culture, their design—everything."

Jim finished his tea and removed a few stray flakes of tea from his bottom lip with his finger. "That's an awful big leap—that you admire their culture and that you had a past life there?"

Frank rolled his eyes. "I feel at home in this environment. I grew up in Maryland, with white-bread family. Hell, I don't even think I saw my first oriental until I was a teenager. When I look at the weapons, the dress and pictures..." He trailed off, closing his eyes. "I swear that I can remember being on horseback in the midst of battle, our flags flying and my sword covered in fresh blood. Archers are firing arrows swiftly towards the battlefield... I can almost see our enemy cut down and the survivors fleeing away from us."

Jim stood up from the couch, looked at his naked wrist and said, "Gosh, look at the time!"

Frank laughed. "I knew you wouldn't believe me... *dickhead*."

Jim put his cup down on the tray. "I don't have the brains to believe in much. No matter what I believe, you have the coolest décor I've ever seen."

Frank got up off the couch and put a ball cap on his head and began fishing his feet into a pair of docksider shoes.

"Where are you going?"

"We're going to pay a visit to Boardman."

Jim pulled his green Seat 850 into the barracks parking lot. It was six o'clock and single sailors were up and about, getting ready to have an exciting evening of partying out in town. The air was still warm, and since Jim's beater had no air conditioning, their backs were sweaty from the vinyl seats. Frank's head sparkled with droplets in the afternoon sun.

Jim looked at the barracks building. It was white, and three stories of identical rooms. "Which one is Boardman's?"

Frank cocked a head sideways trying to remember the room number. "Aw, screw it. Hey! You!"

A sailor was sitting on the balcony drinking beer. At his feet was a red and white cooler, surrounded by empty cardboard six-pack carriers. He looked down and he stood up uncertainly. An older man with a military haircut must have some type of rank. "Yes — Yes sir?"

"Do you know a *dork* named Boardman?"

The sailor pointed down to the ground floor. "Yes sir-- room 104."

Frank said, "Great. Thanks, pal." Both men walked to the sidewalk leading to the ground floor rooms and stopped outside 104.

Frank beat on the door with his fist in rapid succession as hard as his hand could take the pain. "Boardman! Open up!"

Something inside the room sounded like it fell over. There was some quick scuffling noises and the door opened. Boardman stood at the door in a white T-shirt and baggy pair of shorts. His round glasses always gave him a blank look and his mouth was agape. He looked at Frank, then at Jim and a sour expression came over his face. "What is it now *Frank*?"

Frank's face turned hot. He was a millimeter away from reminding him how to address an officer and *then* box his ears. He took a calming breath and looked at Jim. "It's after work, fuck it." He turned back towards the door. "Boardman, stop picking your balls, you have a new mission."

Frank pushed Boardman out of the way as he barreled past. "Jesus! What a mess! Were you in here jerking off?"

Boardman looked pained as Frank made himself at home in his room. "Actually, Frank — y'know, I haven't felt the need in a long time."

"Riiight." Said Frank poking around at the magazines spread out on one of the cabinets.

Boardman turned to Jim and shrugged. "You might as well come in too."

Jim walked into the dim room and noticed that a desktop computer was sitting on the desk nearest the window. "Is that a Commodore?"

Boardman looked at Jim with a wry smile. "Well, yeah—she's my baby. It's a 64."

Jim walked over and noticed that it had two monitors, one color the other an amber monochrome. There were wires, connectors and microchips scattered on the desk. A small whisp of smoke rose in the air from a soldering iron. "*Two* monitors?"

Boardman started out with a couple of stammers, then launched into an excited commentary about his system, revealing his passion with electronics. "Well, uh—one is just a console running off the serial port. I'm trying to mod the CPU to accept 128-bit memory spaces. Got the plans from *Electronics Journal*. Supposedly, Commodore is going to release a 128-bit system later next year, but I don't feel like waiting."

Frank was leaning up against one of the bunk beds flipping through one of Boardman's journals with complete disinterest in the articles or schematics. "You can tell by one's hobbies whether one is a genius or lackluster shit." He tossed the journal onto the bed and leveled his eyes at Boardman. "You, my geeky friend, are simply a turd." Boardman didn't break from his stoic expression. Frank leaned forward, hoping for a reaction.

Jim finally broke the silence. "I wouldn't worry about it Mr. Boardman. Frank sits at home all day polishing his sword, if you know what I mean."

Boardman walked over to the desk and switched off the soldering iron, with a growing smile across his face. "Yeah, I kinda figured him to be the sword-polishing type." He leaned against the desk and appraised Frank's face. He had the glaring eyes of a man that was confident yet sarcastic. His smile wasn't the genuine variety that you warm up to, but one to be wary of. "Frank, are you going to tell me what this *mission* is about?"

Frank sniffed indignantly and then noticed the half-size refrigerator. He kicked it open with his shoe and marveled at the interior. "Beer! Christ... Cruzcampo gives me a headache, but I'm too damned hot to care." He fished out two bottles and tossed one to Jim.

Boardman cleared his throat. "Those belong to my roommate, not me."

Frank had already slugged the top of the bottle against the edge of the dresser, popping off the cap and leaving a gouge in the wood's surface. "Roommate? I don't see any roommate. Finders-keepers I always say."

Boardman nodded towards the bathroom. "In there, taking a shower."

Frank fluttered his eyelids and with a coy expression said, "Why aren't you in there soaping him up? Heh! Hey Jim! Do you know why Boardman prefers liquid soap? 'Cause it takes longer to pick up!" He took a big pull from his beer, sighed at the cool refreshment and belched. Jim shook his head, walked over and put his bottle back in the refrigerator.

Frank looked agitated at both of the men. "What a couple of pussies! Oh, all right. We'll stop at the shoppette and I'll buy a replacement six pack."

Somewhere in the bathroom the water stopped running. The curtain was pulled back, announced by the abrupt, rhythmic clattering of the rings across the metal bar.

"It's not too late, Boardman — you go force your way into the bathroom and lick the water off your bunkmate."

Boardman bent down, picking up the bottle cap and in the same movement, tossed it into the trashcan. "Believe me, I do it all the time. By the way, don't throw trash on the floor — we don't like an untidy room."

"Ooh!" squealed Frank. He was laughing for Jim's benefit, but Jim didn't find any of this funny.

The door opened and a lithe, young woman stepped out wearing nothing but a towel. She had short, blonde hair and it was evident that although slim, was quite athletic. She walked in and noticed the men. Undaunted, she walked towards Boardman and slid behind him, wrapping her tanned arms around his neck. Her eyes fell on Frank and then his beer.

Frank looked like he wanted to crawl under a rock. A tinge of red crept up from his neck and began to liberally flow over his embarrassed head.

Jim lowered his eyes and raised his hand "Hello."

Boardman reached up and grasped one of her hands within his. "Guys, this is Cristina. Cristina, this is Frank, my *jefe*. I let him have one of your Cruzcampos. And this is...?"

Jim suddenly forgot that he never introduced himself and began growing the same red affliction as Frank. "I'm sorry! I'm Jim—Jim Smith! Frank? Uh, we better wait for Mr. Boardman outside."

Frank nodded and both men swept out of the room saying "excuse me" and "beg your pardon" to the girl as they passed. Jim closed the door behind him and joined Frank on the sidewalk. Frank was holding the side of the bottle to his temple.

"Jesus H. Christ!" gasped Frank. Did you catch the gams on that girl? Her legs ran all the way to her collarbone!"

Jim could only nod alongside Frank. "Yes, she was quite stunning."

Frank swallowed the rest of the beer and chucked it into a nearby trashcan. "I feel like such a dick."

"Well, I noticed you took the beer with you."

Frank looked at Jim with an impish smile. "Well, I was already busted..."

Boardman walked out of the room, now sporting jeans and tennis shoes. "What's this about?"

Frank looked at him with a lost expression. He finally remembered why they came to see him. "Oh, shit. Right. You're off restriction."

Boardman cocked his head slightly waiting for the catch. He didn't trust Frank. "Really? I can use my lab again?"

"*My* lab, and the answer's yes. But first, you have to come up with a solution for our friend here."

Jim walked up with his hand out. "I'm sorry I didn't introduce myself before—please call me Jim."

Boardman grasped his hand. "Nothing to worry about. I'm Jared."

Frank could not contain himself—not for one second more. "Who the hell is she?"

Boardman said, "We'll talk in the car."

Jim's car started after the engine cranked for close to a minute. Frank sat in the passenger seat with his arm grasping the top of Jim's seat. The short drive to the Seabee camp was filled with Frank's stories about being young and 'up to his adam's apple in pussy.' While he shot out commentary, he would take a few glances back at Jared, sitting in the backseat. "...Yeah, life was darned good back when I was a single marine barely out of my teens." Boardman wasn't looking at Frank at all—just looking out the small window near his head. The curiosity was eating Frank alive. "Allright—spill the beans—who was that stunning *piece* back in your room?"

Jared's face shot toward's Frank. "Don't you *dare* talk that way about her!"
Frank pulled his face back a bit, shocked by his sudden lashing out. It only slightly diminished his grin.

Jared exhaled, then continued with a slightly lesser tone. "Cristina is my girl. We've been together for about six months. I'd appreciate it if you would only shit on me and leave her out of any of your sarcastic comments."

Frank reached out and patted Jared's knee. "Point taken—didn't mean the disrespect—to be honest I haven't seen a more beautiful girl in the last five years!"

Jared was back to looking out of the other window, sulking.

Jim looked back at him in the rear view mirror. "I agree, Jared. She is quite… stunning." Jim could feel Frank's eyes and accompanying grin on him after he used the same adjective about Boardman's girlfriend.

Jared looked at both of them. "Well Frank, you would have figured it out anyway, but here goes. She's not an American."

Frank was back to having his game face on—not the slightest hint of a smile. "You said she was your *roommate*. Does this girl live with you in the barracks?"

Jared nodded. "She works at the air terminal during the day—that's why she has access to the base. In the afternoons, she teaches aerobics at the gym. We were going to move in together out in town but that all changed when you grounded me."

Frank looked out of the window for a short moment but saw nothing. He maintained a death grip on Jim's headrest since Boardman's revelation about the nationality of his roommate. He tried to limit his anger at the young man by wondering what he would have done in the same situation. "One thing—what do you do when you get assigned another male roommate? I know that in today's *progressive,* faggot Navy— you can't have a female staying in the same room."

"Ruth drafted a letter to billeting that I was to have my own room."

Frank spun around, with a wild look on his face. "She did whaaat!"

"She insisted on it. She did it all on her own—it even said that I was exempt from inspections."

Frank looked from Jared to Jim. Jim was staring straight ahead and trying to stay in his lane. "This... is... pure *bullshit*! She and I are going to have serious words!"

Jared felt ashamed. He really liked Ruth and she was like a mother figure to him. "Frank, c'mon—don't get her into trouble—she's almost sixty." He inhaled and licked his lips. "You aren't going to make her move out are you?"

Frank was wiping fresh sweat from the dome of his head. "Jesus! Why do I get into this shit?"

Jim pulled the wheezing Seat into the Seabee camp where the warehouse and Boardman's lab were located. Frank pointed to the modern warehouse and told him to drive towards the back. At the rear, there was a red steel door with 'Authorized entry only' painted across the middle in big, white letters. Jim turned off the key and the diminutive engine coughed once, then died with a sputter.

Frank got out and held the door open for Jared, who was trying to untangle himself from the tiny back seat. The entire time, Frank was glaring at him. When Jared freed himself, he stood directly in Frank's view. Frank slammed the door shut. "What they don't know won't hurt them. *If* someone does find out, she'll have to go without exception."

Jared couldn't help but smile and nodded to Frank. "I promise —no one will. And thanks, Commander."

Frank roared. "Did ya hear that Jim? This *lucky* fucker is practically kissing my ass now! Commander!" He got closer to Jared's face. "Keep an eye on her—if she decides to walk down the aisle with me, I want you part of my honor guard. After all, I'm a *real* man!"

"If it makes you feel any better, I don't have the slightest clue why she loves me either." He looked down at Frank's gut. "Maybe if you lost forty or so pounds and grew a hell of a lot of hair... but right now I don't feel threatened."

Frank threw an arm around Jared and walked him toward the building. "You really surprised me today, Boardman! Never in my wildest dreams..." Frank was digging through his pockets. "Fuck! Jim? We gotta drop by my office, I left my key in my desk."

Boardman fished out a key from his pocket and handed it to Frank. Frank's jovial expression was gone. "Let me guess," Frank muttered. "Ruth gave this to you?"

Jared nodded and raised both palms toward Frank. "I have not opened this door since I've been restricted. She gave it to me just in case."

Frank nodded slowly while glaring into Jared's eyes. "Yeah, and I'm just the big idiot."

Jared frowned. "Honest!"

Frank spun the key on the chain and then walked over to the door. He inserted the key and turned the deadbolt. "Uh. You remember the combo?"

Jared smiled. "Of course. Bottom two buttons, top two, middle." Frank poked his fingers into the X07 lock and then turned the big knob. The door opened to the dark warehouse. Frank walked in, fiddled with switches on the near wall and managed to turn on the escort required flashing light and the extractor fan.

"Other side, first three switches. Here—let me do it." Jared walked in, flipped the switches and the lights came on. Jared switched off the flashing blue light and turned off the fan. "C'mon in."

Jim followed Frank through the door and was amazed at how neat and orderly everything was inside. There were several racks holding different-shaped extruded tubes, cylinders and hefty blocks of different metals. Welding gear of every imaginable type were lined up against the wall just beneath the associated masks and goggles attached to the wall above them. The entire far wall was a series of eight workbenches that sported a work surface made of hard rubber. The wall above them sparkled with chrome tools. There were several smaller rooms containing gas cylinders and one was labeled 'paint booth – protection required at all times'. Lathes, drills and presses stood at attention all over the warehouse—everything looked untouched.

Frank stood next to Jim. "Amazing huh? I bet someone could build a space shuttle in here."

Jim looked around the massive warehouse. Jared was moving a pushcart towards some of the back racks and selecting different objects. He was wearing protective gloves and had already placed plastic goggles around his neck and a yellow ear protection headset was clinging to the cart's handlebar. "How much did this cost?"

Frank sat halfway onto one of the benches and looked around at the machinery. "They didn't say when I got here—Boardman probably knows. NISE East installed everything here—including the armory, which takes up almost half of the warehouse—that's it on the far side. There's a shooting range about 100 yards away too. I'd say the whole thing cost around 8-10 million dollars. See that machine nearest the cage? That fucker alone is worth almost a million bucks."

Jim looked at the rectangular behemoth against the wall. It was painted white with HITACHI painted in large red letters on the side. There were several warnings painted on the ends and sides, with banded yellow/black strips running around the orifices. It looked like a small carwash. There was a control panel, switches and lights on one side and several rubber and Plexiglas doors along the length. "What is it?"

Frank reached over and grabbed a small screwdriver from the wall. He began cleaning the muck from under his fingernails with the flat edge. "That thing will take any pattern you give it, any digitized drawing or even a series of commands and cut a perfect copy out of solid metal—usually aluminum. I watched Boardman cut a lightened rifle stock with side cavities for storage—the damned thing started out as a 9-pound block of aluminum and took four hours. When it was finished it was polished and perfect—not even a rough spot—seamless."

Boardman had pushed the cart towards the bench and was putting on a long, rubber apron. "Frank, make sure that tool goes back where it belongs."

Frank held the tip out to Jared's face. "Want to lick it clean before it goes back? No?" He turned to place it back in the holder, amongst several similar screwdrivers, all arranged by size and type. He noticed that they were all neatly aligned with their 'Craftsman' logos facing forward. He purposely stuck his borrowed one in the holder with the logo facing the wall. With a grunt of approval, he turned to Boardman. "What have you come up with?"

Jared picked up a large black binder notebook with technical drawings protected by plastic inserts. He opened the binder on the table and flipped through several pages. "Let's see... Here. This is it."

Frank and Jim both leaned over at the same time towards the drawing.

Jared pointed to the side view of a rifle. "RS6 paintball rifle. Manufactured by the Swiss to train snipers. They're ungainly, limited by gravity feed and tend to jam."

Jim stood up and looked at Jared. "Paintballs? Those aren't very affective against bad people are they?"

Boardman grinned. "This won't be shooting paint. The one I'm going to make will fire these." He held out his palm. In the center, were three metal balls no bigger than peas and shining like polished gold. He dropped them into Jim's open hand.

Jim was surprised how heavy they were.

Jared picked up the safety goggles and placed them high on his forehead. "Brass. Your weapon will have a slightly smaller barrel and will expend six of those balls every second in automatic mode or one per trigger pull in manual."

Jim stood wondering how effective these will be against someone prone to violence. "Will these break skin?"

Jared looked at Frank, then back at Jim. "Actually, unless they lodge in thick bone, they will probably go right through your target—it all depends on the pressure setting. I'll shorten the barrel down to one foot—that ought to do the job in a tight urban setting, and I'll include a collapsible stock. The whole thing should weigh around four pounds dry."

Jim looked at Jared and handed back the pellets. "Wow! You'd really make this for me?"

Jared looked at Frank. "Does this sound like what he needs?"

Frank nodded. "Better make three of them though—you never know if one will break."

Jared retrieved his mechanical pencil from the pages and slid it into one of the thin holsters on the front of his apron. "Why a third?"

Frank's eyes lit up. "I might want one too."

Jared looked up at the wall clock. It was approaching eight in the evening. "I should be done by ten. Where can I find you guys?"

Frank looked at Jim with raised eyebrows. "Windjammer club? I'm in the mood for a few pitchers of Sangria."

Jim shook his head. "This is too much—are you sure it's no problem?"

Jared was removing the technical drawing from the plastic insert. "Are you kidding? I'm in my world now. —Don't get me wrong...I love Cristina and all, but my real life's passion is this right here." He thought about it for a moment. "Now, if Frank would let me keep Cristina here…"

"Wrong!" Frank was pushing Jim out the door. "She can stay in the barracks with all of those other horny sailors nearby—think about that, Boardman! That ought to motivate you to get done all the quicker!"

Jared began placing the aluminum tubing next to a jig and then dragged over the arc welder. His mind was neither on his lovely girl nor on the two men that just left, just his particular form of art that begged for perfection. He grabbed a rotary grinder/cutter from the wall, plugged it into one of many protective power slots running against the back of the workbench and fired it up with a flick of the side pressure switch. As the grinder began to sing against the yielding metal, Jared thought, *It's good to be home.*

Chapter Sixteen:
The Opening

Rip poked his head into the room marked 'Earth Sciences' and saw Kayanan and Hank arguing over a long piece of graph paper marked with wavy lines. "Anything?"

Kayanan looked up to answer but Hank butted in. "Just some preliminary vibrations—Ricky thinks it's just the national rail heading to Granada."

"Is that ...spyrograph calibrated?"

Kayanan checked off two lines from the grid with a red colored pencil without looking up. "Seismograph, and yes, it was done yesterday."

Rip looked up at the wall clock and fumbled for his glasses. *Shit.* He remembered that he left them in the living room and squinted. "Does that say 11:40? It probably is the train. Most likely, we won't pick up anything until just before he gets released anyway. Keep checking—I'll see if Simon got back yet."

Kayanan handed the paper to Hank. "Are you sure that he gets out at two in the morning?"

"That's the best guess—Seth mentioned the calculation in arc years and it's difficult to translate to standard Earth rotations—Gellan's software made the computation. Either way, Rothiel's boys have been maintaining a vigil at the location for the past month. I think it's tonight."

Hank had gone back to look at reel two and grumbled, "It's not a damned train..."

Rip walked down the hallway to the living room sat down in his brown, leather easy chair. He pulled a fresh Cuban out of his silver cigar case, bit off the end, and spat it into the empty fireplace. He mulled over the evening's events. In a way, he felt anxious, almost excited about the return of Rothiel. *Could he have changed somehow? What if they open his prison and he's dead?* Deep down he knew that Rothiel was alive and counting the minutes now, on when he would introduce hell to the world.

He clucked his tongue in his mouth and flames erupted, puffing out his cheeks suddenly and minute flames shot out of his nostrils. He placed the end of the cigar in his mouth and gently exhaled, engulfing the end in a rush of blue flame. When the end of the cigar glowed red with bright yellow flecks, he removed the cigar and closed his mouth. He waited until all of the air in his mouth was consumed and the flames died a reluctant death. *Not too many of these to enjoy now,* thought Rip. His time was almost up and he knew it. He carefully groomed the ages of the key members of the Lodge and decided to wait for his own demise. *Besides,* thought Rip, *I'm so much more powerful with all this extra body fat.*

The front gate alarm chimed and the black and white monitor illuminated displaying a man straddling a moped. Gellan walked over, scrutinized the monitor and the numbers that the rider had entered on the keypad. "Simon's back from the animal hospital." Gellan pushed the green OPEN button on the console and the monitor showed Simon gunning the throttle through the opening gate. Gellan waited until he cleared the gates and pushed the red CLOSE button.

Rip pulled a lungful of the noxious smoke and blew it toward the wrought iron chandelier on the ceiling. "Gellan, do me a favor and call the team for an impromptu meeting. I just want to go over the game plan for tonight with guys."

Gellan walked town the hallway to gather the rest of the men. The front door opened and Simon walked in. He removed his helmet and placed it on the nearby coat rack. His hair was sweaty from the warm, musty air. The typical sea breezes, which usually cool off the night air, hadn't arrived this week.

"Go ahead and take a seat," said Rip. "—We're going to go over a few rules before we head out to the grove. The rest of the guys are on their way over. You—weren't followed were you?"

Simon looked startled and shook his head no. He kept looking into Rip's face with concern.

"No need to worry, I think," rumbled Rip while glancing at the clock. "I'm sure Valgiernas will discover our hideout sooner or later, but with tonight's festivities he's probably making preparations at the grove.

Big Lee shuffled into the room holding his Walkman and fiddling with the controls. He walked over to his concrete chair and plopped down. "'Zup Simon?" he said, not looking up from his tape player. Simon ran fingers through his damp hair and gave a small wave.

Hank, Ricardo and Filthy walked into the room and sat on the same large couch in front of the iron and glass coffee table.

Gellan walked into the room guiding Seth on his right arm. Seth was wearing his characteristic black eye mask and was clad in a grey sweater and black slacks. Gellan maneuvered him to the empty chair near Rip. Seth took his seat and crossed his right leg over his left. "Hi guys."

There was an irregular echo of the rest of the men returning his greeting and a few "How ya feeling?" from most of them. Rip seemed generally interested in his health and scrutinized the color in the lower half of his face. "Rick? He looks pretty damned good doesn't he?"

Kayanan nodded. "His CAT scan was negative. His vitals were fine, so I put him on some vitamins and he's back to eating normal food."

"I feel fine guys," broke in Seth. "The vitamins taste like a rusty toilet seat though."

Rip leaned over the table and picked up his steno pad. He was absorbed by thoughts of Rothiel and hadn't quite heard what Seth said. "Glad to hear it Seth. All-right, let's get this meeting started." He flipped through the first few pages and scanned the page. He was able to filter out some Hank's whispered comments and stifled snickering out while he re-read his topics. "Ah. Gideon? How are you coming along with the formula to reanimate Filo?"

Filthy shifted in his chair and absently scratched at the bald spot on the back of his head. "No offense Rip," whined Filthy, "I wouldn't bet your ass that this stuff would work."

Rip looked dead into Filthy's eyes and waited for the answer he was waiting for.

"Yes. Yes! I made the stupid formula. I even had to drive all the way to Estepona to get a few fresh branches from a white ash tree. There were a couple of trees at a nature park dedicated to survivors of the Holocaust. How does that make you feel?"

Rip laid the notepad on his lap and said in an even voice, "I will be gone soon. Probably in a week. Our situation will be greatly improved if we can revive Filo. I'd like to give it shot tomorrow—will you be ready by then?"

Filthy was chewing his gum rapidly. "Sure—sure. Holocaust survivors, Rip—I'm doomed. My number five is certain to turn into a six when this is all over."

Rip chuckled and shook his head. "You didn't *kill* the damned trees did you? You were only supposed to get a few branches."

Filthy rolled his eyes and shrugged. "I forgot to bring a saw, OK? I had to tear them off. It wasn't pretty."

The others were laughing heartily at this point and Filthy's face looked hurt.

Rip bit his lip so he wouldn't laugh his head off and tried to think of something serious. "Gideon, I'm sure everything will be just fine. Let's try the mixture out tomorrow morning at around ten. Rick? I'd like you to be present as well."

Kayanan nodded and lightly patted Filthy on his back.

Rip continued, "Well, we know that Valgiernas, Hale and that *prick* Protaxsis will be playing nursemaid to Rothiel. I'd like to discuss tonight what precautions we need to keep in mind for these guys. Let's start with Valgiernas—Rick, he's your baby—what do you think about him?"

Kayanan sat forward and looked at the shining surface of the coffee table as he thought. "He's going to be very adept with weaponry... I think he may even employ explosives as well. He likes to throw a lot of lead around, but is stealthy before he pulls the trigger. I think things will be different now that our fight will take place in a concrete jungle instead of a battle in north Africa. I've been anticipating him for a long time."

"That, and he's at the end of his expiration date." Echoed Seth. "He's almost fifty—I doubt that he's as nimble or quiet as Rick is."

Kayanan rubbed his chin as he thought about Valgiernas. He remembered back to the mid 1800's when Valgiernas, using the name Tom Barrett, terrorized the town of Laramie, Wyoming. When newspaper reports reached the lodge, then located in East Moline, Illinois, the articles were rife with the mayhem and terror Valgiernas was inflicting on the townspeople. Much to Rip's chagrin at the time, Kayanan went missing. He journeyed west almost without pause arriving in the earliest scheduled coach, just outside the town's center, a saloon named "Barrett's Paradise". He strode into the bar and within the first few seconds, killed the bartender who was sweeping the floor. The bartender was nursing the typical symptoms of a debilitating hangover and had misjudged Kayanan by growling, "No china-men allowed—git out!" Kayanan tore the broom out of the barman's hands, snapped it in half and drove the jagged end through the burly man's face. His fat quivering body struck the floor face down, intermittently shaking as his blood spread across the wood floor. The last smell his mind registered before his brain shut down was the sour smell of beer and spent chewing tobacco.

Kayanan went up the stairs taking steps two at a time with each stride. As he arrived at the top of the steps, he had opened the buttons of his front coat, revealing his polished, edged arsenal. He cleansed his mind of anything that could slow him down and placed two fingers to his jugular. His pulse was slightly high, so he dropped his hands to his sides. He closed his eyes, and imagined that he was standing barefoot on cool grass. He let the individual fingers of grass support him while others nearby tickled the sides of his feet in the soft wind. Another momentary check of his pulse. He opened his eyes and looked down at his vest—everything was ready for him to begin.

He approached the nearest door and wafted air from the doorknob upward to his sensitive nose. Close. Not quite. He walked to the second door and abruptly smelled the sharp, metallic smell of someone that enjoyed pulling triggers and as a consequence, impregnates their skin with the acrid particles of gunpowder. He stepped back, pulled out a large knife with a double-edged blade and kicked in the door. The instant the door crashed open, he hurled the knife, windmilling it into the room, burying itself into the forehead of Valgiernas with such force that it split the hefty oak headboard behind him. Valgiernas stared blankly at Kayanan without emotion or movement. His right hand had dropped to the pillow nearest him, toward the guns that were just inches away, hanging from the post of the headboard. His body laid still as the purple origin number '13' on his chest began to slowly fade away.

Tied to the opposite side of the headboard was a battered and bruised whore who did not let out a peep when the knife cleaved her john's head in two. Her hands were grayish-purple and were tied to the post over her head with barbed wire. Serpentine streaks of clotted blood traveled downwards to her shoulders. Her once-golden hair was a matted nest of dried blood, tears and snot. Kayanan walked over and retrieved a small knife with a slightly curved blade. He cut through the wire with a quick flick of his wrist and freed her arms. She slumped to the floor and started sobbing. For a moment, Kayanan wondered if it would have been for the best to kill her as well. "Take his money—he won't be needing it. ...And take my advice and leave this place." He turned and left, walking down the stairwell where her sobs dwindled to silence.

"Ricardo?" Rip had a concerned look on his face. "Was there anything else that you can come up with?"

Kayanan shook his head. "Sorry—zoned out for a minute. Last time we met, he used percussion grenades to try to shake me up."

"Egypt, right? Back in '40? Did it work?"

Kayanan sat back against the couch. "It only deafened my right ear. He ended up taking his own life when I got close enough to finish him off."

"Well, let's hope he saves himself and all of us a lot of heartache by doing the same-- and soon." Rip looked back at his pad. "Let's see who the next bastard on the list is... Hale. Hank? This guy has your name all over him—if you can find it among all the scar tissue."

Hank looked like a child just moments away from opening up his Christmas presents. "How old did Seth say he was-- 34?"

Rip nodded. "Let's see—he had the gift of strength but tended to wind early if I remember right."

Hank rubbed his hands together. "There, I've got him beat. He's probably still into hurting himself as well—"

Rip jumped in, "Tut tut! I'm sure that Valgiernas has put a stop to that by now, as he'll want everyone fit for any confrontation. Do you have any issues that we should know about?"

Hank smirked and rolled his eyes. "No *Papa Rip*, I'm just fine."

Rip continued unabated, "Next on the list is, ahhh. Prestor— hell, this guy is 61 years old! Huh! Someone make a note to have him fall and break his hip early on and we won't have any problems!"

Hank grunted, "You're not that sprightly either Methuselah!"

Rip's face became as stone. "What are you talking about—I'm only fifty." He noticed the way everyone looked at him with suspicion. Big Lee began laughing heartily, still fiddling with the tape player.

Rip removed his bifocals to make a point. "Well, I'm still in my fifties anyways—what difference does it make. Gideon? What can you tell us about this guy?"

Filthy was bending over the table, grabbing a fat handful of cashews from the candy dish. He noticed the room looking at him. "What do you want to know?"

Rip glanced at this steno pad—unable to make out some of his own writing, he reluctantly put his glasses back on. "As I recall, you and Prestor had similar gifts."

Filthy cleared his throat and began, "I wouldn't place him into the same category, Rip. I am able to 'convince' people to do or to accept things. He's more like a mentalist that puts people into a narcotic trance."

Rip's brow furrowed. "We haven't much information on Prestor —you were the last to meet up with him—*shit* I can't read this." Rip dropped the pad in his lap and looked straight at Filthy. "When was the last time you saw him?"

Filthy looked blankly at the ceiling and exhaled. "I... think the last time was the world's fair in Chicago—the Columbian fair. I was conning people out of money at the time and he was flat out fleecing people, as they stood immobilized. It's kind of funny how we ended up in the same location at the same time." No one in the room saw the humor. "Erm. Well, he always tended to dress up like a priest—it was the same way in Italy too. This time I think he was a Methodist preacher, all dressed in black. We met up near the electric boat launch and we more or less recognized each other—I guess by our abilities. Our chat started off amicably enough, but it just couldn't be helped I guess. I can't remember who threw the first punch, as it were, but I remember his tactic was strange whistling and humming."

Some in the room looked skeptical. "No really—he started this rather mad humming and people all around us started either teetering or dropping like flies. The more he kept it up, the more people began to get sick—you know, vomiting and such. I remember that a lot of my commands were not doing much good, but it was taking the color out of his face. Finally he reached into his coat pocket and pulled out a revolver. It was strange, him pointing a pistol at me with his right hand while holding a bible in his left. Anyways, I was panic stricken and yelled for help, but by that time, everyone around us were staggering around like zombies or lying on the ground all glassy-eyed."

Everyone in the living room was laughing and practically in tears after listening to Filthy's story. Hank couldn't take much more and cried out, "For shit's sake man! What did you end up doing?"

"Well, lucky for me, when he pulled the trigger the damn thing didn't fire. He cocked it again and pulled but nothing happened. I yelled at him to stop and he did. I turned to run and I noticed that his eyes weren't following me—I figured that he finally caved. I walked back and waved my hand in front of his eyes—he was out. I was so desperate at the time that all I could think to do was plunge him face first over the rail and into the decorative pond. I held his bony ankles and he drowned without the slightest kick."

"Jesus!" said Rip while making notes in his notepad. "I guess that if we just poke cotton in our ears, we shouldn't have any problems."

Filthy corrected him. "Uh, Actually, I don't think that it will work—I felt as though the sounds that he was making were causing skin or maybe the eyes to vibrate in such a way to cause nervous collapse. As I recall, he never had to go hunting as any animal nearby could be lulled into a fit."

Rip contemplated this last part—if it was true that it was a type of vibration, they could all be in trouble. "Ricardo? How hard would it be for you to take this guy's voice box or lower jaw out?"

"As long as his humming or whistling doesn't take affect right away, I think I could get the job done."

Rip thought about it. Ricardo would probably have his hands full with Valgiernas. "Rick? If you get in a situation with Valgiernas, I want Simon standing in Prestor's line of fire. That way his hard surface may protect you while you throw over his shoulder. Make sense?"

Simon and Ricardo both nodded, Simon giving Kayanan thumbs up.

Rip returned to his note pad. "And, last but not least, we have Protaxsis. Hmm. This weirdo is only 44, and as we have extensively noted in the library, he has the extraordinary ability to force genetic change on animals. Gellan? Give the boys a better explanation."

"Sure," said Gellan, walking over to the fireplace. He nodded to the group. "Protaxsis has been able to tie animals together and in many cases make genes 'jump' from one beast only to get inherited by the other. It's almost immediate—the new creature's DNA is a combination of the hosts and future cell multiplication contains the same mixture. With the data that we have available, we know that only around 10% of his experiments actually take. In the majority of cases, the chimaeras die because of some subtle incompatibility or disease. His most successful experiments have traditionally been with humans. They tend to have less parasites and are most easily managed in the animal kingdom."

Rip broke in. "Gellan, why don't you refresh them on the outcome of Emperor Shi's war."

Gellan nodded. "As many of you will probably still faintly remember to some degree, Protaxsis' greatest battle was his near-victory against Emperor Shi Huangdi in 216 b.c. In that battle, he cooked up a batch of near-invincible creatures—primarily of Mongol stock, that slaughtered most of the Emperor's soldiers and demolished the southern wall of his fortress. His army had fought until the nighttime when in the darkness, the creatures became cold and still to the point of being lifeless. At first, the soldiers believed that the creatures were clad in some type of durable armor that prevented arrows from harming them. Upon closer inspection, it turned out to be skin that had grown thick and rigid. Only strong pikes or stout sharpened swords were able to pierce their skin. Since they were so incapacitated, most were dragged to a large bonfire and burned."

Hank kicked one leg over the other and interrupted. "Gel? I seem to remember a follow-up war where some of Rip's phantom soldiers were used."

Gellan nodded and glanced at Rip. Rip motioned for him to continue with nothing more than a nod and an expressed lower lip. "Yes. Later in 213 B.C., Protaxsis brought his second army into play. They were very similar to the first but their armor was thinner, allowing them to conserve energy and fight for longer periods. From the first war, there were almost two thousand of Emperor Shi's soldiers cut down and the opposing horde was numbered between two hundred and four hundred. Rip had kept four of the creatures alive to study and a year later was able to make use of the first war's dead to help fight the second onslaught."

Big Lee's attention was diverted from his walkman. "What? You were able to use the dead?" He looked unconvinced. "How?"

When Rip saw all eyes converge on him, he decided to explain the circumstances to his full ability. "Before I begin, I have to confess, that I currently don't understand how this was done. I vaguely remember working night and day under severe stress and anxiety while pouring through our library looking for a solution. What I found surprised me to say the least. Apparently, Filo was able to reanimate humans against the same foe that had previously slain them. Most of it was mumbo-jumbo, but it worked... and damned well. Our dead were cremated by then so I took some of the ash from one body and placed it in a clay pot. Following Filo's instructions and several trial and error periods, I discovered that when the pot was introduced near one of

Protaxsis' creatures, it not only began to shake, but it began to transform."

Kayanan spoke up first. "Transform? As in moving about or changing shape?"

"Not only changing," said Rip with his index finger pointed up for emphasis. "But it was attempting to change into a face—namely the face from the fallen soldier."

Then men began to murmur amongst themselves. Big Lee shifted in his hulking chair and scrutinized Rip's face. "The clay soldiers—that's what they were for. I thought that they were some kind of... robot or something."

Rip chuckled. "Huh! Not quite, Corey. I had survivors from each family guide artisans who created terra cotta reproductions of each dead soldier. They were all hollow. Inside, a thin mixture of blood from each of their family members as well as hair and some expressed tears were used to coat the insides. The coating was held in place by a weave made from corn silk. The dead soldier's ashes were then introduced.

If they preferred a specific weapon in life, they were given the same in death. I didn't know what to expect, but when one of the test soldiers was wheeled into the fortress near an iron cage holding one of the creatures, the soldier shot off the dolly and began tearing the cage apart to kill the creature. One of the guards, worried that the statue would liberate the creature and in turn, get us all killed, attempted to break off the soldier's arms and head using an iron axe. The clay warrior continued to tear at the cage and the blows from the axe did not seem to make a difference—wherever the clay was smashed, the clay would rapidly heal around the area. In the end, it collapsed the wall of the cage, entered inside and rent the creature in two with only its hands. When the lifeblood of the creature spilled onto the floor and its legs ceased from kicking, the statue stood back in its original pose and did not move another inch. I know, I know—hard to believe, but it's true. We began to turn them out as fast as we possibly could. I remember working night and day until we dropped. We were allotted three hours sleep per day and then back to a tireless day's work to complete the statues and weapons.

I hated the Emperor for his merciless driving until one day when we had nearly completed the last few statues. A rider rode into the city bearing a black arrow hanging out of his chest. His last few words indicated that over a thousand were on their way here. We pulled him off the horse and removed the arrow. Then we noticed his eyes."

The mood in the room became silent. The uneasy tension seemed to touch bone. The clock above the mantle seemed to tick louder.

Rip used this moment to prolong the wait and took another drag off his cigar. He coughed, exhaled and put the cigar back down on the ashtray. "Anyways, the iris's of his eyes were almost white. His skin was becoming hard and leathery and his hair was dropping off in clumps. I lifted one of his hands to check his pulse and noticed that his fingernails were sliding off with ease. I told the guards to carry him to my lab immediately. They picked him up and when we arrived to the outer doors of the fortress, the clay soldiers that were already in place erupted into life and hacked the man apart. In their sheer speed, some of the guards lost fingers and one lost an arm from the elbow down. I yelled at them to back away and let them do their work. The rider expired right away—the soldiers ceased their attack, stood erect and halted. At that moment I knew that this rider was not suffering from a disease or poison meant to kill the enemy, but was slowly turning into one of Protaxsis' minions while we watched. I returned to the place where the rider fell and retrieved the arrow from the ground. The shaft was hollow and packed with something similar to cotton. I realized that the cotton was not saturated with the rider's blood, but something different.

The next day, one of the guards on the south wall raised the alarm. The horde was coming over the Cho Zhu pass and converging on the fortress. Only the day before, the fallen rider had estimated that there were a thousand of them but he was mistaken—from what I could estimate, there appeared to be at least three or four thousand of the damn things. Every man available suited up in their armor and weapons dispersed. Fear was in everyone's eyes—except for our small group who knew that a new life was just a few moments away and we would be back to our familiar state—shitting on ourselves and drinking out of some lady's tits. I went to the vault and locked Filo away behind a stone wall bearing his inscription. In the event that we're all killed and there's no one to take over his care, he is hidden as best as possible until I can come back as an adult and reclaim him. I remember talking to him, hoping that his recipe would make a difference, when I heard the rattling. The oil lamp on the floor was shaking and then a low noise grew louder as if it was a long, endless course of thunder. I closed the wall and ran upstairs. The clay soldiers had all come to life and were all running full tilt out of the main door of the fortress, knocking down guards who were too close and spilling out of the gate with their weapons drawn. The last group to leave the fortress was 130 archers. They left the gate walking in perfect step and lined up as neat as a pin just outside the wall. They knelt on one knee and simultaneously drew their first arrow.

At that point, I really can't say that I remember being concerned —I was more shocked. The horde remained approximately 1,000 yards away from the fortress—it looked like the ground had changed from grass to shiny black stones. As the soldiers ran at them, they didn't appear to notice—they kept their same speed, marching towards the fortress. Just before the soldiers impacted the first line, the archers released their arrows. The arrows struck the creatures and a great hiss rose up in the air—no screams or shouting, just a loud hiss like standing next to a waterfall. The soldiers slammed into the horde and began hacking and slashing at them. It was as if the entire horde was blind and at that moment realized that the soldiers were upon them.

We realized that the horde could see us just fine because they could only register our body heat. The clay soldiers were a minor distraction to our signatures peering at them over the wall. The attack was brutal and lasted most of the day. By evening, most of the statues had fallen silent—some laid on their backs on the slick battlefield. A thick, almost tarry liquid coated the ground and killed all plant life that it touched. Horses would not venture out on the battlefield—none could be rode on that ground for years afterwards. We did not lose a single human fatality except for the first rider."

Hank stood up from the couch and looked at Gellan and Rip. "Well—it seems obvious! These things are still around aren't they?"

Rip picked up his cigar and took another pull—all the while shaking his head. "It's not that simple." Smoke curled up from his nose as he exhaled. "The original treatment was over two thousand years ago—odds are they won't be effective today. The reason for bringing this up is because it was Protaxsis greatest achievement—he almost won. I am betting that he is generating something similar this time around. I'd like to remind you all about Mycenae—we didn't get there in time and at some point, the entire city melted down everything made of metal to make weapons, but was entirely wiped out—no trace whatsoever."

Hank looked annoyed at hearing this. "Well, aren't you at least going to give it a try?"

Rip nodded at Hank and pointed to the area of the couch that Hank left empty. Reluctantly, Hank returned to his seat.

Rip waited a few more seconds until Hank finished bitching to Simon and continued. "We are in luck. Brother Qin is in tight with the Chinese mafia in Almeria. Other than opium smuggling, they ship antiquities from mainland China. There are currently three soldiers in the museum of Madrid, which Qin is securing one of them for our benefit to use in testing. He is also working on securing around six more that are in good condition from a display in Marbella—We should have them in about four months—I just hope that we have enough time."

Rip bent over the coffee table to place his cigar in the ashtray and noticed something shaking the surface of the cognac in his glass. He watched it for a second, and then raised his head. "Ricardo—you'd better go check your equipment."

Kayanan bolted from the couch and ran to the environmental lab. When he opened the door, he was shocked by the seismograph's display. Red ink flew in arcing sweeps across the graph page and a black line registered the same amplitude next to it. Kayanan tore off the spent sheet and ran back to the living room, all the while studying the lines of the graph.

"This has got to be it," he said, holding up the paper. "Red is our monitoring station in Puerto Real and black is our station in Jerez. Red is picking up the primary and echo noises and Jerez is hearing the primaries clean."

Rip looked at Kayanan as if he had just read out the ingredients of hemorrhoid medicine.

Kayanan broke it down in easier terms. "We can barely feel the tremors, but something is causing significant activity just due west."

The men began getting ready in earnest. Hank had arrived wearing a dark jacket and a 12-gauge auto-loading shotgun. The pockets of the jacket were bulging with spare shells. In his left hand, he was carrying an ammunition can labeled, 'Grenades, 12/Percussion, 12/ Fragmentary'. Gideon Blunt had driven the 6 1/2 ton truck to the front of the Villa and Big Lee was stepping up into the rear bed and settling down with his dog under his arm. The truck had enormous carrying power and the springs barely flexed when Big Lee stepped up. Kayanan double-checked the sensitive night vision equipment and cameras that were loaded in the back inside two large canvas bags.

Gideon turned westbound on the A340 and headed towards Estepona. The night air was at last cool, but still. The miniature bodies of mosquitos exploded onto the windshield as the truck picked up speed. Rip and Gideon had made the trip previously just to check out the surroundings. The Grove, as it was called, was a large olive farm located next to a lake surrounded by a valley made of high granite cliffs. Gideon peered out at a small wooden sign that Rip had made years before. It was weathered with grey flecks of wood splitting on the sides and peeling paint. The sign said '*Cuidado*'. Gideon slowed, and turned the truck onto the dry, graveled road that lead to the southern side of the grove. The truck's diesel engine grunted and clacked up the gentle hill until it reached one of the crests overlooking the thousands of trees.

The truck came to a stop and Gideon turned off the ignition. Rip felt a tickle on the back of his neck and his hand brought back sweat. He was nervous for several reasons—he wasn't sure of what Rothiel would be capable of and he didn't know how tonight's events would play out. Rip heard a dry rumbling sound below. He walked to the side of the hill and gazed down. A portable generator was running at a fast pace, driving several mercury vapor lamps scattered around the grove. Several men were walking around checking instruments on the ground. *At least we didn't have to worry about the truck giving away our arrival,* thought Rip.

Gideon walked up while guiding Seth. "Looks like the welcoming committee is hard at work."

Rip looked at Seth and then around the area. The moon wasn't out, which was good. "Seth? I think it's safe for you to take off your mask—try not to look at the bottom of the hill where all the lights are."

Seth pulled the eyeshade from his face but kept his eyes closed. He squinted and looked down towards the noise from below, but forced himself to look away from the lights. He started scanning around the area. "Oh!"

Rip looked in the same direction that Seth was looking at— nothing. "What do you see?"

"It's that same girl."

"Theo? The blonde one? The one you saw in the fortress a while back?"

"Yes. Good God, is she something to see. I don't know how you can stand to be away from her. Standing next to her is an older man — I don't think that I've seen him before. The boy, Cesar, is standing between the both of them."

Rip scrutinized the direction and tried squinting as well. *No use.* "Do they see us?"

"Hell Rip, they're only about fifty feet away from us. All three are staring right at us and talking to each other."

Bob, Theo and Cesar had been at the grove for several hours. They had all walked through the camp and took a good long look at Rothiel's followers. Luckily, there were no peacocks around to see them. They could observe in complete anonymity — up until the truck drove up. They watched the three men look down into the grove and saw Seth remove his eyeshades. Cesar did not recognize him until he saw his eyes. Even in the darkness, he could tell that his eyes were tired. His face was gaunt, and weary, like he wore his punishment on his very skin like a tattoo that was once colorful and intricate, only to turn faded and corrupt.

When Bob saw that Seth was looking right at them he whispered out of the corner of his mouth, "Looks like you have an admirer, T."

"Shhh. We still don't know if he can *hear* us as well." Said Theo, trying not to stare back at him.

Cesar kept looking straight back at him and wondered if Seth knew that he was the one that helped him the day before. Absently, Cesar put his left hand in his trouser pocket. Because pockets were so new to him, he found that he did this quite a bit during the day. Seth mimicked him by putting his left hand in his own pocket.

"Don't stare back at him," whispered Theo. "We know he can see us — just keep a look out for other visitors."

Bob and Theo were busy conferring softly to each other and scanning the grove for anyone new. Cesar saw Seth remove his hand from his pocket with his fingers and thumb in the OK sign. Just before Cesar looked away to follow Theo's advice, he performed the same for Seth's benefit.

"Yup. It's the same kid."

Rip still looked concerned that just a granny-tossed stone away, stood his former contemporaries. "Are they still looking at us?"

"No. It looks like they're preoccupied with what's going on down there."

Rip tried to think about what they would be most interested in. "What about others?

Seth turned slowly and let his eyes wander around the ridge-line and down amongst the trees. "A few here and there, but further from the center than we are. One interesting thing I just noticed—all of the spooks are fleeing from the center of the grove." Seth stooped down and put his palm flat against the sandy soil nearest Rip's foot. His hands folded around something unseen and he brought it up to Rip. "Caught one."

Rip had never touched one of Seth's spooks before—Hank did, and it freaked him out for days. They were in several shapes and sizes —some apparently menacing and others docile. He looked at Seth's upturned fist that was loosely clenched around something wriggling. "What does it look like?"

Seth held his hand up to his own face. "Uh, similar to a lizard's body but it's covered with silky hair like a weasel. It's got a long tail with a big tuft of hair at the end. It has hairless hands and feet that almost look human-- really big eyes too."

"...Any teeth?"

Seth brought up his index finger to the creature's snout and it turned away. He prodded again and it opened up his mouth and began to chew his finger. "Huh. Really tiny ones—can't even break my skin."

Rip reluctantly held out both hands to accept the strange creature. When Seth placed the creature in his hands, he felt a moment of soft warmth and then it scrambled out of his grip. He tightened his grip as it squirmed, but it shot out of his hands and scurried over his shoulder, continuing down his back. "Shit! It got away!"

Seth looked and saw that the creature was still hanging on to Rip's belt loop and looked agitated. Its long curving tail snaked up and touched the base of Rip's back for a moment before dropping to the ground.

"Ooof! Fuck!" Rip grabbed the small of his back.

"What's wrong?" asked Gideon.

"Aw, *hellll*. Ohhh! I think I just slipped a disc or something." Rip began to twist his back towards each side to try to loosen the discomfort. "It feels like one of my ribs is stabbing my lung!"

Kayanan walked up and said in an even tone. "Everyone down there is going to hear you-- and what the hell happened to your back?"

Seth glanced over at the spook sitting on the branch of a nearby olive tree, its long tail curved around its body. It was staring back at Seth and licking the tip of its tail. "My fault. I caught a spook and put it in Rip's hand. I guess it's one of his defense mechanisms. Rip doesn't have a hole in his shirt or anything—maybe it zapped him with electricity or something."

Kayanan walked Rip to the back of the truck telling him to keep it down. Enano, Big Lee's dog walked up to Seth and began sniffing his ankle. Seth reached down and scratched the top of his head and could feel the wind moving from the dog's wagging tail. He looked down at the dog and a gleam from the dog's eyes shot into his own, causing pain like a cold steel nail driving deep into each socket. Seth looked away and opened his eyes. The center of his vision was black— he only had some peripheral vision, but with some relief, the pain began to recede. "Whoa boy—I forgot how shiny your eyes are." He reached back down and started scratching the dog's head again. He blinked frequently and rotated his eyes at the dark night. The dark spots were diminishing. He looked back to the right and caught Cesar's gaze. The boy nodded to him, with a clear look of worry on his brow. Seth nodded back and pulled his eyeshade down over his eyes.

"Jesus, that's better," said Rip, walking back to the edge while rotating his right shoulder. "Ricardo popped my back against the truck bed down to the base of my spine—it hurt like hell at first."

Seth smiled as he rubbed at his temple. "Glad to hear it. I thought I heard the sound of lumber snapping."

"I don't know what in Bozo's name your damn spook did, but I swear it sucked a bone out of my back." He looked around his feet. "Any more of the damned things around?"

Seth lifted the bottom edge of his shade to glance at the ground and then let it snap back against his face. "No. The ones that are walking around are the benign ones."

"What do you mean by benign—they just bite you to death instead?"

Seth laughed. "Have you ever eaten pieces of some snack and everything tastes fine? Then, out of the blue, you pop another into your mouth and it tastes like a goat's ass? That's what I mean by benign."

Rip looked disgusted. "You mean to tell me that spooks taste horrid?"

"No. Worse. That's what happens when one of them slobbers on, mates with or shits on your food."

A cry from below got their attention. Down in the clearing there was a flurry of activity. Kayanan handed his binoculars to Rip, who placed them to his furrowed brow and looked down. The earth was shifting and boiling and at once, Rip recognized a man shoving people away from the perimeter. Valgiernas. "Well, well. It looks like your friend is down there directing the rescue."

Kayanan was watching the spectacle next to Rip. Seth had removed his eyeshade and was half shielding his vision with his palm to avoid any inadvertent reflection. "Can't make out a damn thing. What do you guys see?"

Rip chewed his bottom lip a moment. "The ground is coming apart—or ripping itself up. Wait! There it is! It must be. There's something like an egg or ball pushing out of the ground—hell, it's big."

Seth was looking at all sides to see what activity he could pick out in the darkness. The spooks that were migrating from the grove were now scurrying at a frantic pace towards the surrounding tree line. "How big?"

Kayanan switched to a high-powered spotter's scope. "Enough for Big Lee to fit in—maybe his damn dog too. ...Okay, It's definitely a large ball—kinda rough on the outside, like it's all wrinkled or covered in weird swirls or something. Look's like it's come to a stop. Valgiernas is walking up—looks like he's going to touch... Whoa! It must be hot, because he just burned himself. I can't see what he's doing now—he's standing right next to it."

Kayanan scratched his head and looked at Rip. "Looks to me like he's listening with a stethoscope perhaps—hard to see from here. Yes, it's definitely a stethoscope and he's banging on the outside of the sphere with the butt of a pistol."

Valgiernas took off the stethoscope and yelled at one of the attendants standing by one of the floodlights, "Bring me a cold chisel and hammer—now!"

One of the men brought up the tools. "Is he alive lord?"

Valgiernas paced around the steaming sphere looking for a likely spot to make the first cut. The surface was a rough and wavy — from the lack of noise it made with his pistol butt, the rock felt thick. His voice betrayed his uncertainty and his panic. "He's alive, but I can't make out what he's saying. Be ready with the water and blankets — on your life, do not touch him until I say so!"

He raised the chisel and touched it against the surface. He brought the block hammer back and grunted as the hammer slammed against the chisel. It did not scratch the surface and seemed to reflect all of the energy backwards, repelling the hammer away from the chisel. Valgiernas stepped back and began searching around the stone. He could find no defect, no grain or area of weakness that might make parting the stone easier.

Inside the clouds that encroached the horizon a distant crack of thunder rang out. The beige sphere of stone pulsed, and then changed to a dark greenish-black. The surface changed from a porous, light texture to a glassy, hardened structure with a hue that resembled gangrene or a severe bruise. Valgiernas began walking backwards, dropping the hammer and chisel. "Ready yourselves!" In the center of the sphere, a glowing yellow spot, no wider than a finger began to appear on the outside. It began to move, trailing a bright orange line and curling smoke from the surface. The finger continued slowly across the top of the sphere and without pause down the other side. Another large crack echoed through the valley but came directly from within the sphere. A smaller series of cracks announced the two halves separating.

The two sides fell apart bathing the onlookers in a sour, dank stench. Something was shivering in the center of the left shell and screaming weakly with a hoarse voice. It was pale white and quivering. It shined as if damp or covered with a slimy sheen. It was difficult to make out as a human form, but as their eyes adjusted to what they were seeing it was obvious that it was the naked body of a thin man — mostly bone covered with tight skin. The hands and feet were a dark color. Valgiernas saw that the fingers and toes were freshly bleeding. He heard a hoarse wail from the creature that he could barely understand. He thought he heard the origin word for light. "Cut the lights, damn you, now!" Valgiernas threw the closest man toward the ring of floodlights and snatched the blankets from the attendant holding them. His eyes were stinging from the fetid smell. It smelled of human excrement, rotten eggs and the sour smell of vomit. He draped the blanket gently over the creature and the lights were extinguished. "Master—I am here —it's me, Valgiernas." The hoarse wails died with the lights. Low muttering was heard, but Valgiernas could not understand them— perhaps a word here or there. He tried to remember a greeting in origin but could not remember any. "Rothiel? Master?" He was met with a hiss and a flurry of words—of which, only one that he could understand —'*home*'.

"Jesus… H. Christ." Muttered Rip, staring through his binoculars. "Ricardo? What in hell am I seeing here?"

Ricardo didn't answer right away, as he tried to make sense of what he was looking at. The strain of anticipation was too much for Seth as well. "Rick? What's going on—Rip?"

Ricardo cleared his throat before speaking. "Um. Well, that was different than I imagined—I thought his cell would open with Rothiel sitting on a throne."

Rip echoed with a short, "No shit."

Ricardo remembered that Seth was unable to see. "Sorry Seth— Rothiel's rock cell opened—snapped in half, I guess would be the best description. Anyways, in one half of the shell, there was something moving—at first it looked like a sheet or something. Rothiel is paler than the insides of a clam and worse looking. From up here it looks like he's injured—I saw his lower jaw streaked with blood—his hands too."

"Did they douse the lights?" Seth lifted the edge of his eyeshade and saw that the lights had gone out.

Rip lowered his binoculars. "Shit. Now I can't see a damned thing. I hope Big Lee and Filthy are getting everything with the IR cameras."

Seth took his shades off and peered down the valley. "Weird—I can see them gathering something—must be Rothiel, up inside some blankets and placing him inside a van. That looks like Valgiernas near the shell. He's looking inside it—" Seth closed his eyes as soon as the pain struck. Valgiernas had turned on a flashlight and was examining the inside of the sphere.

Seth pulled down his shades and Ricardo was already by his side. "Did it get you?

"Whew! No, but close. My *eyes* are ringing. Strangest thing though—I swear that I could see something inside."

Kayanan jogged to the truck and saw the van rumbling over the loose rock on its way to the main road. Valgiernas was behind the wheel. Four other cars were following and a small herd of people was busy removing the lights and tents that dotted the area. Corey and Filthy were loading the equipment into the truck and Rip climbed into the cab. Corey reached down and picked up his dog.

When Corey brought the dog chest high to place him in the back, the dog took the opportunity to lick his master's face. "Cut it out! 'Nano—can't see a damn thing." Corey placed the dog into the bed of the truck and the dog came to a rest on top of both aluminum tripods, crushing them flat.

Filthy was attempting to shove the dog off of the tripods, but it was like pushing a fur-covered anvil. "Shit! Corey! Rip is going to blow his top when he sees this. Move it Enano!" The dog looked dejectedly at Filthy, got up on his feet and lumbered towards the cab. Each step of Enano's paws made the massive diesel truck tremble. Both tripods were beyond repair. Filthy picked up the expensive one and showed it to Corey. "It's bent like a frigging banana! I'm not taking the rap for your dog Corey!"

Corey gave a deep laugh and chucked both out of the truck onto the ground. "Didn't you pay attention? Look who was just let loose into the world? Those cheap-ass tripods don't mean 'nuthin." Corey placed a fat hand on the back of the truck, stepped up onto the thick steel bumper and strode aboard. The truck's suspension lurched from the extraordinary weight. Corey strode delicately towards the back of the cab to sit down. His dog was panting throughout the warm night but was wagging his tail with a soft thumping sound as it struck the bed of the truck. Corey picked up the dog and placed him on his lap as if he was as light as a snowflake.

With the truck loaded up, Filthy switched on the massive Cummins diesel engine and was careful not to rev the motor or make excessive noise. He backed the truck away from the edge of the valley and continued down the path towards the road. Filthy drove a few hundred yards away from the grove before switching on the headlights. Seth sat in the middle with his black eyeshade firmly in place with his jaw set firm. He was tracing some unknown designs on his knee with his index finger and would stop for a moment, cock his head and start over again. Rip realized that none of the men were speaking. He exhaled a relieved breath and looked out the rear window. Hank was sitting on one side of the truck next to Simon. Strangely enough, Hank was silent. Kayanan was sitting next to Corey in deep thought. He looked up when he noticed that Rip was looking at him. *His face looks so worried. I hope I can change all of that soon.*

Rip looked over at Filthy. "What are your thoughts Gideon?"

Filthy muttered, "…I think Big Lee should pay for them that's for *damn* sure."

Rip looked over at Seth for clarification, but Seth looked like he was in his own world. "What?"

"Sorry—Rip, I was just lost in thought." Filthy looked at Rip. "You mean with Rothiel? Strange… *real* strange. I honestly thought that he would rip the stone apart from inside and then destroy the entire planet. I-- I never expected him to look so…weak."

Seth's face was positioned straight ahead, but with his shade on, it was hard to judge his interest or emotion. He spoke with sudden urgency. "Did you train the camera on him as well as the shells?"

"Hmm?" Filthy was watching the road and glanced at Seth at quick intervals. "The shells—you mean the halves of that… ball thing? Yeah I got it on camera two. Hank was on the other side and he said that he had a clear view of everything with camera one. Why?"

Seth didn't say anything for a few seconds. "I saw something. I'm not sure what it was, but I know Valgiernas saw it as well."

Rip was watching Seth with deep interest. "Seth? What was it you think you saw?"

"I saw… I saw pictures or writing—maybe both. It was for a brief second, but I'm sure of it."

Rip wanted a cigar more than anything. *Hell*, he thought, *it's just another twenty minutes to the fortress. I've got to keep clear-headed.* "I'll send someone to check out the halves tomorrow—probably Hank and Simon."

There was a loud banging on the outside of the truck and Kayanan was shouting something. Rip slid open the rear window and Kayanan's face arrived to within an inch of Rip's nose. "Rip, we're being followed! Rip shot a look behind the truck and just saw headlights. Before he could ask any questions, Kayanan insisted, "Believe me! It's one of the cars from the grove."

Gideon's face was pale. "Rip! Do I keep driving? They can't know about the fortress!"

Rip turned to Kayanan. "Rick—have Hank and Simon stop the car, then you flank for any survivors. Try not to kill any of them. Gideon? Stop the truck".

Gideon pulled the truck to the shoulder of the highway and Enano began a low growl. The dog was up on his feet shaking from his snout to his tail. Corey had a fat grip on Enano's scruff and murmured, "Not our fight boy—we's just gonna watch."

Hank was on his feet. He had taken off his jacket and was rolling up his sleeves while judging the distance of the car behind them. The car had pulled to a stop over on the shoulder 100 yards behind. Simon had removed his shirt and shoes and pulled himself into a tight ball on the bed of the truck. His chin was buried between his knees and both arms were wrapped around his legs.

"Pull the emergency brake, Gideon," said Rip as he got out of the truck and reached for a cigar. After a loud pop, his mouth and nostrils filled with flame and he lit his cigar in his peculiar way. Hank looked down at Rip for approval. Rip chewed the fat cigar between his teeth and nodded at him.

Hank looked down at Simon and said, "Ready?"

Simon's deep-blue eyes began to deaden and the blue faded to milky white. Even his hair turned a lighter tone and ceased to wave in the wind. Hank tapped the side of Simon's face with his fingertip. Satisfied that Simon was ready for the short journey, he wrapped his right hand around Simon's upper arm and hefted Simon up off the floor of the truck bed. He steadied Simon with his left hand to keep him straight, braced his right leg against the back of the truck bed and cocked the human cannonball just over his shoulder. Hank took a series of short puffs, inhaled then hurled Simon towards the car with ferocious speed.

When he released Simon into the night air, Hank's body followed the movement, now devoid almost entirely of weight. Big Lee's hand struck out and grasped Hank's ankle and held him immobile. Simon hurtled through the black sky and struck the ground once kicking up dust and gravel and continued unimpeded towards the car. The driver's side door shot open the same instant that Simon's body slammed into the front of the car, exploding the glass from all sides.

A bloody hand fumbled out of the window for the door handle but could not get the door unstuck. As Simon could feel his weight subside from the over 1,000 pounds that Hank was able to tack on to his mass compared to his normal 160 pounds dry, Simon unrolled from the ground and sat up. He was near the front of the vehicle and as usual, surprised by the destruction. Getting to his feet, he looked at the driver and saw that he was killed on impact. He was brushing grit off of his shoulders when he heard Hank yell out. Simon looked to the other side of the car and noticed the wounded passenger had a gun in his shaking hand and was pulling the trigger.

The passenger did not know what struck the car—he only saw a rolling mass rushing towards them. It was a massive blur that seemed to take a familiar shape as it hurtled under the street lamps. The force was so great that his left arm, which was braced against the dashboard, broke in two. His jawbone slammed against his chest and sheared off the tops of three of his molars. As his vision cleared, he thought he saw someone approach the car and he reached for the pistol in his ankle holster. The man was looking at Felipe, the driver who was either unconscious or dead. He leveled the gun at the man's face and just before he pulled the trigger, he thought that he saw the man's blue eyes turn white. The slug impacted the man's forehead but did not make a hole- it simply rocked him slightly backwards. He felt his finger tighten around the trigger for a second shot and felt the cold slap of metal on his wrist that sent waves of pain up his arm. The gun had disappeared. Even though he could still feel it, his hand too, was missing. It lay in his lap gently drowning in the coursing blood running from his stump. An oriental man reached inside and gripped a handful of his hair and shoved his head back against the seat and kept a large knife against his throat.

"You okay Simon?" Kayanan took just a few seconds to flank the car but was not quick enough to get back around by the time Simon got up from the pavement. It looked like he froze quick enough to avoid harm, but he couldn't be sure. Simon nodded and wiped the palm of his hand against his forehead. It was dirty from Hank's wild ride, but the bullet did not harm him. Kayanan looked into the car and saw just the two. He could tell by the driver's eyes and stillness that he was not breathing and probably past the point of no return. *"No te muevas,"* he said in Spanish, "Or I'll take your other hand, then your head." The passenger looked in agony but did not move. Kayanan took a cursory look around the car and saw that there were no more weapons. He removed his knife from the throat of the passenger and returned it to the sheath on his back.

Rip walked up to the car puffing on his cigar. "Well, well! Nice throw Hank!" He walked around to the side where Kayanan stood next to the wounded passenger. "And what's this pretty piece of work?"

Kayanan was coiling up a length of wire while looking at the man. "Don't know who or what he is yet—looks like his left arm is broken and he may have some broken ribs by the way he's leaning in his seat."

"And that?" Rip was pointing at the bloodied hand lying on the man's lap.

"Strangest thing—after it shot at Simon, it just sort of—came off."

The man let out a long groan let out a series of short gasps.

Rip reached in and used his thumb to spread the passenger's eyelids open. "Hm. Yep. We're taking this one with us. Ricardo, why don't you stop this guy's bleeding and get him stabilized. Get him loaded into the truck and we'll be on our way." He looked over and saw Hank handing Simon his clothes and admiring his handiwork with the car. "Hank, come get the door off this wreck and help get our ugly guest into the truck. Oh, and don't let any of this blood get on you—*I mean it.*"

Chapter Seventeen:
Boardman's bang-stick

Jim and Frank sat in their plush, rounded chairs in the main
room of the Windjammer club. In front of them were two empty
pitchers of Sangria, replete with melting ice and the rinds of several
oranges and lemons. The third pitcher was half full and was vacant of
fruit and much of the ice—Frank rather rudely insisted that he was
being shafted on his purchasing power of alcohol.

Frank picked up the pitcher and Jim simultaneously placed his
hand over the top of his glass. "Frank—stop. I've got to drive,
remember?" Frank answered by pouring the liquid over Jim's fingers,
until he finally removed his hand and let Frank get his way.

"Fucking shame, Smitty. I mean, look around you. Beautiful
women and loud music and you want to play sissy."

Jim looked around the room and his head swam. He saw at the
table across from them the same ladies from the charity run that were
the size of refrigerators. They were downing pitchers of beer and
giving Frank what he liked to call, '*whore-eyes*'.

"Jesus Frank, I bet there's not a single girl in here that weighs
less than you do."

Boardman walked into the club and looked around the dimly lit
room. To the right was his commander, waving to fat chicks at a nearby
table. When Frank noticed that Boardman was watching, his hand fell
to his lap like a stone.

"Time to go Jimmy- *monsieur* John Holmes just walked in!"

Both men got up from their chairs slowly and Frank finished his
glass. Jim walked towards Boardman with an ungainly stride while
Frank had a last minute chat with the fat-girl table.

"Hey Jared, would you like a drink or something?"

"No thanks man—" Jared noticed that Frank was kissing the
hand of one of the laughing blondes and as she giggled, several pounds
of flesh heaved to and fro from under her arms. "Oh man. I'm not
going to let him forget this one. Anyways, I've finished and tested all
three—they turned out better than I thought."

Frank trotted up to Boardman with droplets of sweat shining
from his brow. "Let's hurry this up, I think they're interested."

Boardman looked at him with distaste. "Frank if you bed that overfed hippo I am personally going to shoot you with one of my rifles."

"Aw, fuck it—let's see what you got."

The three men walked out into the parking lot towards the duty van that Boardman drove from the engineering lab. He unlocked the back double doors and pulled out one of the plastic Hardigg cases and placed it gently on the parking lot surface. He flipped open the locks and opened the case. Inside, was a black rifle with a short barrel, surrounded by grey foam padding cut to the exact size and shape. The rifle was surrounded by white canisters of some type, four black clips and a clear plastic case filled with the brass spheres that he saw at the facility.

Frank hissed. "Why did you paint them black—they look better shiny!"

"This is the only one that's blacked out—you never know if he wants to be unnoticed in the dark." Jared waited for some type of acknowledgement from his boss.

"What in hell are you waiting for? Show us how the fucking thing works?"

Boardman removed the rifle from the case and pointed it straight at Frank's belly until Frank's right eyebrow rose changing his face to a *'do you really want me to kick your ass?'* expression. Smirking, Boardman moved it to the side while he slapped in one of the rounded clips at an angle to the right of the sight. He removed one of the canisters from the case and held it up to Jim. "Standard refrigerant— Freon." He screwed the cylinder into the back of the rifle until a slight hissing noise died from the seal. Boardman pointed to a red locking mechanism for emphasis, pushed it inwards and then swiveled the stock in place over the canister. "Couldn't be any easier—each clip holds fifty balls and is gravity fed—important to remember. If the rifle is at a whacky angle the balls can't feed in-- you are only going to fire air."

Boardman turned toward the rear of the parking lot towards a large grove of pine trees. "See these settings near the nozzle of the canister? Green indicates that it will stun a small animal and hurt like hell if it hits you. Yellow means that it will pierce skin and probably stop in muscle. Red? Red will go right through you if up close... with the exception of one of Frank's new girlfriends." He pushed the selector to yellow. "Notice the red dots behind the trigger—one dot means single shot per pull, three dots mean just that-- three. The red circle you see opposite? That's wide open."

Boardman selected the red circle, aimed at a pine tree sixty yards away and pulled the trigger. Jim was surprised by the sound. The tree erupted in white flashes as the outer bark exploded off leaving just the rubbery white under layers and bare wood.

Jim walked over to the tree and ran a hand over the destruction. Rough bark was stripped free with terrific force and two brass balls were still embedded in the pale wood.

Jim walked back thinking about what that gun would do to gypsies—especially in the third setting. "Frank, you gotta see what it did to that tree."

Boardman pushed the safety to 'on' and was handing the weapon to Jim when Frank pushed Boardman back with a thick hand and grabbed the rifle out of his hand. "Daddy's turn. Go play with yourself Boardman." Copying his marine training 17 years ago, Frank snapped the rifle up to his cheek and aimed at the same tree. After a couple of seconds of trigger squeezing, Frank looked down and snapped off the safety. Nothing. He double checked the safety, jiggled the trigger and said, "Good going—this piece of shit is already broken."

Boardman walked up to Frank and slapped the top of his bald pate. "Ooh! Big bad man with the gun is gonna hurt me!" Frank countered by trying to swing the rifle by the nylon strap at Boardman but with his shaky reflexes only earned another slap.

"Cut it out dickhead! Fix the fucking gun so I can blow your head off!"

Boardman carefully took the rifle from Frank, making sure that he wouldn't get caught off balance and took a few safety steps away from him and brought the rifle up to Jim's attention.

"Safety first, I like to say. See how you grip the underside just below the barrel? There are buttons on each side. They must be pushed in at the same time while your other hand is on the grip. If not, the rifle stays locked. This way, if someone takes it away from you, most likely you won't get shot with it." Boardman then tossed it back to Frank who was caught off guard, but managed to catch it after a couple of mad snatches.

Frank looked back at Boardman silently mouthing *Motherfucker* and then glanced down at the weapon while he pushed both buttons.

"Frank, you have to hold the grip while—"

"I know! I know, goddammit!" Frank grabbed the grip with his right, looked down and with care, pushed both buttons. The rifle emitted a satisfying thud as the pressure chamber charged with gas. "Now we're talking!" Frank looked up at the tree and aimed. He pulled the trigger and the same low but audible crack shot out from the end of the rifle. He had missed the tree. He pulled the trigger again and another single shot spat out of the weapon. "Shit—it's set back to single..." He fumbled with the shot selector and moved it to the red circle. Again, he brought the weapon to his cheek and pulled the trigger. It didn't budge.

Boardman sighed. "Frank if you let go of the grip..."

"Goddamn gun! This is bullshit! He lowered the gun, made sure his right hand was choking the grip and then pushed both buttons again. *Chisss.* Again the chamber was prepared for the next volley. Without bothering to aim, he leveled the rifle waist high towards the tree and squeezed. As with Boardman's firing, the noise was loud and satisfying. The tree's bark exploded and tatters of fibers windmilled away from the trunk. The clip ran out and the gun stopped just as abruptly as it started. The end of the barrel grew a faint layer of frost from the propellant, and a thin sliver of fog was dwindling out of the end. "Jim! Let's find this gypsy fuck right now!"

Jim noticed that some people had come out of the club and were gawking at the bald man holding what looked like an assault rifle. "Frank, I think we should call it a night."

Frank's eye caught sight of the spectators and walked briskly back to Boardman handing him the weapon. "Enough fun for tonight— I get one of the shiny ones."

Boardman dropped off Jim in front of his apartment building. "Are you sure you can manage with the case?"

Jim pulled the black case from the back of the van and shut the double doors. "I'll be fine, Jared." Jim put the case down on the sidewalk and walked back over to the driver. "Really Jared, I can't thank you enough for this."

Boardman yawned and looked at the clock on the dashboard. "No problem—just be careful with it—I'd feel really bad if you shot an innocent with this thing. Just do what I do—hold your breath and count to three before you take the shot. There's nothing wrong with holding someone in your crosshairs for three extra seconds."

Boardman feigned a salute with his index finger and pulled the transmission lever into drive. Jim walked back to the sidewalk and watched the van lumber off into the night. Jim looked at his watch and noticed that it was almost four in the morning. People were still heading toward the local discos on an evening of limitless partying. Jim picked up the case and his head swam. *Too much Sangria,* he thought. *Gotta get to bed.*

He fumbled with his keys and while placing them in the lock and noticed a taped note from Manoli on his door.

> *Oye Tonto,*
> *We took Elena to the house*
> *in the campo. Come and stay the*
> *weekend with us there. It's too hot*
> *in Rota. Nino said bring ice from*
> *the base.*
> *Manoli*

Jim pulled the note from the door and lumbered his way inside. He placed the case on the floor near the bed and opened it. *Amazing work- he did this all in just a few hours? I just hope I don't have to use it.*

He laid back on the bed and watched the room dim as his eyelids gave up the fight first. He dreamt of Frank chugging Sangria out of glass pitchers, wearing a stained, white toga. He had bunches of grapes festooned around his head and fat blondes with rolls of fat were giggling and taking turns licking the top of his head.

Chapter Eighteen:
Awakening Filo

Rip stayed up late reviewing the videotapes of the previous night's event. What he found most intriguing was what Seth mentioned about Rothiel's prison—that there was writing inside of the shell. He went frame-by-frame through camera 2's footage as it had the most direct angle of the two halves. *There was something there*, He thought and he played with the controls on the television. *It's in tight rows and it looks like carved origin script. Can't make a damn thing out though.*

He fell asleep in the chair at some point past five in the morning. When the sun peeked out across the horizon, he stirred, mumbled "aw, hell." And walked to bed.

By seven he was wide-awake again. He got up, walked to the chow hall and was greeted by several of the children already cooking and preparing the day's breakfast.

"Eggs Rip?" asked Mikey from behind the counter. Mikey was only 12 years old, but already needed to start shaving as he had what Rip jokingly called a 'Puerto Rican girlie mustache'.

"No thanks kiddo—just going to get some coffee. Is Gideon and Ricardo walking around yet?"

"Yup. Both have already eaten and went down to the medical lab for a few supplies and they're going to meet you in your library."

Rip grabbed a styrofoam cup and flipped open the valve on the large coffee dispenser. "Mikey, when Juani gets in, tell her that we are going to need the arrangements for three to go to Melilla. Big Lee is one of the three, so that means we go by boat. Oh—tell her that she's leaving for Florida to pick up Sharky tomorrow and then on to Virginia to pick up our savant. She'll be traveling with the usual, Gideon and Hank. Remind her that it's not a shopping trip."

Still groggy from lack of sleep, Rip walked down the steps to the third underground level where most of the paper archives and artifacts were stored. Filodraxes spent the last forty years sleeping amongst the writings, maps and knowledge of the past.

Rip walked up to the vault door and noticed that it was open and the security panel was logged 'safe'. Rip stepped in and closed the door behind him. "Boys, make sure this door is *always* closed—we don't want any of the humidity from outside to get in here."

Kayanan and Gellan looked up the moment Rip walked in and nodded. They were both examining the objects that Filthy brought in as well as comparing the notes that were taken at Seth's last reading. Kayanan stood up and put the clipboard down. "Sorry Rip—we just walked in ourselves—we haven't even uncovered Filo yet."

Rip walked over to the wall where a large iron door hung, resembling a large, baker's oven. "When was the last time you boys saw him?" He grabbed the iron handle and pulled. The door swung open, groaning from the hinges until it was wide enough to clear the body. Inside, Filodraxes' corpse was covered in thick blankets and resting inside the bottom half of a gilded wood sarcophagus.

Gellan wheeled the stainless steel gurney over to the wall and placed it just underneath the opening. "Gosh, I don't know, Rip—I'd have to say probably since I was a teenager, at least." Kayanan and Gideon nodded their heads in agreement.

"Just don't forget who this man is. He was our greatest leader and is more important than any one of us—you should have visited more often."

"C'mon Rip," Filthy whined. "He's almost dead anyway, what does it matter?"

Rip glared at Filthy. "He's still alive! I'll tell you something too, Gideon—you better make damn sure that you followed the recipe correctly! If, God willing, we can bring him back, you had better treat him with the utmost respect."

Gellan nodded reluctantly, reached in and carefully pulled the sarcophagus out and slid it on top of the gurney.

Rip pointed towards the lab table, brimming with the ingredients. "Let's get him over near the table."

Rip reached over and pulled out two latex surgical gloves from the dispenser on the wall. The other three followed suit under Rip's glare. Rip closed his eyes for a few moments to clear his head and then removed the blankets from the top of the sarcophagus one at a time and placed them on an adjacent table. The blankets were old and musty. They were probably hundreds if not thousands of years old and the thick threads looked like they were ready to give away at the slightest tug. Rip reached the last layer, which was a sheet of sheer muslin that covered the open top. Underneath, Filodraxes' sharp features were visible.

Rip folded back the muslin and then placed it on the table with the blankets. Surrounding the body were several modern dial gauges measuring humidity and temperature. Rip removed them and scrutinized the readings for a few seconds, then placed them on the table.

Filodraxes was practically a mummy, emaciated to a leathery depleted form. The head was almost hairless, with a wisp of fine hair visible here and there. The nose was withered to a slender point and the jagged mouth was frozen in a silent groan of despair. Rip reached in and carefully opened the front of his embroidered robe, revealing his chest. The skin was the color of dried tobacco leaf and his breastbone and ribs were pronounced under the tight skin.

Rip looked up at the men who were staring at the strange sight. "Notice how he still breathes." The shock in their eyes made Rip smile.

Kayanan approached closer, intrigued by the breathing corpse. "Is his heart beating?"

Rip shrugged. "For the past couple of hundred years, I haven't been able to tell. I think it may still be moving though, however slight."

Kayanan placed a gloved hand gently on top of Filo's breastbone. "His breathing, although slow, is quite regular. Curious."

Rip walked over to the table and looked at the ingredients. "Where are we with this stuff?"

Filthy pulled himself away from Filo's sleeping form and walked over to the table. "Um. Yes, the ingredients are all... here. Uh, coffee's still brewing over there and we should have enough of everything to repeat the experiment if needed."

Gideon fell silent for a moment, but he kept looking back at Filo's body and back at Rip like he wanted to say something else.

"Ricardo? What have you brought for today's science experiment?" Rip said.

Kayanan removed his hand from Filo's chest and walked over to the table. "I have the defib-kit and it's already charged and ready to go. I have intubation kits as well as various injections such as adrenaline and atropine. Um, over here are histamine blockers, antibiotics and various general anesthetics. I have bags of saline, but it doesn't look like I'll find any veins to stick them into. Let's see... oxygen, bags of various blood for transfusion and various antibiotics."

Rip nodded his head. He barely understood half of what Kayanan said, but it sounded like he was confident. "Gellan? What are we missing?"

"Nothing." Gellan was plugging in various monitors into the wall sockets. "EEG's to check for brain activity, heart monitors for obvious reasons, I've brought in a portable X-ray unit and sonogram in case we get some of the organs to function. I figure that between the two, we can find out which organs are or aren't functioning."

Filthy leaned against the table and looked back at Filo's body. "Guys, I've seen a lot in life, but I have never seen something like that... come back. What if he does come back—what if he's like a zombie or nuts?"

Rip thought about what he said for a moment and said, "Either way we have to find out. I don't mind telling you boys, but we're up against something that we may not be able to win. We've fought their like before and most times we came out on top. Now Rothiel is in the mix and I just don't see the odds in our favor." Rip finished the coffee from his cup and tossed it into the trashcan. "Let's get started."

Kayanan picked up the clipboard, double-checked a few items and said, "OK, me and Gideon will begin rubbing down his skin with the mixture of oils while Gellan finishes with the wood dust and coffee. Rip? Are we going to be able to roll Filo onto his sides?"

Rip chewed on his lower lip while thinking for a short moment. "Beats me. I haven't removed him from the sarcophagus for the past 12 years."

Kayanan walked over to the intercom and pushed the grey button on the bottom. "Hank? Please come to Rip's library on level three."

Rip shot a glance at Kayanan. "What do we need him for?"

"Hank can lower his weight—it'll make it much safer to move him around."

"Good thinking—I just want it quiet in here." Rip rubbed his temples while he thought about having Hank mouth off all morning. "One thing—once we get Filo good 'n oiled up, Hank leaves."

Gellan picked up a beaker containing the compound of oils and dipped in a cotton swab. He painted a thin line down the skin on the top of Filo's shriveled right hand. He jumped back so suddenly that he almost dropped the beaker. "Rip! Look at his hand!"

The men crowded over the body and Rip brought his face close. All of the skin was dry and brown with the consistency of a weakened paper sack, with the exception of a thin line of skin that appeared to gently swell away from the surrounding areas. After several seconds, the strip of skin bulged slightly higher and looked considerably healthier than the rest of him.

Rip's eyes narrowed. "All that from one small swipe? Let's rub some on his face."

Gellan reached over to the small table and selected a cotton ball. He dipped it liberally into the oily solution, glanced at Rip and exhaled. He looked at the face of Filo and looked for the best area for a test. He noticed that the ears were flat and desiccated similar to a smoked pig's ear. He gently drew the moist ball over the ear and lobe, letting the oil saturate. The ear was damp, but the reaction wasn't as swift as the area of skin on the hand. Slowly, the ear began to absorb the oil and become pliable. The hardened, almost rawhide-like texture began to yield and soften. Gellan took a gloved finger and touched the lobe. It had filled out and could now be wiggled from his touch freely. "Rip, it feels normal!"

Hank walked through the doorway in gym shorts and a mangy shirt that looked like he had slept in. His long hair was unkempt and wasn't yet tied back in his typical ponytail. He moved some stray hair out of the way while taking intermittent bites out of a pop tart. "You guys wanted me for something? Hey! How's the stiff?"

Rip pulled himself away from the sarcophagus, while giving the three the 'mums the word' look. He walked up to Hank and pointed to Hanks breakfast. "There's no eating in here. Ever."

Hank shrugged and shoved the two tarts completely into his mouth. He balled up the wrapper and tossed it into the trashcan. After mumbling a distorted "No problem!" he began to choke down the food. Rip turned around scowling and headed back to the table as Hank beamed a strawberry stained grin over his shoulder.

"Hank, we need a favor," Rip growled over his shoulder. "Are you paying attention?"

"Lighten up man! I was just looking at Mr. Jerky over there."

Hank walked over to the table and looked down at the body with a smile on his face. Something was clearly very funny to him and Rip wanted to slap it out of him.

"Hank," Rip sighed. "We need to cover Filo with this oil. We'd like you to suck the weight out of him so we can safely move him."

"No problem. Jesus, Rip—he looks even uglier than you."

Rip felt the throb in his right temple spike and thought he felt something inside his head give way. Before he could react to the trite comment, Hank continued with some helpful logic. "I don't know how much he weighs, but I can comfortably hold someone that's around 160-180 pounds for close to an hour."

Kayanan was setting up the cotton balls around the table so that they could all work quickly. "He weighs seventy one pounds. Gellan and I can probably coat him in less than a minute—just tell us when you can't hold on to his weight any longer."

Hank laughed. "Seventy pounds? Hell, I can hold that for the rest of the day! You want me to start now?"

Rip nodded. Gellan, Filthy and Kayanan were looking at him for his signal.

Hank breathed in and stared at the body on the table. His hearing deafened slightly and he could feel the extra weight flow into his body. He nodded and kept his breathing steady.

Kayanan placed his right hand on Filo's shoulder and tried to slide his left under Filo's left buttock. Filo's body lurched up slightly from the sarcophagus and Kayanan gripped the shoulder more firmly to make sure he didn't lose his hold. Filo's body moved easily upwards as if it was a helium balloon that had lost enough of its gas to reach equilibrium. Kayanan rotated the body gently and nodded to Gellan. Gellan gently grasped one of the ankles with his right hand and brought up the balls of cotton saturated with the oils.

They worked swiftly, sliding the liquid up and down the lengths of Filo's legs, around his buttocks and around the back. Hank watched with amazement as the skin returned to its natural state following each stroke of the oil. Rip kept a close eye on Hank to make sure that he didn't lose his concentration. Hank kept his breathing steady and felt just slight pressure. Seventy pounds was nothing for him—he had been able to accommodate close to a ton of weight in a former life when moving groups of men up the face of a cliff in Normandy. *The krauts were pretty damned surprised then* he thought. Lately, he hadn't been able to totally absorb Big Lee's weight though—it was just impossible.

"Should we give him two coats Rip?" asked Kayanan while busily working the oils into the back of Filo's wrinkled neck.

Rip looked at Hank's face for his opinion. Hank nodded back and blew Rip a small kiss. Rip checked the clock on the wall. It had been almost a minute. "Go ahead Ricardo—don't rush anything."

Kayanan went back to the feet and continued up the body and slid the saturated cotton around the skin. "Gellan, I can make out some veins in the ankles. When we get done, I'd like to see if we can get a drip into him." He continued working up the spine and noticed a small abrasion near the shoulder blade that was weeping capillary fluid. "Look's like some of the circulatory is coming back too." He pushed a finger gently into the skin around the shoulder blade and it was getting spongy. "Allright. Let's set him down on the bed and continue with the oils on the front."

They gently guided his body over the bed and lowered it to the mattress. When Kayanan gave the nod, Hank let everything go. It felt like sand running out of his body at the fingertips and feet. The weight returned to Filo's body slowly and his body began to push downwards against the cushion. Gellan and Kayanan continued with the oils along the head, neck and chest. When they had slathered the oil across the chest and ribs and made their way past his navel, Filo's breathing became more pronounced.

Kayanan placed his stethoscope directly over Filo's chest and listened. "I think... yes, it must be. I can hear a slight heartbeat." He placed the earpieces of the stethoscope around his neck and continued swabbing down Filo's body with the oil. They arrived at the tips of his toes and stepped back to admire the work. Filo's body was still a breathing corpse, but the oils had taken off thousands of years. He was looking better by the minute. Kayanan used his thumb to gently test one of Filo's eyelids, but it was still tough and firmly set together. He reworked more oil around the face, paying extra attention to the eyelids, nose and mouth. He rechecked one of the eyelids and it slid gently open. The eye underneath was gray and mottled. No trace of iris or pupil.

Gellan was observing Kayanan's examinations and said, "We need to give it some time, Ricardo. Let's set him up with an IV and I'll get some of the leads attached to his head to try and track any brain activity."

Kayanan dragged over the IV stand and attached a bag. He unraveled the hose and let it dangle over the bed as he selected a needle. He went with one of the smaller varieties, usually used for newborn children's heads, as he wasn't sure what type of vein they would be offered. He double checked one of Filo's hands and found some viable veins beginning to emerge on the top and around the wrist. As he was touching the vein in the top of the hand with his index finger, he noticed that Filo's fingers were now flexible.

"Guys! Take a look!" Gellan was gently rotating Filo's head from side to side. "Looks like he's losing some of his rigidity."

Kayanan removed the plastic cap exposing the needle and with his left hand, swiped clean a small area over the vein. The needle pierced the skin and embedded itself safely into the vein. A small but satisfying shot of blood traveled a short distance up the line. Kayanan taped the line to the top of Filo's hand, then connected the line to the bag of saline solution and started the drip. Slowly, the clear fluid mixed with blood older than five millennia and ran into Filo's veins. "I'd like to obtain a small sample of his blood before we go any further."

Rip thought about any repercussions of taking even the slightest drop of blood from his system before they attempted to revive him.

Kayanan saw the hesitation in Rip's eyes. "I'll only need a small amount. I just want to make sure that there aren't any underlying problems that would prevent us from reviving him. I'd also like to compare his blood with a normal sample."

"Fine. Not too much though… I don't want to deviate from the instructions that Cesar kid gave us." Rip noticed Hank was nosing around over Gellan's shoulder as he was attempting to attach leads to Filo's forehead and temples. "Hank? Thanks for the help. Get out."

Hank looked open mouthed at Rip for a moment, sniggered and sauntered out of the room, slamming the opening bar of the door with heel of his palm.

Rip sat down on one of the aluminum chairs positioned around the room and could feel the pressure slightly decrease. He looked back at Gellan who was flipping switches on some type of monitor — it looked like the EEG. "Seeing anything Gellan?"

Gellan was busily tuning two knobs at the bottom of the display and didn't peel his eyes away for a second. "Yeah. Wow! I'm definitely getting some brain activity, but I can't tell if he's wide-awake or in a coma. The patterns are there but they look really irregular."

Kayanan was drawing blood from the other arm and had just pulled out the syringe and taped a cotton ball over the hole in the crook of Filo's arm. *The blood looked darker than usual, but at least it was liquid*. He removed the needle and placed the vial in a plastic stand on the table. He tore apart a sanitary plastic wrap containing an oxygen mask and connected its line to a portable green oxygen bottle. Near the oxygen, there was a blue bottle with the label '*Sulphur Hexafluoride*. Before putting the mask on Filo's face, he tilted the head slightly back and peered into the mouth with a penlight. The mouth looked moist and the tongue was pliable. *God but his breath smells horrible.* Once he verified that the airway was clear, he placed the mask over Filo's nose and mouth and increased flow until the pressure reading was at the proper setting. Kayanan stopped for a moment to double check his procedures. *Airway's established, his heart is beating and his blood appears to be circulating. I'd better hook up the heart monitor before we continue.*

He pulled the plastic dust cover off of the portable heart monitor and flicked the power switch. A loud, high-pitched beep pealed from the front of the box until he attached the first lead to the side of Filo's rib cage. He attached the second to the top of his chest, just above his left nipple. The heart monitor immediately began to churn out the amplified noises of the heart beating and blood whooshing past fluttering valves. He watched intently at the strip of graph paper slowly ejecting out the front of the machine and marked off a few of the lines of interest as well as annotated the current time. "Ready Rip."

Rip rose uneasily from his chair and massaged the small of his back. *Fucking spook.* "All right boys, you may not be excited about what we're about to do, but whether you realize it or not, this could be our finest moment." He walked towards the table and took a good look at Filo's face. "Amazing. I haven't seen him look like this for so many lifetimes—I barely remember what he looked like before—this really is something. Gentlemen, amongst ourselves, we are formidable in what we know and are able to physically do. Fate has dealt with us in the guise of frail human beings, incapable of remembering that which made us so magnificent. This man you see before you was the most gifted. Unfortunately for him and us, he has been dormant for the majority of our stay here. I only hope that when we revive him..." He noticed a slight uneasy reaction from Filthy. "...*If* we are able to revive him, that he still remembers some of what we have forgotten."

For a moment, Rip was silent. Only the beeping of the monitors and the pulsing, whooshing noises from Filo's augmented heart beats emanated in the room. He looked and saw that Filthy had retrieved the coffee concoction from the percolator and had poured it into a large steel vat. "This kid Cesar... how did he say we were to give him the coffee?"

Filthy picked up his notebook and flipped the pages. "Uh, it says to pour it over his chest and abdomen... and around the neck. That, and make sure that it's just under boiling."

Rip looked around the room and said, "Is everyone ready then?"

Kayanan raised his hand. "I need to fill his lungs with some gas first. Should only take a few seconds."

Rip flipped back a few pages of his notepad and squinted. "Gas? What gas are we talking about?"

"Sulphur Hexafluoride. It's a heavy gas that is only used for industrial purposes. ...Honestly I don't have a clue on how this could possibly help." Kayanan waited for a moment to see if Rip needed more clarification, then turned and disconnected the oxygen lead and connected the blue bottle. He turned the valve and heard the audible hiss of gas leaving the cylinder.

"Ricardo? What does Sulphur..." Rip blinked his eyes at his notes for the name of the chemical but couldn't read his own handwriting. "What kind of affect on the human body does this *goddamn* gas have?"

Kayanan thought about it for a second. "Nothing. It has the reverse effect that Helium does. Instead of making the pitch of your voice high, it makes it very deep. Hank used this quite a bit to make crank calls during college. The only difference, and one you must keep in mind, is how heavy it is compared to atmospheric gasses. After this gas is in your lungs, you must bend over at the waist and exhale it out."

Rip's mind flashed back a dozen years ago when he repeatedly received calls from a 'Milton J. Futtbucker' who woke him at all hours of the night. He had a very deep voice. "Well I'll be a son of a bitch."

Filthy pulled on two thick potholders and carried the vat over to the table. Steam rose in abundance over the surface and fine flecks of wood dust spiraled and swirled in the dark brown fluid. He placed it carefully on the surface of the table nearest Filo's bed and then looked around. "It's going to make one hell of a mess."

Gellan walked around looking at the hospital bed looking for a way of containing the coffee mixture. "What if we heap sheets around him?"

Rip shook his head. "What else we got?"

Kayanan was opening up a medical cabinet and crouching down towards the bottom shelf. "We've got a lot of these." He rose with handfuls of cheesecloth. "We can just place them around his torso and lay bunches of it around his body. It should soak up the coffee and keep him saturated at the same time."

Filthy wagged his finger at the cheesecloth. "No, no no! That's not going to work! It's still going to get all over the bed and on the floor!"

Rip glanced up at the clock. Things have to start moving quickly. "Fuck the floor. Go ahead Ricardo, pack him with the cloth."

"But I'm the one that cleans up on this level!" Yammered Filthy. "Do any of you know how hard it is to get coffee stains up from linoleum?"

Kayanan had already begun to unravel and pack Filo with the cloth. Gellan joined in alongside him. "Don't worry Gideon. If it's such a problem, I'll do it for you!"

The heart monitor skipped a beat and Filo's chest jerked slightly. Rip was alarmed because Kayanan had stopped wrapping and was watching the monitor closely. "Tell me that he's OK? What in hell was that?"

Kayanan spun around, pulled off Filo's mask and returned to packing the cloth, but with more intensity. "Let's move! I was afraid of this—his body is being deprived oxygen because of the gas."

Rip pointed his finger at Filthy. "Begin ladling the coffee on him. Now!"

Filthy picked up the soup ladle and filled it with the coffee. He remembered from Seth's session that it was to be poured all over his chest and neck. He poured the first ladle full on the middle of Filo's abdomen. Nothing happened.

"Keep going! Get that stuff all over him now!" Rip growled.

Filthy began reaching in, and slopping the coffee over the man's body more frantically. Coffee was spattering all over the floor and himself. Steam rose off the saturated cloth and at once the heart machine went dead with a long beep.

"Relax, guys!" Barked out Kayanan. "The coffee just shorted out the leads to the heart machine." He put on his stethoscope and monitored Filo's heart manually. Rip's hands were gripping the sidebars of the bed. With all of his worrying and stress, it was the only way to keep them from shaking. He began whispering an old song in origin that was meant to keep up high spirits before war or during calamity. He silently cursed himself that he couldn't remember all of the words or understand all of their meanings.

Gellan snapped his fingers twice near Kayanan's face and pointed to Filo's face. Gellan's eyes were wide with shock. Kayanan glanced at Filo's face and saw nothing. "What?" Kayanan whispered. A moment later, during one of Filo's slow exhales, he saw it as well. Green smoke softly rose from Filo's mouth and nostrils. It dissolved into the air just a few inches above his face, but the color was unmistakable. When Kayanan looked back down at his stethoscope he noticed the dark shape of the origin number 12 darkening on Filo's chest. Rip saw it too and bent over Filo's body for a closer look.

Gellan kept shooting glances at the EEG and finally clicked on his penlight and pulled back one of Filo's eyelids. It was unmistakable. He now had a perfectly formed iris and pupil, but the whites of his eyes were blood red. Gellan shot a glance at Kayanan who was also riveted at the sight of the eye. Gellan flashed the light into the eye and found no reaction. He opened the other eye and found it in the same condition. He flashed the light over the pupil and for an instant, thought that the pupil contracted. He went back to his right eye and flashed the light. *The pupil contracted!* Just before he could yell out the news, the eye looked sideways and glared directly into Gellan's soul.

"Jesus! Hey! He's looking around!" Rip was practically jumping out of his shoes, but his grip remained locked on the bed, shaking it violently. "Is he awake? Can he hear us?"

Kayanan saw that the mouth trembled slightly and the eyelids fluttered. His gaze remained on Gellan's face and his eyebrows knitted together for a short moment. Kayanan moved his face closer to Filo's and clicked his fingers. "Filo- Filodraxes! Can you hear me?" The red eyes fluttered again, and at one point rotated back in their sockets as if overcome by tiredness. His lids opened and now he was looking straight at Kayanan. He couldn't tell whether Filo was exhibiting a feeling of fright, anger or both.

Rip opened his mouth and began speaking in the language of origin. His voice fluctuated and sounded like two or more voices speaking at the same time, with pops and clicks. "Lord Filodraxes, forgive our intrusion and allow us your council." At once, Filodraxes' face became neutral and his head slowly followed the direction of Rip's gravelly voice. Filo's mouth trembled and his tongue shook briefly, but it was clear that his energy was almost spent. He gurgled a low groan and began a light cough.

"The gas!" Kayanan reconnected the line to the green oxygen bottle. "Rip, we've got to get this gas out of his body and get some oxygen into him fast!" Kayan kicked the foot pedal on the side of the bed and rapidly lowered the head of the bed at an angle. "Keep talking to him!" He gently turned Filo's head to the side and made sure that the angle would keep the gas pouring out of him. The green smoke subsided and Kayanan could tell from his stethoscope that his heart rate was beginning to stabilize.

"Lord Filodraxes, I am your faithful servant, Danhieras. Please lie still as we are trying to cure your condition. With me are your faithful servants, Kainaan Toth, Gaeliin and Gideon."

"What's he saying to him?" Gideon was moving the vat of coffee out of the way and watching Kayanan replace the mask over Filo's face. "I distinctly heard our names and something about him needing a shit."

Gellan looked pained at Filthy. "You had better take the time to learn your language before it is gone forever. Rip is just telling him who we are and that we're trying to help."

Rip had grasped Filo's hand and was softly asking him if he understood what he was saying. The hand minutely grasped his own, but he could feel him fading. "What's going on? Is he falling back into a coma?"

Gellan glanced at the EEG and said, "No. I think that he doesn't have the energy to stay awake, that's all." Kayanan nodded and continued to monitor his heart with the stethoscope.

Filo's eyes began rolling back and his eyelids fluttered. He was out.

Kayanan began stripping off the damp cheesecloth and throwing it into the wastebasket. He was surprised by how much his body recovered when the cloth was removed. Although his skin was still somewhat wrinkled, it changed considerably to a healthy thickness and tone. "How old was he when he passed into a coma?"

Rip thought back to when this all came to a head. "I'm not really sure—I'll need to check the library. I think I was his emissary to Nineveh at the time and he was older than I was—he must have been in his upper forties or early fifties."

"Well, he's looking very good for a former mummy. I think we should keep watch on him in the ICU for the next few days until he stabilizes." Kayanan reconnected the heart monitor and with care, slid a blood pressure cuff up his arm. He checked his pressure and pulse. "The pressure's weak, but then again, he hardly weighs anything. We should keep him on saline with dextrose and see if we can bring him around tomorrow to give him some nourishment. ...His temperature is coming up nicely too."

Rip could feel his knees giving away. A large amount of stress was taken off of his shoulders. "So mote it be. Guys, great work today —I feel it. I honestly think he's back. Gideon? Please go upstairs and tell... is Claire on duty in the infirmary today? Go up and let them know that we're checking in a new patient for ICU and that he requires around the clock care. Scoot."

Filthy nodded, wiped the sweat from his brow and walked out of the room.

Rip smiled down at the sleeping form and then locked eyes on Kayanan and Gellan. "Gentlemen, I'll be traveling to Malaga this afternoon, as we need to enlist the help of Big Lee's son before we lose him again. I want you, Ricardo to come with us. Gellan, I'd like you to remain here and look after Filo."

Gellan nodded while pulling a clean sheet over Filo's sleeping form. "How long do you thing you'll be gone?"

"Hmm. Probably just a couple of days. We'll be taking the truck down there because of Big Lee's heavy ass. Just in case we get lucky and can bring Diano back with us, be on standby to fly a cargo plane there for a pick up." Rip looked up at the clock. It was just after nine in the morning. "Guys? I'm out of it. I'm going upstairs for a fatboy nap. Ricardo? Do me a favor and get the truck ready for the trip and make sure Big Lee's ready. The dog stays here, by the way—no exceptions."

"I'll take care of it. Go get yourself some rest and we'll leave at around two this afternoon." Kayanan was still examining the fingertips of his new patient and putting things away.

Rip walked out of the room and trudged up the stairs.

"What do you mean I'm leaving tomorrow to pick up another brat?" Juani Macías was standing at the top of the steps with her hands on her hips. She was in her mid-thirties and took very good care of herself. If she couldn't be contacted at home, she was usually found at the beach enjoying all of the attention from younger guys.

"Good morning Juani. Nice dress, is that orange?"

Juani's face brightened. "Yes! Isn't it beautiful? Matching shoes and purse as well!"

"I don't know," yawned Rip. "... makes you look like a Butano bottle." Rip was making his way past her to get some much-needed sleep.

"So who is this *niño* we're picking up?" Huffed Juani, clearly upset by Rip's comment. She was cutest when angry, but you had to pay for that luxury.

"It's Sharky." Rip sighed in an apologetic way. "You remember? The old guy that was so good at managing our stores and equipment?"

"Ahhh—*si!* He died a couple of years ago no?"

Rip nodded. "Yes, him. It's been almost two, really. It'll be nice to get him back won't it?"

Juani nodded. "Hank does a shitty job and he always loses receipts."

Rip gave an exhausted sigh. "Yes, a *very* shitty job. Anyways, You, Gideon and Hank need to fly to Florida to pick him up, so get Tyler to make the necessary documents. You'll need an identikit to make Sharky's passport when you get there. On the way back, fly into Dulles and pick up our new sav—um, a guy named Louis Plak. Gideon will handle the discussions, as always, you'll be acting as Sharky's mother."

Juani drummed her manicured nails on her hips as she thought. "How many days will this trip be?"

"Juani, I don't want any more shopping sprees on these trips. When you went to pick up Claire, you spent four days shopping!"

Juani launched briefly into some typical Spanish swearwords before reverting back into English. "Her good-for-nothing parents did not have decent clothes for her to wear! And then, in case you can't remember well, my bags were stolen! What do you expect me to wear, flour sacks?"

"You picked up Claire in Las Vegas! I find it funny that you need two extra days just to buy her clothes. --Her shoes alone cost over four hundred dollars! And why did she need two bathing suits for Christ's sake? Calm down! Let me finish! It just seems odd to me that when we send you to pick up a child in the steppes of Russia, you are back as quick as greased lightning, but when you hit a touristy spot we need all of Hank's strength to drag you out of there!"

Juani jabbed her index finger repeatedly into Rip's belly. "I have worked for this *organizacíon de locos* for over ten years! Your men repeatedly come onto me like I'm the only woman they've ever seen and I'm expected to keep my mouth shut about who you all are! When was the last time I had a real vacation? Huh? If you don't like how I work, you can just find someone else!"

Rip felt bad about bringing up the spending and now just wanted her to calm down. Their organization would be nothing without her managerial skills. "I'm sorry Juani—really. I've been under a lot of stress these days. Tell you what, when you come back from this trip, we'll book you a cruise or something. Ok? I'll tell Gideon to back off as well. I always make it clear that there is to be no fraternization with staff—honest!"

Juani calmed down, but her face was set like stone. She stood back with her arms crossed giving Rip a stern look. "*Vale*. We'll talk about a suitable vacation for me when I get back. I want an extra day in Washington though."

Rip squeezed the bridge of his nose while he tried to keep from blowing his stack. Per diem rates in Washington were among the highest in the US. "All right. Just stay out of expensive hotels and keep an eye on Sharky. I don't know much about this new guy Louis, but I'll make sure Gideon and Hank take care of him." He looked into her dark eyes for a few seconds. He normally avoided direct eye contact with her or other women that he found attractive so that emotion would never betray his position. "Thank you my dear." He gave a short bow and sighed, "Now if you'll excuse me, my pillow is calling me."

Juani leaned over and kissed his cheek. "*Sueños dulces, Reep.*" She turned and walked towards her office with an elegant, but purposeful stride. Rip found himself staring at her long, tanned legs. *Oh to be twenty years younger. I'd take her shopping any day.* He walked into his room and collapsed on his unmade bed. He thought about Filodraxes and hoped he did the right thing.

Rip rolled softly to sleep and dreamed restlessly. His dreams were dark and uncertain, clouded by doubt and wrapped tight in a covering of cold, unforgiving fear. At the worst point, he found himself chained to a dungeon wall and was unable to bring on his flame. Try as he might, he couldn't explode the wall or melt the iron on his manacles. He begged the flame to come forth but not one sputter, not one spark would accommodate him. Rothiel entered the room, young and confident as ever. Behind him was Ricardo, blindfolded, bound and gagged. He was tethered around his neck by a rough rope and he was dragged across the floor by Valgiernas. Rothiel watched Rip's face with rising mirth while Valgiernas, slowly sawed through Ricardo's throat with a long knife. More struggling, and all in vain. Next was Hank, then Gellan. All were trussed the same and all appeared to be powerless.

Rip awoke to rough shaking. Kayanan was holding his shoulders with his nose bunched up. "Rip! Wake up! You're going to ignite! Rip sat up in bed, completely soaked. His skin had excreted the volatile liquids that burn with unnatural intensity. It hadn't gone off, but it could have at any moment. Kayanan buried his nose into his sleeve as his nose and lungs couldn't stand the strong vapors. "Hurry! Get up and let us get these sheets out of here."

Rip stood up with a groggy lurch and noticed that the sun had already past noon and was traveling to the west on its way towards night. "Sorry boys, I... had a bad dream. Alarms go off?"

Big Lee was grabbing the sheets and wrinkling his nose. "Hoo! What do you think? Damn thing went squawking like crazy and when we run in, you're shaking your ass off in bed! Scared the living hell out of us."

Kayanan was opening up the windows and fanning the air. "Honestly—we thought you were going to blow. Are you OK?"

Rip shuffled around the room and slowly rotated his head to wake up. "Yes, I'm fine. I'd better step outside and burn off some of this stuff before I jump in the shower—damned stuff doesn't react well to soap and water."

"Just make sure you go downwind—it's so damned hot, I don't want you setting the house on fire." Big Lee took the sheets and shoved them into a rolling hamper.

Rip walked out of the room and shielded his eyes with his hands. He took with him a pair of clean shorts and a T-shirt. He walked outside and looked around for a reasonable spot. *Over near the games field—no trees. As likely a spot as ever.* He went over to the sand pit that held the horseshoe trap and stood in the sand. No one was watching, so he hung the clean clothes on top of one of the pegs, kicked off his sandals and took several paces away from them. He reflected on his nightmare where he couldn't get any of his fuel working. *Damn near blew up the fortress. Good thing Gellan insisted that those sniffer alarms get installed.* He shivered, opened his arms wide and immediately erupted into flame. He was surprised at the intensity—he must have sweated out quite a large amount. The fire seemed to surge and surge ever greater. He couldn't feel anything, not even the heat from the inferno that engulfed his body, but he was worried about accidentally burning the clean clothes that he had brought with him. His older clothes were now just a memory. His right foot touched against something in the sand. A horseshoe. Curiosity got the best of him and he bent down and picked it up. After two short seconds it began to glow cherry red in his hands. He thought back in the dream. *Couldn't shake the manacles.* He kicked up the fire on his body and in an instant, the horseshoe flashed white-hot and began to melt. It's bright orange liquid fell between his outstretched fingers and rained down on the sand. He shook any residual melted iron from his palms and relaxed. The flames began dying down and began turning a soft hue of blue that began to die off around his body. A few seconds later, the fire had gone out. He stepped out of the sand pit and saw what was left of the smoldering sand, which had fused into a hot, reddish gel. Areas that had already cooled off were now forming a glossy green glass where he had been standing. Since he was naked, he quickly dressed himself and put his sandals back on. Something about burning off excess fuel always made him feel fresh, anew. He walked back to the house and Kayanan and Big Lee was waiting for him.

"Sorry boys. I hadn't gotten much sleep in the past few days."

"I don't think many of us have either." Big Lee was carrying out some large, locked boxes out to the truck. "It would be a shame to lose all of this preparation from a single bad dream." Big Lee stopped and looked Rip directly in the eye. "Seriously man, if you think that you may go nuke on us, you may want to think about sleeping outside."

Rip laughed. "No, it wasn't that bad. It was just fuel leaking out of my pores—self-destructing is much different. The fire burns from the inside out, and that is easily controllable." He turned to Kayanan. "How's our newest patient?

He's asleep. He looks a lot better now than he did when you last saw him. He woke up for a few minutes too."

"Did he say anything?"

Kayanan shook his head. "A good percentage of his tissues are restored—his nerves haven't completely recovered yet. I don't think he'll be able to talk for at least a couple more days."

"What about the sack of shit we picked up on the highway?"

"Just checked up on him before the alarms went off. His name is Manolo and he's from Rota. He said that he needs his medicine, something called '*Cambio*'."

"Change? What is it, a drug or something?"

"Not sure. Either way it's causing a physical change to his body. He's losing his cool over this stuff and switches from begging to threatening us if he doesn't get his fix."

"Sounds like Protraxsis's work. Tell Gellan to keep him on non-reactive food and water until we get back." Rip walked into the Villa and took off his sandals. Gimme a minute to take a shower and then we'll hit the road."

Chapter Nineteen:
Go ask Dad

Bob White paced outside the front doors of the temple, nervously snapping his fingers, mumbling and in general, trying to figure out how to phrase the right question. He would be asked what he observed at Rothiels release on Earth. Bob knew full well that God was entirely aware of the events the previous evening and this was just an exercise or test that he must endure. He knew what he wanted to ask: 'Lord? May I have your permission to advise some of the exiles that Rothiel's followers are close to finding their ranch?' *Hmpf. Sure. He'll definitely be responsive on that one! Hell, he may just exile me along with them for asking a question that ridiculous.* He paced, and then paced some more, walking in lazy circles along the polished marble. He wasn't aware of the natural beauty around him or the folks passing by calling out "Hi Bob!" He was still buried inside his mind, trying his best to find a way of asking the Big Boss to cut him some slack and let him contact Rip's team.

A delicate chime emanated from Bob's patch and he pulled it out of his vest pocket and flipped open the top. He scrutinized the hands of the clock with a frown, snapped it shut and turned towards the building for the meeting. *Time's up. Looks like I have to wing it.*

An old man opened the door for him in an immaculate black suit. "Good morning Bob, it's good to see you again."

"Hello Phillip, same here. How've you been?"

Phillip stopped for a moment and looked at Bob with concern. "Do you mean from just two days ago, when you were last here?"

Bob looked embarrassed. "Sorry. I've... I have a lot on my mind and now with this meeting, I honestly don't... I don't know how to begin."

Phillip turned directly toward Bob, while he scrutinized Bob's face. "Why don't you tell me what your problem is? Perhaps I can give some small advice?"

Bob looked over Phillip's shoulder to see if God was on his way.

"Oh, don't worry. There's plenty of time—he'll be another few minutes." He pointed to the meeting chairs in the center of the room. "Here. Why don't we sit down and have a quick chat?"

Bob sat down and tried to collect his thoughts. He opened his mouth to speak, then stopped, closed it and went back to thinking, while shaking his head. Finally, he asked, "How did you ever do it? When you wanted something and you *knew* to your very core that it went against your boss's rules or principles—how did you find the guts to ask him?"

Phillip laughed robustly. "Bob! Don't you remember all of the times that you came into my office with exactly those requests? I remember several times after you left my office thinking, *why on Earth did I say yes to that?*"

"Well sir, that's my problem. I have something that I feel deep in my bones that is right, but it goes against all of his instructions—he's made them quite clear."

"Let me ask you then Bob, how did you ever get the courage to come and ask me some of those ridiculous things from the past? I know *I* wasn't the easiest man to deal with in the old days." Phillip laughed again, remembering Bob's persistence.

"Well, please don't take this the wrong way, but you've always looked very similar to my Father. I've had many bosses in the past that I've had problems with, but because of your... appearance and mannerisms, I've always felt that... I could just go and *see Dad.*"

"Huh!" Chortled Phillip. He sat forward in his chair and smiled. "Well Bob, I must say that I feel honored by that sentiment. You are in your particular position because God knows your abilities better than anyone in the two worlds. Now listen to me: You go and approach The Creator with your request and be honest and forthright. This is what your father would want his son to do."

Bob nodded and an appreciative smile grew across his face. "Thanks Phillip. ...I feel better about it, knowing your opinion—seriously, I think—*I know* I can do this."

Phillip reached over and grasped Bob's hand in a firm handshake. "Good man!" He looked over at the wall clock and noted the time. "Ahh. I'll just go and announce you, master White!" He stood, patted Bob on the shoulder and crossed the foyer towards the main entry. When he walked through the main archway and stopped at the large office door. He knocked twice on the door, opened it and stepped through. When he walked through the doorway and closed the door behind him, he no longer looked like Phillip. He was the creator again. He turned to the older gentleman sitting on the couch who watched him enter through the door. "Thank you Phillip, we had a good chat." He pointed to the wall display. "—Were you observing?"

Rising from the couch, Phillip Walker, retired Navy Vice Admiral, nodded. "Yes my Lord, thank you. I have always suspected Bob seeing me as a father figure. He's a good man, that Bob White."

"Undoubtedly. Some people display their stress openly, but with Bob it's sometimes tricky to tell. Today was different—I could hear his hands wringing ever since he returned from the grove!" The creator glanced up at the clock. "Well, I'm going to head back to him—I gather he has a difficult thing to ask me today."

"Shall I bring you two anything?" said Phillip rising from the couch.

"No. I don't think that it will be necessary. Mr. White will be finished in just a minute." God turned and walked back towards the foyer and Bob White rose to meet him.

Bob gave a short bow. "Good afternoon Lord. I am here to give you my report on last night's events."

"Have a seat Bob." God took the seat across from him and appraised Bob's face. He was just sitting across from him only a minute ago, but now his face was clouded in worry. Folding his hands in front of him, God began. "I gather you have something that you want to ask me?"

Bob thought back to what Phillip said. He cleared his throat and shifted in his seat. "Um. Yes. Lord, I would appreciate your permission to make a small—I mean we need to make a temporary contact with the exiles—to Danhieras' group I mean. You see—they are probably unaware that... they may be in danger. I thought it best to slip them a note or something..."

God sat forward in his chair with a stern look on his face. "Robert? You are asking for permission to *contact* the exiles? Is that what you are trying to say?"

Bob felt as if his ship was sinking. "Lord, I'm not asking for long-lasting communication, just a moment where I can pass on a short message. Nothing more—I feel that this is very necessary."

"You feel that this is necessary."

Bob felt that he needed to accentuate how important this approval was to him. He centered his gaze on the creators face, and with a steady and even tone said, "My Lord, I feel that it is crucial."

God sat back in his chair and thought about the back office where Phillip was sitting. In the back of his head, he could see Phillip sitting forward looking at the wall picture, almost on the edge of the couch. He was gently nodding his head in anticipation.

"Sure. Why not?"

Bob sat as straight as a rail in his chair, speechless.

God stood up, adjusted his suit cuffs and was beginning to walk back to the office when he turned slightly. "Was there anything else, Bob?"

"Uh. N... No sir. No sir! Thank you!"

God faced Bob and nodded. "Well then, be on your way and keep up the good work. One word though—*discretion*. There is to be no *frequent* contact. I'm only allowing this level of interface because of a new development. One of Rothiel's followers has been gaining access to this world through the willow tree. You should pass on to your exiles what Rothiel's followers are doing and that it's in everyone's interest to put a stop to it."

Bob's head was swimming. *He said yes!* "Certainly! ...Lord? Just how are they gaining access to the willow tree?"

God smiled. "I'm sure that once you put your heads together, you'll be able to figure it out."

Bob bowed and when he looked back up, he was alone in the foyer.

He turned 90 degrees and with his eyes wide, bolted out the door towards the park where Theo, Tieran and Cesar were waiting to hear what they thought would be bad news. *They're just not going to believe this.* Thought Bob, sporting a huge grin on his face.

"You're either joking or out of your mind, Bob!" laughed Theo as she stood by the park playground waiting for Cesar to arrive. "He's told us since he formed our team that contact with the exiles was a rule never to be broken."

Bob felt liberated, unfettered and charged full of energy like never before. "I still can't believe it, Theo—he looked right at me and gave the OK. I swear, for a short moment that there wasn't a chance in seven levels of Chinese Hell that he would approve."

"This is fantastic," beamed Theo. "We have to tell Tieran right away." She looked towards the pier and saw Cesar with his new friend. "Bob, you may want to wait a bit though."

Bob had his patch out and had already said, "Tieran. Contact".

The image of Tieran filled the view. "Bob! I see you're still with us!"

Bob saw Cesar walking towards him waving and the child Aaron was walking beside him. Bob snapped the patch shut and stuffed it into his vest pocket without saying another word. He waved back and mumbled out the side of his mouth, "Why didn't you say something?"

Theo hissed under her breath while smiling, "I just saw them myself—act natural."

Both were eating ice cream and giggling about something funny that happened on the water. Cesar remembered that Bob had a meeting with the creator. "How did your briefing go?"

"Just fine, Cesar. Just fine. Aaron, good to see you. How was your boat ride?"

"Fine."

The boy just kept watching Bob's face with his pale blue eyes— they seemed to burn straight through Bob's soul. *Is he doing this to me on purpose?*

Aaron turned to Cesar. "I'd better get going. Are you going back to the park tomorrow Cesar?"

Cesar was getting his face wiped clean by Theo but still managed an answer. "Sure! Same time OK?"

Aaron snickered at Cesar's predicament. "Okay! Tomorrow then. Bye!" Aaron turned and ran off towards the bridge leading out of the park and into the city.

Theo finished wiping up Cesar's face. "Where does your friend live?"

Cesar threw the remainder of his ice cream and Theo's napkin into a nearby trashcan. He did a double take when he realized that as soon as his trash entered the can it disappeared. "Huh? Oh yeah, he lives with his grandmother not too far from here. What happens to the trash?"

Bob fished out his patch and called up Tieran's face again. "It all gets sent to the French!"

"Don't listen to him!" admonished Theo. "You know how everything is made up of molecules, and even smaller than them are atoms? Well, on Earth, when an animal or garbage decays, the molecules degrade into other chemicals and compounds. The atoms themselves simply turn into other things. In our world it's the same except the transition is immediate. It either gets turned into other items or converted directly into energy—depending on the balance of the world."

"—I am not shitting you! He recognized my leadership and approved it!" said Bob towards Tieran's image. "I should have asked him for your job while I was at it—I'm sure he would have preferred someone superior like myself in charge of the Armory!"

"Keep dreaming Bob. He probably helped you because he felt bad that you were doing a lousy job!"

"Gotta go, Tieran. I'm an important man now, and have things to do. Dinner tonight at the pergola?"

"Sure, but without coffee. Why don't you stick with water?"

"*Mister* White signing off. See you at eight." With that, Bob closed his patch and stuck it back in his vest and patted it twice in his pocket.

"Look at him", said Theo. "It looks like all of his buttons are going to pop right off his chest."

"What's going on?" asked Cesar with a wry grin on his face."

"Bob went to see the Creator this morning and asked him if he could communicate with the exiles. He gave him permission to do so."

Cesar jumped with excitement. "With who? When?"

Bob put a finger up to his lips to calm him down. "I don't want anyone other than us three—and Tieran to know about this. We'll brainstorm later on the specifics, but I'd like to get Tieran's input on this area as well. There are a couple of things going on that we are to figure out—most importantly is how Rothiel's followers gain access to the willow tree."

Theo looked over at the tree with her brows knitted. "What? How are they gaining access to the tree?" She grasped her pendant and twisted it apart until it unfolded to resemble her spectacles. She placed them on the bridge of her nose and asked "Exiles accessing the willow tree—report." She looked at something that she couldn't comprehend. "It says that none of the exiles have arrived in the tree. I don't get it."

Bob nodded, twiddling with the chain on his patch. "I have already done a few searches and everything came back negative. I think what we need to do is backtrack and find out the disposition of all of the exiles—where they are and what they are doing. I've already divided the list of names amongst our patches. You'll find them under your *Bob* folder. I say we take a few hours of looking at each of them and try to determine which ones are capable of accessing it."

Theo nodded and went to work, muttering to her patch and reading off the names.

Cesar had retrieved his patch and retrieved the list. *Wow, there were so many of them.*

Chapter Twenty:
Sharky and the Savant

The rental car pulled up outside Winged Foot Drive in Fort Myers, Florida. It was sunny but not as hot as it had been in Spain. Juani was busy applying lipstick in the rearview mirror while Hank and Gideon discussed their plan to snatch Sharky.

Hank got out of the car and pulled the child seat out of the trunk and began fastening it in the back seat. "I'm just saying that I think it's better when you use the angle that the kid is the next Dalai Lama—or some similar shit, and that we're taking him to Tibet to sit on a throne."

Gideon got out and ran a hand across his greased, thinning hair. As usual, he wore his trademark brown suit that made him look like a smarmy lawyer. "Naw. I'm going with the 'Thanks for watching junior —my wife missed him very much and now we're here to collect.' Besides, once they believe that Sharky was never their kid, they'll adjust better."

Juani got out of the car and pulled her skirt lower and brushed the wrinkles away from her immaculate jacket. "Le's go. We have to go to the airport before three to catch our *avión* to Washington."

Hank slammed the door. "I *know* why you are in such a rush— the summer sales are on and you want to go to Georgetown for shopping."

Juani winked, patted her purse and walked up the sidewalk with Gideon.

Mrs. Van Allen heard her doorbell ring and peeped through her screen door. Gideon's smiling face drew near. He glanced down at his notepad. "Vivian! Good to see you again! We're just here to pick up...Jeremy—that's it! We're here to bring the little guy home."

Vivian had the impression that she knew the man in the brown suit and felt strangely comfortable with him. She opened the door. "I'm sorry, your name is?"

Gideon walked into her house and said his name, but she had already forgotten. "So where is the little tyke?"

Juani walked in and saw the boy sitting in his highchair excitedly trying to get out of it. She picked up a paper towel and wiped the creamed banana from his lips and lifted him out. She gave him a hug and kissed his cheek. He helped himself to twin handfuls of her breasts.

Vivian became confused. "Who is this woman... what did you say your name was..."

Gideon laughed and walked over to Juani. "Why this is my lovely wife... uh, *Mary*." He tried to put his arm around her waist and Juani stepped away. She was busy placing Sharky in a more innocent position where he couldn't cop another feel.

Vivian felt confused. "But... I'm his... mother? Aren't I?"

Ted Van Allen, half dressed in his State Trooper uniform came out of the bedroom with a sour look on his face. "What in hell are you doing with my son?"

Gideon smiled and looked directly into his eyes. The anger died off and he became as pliable as his wife. "That's *my* son, officer. Thanks for taking care of him for us, but he's coming home with mom 'n pop."

Ted stood there for a moment, blinked and said, "Sure. Anytime."

Gideon went around and picked up the baby pictures held in small frames around the room. "Do you have any of his albums?"

Vivian went to the bedroom and came out with two. "Here you are. You have a very beautiful son."

Juani turned on her heels and walked outside with Sharky. Gideon carried the pictures outside and threw them in the trunk. They would stop by a dumpster on the way to the airport and get rid of them. The childless Van Allen's stood on the doorstep, waving goodbye as Juani placed the boy in the car seat and then sat down next to him.

After the car drove away, the Van Allen's sat down to the breakfast table and engaged in idle chat as they ate. "Their son was very cute," said Vivian.

Ted pulled the sports section from the paper and grunted. "Didn't look anything like the father though."

"Well, it sure took you assholes long enough to come get me," said Sharky with a toothless lisp as the car sped out of San Carlos Park. "How's everyone doing?"

"We're fine," added Juani with attitude. "*Si tocas* my tits again, you are going to get slapped."

Hank turned onto I-75 and continued to the airport. "We were tied up. Rip thinks he found Diano and is on his way to go get him. Do you need a change? We got diapers in the trunk."

Sharky shook his head, but couldn't get the grin off his face. "I could use some milk, but I'm guessing Juani may not be in the mood."

Juani just clucked her tongue and gave Sharky a stern look.

"Are we headed to Spain?" asked Sharky.

Gideon shook his head and pulled out his instant camera. He had to get Sharky's passport ready. "First we have to pick up a Savant in Maryland."

"Interesting," said Sharky, kicking his small legs in the child seat. "We haven't had one of those in centuries. Should make things a lot easier."

Silver Spring, Maryland

Hank pulled off the beltway at the Silver Spring exit, following the road towards the Walter Reed Army Medical Center. He took his eyes off the road in small glances as he tried to make sense of the map. "Shit. This is it—I thought I passed it. Are you ready?"

"Yeah," said Filthy, scrutinizing the notes that Rip and Gellan prepared before their journey. "It looks like we can spend up to 50k per year for this guy. Rip's feeling a bit generous don't you think?"

"All we gotta do is pick this guy up, drag Juani out of the Tyson's Corner Mall and we're home free." Hank pulled into the short driveway, in front of a modest, white two-story home.

Both men got out and walked up to the porch. Filthy was holding his briefcase and he pushed the doorbell.

Laurie Plak opened the door with fat forearms. She glared at both men. "We ain't buyin."

"Actually, Mrs. Plak, we're the ones that are buying," said Filthy with his friendliest smile. "Is Mr. Plak in?"

"Where else would he be?" She yelled towards the inside of the house. "He was laid off yesterday—the second time in six months. If my no-good husband had a brain, he could at least hold a job!"

"Goodness!" Said Filthy. Then it's fortunate for you that we've come. You see, we're here to offer your husband a job!"

Laurie wiped her hands with her dishrag and looked sideways at Filthy. "How much does it pay?"

"Well, ma'am, how much did he make with GTB?"

"Huh!" laughed Laurie. "That's none of your business—what is he worth to you?"

Filthy opened his briefcase and pulled out the typed paper. "We are willing to pay fifty thousand for the first year with at least a six percent raise for each year afterwards." He handed her two checks. "These are for his first two pay periods. He has to work on an oil derrick in the Atlantic, so we'll send the other checks directly to you..."

"Louis honey, come down and meet these nice gentlemen!" She turned to them. "Would you like to come inside—something to drink perhaps?

Hank looked back towards the car. "Uh. Actually, we gotta hang out near the car. We have a baby asleep in the backseat."

Laurie looked at both men with hooded eyes. *Fags or something. Either way*, she thought, *at least her husband would be out of the picture. Her boyfriend could move in too.*

A short man in his 40's with thinning hair, thick glasses and buckteeth came downstairs holding a phone book. He was slightly pudgy with thin arms. He dutifully walked to the door and said in a friendly tone, "I'm Louis Plak. I write Fortran."

"Jesus Lou!" Said Laurie, snatching away the phone book. "These men are here to hire you, not listen to your stupid hobbies." She tossed the book onto an unkempt couch and looked at them apologetically. "Sorry—he likes to read... the phone book."

Filthy pulled out the fake contract and handed it to Louis. "Mr. Plak, if you'll just sign and date here, we can hire you today. We have a flight leaving in four hours. We'll be paying you double what you made with GTB, Inc. and it will be tax-free since you will be working outside the United States. Is this acceptable to you?"

Laurie was already pushing Louis over to the coffee table and placing a pen in his hand. "It will only take me a moment to pack his bag—here—sign the damn paper."

Filthy smiled and shook his head. "Not to worry madam. All clothing will be provided at the facility. He can just put on a clean shirt and we'll be on our way."

Hank drove the car onto I-495 with Louis Plak sitting next to Sharky. Sharky snored softly in his child seat and drooled onto his yellow bib. Hank kept glancing into his rearview mirror at Louis. Mr.

Plak just watched the license plates on other cars driving down the highway. At some points he would look surprised at some of the numbers, shake his head and mutter to himself.

"Looking forward to working on an oil rig Mr. Plak?"

Louis looked confused. "I thought we were going to Spain?"

Diana's cave, Mount Gurugu,
Morocco, 1986

Chapter Twenty One:
Melilla

The large truck pulled into the parking lot of the Hotel
Bajondillo, in Torremolinos. Torremolinos was known as 'T-town' and
was one of the better vacation spots for singles looking for Europe's
Adult Disneyland genre. The hotel sat at the bottom of a cliff, with a
huge, winding staircase that led scrambling up the Cliffside to the main
town. The staircase was packed with bars and restaurants, all clinging
to the cliffs and giving the patrons immaculate views of the
Mediterranean.

Rip got out of the passenger side, did a quick check for
unwanted observers and when satisfied that there were none, struck up
his cigar. "Gads what a long trip!" He stretched his back and rotated
his left arm. "Still hurts a bit Ricardo. When is this damn pain going to
subside?"

Ricardo was locking the cab of the truck and began grabbing
luggage that Big Lee was passing down to him. "Well, you wouldn't let
me do a bone density scan back at the fortress, so I really don't know.
It should feel better than back at the grove, doesn't it?"

Rip thought back at the agony he felt when Seth's spook jabbed
him. "*Jesus yes*! It's only a twinge, but it still aches every time I
breathe in."

Are you going to stop flapping your jowls and help unload?"
Big Lee was holding out a big Samsonite case towards Rip.

"Um-- Hey Ricardo? Help this big sissy with the bags—I'll
head to the front desk and make sure that Tyler didn't screw up our
reservations."

When the last bag was down, Big Lee stepped down off the
back of the truck. The night air was warm, but there was a steady
stream of tourists heading up the cliff to begin a night's drinking and
dancing. Ricardo placed a hand on Big Lee's shoulder. "I'd forget
about those stairs if I were you."

"Fuck it. ...Too tired."

The men walked to the main entry of the hotel and Rip had
already retrieved the keys. They rented a small apartment on the
ground floor and found their room decorated in the typical 1960's

fashion. The furniture was dark oak, surrounded by cheesy paintings on the walls and the cheapest bedspreads bought from the weekly gypsy market. When they got inside, Rip walked over and closed the drapes on the windows of the living room, while Ricardo and Big Lee moved the furniture out of the way. When a good amount of the floor was clear, Big Lee opened a large, boxy aluminum case containing a thin mattress and dozens of thick, black rubber blocks that interlocked like puzzle pieces. He went to work assembling them as a base for the floor and then laid the mattress on top. The pillow was a small beanbag chair covered in cotton cloth. Ricardo and Rip said 'good night' to each other and headed off to separate bedrooms. Ricardo reminded Rip as an afterthought, "Remember to turn on your portable nitrogen detector before you *think* about sleeping." Big Lee laid down on his temporary bed, pulled a thin sheet over himself and began snoring loudly.

The three were up by five-thirty and had the truck loaded by six. Kayanan drove the 16 miles to Malaga's main port where the large white and blue ferry, *Reina de Scirocco* awaited them. Kayanan presented their tickets and passports, followed by a brief inspection of the truck. "*Que llevas?*" asked the guardia civil officer pointing to the truck with his bottom lip.

"Nada. We might buy an airplane engine from the Moroccans when we get there."

The guardia handed back their passports, waved them through and said, "*Vale, adelante.*" Kayanan fired up the truck and maneuvered slowly up the ramp that led into the side of the ship. When inside, he followed the painted yellow line on the deck identifying the separate lanes. A man controlling the flow of traffic waved them to an open space, just behind a larger truck until they were just inches apart. "*Yasta! Ponte freno!*"

The two men exited the cab and signaled Big Lee to come down from the back. The three of them walked towards the main plaza of the ship where children were busily chasing each other and adults smoked and chattered on in Spanish. "Man, how long is this trip?" asked Big Lee while looking out across the Mediterranean.

Kayanan looked at his paper schedule and squinted. "Eight hours. The boat should pull away in about an hour."

"I hope to hell that there's some damn food on this thing!"

Rip already had his morning cigar lit and glanced up the metal stairs to the boat's restaurant. "Hmph. There's food, but from the looks of those stairs, you'll be staying down here. Don't bitch, Corey — Ricardo and I will bring food and drink for you."

"Gonna be a looong trip, tha's all." The big man was something of a celebrity on the ship as he was easily two heads taller than anyone on board. He looked at the bench seats inboard and noticed that the frames were steel, but with wooden planks running across. "Shit, I can't even sit on a chair in this damned boat. Guys? If you want me, I'll be laying down napping in the back of the truck." Rip gave a slight wave and the big man shuffled off towards the garage.

Rip flicked the stub of his cigar into the rippling sea. "Ricardo — why don't we score some breakfast for ourselves and we'll get a little something for *fat boy* while we're at it?"

An hour later, the ship pulled away with some fanfare, mostly the children erupted into a festive mood as the ship began cutting its way through the Alboran sea. The cool breeze poured across the deck providing much-needed relief from the hot summer sun. Rip looked back and admired the granite hills plunging down towards cascading white villas halfway down, then to the beach, which was packed with tall apartment buildings.

"Hm. Always a classed society for you people."

Ricardo turned to see what Rip was talking about.

Rip pointed to the hills. "The wealthy live in those big white villas on the sides of the hill with uninterrupted views of the sea, the middle class live on the outskirts of the city in dumpy villas with only views of their neighbors and the poor live in a concrete jungle at the bottom, packed in like sardines."

After taking a sip from his tea, Kayanan nodded. "Hasn't it always been the same?"

"Yup. Wealth starts from the top down and crime and misery from the bottom up, in a never-ending tug of war. The human race is fascinating in that they shall always repeat themselves in how they build societies."

Rip looked towards the bow and stared at the horizon. "Tomorrow we will probably be face-to-face with Diano. Are you ready for him?"

Kayanan was quiet for a few seconds. "I think so. I have to be honest, I'm not looking forward to this."

"You two were great friends—you helped raise him, didn't you?"

Kayanan nodded.

"Well, what's the problem?"

"Don't get me wrong Rip, I am excited to see him again, but there is a good chance that he won't see things our way-- and it will end in shedding his blood."

Rip understood what he was feeling. He felt like one of Diano's uncles himself. "If the time comes, you can take him can't you?"

"Sure. I'm in the best condition that I've ever been in. But this time we have a singular problem—his father is with us. What happens if Corey decides he can't let his son die?"

Rip's eyebrows furrowed. "We've discussed this—I'd handle Corey if things got rough. If things get pear-shaped, keep clear from Corey and I'll make sure that he lays down for awhile."

Kayanan pushed away his cup and sat in deep thought for over ten minutes. "You will do everything you can to convince Diano to join us?"

"Of course! That boy is almost as powerful as Corey is. Can you imagine the two of them fighting against anything that Rothiel's got? He doesn't stand a chance!"

The two men brought down a half-dozen hamburgers and a foil wrapped container filled with greasy french-fries to the garage. Big Lee was snoring in the back and small children were standing up on the bumper to get a look at the sleeping giant and snickering. "*Fuera!*" yelled Rip, and the children scampered back to the main deck. Big Lee stirred and sat up. "Food! Doesn't smell too good, but hand it over!" He chewed his way through two of the burgers and half of the french-fries before he asked, "How much further?"

Kayanan looked at his watch and then looked outside. "Sun's going down, so we have about two more hours. We should be able to see the northern coast of Morocco by now. Want to come and see?"

"Knock yourselves out—I'll stay right here."

The ferry pulled into the small, coastal city of Melilla, and parked parallel to the large pier directly in front of a huge 16th century fortress, which loomed high over the port. It was lit up in yellow lights that provided a striking contrast to the burgeoning mass of white houses that sprawled over the countryside above.

The three were waiting in the garage for the door to open. Big Lee was getting hungry again. "This place is part of Spain?"

Kayanan was flipping through a tourist guidebook. "Yeah. Says here that in 1492, an emissary from the Duke of Medina Sidonia sent Don Pedro de Estopinion to conquer Moorish territory, in order to defend the mainland against another Moorish invasion. Apparently, this city is twenty kilometers square."

Rip was squinting into the night sky. "Looks like there's red lights on top of the mountain. Is that the mountain Seth mentioned? I forget the name."

Kayanan looked at the map. "Probably. It's called by the locals, Gurugú and is northern-most section of the Atlas range." Kayanan was looking up at the mountain thinking about Diano. "Corey? How did Diano end up killing you the last time you met?"

Big Lee smiled. "Well, you know how Diano is. After I found him, he was really indignant—blamed his situation on me and everyone else. Talking didn't seem to make a difference so he wanted to tussle. We beat on each other for the better part of a day. He was much stronger than I remembered. Anyways, he began to tire down, so we sat down for a meal. His slaves... or servants, whatever they were, brought out the food. They brought lots of wine and I was getting *real* tired. I remember waking up a couple of times with him trying to kill me, so I reached out and grabbed onto his right horn to hold him off. I guess I was too groggy. I ended up ripping it off of his head. After that, everything started to get dark and I woke up as a baby."

Rip nodded. "All right. Rule number one: no dining."

The white truck drove into Melilla and after asking directions twice, made a turn onto *Candido Lobera* and pulled into Hotel Parador.

After a fitful night's sleep for all, the three men ate breakfast at the hotel and then walked into the center of town. Although not too distant from Torremolinos, Melilla was several degrees warmer. The heat radiated from the sidewalks and Rip and Big Lee were covered in sweat within minutes of stepping outside the hotel.

Rip asked three people in the park about a witch named Luisa and received dirty looks. The three men continued until they saw a large Mercado brimming with people. It was similar to a large auditorium, selling different varieties of meat, vegetables, fruits and an area separate from the others that sold fish. The latter had herds of cats roaming around looking for handouts.

Big Lee was eating fruit out of paper sacks and following the other two as they canvassed the people shopping. A young Moroccan seller of nuts and spices overheard Rip. "You are looking for the *Bruja*, Luisa?" He was dressed in modern clothes, but sported the white, lace skullcap that covered the top of his head in Muslim tradition. He walked over to them and shook Rip's hand. "My name is Ali! I can help you! What do you need her for? She lives up on the hill in a barrio." He walked them to one of the doors of the market. "I'll take you, but you have to pay me some money, yes?"

Rip nodded and said, "How much is this going to cost me?"

"Why don't you give me ten mil?"

Rip broke into a flurry of perfect Spanish, "*Que dice! Estas loco? Yo no lo pago diez mil pesetas por algo tan estupido!*"

Ali laughed. "I'm sorry, I didn't know you were Spanish." He looked at Kayanan and Big Lee. "...Are they Spanish?"

"I'll give you five. Take it or leave it."

He took the money and walked them up rows of stairs leading up to the higher barrios. Rip wiped sweat off of his forehead as he made his way up the stairs. The young nut seller didn't seem bothered by the heat and loudly jabbered to Rip during the journey. "Why do you need the *bruja*? Usually she puts curses on people or gives young women abortions. My sister in-law once asked her to put a curse on my brother so that he wouldn't cheat on her. The *bruja* told her to wait until he was asleep and then tie a string onto his penis—" He stopped in his tracks with his mouth open and eyes filled with fear.

Standing in front of him were two young women, one with fair skin, blonde hair and blue eyes, the other olive-skinned, with dark black hair and dark eyes. They were both wearing delicate white dresses and were both exceedingly beautiful. They were both glaring at him. Just behind them was a plump lady in her fifties with big round glasses. She had short curly blonde hair and was stuffed in a dress that was at least one size too small. She was standing at a booth buying flowers and had been watching Ali approach.

Ali pulled off his white skullcap, "*Perdoname! Perdoname!*" turned and fled back down the hill.

The young brunette shouted at the retreating Ali, "*Gilipolla! Eres un cobarde!*"

"*Niñas, callaos.*" The mother walked over to the three men and looked at them with a sour expression on her face. "*Que quieres? Hm?*"

Rip looked at Kayanan and Big Lee and raised his eyebrows. He turned to the lady and gave a slight bow. "Good morning. I am Rip Damhorst, and these are my sons, Ricardo and Corey."

The chubby lady looked at the two men standing behind him with distaste. "Let me guess, you want your cheating wife killed."

Rip laughed politely shaking his head and tried to talk as low as possible. "We're here on urgent business. We need to see one of your... acquaintances. His name is Diano?"

She kept the frown on her face. "I don't know anyone by that name. *Chicas! Nos vamos!*" She turned and started back up the hill. The two girls followed and glanced back towards Rip with confused expressions on their faces.

Rip shrugged and said, "Let's go." The three men walked up the same hill following the witch and her two daughters.

When it became apparent to Luisa that the three were following them, she abruptly turned and spat on the sidewalk in front of Rip's feet. "Eh! If you walk any further, I will send the three of you to hell!"

Rip snickered and looked at Ricardo as if it was a joke. His face became stern and he opened his mouth wide. Blue flame roared from his throat and reached out several feet towards the witch, making her stumble slightly backwards. For effect, he closed his mouth, made a couple of chewing motions and then spat an orb of flame the size of a ping-pong ball on the sidewalk between himself and the witch. The fire sputtered and crackled, burning with severe intensity for a moment and then slowly died out, leaving behind black soot. "I'm the one holding the keys to hell, dear lady. I suggest you hear what we have to say."

Kayanan was watching the two younger girls. He had his bridge in his right hand and was holding it behind his back. He looked calm, but his stance was in preparation for attack.

Rip looked over at the two young women and they were both facing each other with their hands locked together. They were both whispering a chant in unison. They both looked scared but purposeful. "We're not here to harm anyone. We just want to discuss Diano, that's all."

During the entire encounter, Big Lee continued to gobble dates out of his paper sack. He looked bored.

Luisa turned up her nose. "*Esta bien*. Follow me. *Chicas*—go open the house and make sure there are no visitors at our door." The two girls released each other's hands and approached their mother. They didn't trust the three men and tried to argue with her to let them stay with her. "*De prisa!* I'll be fine!" The two girls gave another angry look at the three strangers and ran up the steps to their barrio.

Luisa led the three in silence up the stairs to her barrio. Children did not dare to run across her path and if she approached, they ran into the sanctity of their homes. Women sweeping the sidewalks in front of their houses would stop and rush inside, closing their doors behind them. When they turned the corner towards Luisa's home, the dark-haired daughter was standing just outside her door. Luisa walked to her door and appraised the neighborhood for prying eyes. "Come in."

Rip was expecting skulls with candle wax dripping like thick blood out of the sockets, bats and cobwebs, but instead found a typical Spanish home. It was compact but clean. She led them to a back terrace that was shaded from the sun. She sat down at oval patio table and invited the three to join her. Big Lee walked over to the far wall, squatted down and sat on the floor. All the while, Luisa watched the big man sink down to his buttocks on her tile patio.

"Believe me, you don't want him sitting on your furniture." Rip was jovial and admired the view of the white houses sloping down towards the sea. "Thank you for talking with us. We are old friends of Diano. We'd like to see him."

"First, tell me of this... Diano. What does he look like?"

Rip looked at her with a slight smile on his face. She didn't return anything but a sour expression. Rip sighed. "OK, we can go this route if you want. Let's see—he's about eight feet tall, has one horn on his head—did I mention he resembles a bull? --Oh, and by the way, and tends to like human flesh. Good enough description?"

Ricardo chimed in, "Actually Rip, the last time we've seen him he was a little over eleven feet tall. His other horn probably grew back by now too."

"Right. Thanks Ricardo." Rip looked at the lady to see if her expression changed. It didn't.

"I'm sorry. You are wasting your time and mine. I do not know of a Diano or anything that fits your description."

Rip sat back in his chair and carefully chewed at his inside cheek as he appraised her. He was starting to get agitated. "See Corey over there? That's Diano's father." Big Lee looked up and gave a single, uninterested wave. "He just wants to see his son. He knows that he lives up on Gurugú and if he needs to tear this city and that mountain apart, he's going to find him."

The witch stood up from the table and walked over to a shelf where a black Chinese vase sat. She picked it up and walked back to the table and dumped it over the table. Small white plastic tiles fell out with symbols on them. She used both hands to mix them up as if spreading bread dough and then with large handfuls, dropped them back into the vase. When they were all back inside the vase, she held it towards Rip. "Take one."

Rip thought for a moment, shrugged and reached in. He grasped a tile and pulled it out. It was the symbol of a crown. She passed the vase over to Kayanan, who reached in and pulled out a tile with a symbol of a worn, battered shield. She then walked over to Big Lee and shook the vase in front of him. He stuck his fingers into the top of the vase, but his hand could not enter. She ended up turning the vase slightly at an angle so that his fingertips could touch the tiles. He pulled out a tile embossed with the symbol of a tree.

She returned to the table with the three tiles. She scrutinized Kayanan's tile the longest. "Who are you?"

Kayanan looked at Rip then answered. "I am Ricardo Kayanan. I am a doctor of medicine and am here to give protection to Rip if he needs it."

She looked at him for a few moments with distrust. She then looked at Big Lee's tile. She dropped it back into the vase, placed her hand inside and stirred the tiles. She walked back over and had Big Lee repeat the procedure. Again, he pulled out the tree. She walked back over looking at the tile and back at Big Lee. Finally she looked at Rip with an uncertain look. "This... Diano has told me that he is several thousand years old. How old is that big man?"

Rip grinned. "Corey Lee is a youngster of twenty-three. He'll be twenty-four next month. He may be young, but I assure you, he *is* Diano's father."

Luisa put all the tiles back in and handed the vase to the blonde girl. "How is this possible."

"We live inconspicuously amongst humanity. We came from brighter, divine beginnings, but are now here, paying restitution for the crime of betrayal. Diano came from a time of greatness and all like him were slaughtered. He was allowed to live because he had better foresight than the rest of us, however he has been forced to live in hiding. We know that he lives somewhere on that mountain. Will you take us to see him?"

Luisa was pensive for a moment. "Do you promise not to kill him?"

The men looked at each other. Rip cleared his throat. "Doña Luisa, I have no desire to kill Diano—only to enlist his help. If he insists on causing us harm, however we must defend ourselves."

Luisa called out to her daughters, "*Alexandra! Maria! Ven aqui.*"

The two girls walked closer to the table. "These are my twins. The dark one is Alexandra and *mi rubia* is Maria. I call them 'salt and pepper'."

The two nodded to the men. Maria said lowly, "*Encantada.*"

Luisa whispered to Alexandra, "Bring me the ash."

The dark haired girl walked back into the house and after a few seconds returned with a deep plate, filled with grey ash. Luisa stood up from the table and took the plate from her daughter. She walked over to Rip. "Promise me that you will not kill Diano."

Rip looked curiously at the ash. "Sure. I promise."

"Now stick your thumb into the ash."

Rip cautiously pushed his thumb into the ash and after a short moment, pulled it back out. It was covered with a fine layer of gray ash.

She walked the plate over to Kayanan and Big Lee and had them do the same.

"*Bueno.*" Said Luisa handing the plate back to Alexandra. "I hope you are all men of your word. Maria—the water." Maria brought out a white ceramic bowl filled with water, which she handed to her mother. Luisa took it over to Big Lee who was busy examining the gray ash stuck to his thumb. "Put your thumb in the water."

Big Lee shrugged and stuck in his thumb. When he pulled it out it was clean. All of the ash had left his thumb and was slowly falling to the bottom of the bowl.

She brought the bowl back over to the table and motioned for the others to do the same. Rip and Kayanan stuck their thumbs into the bowl at the same time and the moment the ash touched the water, it brightened to the color and consistency of fresh blood. They both snatched their thumbs out and although they felt no pain, blood coated their thumbs.

"*Lo sabia!*" Shrieked Luisa, backing away from the table. "You *are* here to kill him!"

Big Lee had gotten to his feet and was looking from his thumb back towards the other two men. "What in hell's going on? Rip?"

Rip's face was getting flustered. He stood up from his chair so suddenly, that the chair fell back and clattered on the tile floor. "Señora! I am not planning on killing Diano! Corey, sit back down! Matter of fact *dear lady*, I absolutely need his help! If *however*, he refuses to join us or if he attempts to harm us, we will not have a choice!"

The two girls stood next to their mother, eyes wild with apprehension. Luisa stood her ground with her lips pursed in anger. She considered what Rip said for quite some time as her eyes darted between Rip and Kayanan. "You say that if he does not join you he shall be destroyed? Why? What is so important?"

Rip looked over at Corey who was still on his feet. Corey's jaw was set firm and his face was shrouded in concern. "Rip. Tell me what's going on man."

Rip scratched his head with agitation and took a deep breath. When he spoke, it wasn't in Spanish, but in origin. "My son, Diano is important to all of us. I taught him our language and writing—remember? I love that boy and want no harm to come to him, not one scratch. Now we've got to concentrate on what we know today. Rothiel is loose upon the Earth and we are going to need all of the help that is possible. We are all considered betrayers of Rothiel and *especially* your son—after all it was Diano that informed the Creator of his plans. If we cannot convince Diano to join us, I guarantee you that the minimum Rothiel will do is kill him on the spot. I suspect however, that he will want to change him into one of Protaxsis' creatures. His creations are dangerous enough when made from mere animals or humans. Just try to imagine if Diano was one of those things."

Corey sank back down to his haunches and shook his head. "Rip, I know what you're saying man. I just... I just don't want to see

my son die, that's all. I know I can convince him to come back with us
—just please, please give me a chance."

The women watched the men communicate with the mixture of
strange voices, popping and clicking noises. At some points, it sounded
like a roomful of people speaking at the same time. Luisa had heard the
strange language from Diano when she first met him. "What are you
two talking about? Well?"

Rip bent down, picked up his chair and sat down. He looked
over at the sullen Big Lee and nodded to him. "Doña Luisa, I'm sorry,
but we had a few last minute items to discuss. I believe that Corey and
I agree with each other that if all attempts to convince him to join us
fail, that we'll have no other choice than to put an end to him."

Luisa looked over at Big Lee, who was rubbing his head while
looking at the floor. "This is just a lie! You call yourself his father!
How can you agree to kill your own son?"

Big Lee looked up at her. "Rothiel is evil. If he is able to use
his evil on my son, all of mankind will die."

Luisa stopped. She had heard this name before. "I don't
understand you. Who is this person?"

Big Lee chuckled for a moment thinking about him. "Now?
Just a man. One thing I know about him-- he is going to kill all of
you... the first chance he gets."

Luisa looked at the ash and contemplated testing them again.
She felt confident that if hostilities broke out, Diano would be able to
kill them—if not, she would take care of things herself. She just didn't
want to damage Diano in the process—after all, he is quite valuable.
"We will go now. Excuse me a moment, I have to change first. Niñas!
Give them something to drink while I change."

Luisa walked back into the house and Alexandra followed to
bring refreshment. Rip grasped her arm gently. "That won't be
necessary—we're fine."

"You don't even want water?"

"No. We're fine. We're not thirsty."

Big Lee broke out in hearty laughter. "Huh! Just tell her the
truth, that we don't trust her Mama!"

She glared at Big Lee and Rip stood up from his chair. "My
apologies dear, all of this heat has gone to his head. We're fine."

Luisa emerged wearing the same tan skirt, but was now sporting
a bright red top. She held in her hands a large white hat and a rolled-up

red handkerchief that was in the shape of a Chinese spring roll. She led them out of her house and down the hill to the taxi stands.

Rip noticed where she was going and stopped her. "Doña Luisa? We cannot take a taxi. Big Lee couldn't possibly fit inside one."

She frowned. "He's not that fat—we'll get a small van."

"Believe me, there's no chance that he can go in a cab. If you'd like, we can go in our truck over there."

She appraised the situation. "Do you have air conditioning?"

Rip laughed. "Of course! Right this way Señora."

They walked the short distance towards the hotel and climbed inside the large truck. Big Lee stepped up into the bed of the truck and sat down near the window. Kayanan started the massive diesel engine and turned on the air conditioning. He backed out of the parking lot and continued down the hill towards the center of town.

"*Ay! Que frescito!*" said Luisa, holding her hands towards the vents, blowing chilled air. She was still holding the rolled up hankerchief.

As Kayanan drove, Rip watched the roll of cloth and pointed towards the marina while asking in origin, "Ricardo? What the fuck is that she's holding?"

Kayanan glanced over at the object for a moment and heard her instructions to turn right. He nodded his head and replied in the same tongue, "Not sure—look's like a *Jack*."

"Jack? Is it like a sap or something?"

"No. It's a voodoo-type object called that's also called a John the Conqueror. It's red cloth containing either ash or dirt from a cemetery—I forget which. In the center is a silver coin. It's used to ward off evil."

Luisa gestured to Kayanan to take the next right.

Rip pulled out his reading glasses and flipped through a magazine that was left on the dashboard. "Hmm. Do me a favor and watch our backs." Mumbled Rip. "I don't trust this crazy old bitch one bit. Watching what happened up in her house made me think that she may not be all that benign."

The truck rambled toward a large sign warning that they were approaching the border to Morocco. Rip put the magazine down and turned to Luisa. "Do we need anything special to cross the border?"

She pulled out her Spanish ID card. You'll need one of these or a passport."

Rip opened up the glove box and pulled out the three passports. They were Spanish and expertly done two days earlier by a seven-year-old craftsman named Tyler. Rip slid open the rear window and handed Big Lee his fake passport.

They were waved through the first gate on the Spanish side of the border and continued slowly to the second. When they arrived at the border control on the Moroccan side, a ratty looking guard walked up and scrutinized them. *"Donde vas?"*

Rip rolled down his window, but before he could answer, the plump lady sitting in the middle replied, "To the pine forest, to buy fruit."

The Moroccan guard waved the men on with a curt, *"Vete."* The truck chugged along the dusty, pockmarked road towards the looming mountain of Gurugú.

Rip noticed the change in scenery since leaving Melilla. "Where did all of the greenery go?"

Luisa spat out a volley of curses. "Those *Moros* turn everything they have into garbage. Just 100 years ago, all of this land belonged to the Spanish and was filled with trees and flowers. Just forty years ago, all this was given back to them and they've destroyed it. Now they're flowing into my city like sewer rats and doing the same to Melilla."

Rip sighed and looked over at the pristine highway that was running parallel to the bumpy road they were driving on. "Why aren't we using that nice road over there?"

"Gilipolla Hassan II!" spat Luisa. "That is the king's private highway. You'll never see anyone on that road unless he's driving at three hundred kilometers per hour in one of his sports cars."

After an hour, she signaled to take the next right, a dirt road that broke off towards the mountain. The dirt road was somewhat smoother than the paved road, much to Rip's surprise. Sheep hugged the steep, barren hills and from Rip's perspective appeared like flecks of popcorn strewn over the land.

"Alli. We are going to that grove of pine trees." Luisa said.

Kayanan looked from the road to the lady sitting next to him. "Is that where Diano is?"

"No. That is as far as we go in this thing. We have to walk from there."

The truck pulled to a stop in the middle of the grove, scattering monkeys to the outward edges of the trees. The men got out of the truck and looked around. There were small bits of litter on the ground. Big Lee climbed down from the back of the truck and looked over at Kayanan. Kayanan looked around a bit more and sniffed the air gently. He shook his head.

"*Bueno*. Let's start walking, because it will take quite a while to get there." Luisa began a steady walk up the incline. The men followed and kept close together. Kayanan was in front and watching every angle of the ascent.

Luisa continued chatting while walking and her voice seemed to get louder the higher up they went.

"Why do you think she's so... chatty all of a sudden?" asked Rip.

Kayanan continued to sniff the air and watch for movement. "Isn't it obvious? She's giving Diano a warning. That's why she changed her blouse to a bright red one and is speaking louder---"

Kayanan stopped and crouched down. He could smell him. It wasn't an older scent—it was fresh. He couldn't be sure how close he was, but it was too dangerous to ignore. "Rip, he's close."

Luisa stopped yammering and turned to see why the men stopped.

"Don't be alarmed *Señora*", said Rip. "Corey has to make himself presentable to meet his son."

Kayanan was helping Big Lee remove his sweat-stained shirt and kicked aside his thick, black sandals. Luisa saw that encompassing all of Big Lee's arms and back were jagged scars, twisting around his torso like a darkened, thorny vine. At once, his skin began to tremble and swim until she saw large areas of his flesh begin to come undone.

Several soft noises like the popping of bones filled the air. Big Lee grimaced and began to get larger. At first, just his shoulders and arms rippled and popped until the scars that she first observed opened as seams, spilling out more skin and muscle underneath. Big Lee took larger and larger breaths and grunted with each movement of his flesh. He began using his hands to pull his seams apart and help unfold the flesh and pull bone straight. His face was a cycle of pain and relief and even the skin on his face began to tremble and become misshapen. His jaw popped and the left side of his face was almost twice the size of the right. Then the right swelled to equal size. His hands found the top of his head and he began to coax the sides, as a seam appeared to run down the center of his head into a Y-shape just above his eyebrows. The seam opened and a darkened, blunt horn began to emerge.

Luisa stood in shock, watching the man become larger and larger. He was from first appearance, an obese man and now appeared to be made completely of solid muscle. His chest split open and spread, then again and again.

After a minute, he was done. He stood easily fifteen feet tall and the horn on the top of his head was a foot long by itself. He was wearing light, shiny sweatpants before before the transformation that now stretched to low shorts that looked painted onto his body. His skin was covered in gooseflesh and he shivered slightly as Kayanan spoke to him in their strange language.

Rip had folded Big Lee's shirt and stuffed it into Kayanan's backpack. He turned to the shocked woman with a grin on his face. "Now, can you see the resemblance? Don't worry about the shivering. When he unfolds he gets a case of the chillies. It'll go away in a minute or so."

Kayanan had removed his shirt and had a simple white sleeveless t-shirt underneath. He was scanning the horizon and clipping a black nylon vest over his shoulders. He connected the vest in the center of his abdomen using Koch fittings. The vest was adorned with gleaming objects that looked like butterfly wings and loops of twisted steel wire hung coiled over the vest and on his right hip. He had slipped on leather guards on his wrists and pulled the laces firm. He drew on tight fitting leather gloves that were missing the index finger. Lastly, he unsheathed a large knife and carefully slid it into the vest over the small of his back, taking a few seconds to make sure the handle was in the correct position. He nodded to Rip and the two men and shivering giant headed up Gurugú's rocky face towards Luisa.

The woman said nothing, but continued to gawk at Big Lee's enormous size. She realized that he was far larger than the beast that dwelled in the cave and was worried that even with her abilities that she may not be able to kill the three strangers. When the men reached her position, she turned and continued to rattle off commentary in a strong voice. Kayanan looked at Rip and motioned with a shift of his head for him to take his strategic position to the right of Big Lee.

A sharp whistle shot over the cliff and echoed across the rocks. Near the outcrop of boulders stood Diano. He stood two hundred yards distant, watching the approaching group. Even from this distance he was huge. His tawny skin was very close to the color of the dusty surface of Gurugú and his massive hands remained near his sides. He had two horns protruding from the sides of his head; the right one appeared smaller and twisted. He lingered for a moment, turned and stepped back into the darkness.

Rip lightly chewed his lower lip as he contemplated Diano's lack of action. *Why didn't he charge down and attack? Did he recognize Ricardo—or the both of us?*

Thinking along the same lines, Big Lee muttered in origin, "Remember what we talked about. *I* speak with him first. I only want threats or... action as a last resort."

Rip nodded and Luisa glowered at the men with hooded eyes.

When they arrived at the cave, Rip gave a short bow and motioned for Luisa to enter the cave as the gentlemanly thing to do. She shook a finger. "I'll follow you. My eyes are not so good in dark places."

Rip chucked his cigar down the ledge and following Kayanan's silent gaze, took up his predetermined position to the right of Big Lee. Kayanan led the way into the cave silent and cautious. The stench from the cave irritated his nostrils. Diano always had a strong smell, and his chosen diet of raw meat and penchant for drinking blood made for a sickly, sour smell. The cave's entrance was large, but Big Lee still had to duck low as he walked. At one point, his horn struck a stalactite hanging from the ceiling. A loud crack echoed through the cave, but neither object gave away. Big Lee winced and rubbed the top of his head. Kayanan shot Big Lee's an angry look of disbelief and Big Lee shrugged back and mouthed a silent *fuck.* Kayanan crouched down and looked back into the cave's darkness, weaving his head slightly from side to side to get his bearings. After gazing for a few seconds he continued forward into the cave.

Up ahead in the gloom, a slight flash of light appeared and soft light began to glow. The men entered a huge, open area of the cave that was littered with trash, bones and old carpets. Diano had just finished lighting several oil lamps that sat on the ground.

"Future and past—together at last." said Diano as he blew out the match and tossed it on the floor. He spoke in origin. "My prizes are few, but what I keep are priceless. Especially my masterpiece." He walked to an area of scattered junk, reached down and picked up a massive skull with a single horn rising out of the front. "Your previous one has taken quite a beating—I could use a new one."

Diano walked towards the center of the room closer to a lit lamp. The light revealed the many faded tattoos that covered his body as well as the many scars that littered his hide. He wore two heavy earrings that stretched long holes in his lobes. When he reached the center of the room, his muscles were tense. Kayanan silently looped a few feet of thin steel cable around his forearm and stepped out of the shadows towards the right of Diano. Diano growled at the intruder and then noticed his stance. He recognized his old teacher and smiled. Many of his yellowed teeth were broken off flat, but his canines were still long and sharp.

Big Lee couldn't hide the joy in his face. "Diano! Damn! It's so good to see you!" He tapped the side of his head. "If you don't mind—I'll just keep this one for a while longer." Big Lee contemplated the yellowed and battered skull and pointed a thick finger at it. "Just how were you able to kill me anyway?"

Diano's attention shifted slowly to Big Lee. His smile faded to a scowl while he juggled the skull, ultimately tossing it over his shoulder. It clattered and bounced on the ground a few times before coming to a stop near the cave wall. "The *damndest* thing," he growled. "...How to kill something that is virtually impervious to everything you throw at it. ...I got you drunk on strong wine. When you were in the midst of a deep sleep, I hurled your body into the sea. It was in the middle of a storm and the sea was raging."

Diano's face alternated between hate and pleasure as he recalled, "As I watched with satisfaction, your snoring form bobbed above the waves and floated—and yet you continued to sleep. I leaped into the sea and pulled you underneath. I held you under the waves for almost an hour—I can still remember the flashes of lightning that lit up your face. At first you were peacefully sleeping, but holding your breath. Your drunken eyes opened up with concern until you saw my face. I held you below with all my strength and not once did you fight back. A final flash of lightning showed a slight smile across your face as the last of your air escaped. You didn't struggle once."

Diano glared directly into Big Lee's eyes. "I dragged your dead body to the beach, but by then I was too tired to carry you any further. I had to wait four days for your body to soften enough for the crabs to eat your flesh!"

"I've heard just about enough of this shit." Growled Rip, lighting a fresh cigar from his mouth. "It's good to see you son, but your hatred for your Dad is wearing pretty fucking thin after all these years."

Diano scowled at the old man standing to the right of Big Lee. He looked back at Kayanan and then looked back at Rip. "I doubt you're Filodraxes—the last I heard, he still sleeps alongside the dead." Diano walked to the east wall of the cave where a circular diagram was carved into the cave. "I expected guests you see." He ran a gnarled hand over the origin letters and symbols, letting his claws drag across the carved wall. His head spun towards Rip, his fierce eyes reflecting the light from the oil lamps. "He's free isn't he? My calculations were wrong by about 10 years or so. I've been waiting all this time to see who would find me first. By the way you address me with your... air of *familiarity*, I'd say that you were none other than Danhieras."

"None other!" Laughed Rip. "Call me Rip though, and Filodraxes isn't what you'd call dead or sleeping either. He's recovering back home, but I'm sure he sends his regards." Rip held out a fresh cigar to Diano. "Cuban. My absolute favorite."

Diano approached warily and glanced towards Kayanan. He kept his distance, but reached out and took the cigar. Rip nodded in a approving way, holding out his right palm while bright blue flame erupted from the skin. Diano kept his eyes locked on Rip's face as he knelt, picked up an oil lamp and lit the cigar. Rip closed his hand and the flames waned and died. As Diano was getting back up, Rip snapped his fingers and Diano shot backwards, eyes wildly sweeping between the three men with teeth bared. His hands were fanned open with his thick, sharp claws pointed towards Rip.

"Haw!" Laughed Rip, bending down to pick up Diano's fallen cigar. "No one is here to threaten you, boy!" Rip stepped forward with the cigar in his outstretched hand and Diano swatted it away with blinding speed. The show was purely for Kayanan's benefit, to see which hand Diano preferred out of anger and to check his reflexes.

Rip glared at Diano. "Don't you dare forget who I am boy! I am not here to harm you but that doesn't mean that I won't teach you a painful lesson in respect!"

Diano's emotions were running high. His eyes betrayed his inner feelings of love for his former master, hate for his father and fear of what lies ahead. "I know you Danhieras," said Diano with a trembling voice. "I remember what you did in Siberia-- ...I was in western China and I felt the Earth shake."

He began to step slowly backwards. Kayanan continued closer at the same pace. "What about him?" He motioned towards Kayanan. "If you're not here to kill me, then why is he here? Why won't he say something to me?" He turned pleading to Kayanan with a terrified voice. "Master?"

Kayanan's face unfroze and he looked at Rip. His stance remained at the ready.

"Fine." Rip grunted. "Why don't we establish a general truce? Diano? Stand tall, boy. Do you promise on your allegiance to the Creator that you will not attempt to harm us?"

Diano snarled, backing further away. "Do I look like one of his followers to you? Is living in hiding for all these millennia just treatment for his faithful?"

"Bah!" spat Rip. "Given the choices, I'd say that you adhere to his laws which to me, implies respect. Now make the bond before us— or I'll have your former Master take *your* head!"

Diano's scowl slipped away in resignation and he stood slowly wiping tears from his cheeks. "I-- I promise in our Creator not to harm anyone in this room—except for the witch."

Rip stepped toward Diano and grasped his forearm in the old ways of friendship. The top of Rip's head only reached the bottom of Diano's ribcage. Diano was surprised at Rip's lack of fear.

"Ricardo!" Barked Rip. "Come and greet your former pupil!"

Diano watched with relief as Kayanan removed his vest and left his weapons on the floor of the cave. He took four steps and held his palm towards Diano. "Keep your hands at your sides and approach."

Diano wept and dropped to his hands and knees. He gently moved his head forwards until it touched Kayanan's open palm. "Master—I have missed your guidance—greatly."

Kayanan used his hand to wiped away Diano's tears. "We have much to do you and I. But before we can begin, you must make peace with your father."

Diano kept his face down and muttered in broken origin, "He has betrayed us all. I was greatness—I had fame in darkness and light and he betrayed everything that I was—what you all were."

Kayanan lifted the massive beast's face towards his. "And what pupil, have I done differently? We serve our sentence no matter how bitter and we hope to overcome. We endeavor to pay our debts." He pulled down the crew neck of his t-shirt exposing the dark, origin number 3 on his chest. Rip unbuttoned his own shirt and pulled it aside. The origin number 1 stained his left breast like spilled wine on a tablecloth.

Diano looked between the men and then towards the origin number six as big as a dinner plate on Big Lee's chest. "So it's true," said Diano. "The penance of the great Danhieras is coming to an end. Is not my father as pious as the rest?"

"I *said* call me Rip, boy." Said Rip, buttoning his shirt. "It has nothing to do with that. No one knows how we earn our freedom, whether it's sacrifice or duty—we've had four of our kind return home so far."

"As you can see," croaked Diano, "I was not blessed with a number, nor will I ever be able to return home."

Rip cleared his throat. "You were born here son. I realize that the world you were born into is now gone, but that doesn't mean that you have to live... " Rip looked around the cave, "*Jesus*-- like this."

Kayanan put his hand on his former pupil's shoulder. "You have a home with us—where *you* belong. We've been looking for you for hundreds of years—now it's time that you come back with us."

"So what's it going to be, old friend?" asked Rip. "An outcast or hero? Either way Rothiel is going to find you and... well, he's not planning on coffee and doughnuts."

Diano looked confused at Rip's last remark but shook his head and continued, "It won't be easy. I cannot shrink like my father and I--- I tend to stick out."

Rip grinned. "Don't worry my boy, I've got it all figured out. Rick? Help Diano pick up what he wants to bring..." Rip looked around and with a grimace. "—Shit, I hope it's none of this stuff, and torch the rest—I don't want any remnants left to help Rothiel figure out where he's gone. I'm going back to the truck to raise Gellan on the wireless and tell him to get a cargo plane here tonight!"

Rip turned to leave the cave and his eyes locked on Luisa's glare. She stood indignant, with her lips pursed in sour severity. He nodded and tilted his head to the side, waiting for her disapproving comments. "Well? Are you waiting for a tip or something?"

"*Mierda!*" spat Luisa. "I don't know what is going on between you but I want—I *demand* to know what is going on!" Luisa stepped in front of Rip, expecting an answer before he left the darkness of the cave.

Rip fished out his wallet and started thumbing through 20 mil Peseta notes in front of her. He used his best *Madrileño* accent to piss her off, "Your help has been most valuable and all, etc. How much can I offer you for your services? Say 300 mil?"

Her face soured even more and she pointed at Diano. "Where he goes, I go!"

Rip clapped the wallet shut and slapped his palm with it lightly. "*Doña Luisa*, we both know that you are either after wealth or power — or both. Diano isn't yours to keep — may I suggest a kitten or hamster as an appropriate pet. --Let me finish! I am however, prepared to reward you financially both for your troubles and to maintain a degree of silence about Diano."

Kayanan walked up to Rip and interrupted in origin. "She's been feeding him human remains."

Rip glared at him. "What? Did he tell you this?"

"Partly. I can smell it on his skin, but it's not… adult flesh as far as I can tell. He says that she bakes him pies with animal's blood, which he asked her to do. Well, he can tell that it has human blood in it, and since he tends to like it, he hasn't complained."

Rip looked at the old woman and then back at Kayanan. "Not adult flesh? Didn't that kid at the market say that she performed abortions? You — don't think that she's giving it to him do you?

"Could be. I vaguely remember a practice of feeding infant flesh to kings in order to corrupt their minds for control. Kind of a long shot, but based on what we've seen with this woman, I'm betting that she wants control over him."

"Makes sense. Watch her for me — don't let her within spitting distance of Diano until I get back." Rip turned towards Diano and saw him and Big Lee sitting on the floor of the cave talking. Diano was talking softly to his father, who had tears running down his cheeks. *Well I'll be damned*, thought Rip. He walked past Luisa without looking at her, saying, "Think of a number, lady. I'll be right back."

Rip walked down the slope from the cave towards the white truck. His shirt clung to him with sweat and his throat felt dry. He thought about the cool, electrolyte water waiting for him in the cooler and quickened his pace. He didn't know what to expect from this woman, but in case he had to kill her he wanted to be ready.

He climbed up into the back of the truck, popped open the red lid of the cooler and fished out a bottle of water. He took a long pull, enjoying the cold refreshment and the popping he felt in his throat as the electrolytes reacted with the charged acids in his saliva.

"Hello lover."

Rip swung around, dropping the bottle of water on the floor of the truck. She stood in the fading light of dusk, still radiant and lovely as ever. She smiled up at him and laughed that he was so startled.

"Theo?" Rip climbed down from the truck and she reached forward and embraced him in a long kiss. As she hugged him, he could feel her grip shaking. She kissed his mouth and cheeks and rested her head on his shoulder. One of her hands drew small circles in his damp hair, the other held onto his back for dear life.

She wept and looked at him. "I don't have much time, but at least I am allowed to be seen and heard."

"Seth saw you at the grove—you don't know how jealous I was of him at that moment."

Theo placed her finger gently against his lips. "My love, I am here to tell you that Rothiel's men are going to attack your fortress—I only know that it may happen tonight."

Rip looked at the dull red sun, pushing itself slowly below the horizon. Part of him didn't care. He only managed to be with Theo in a rare moment of a lifetime. The last time he saw her, he was 22 and sitting at an outdoor café near his apartment in Copenhagen. She pulled the newspaper away from his startled face, dragged him upstairs and made love to him for almost two straight days. She spoke no words, but Rip knew she was not allowed to communicate with him or any of the exiles. On the last day she kissed him longingly then faded to nothing. His body and bed still smelled of her, so he wrapped himself up in the sheets and wept, knowing he probably wouldn't see her again until the willow tree.

"My God," said Rip. "I can't get back there in time. I don't know if Simon can pull us from here..." Rip held tight to his love and his mind raced with thoughts on how to get to the fortress. He thought of something. "Theo I have an idea—I know you can't help us, but can you place the location of that cave in Simon's mind? You know, just the image of it? If he has that, he can hex us back to the fortress."

"I will my love, but be careful. Some of the ones that are being mobilized are very dangerous. Valgiernas will be leading them."

Rip grasped her for another long kiss and held her face in both of his aged hands. "I'll be seeing you soon, if only for a brief moment."

Theo's face was saddened. "Must you remain for them all?" She pushed her hand into his shirt and rested her palm over the birthmark on his chest.

Rip sighed. "I know my dear, but I've got to correct these wrongs that I-- we have done. It won't be long, I promise."

She stepped back wearing a delicate frown and tears began to erupt in her soft blue eyes. She choked out a soft "I love you."

He nodded and said, "For a moment I thought I was back in Copenhagen."

She managed a broken smile, pointed towards Rip's shirt and faded away.

Rip could feel his heart ache. It was always so difficult for him to act brave in her presence. There was no earthly treasure, admiration of artistic genius, solace in music or rare wine that could quench his thirst, his desire for her. She wore something on her lips that he could still feel taste and smell—he would never remove it, instead allow his body to absorb this most rare of sensations.

He stepped up on the sideboard of the driver's side door and opened it. He sat down behind the steering wheel and clutched the push-to-talk microphone from the multi-wave band radio. He switched on the radio and waited for the radio to warm up. While he waited, he placed his head in his left hand and silently played back his short moment with Theo. He heard the carrier signal from the fortress ping softly from the truck's speakers.

"Gellan, pick up, this is Rip, over."

He waited for a few minutes and before he pushed the microphone button, Gellan's voice crackled over the speaker. "Rip, this is Gellan. I hear you fivers, over."

Switching to origin, Rip focused on the task at hand. "Gellan, listen carefully. Valgiernas is going to attack the fortress soon, perhaps tonight—he may already be nearby. I want you and Gideon to lock down the doors on the buildings, open the pens and for God's sake get those bulls awake and moving. Did you copy all that I've said?"

Gellan's cheerful demeanor had gone. "We're on it Rip! Gideon is rounding up the children and sending them to the basement. I'll get the bulls up and about and Simon is on his way to unlock the arsenal. Over."

Rip looked up the slope to the cave and tried to figure out how long it would take for him to get back. "Negative on Simon. Tell him to go into the living room and open a hex to the cave on Gurugú — I realize that he has no idea where in hell it is, but tell him to do it anyway. Is Simon there next to you? Over."

"Roger — he's right here, over."

"Simon, listen to me. The cave will be in your mind. Just close your eyes and you will see it. Trust me. Give me 15 minutes to get back to the cave and open the hex — it's got to be big because we're bringing Diano back with us. Over."

Chapter Twenty Two:
We Have Visitors

Gellan placed his handset down on the mahogany desk and looked at Simon. Simon's eyes betrayed his apprehension to what lay ahead. "Simon, I need to step outside and get the bulls moving. I'm going to need about five minutes, so I need you to watch the monitors, OK?"

Simon nodded. Gellan stepped outside the side door of the main ranch house and took a moment for his vision to adjust to the darkness outside. The moon was not quite half full, but with the stars there was just enough light to make out the black shapes of the Europe's most deadliest animal, the Spanish fighting bull. Gellan pulled out an old riding crop from one of the sheds and continued to look about. He saw no one.

He jumped the nearest fence and dashed over to where Big Chief usually stood, on a small hill, overlooking the olive trees. Big Chief was the biggest of the lot and originally came from Colmenar, of Miura stock. He was exactly what was needed to get the younger, more impressionable bulls agitated. Gellan dashed past Big Chief and struck his rear quarters with a deft strike from the crop. Big Chief roared a trumpet-like bellow and was hot on Gellan's heels in an instant. There was no chance that he could keep up with Gellan's rapid pace, but Big Chief could run for days without giving up.

Gellan arrived at the pen's large galvanized gate and used the last twenty feet to skid to a stop. He could hear Big Chief's hoof beats ripping up the soil nearby and wasted no time opening the gate and running through to wake up Vavilov and Lebedev, the twins that Rip named after Russian research ships. Gellan whacked both and doubled back towards the approaching Big Chief. When he was within ten feet of Big Chief's charging horns, Gellan leaped over the bull and ran back towards the outer pens. One by one, he woke the bulls and riled them up to the point of attack. He criss-crossed the pens to make sure that they would roam in all directions for their attacker. He was almost struck by the wily Marfil, who was struck by a lightning bolt when young, which splayed the tips of his horns. The encounter with the electron left the bull paranoid and unstable. His grandfather, Tocayo, was killed when he managed to sneak out of his pen and charged a locomotive on its return run from Sevilla.

In all, he woke up all of the 16 bulls that lived at the ranch and opened the pens so that they freely roamed all of the grounds of the fortress. Every blade of grass, olive tree and the very air itself now belonged to them. Spanish fighting bulls are greedier than any monarch, property developer or slumlord. Wherever they find themselves, the very dirt that they stand upon belongs, heart and soul to them and to them alone.

Gellan slipped back inside the fortress and bolted the steel-reinforced door. Simon had his face buried among the rows of monitors of cameras sweeping the grounds and had already switched off the internal lighting of the fortress to red light. Gellan twisted the grey key that initiated electric motors to pull heavy steel shutters across the windows.

"Everything looks good—"Gellan's comment was interrupted by the crack of Randall's sniper rifle on top of the roof. "Well my friend, it looks like you have a job to do. I'll be up on the roof with Randall. Good luck." Two more loud cracks echoed from the roof. Gellan ran out of the room and up the stairwell towards the roof.

Simon walked into the living room and began to slide the couches out of the way. He remembered how big Diano was and he would need to make as much room as possible.

He stared at the wall and tried to think about the cave that Rip was in. He saw nothing. He closed his eyes and tried to imagine what it would look like. More shots from the roof. He could feel sweat trickle down his shirt and his hands were clammy. *This has to work*, thought Simon. *It must.*

Behind Simon, a young woman appeared. She still bore the pain of an obscenely short meeting with her love, but she bit back fresh tears. She was nothing more than an apparition and had no physical touch, but just the same placed her palm on the back of Simon's head.

He felt some warmth and a slight tickle but felt that he was close to remembering something important. In his mind, he saw what looked like an old pumpkin that was carved for Halloween and now old and misshapen. The eyes collapsed into the disintegrating flesh and the mouth yawned open. The color faded and jagged cracks appeared around the growing mouth. It stopped growing and seemed to fade even more until it was nothing but a dark vision with a lightened slope near the base of a mountain. The mouth looked more like an aggravated sore on the face of the hill. *The cave! I can see it*, thought Simon.

He felt like he had been there. He stood up from the floor and faced the wall. The wall was 12 feet high from the floor. *A ten-foot hole should be big enough*, thought Simon. He held out his palm and began to hum.

"Change of plans." Said Rip, almost out of breath. He was covered in sweat and was mopping his brow with the back of his hands. "The fortress is going to be attacked tonight. Simon's going to hex us back, so get ready."

Big Lee rose from the floor. "Who told you this?"

Rip was grateful that the arduous walk diminished his raging erection before he got to the cave entrance. Just the same, he glanced down to make sure. He kept trying to get his breathing back under control and said in a husky tone, "A little birdie told me — don't worry about it. The boys are getting everything shut down as we speak. We'll all be back soon, so let's get everything prepared to go."

"What about the truck? It will get stolen if we leave it here."

"Screw the truck. We'll give the keys over to the hag so she can make some money off it."

The cave began to illuminate, not from the yellow flame of the oil lamps but from the cool, bluish-white symbols that formed an enormous ring on the cave wall.

"OK boys, our ride is here," said Rip. "I'll be going first, followed by Ricardo and Diano. Big Lee, make sure that the *señora* stays put and get your ass through that hole last." Rip fished out the truck's keys and tossed them over to Luisa's feet.

The woman took her eyes off the strange symbols on the cave wall that grew in intensity and looked at the keys at her feet. *"Que es esto?"*

Rip looked at her a moment and then his eyes went back to the symbols. He could feel the pulsing energy of the hex grow stronger.

"The keys to the truck. There are five hundred thousand pesetas in the *ajuantera*—it's all yours.

She looked at the wall. "Are you going someplace?"

Rip walked closer to the wall. "If you must know, we are going back to where we came from—in Canada. Ah, here it comes."

The cave wall hazed and then erupted in soft light as the soot-covered walls disappeared showering the cave with dim red light from the fortress. Simon stood in front of the hole groaning lowly, his face damp in sweaty concentration. Rip stepped forward and was halted by a sharp whistle and shaking of head from Simon. Rip looked at the sides of the hole and they shuddered as if unstable. Rip stood back while Simon concentrated, his brows knitted in frustration. A gunshot rang out from the roof and Kayanan ran forward and somersaulted through the hole into the living room. He sprung to his feet and ran out of view, grasping butterflies from his vest.

"Rick! Dammit!" yelled Rip. He was almost knocked off his feet when Diano tore past him and leaped through the hole just seconds later.

Luisa stood ashen and had already placed her purse strap over her head and between her bosoms. She quickly kicked off her shoes and opened her purse. She dug around and found what she wanted- an object that looked like a greasy, black tomato. She bit into the side and spit the piece of flesh on the cave floor. She squeezed the object until blackened dust began to cough out of the inside. She placed her trembling mouth over the hole of the vile object and crushed it, inhaling deeply the soot-like ash from the inside. The pain was excruciating but she felt as if she was floating. The effects only lasted a few seconds. In her dim vision she saw the hole and willed herself towards it.

Rip watched Simon's face contort as he tried to regain control of the hex. At last, he nodded and Rip took the small hop through the hole. The moment he entered, he felt a sickening acceleration and his nostrils filled with stink. For a split second he felt as if he was trapped in a whirlwind of gnats that forced their way into his eyelids and ears. He felt several quick stings in his face, his hearing blanked out in his left ear and he saw shooting stars in his vision. Instead of standing on the living room floor, he found himself lying on the floor. He watched Big Lee emerge from the wall and peer down towards him in alarm.

"Rip! Damn! Are you all right?" Big Lee's massive fingers were gently tapping against his face.

Simon had sealed the hole and was kneeling beside his prone form. He heard Simon speaking softly, "Rip, I'm so sorry—I don't know what happened—can you say something?"

Rip was not in pain but his head swum. He could feel the floor of the house thrusting upwards as if it was riding huge waves. The left side of his body felt like lead—it felt dead to him as if it was missing entirely. He was able to hiss out a few noises, then a groan. His right hand found it's way to his face and he could feel its warmth on the right side, but not where he touched on the left—it felt like the face of a cadaver. More gunshots. He could hear Gellan screaming about something being everywhere. Big Lee gave a worried look to Rip and then got up and scrambled outside.

Valgiernas had sent five teams in different directions towards the fortress. He knew that the majority of the structure would be underground, away from prying eyes. Each team was made up of nine men—or at least they were once men. Two of each team was stage II addicts that would do anything for another hit of Protaxsis' wonder drug. Three were drone class workers that had great strength, almost impervious skin but were slow. They were largely flat on one side, and misshapen to the form of a large flea. Their specialty was that they could chew their way through fences, doors and soldiers legs on their ceaseless march into the enemy's ranks and most ammunition simply bounced off their thick hides.

Three more were of the advanced stage hunters that no longer resembled humans, but a large, spiny cricket that dragged its body along the ground by four powerful legs underneath its abdomen. A powerful, neurological venom dripped from the ends of the hundreds of spines that could be ejected towards anything that was close enough. They would take down anyone in their way while using the drones as shields. When someone was captured, the advanced stage creations would feed on them or drag them from curving, gnarled hooks trailing from their abdomen—more troops for Protaxsis' army. Finally, each team consisted of a Bishop, the highest order of Protaxsis' creations. They walked upright, were fast and stealthy. They were lightly armored but well armed with extremely sharp claws on their arms and legs.

They were the control mechanism of the others and hissed orders to the drones and advanced stage creatures. When the battle was over and the situation was stabilized the Bishops walked in to slaughter whom they wished or injected the wonder drug into immobilized recipients.

Valgiernas sat perched on the roof of his van, peering at the darkened buildings with night-vision binoculars. He watched two men on the roof of the fortress sniping ineffectually at his drones as they marched steadily over the main walls of the ranch and continued up the grass towards the main house. Outside the walls, the dark silhouettes of the Bishops hissed orders for the stage II's and hunters to climb over the walls and enjoy the cover that the drones provided. While Valgiernas watched through his night-vision binoculars, he finished screwing on the small tripod to his sniper rifle. He watched the two men on the roof with great interest — he hoped to eliminate his only threat the moment he could get a clear shot. The two on the roof couldn't be him — he remembered well his movements — stealthy, cautious and explosive. There was a tall, skinny one on the roof opening up with automatic machine gun fire and another that was carefully aiming with a high-powered rifle. *No, it wasn't one of them.*

A gleam of something appeared out of the corner of his view. He followed with his binoculars and noticed the side door had been thrown open. *Strange.* He didn't see anything come out. A small, almost unnoticed gleam of metal made his heart skip a beat. He saw something flash behind a tree about 100 yards from the door. He could almost make out a shoulder of someone. He felt a chill and attempted to zoom the binoculars in a bit more — they were zoomed as close as he could get. He saw a drone lying on its side on the lawn just below the tree — some of its legs were kicking slowly. He saw a thin, shining cable slowly snaking back up the tree to its owner. *Shit. That must be him.*

Out of the same door, a hulking figure dashed out. The heat coming off the creature made him stand out considerably. *Diano. Rothiel will indeed be pleased.* Valgiernas lifted the sniper rifle and turned off the safety. He continued to follow the creature as it trotted to the tree where the drone lay dying. It crouched to examine it while cautiously turning its ears in all directions. Diano's face jerked upwards in surprise towards the tree. *That must be Kainaan Toth talking with it.* At once, two light green dots appeared from the tree and bored into Valgiernas' very soul. The lights disappeared and a dark shape dropped from the tree next to Diano. He watched as Diano's face scowled and both figures dashed towards the direction of the wall nearest the van.

"Move!" shrieked Valgiernas to his driver as he jumped back down into the van. The driver, once a gypsy known as Cordón sported the colorless iris and pallid skin of a type II addict, fired up the engine and raced the van off the shoulder of the road towards the highway. Valgiernas kicked open the back doors of the van and leveled the rifle towards the dark shapes racing towards him. He fired a burst of three rounds at the shapes and a whizzing disk of metal crashed into some supplies next to him. Attached to the blade was a thin cable, which wrenched the gleaming object out of the van, along with some of the supplies in a crate.

"Faster! Faster damn you!" shrieked Valgiernas as he could make out Diano approaching within 100 yards of the van, his legs pumping like mad and saliva streaming out of the sides of his mouth. The van began to gain and in a blink, Diano melted back into the darkness.

"Where do we go, master?" asked the driver.

Valgiernas put the rifle down and took stock of what had struck the inside of the van. It was gone, but it took some things with it. *An entire box of CamBio*. He hoped that his soldiers could kill Kainaan and Diano but he doubted it. His soldiers were probably all dead by now. He brushed his fingers through his grey hair, sopping with sweat. "Back to Rota. And not another word."

Simon grabbed a flashlight passed the light into Rip's right eye. It dilated normally. He checked Rip's left eye and received no response. "Rip," he said close to his ear. "I think you may have had a stroke. I've got to get down to my lab." Rip tried to acknowledge but just managed a sigh. Simon ran down to the stairwell among the sounds of gunfire.

Rip's eyes lolled around as he tried to breathe normally. It was a long time since he last heard the sound of Simon's voice. His body felt like it weighed 500 pounds. He tried to lift his head from the terrazzo floor but was unsuccessful. Try as he might, he couldn't release his body from the vise-like grip of gravity. He noticed movement out of the corner of his right eye — he thought it was a mound of ash moving about, but it was Luisa, getting up off the floor with a cough and low grunt. Her dress was disheveled and filthy, her hair was a rat's nest. She shuffled past Rip in her bare feet and fidgeted around in her purse. She looked down at Rip and snarled. Her teeth were as black as coal and when she walked past muttered, "I shit in your milk."

Luisa stepped out of the side door of the house and gazed into the darkness. She pulled a mint out of her purse and popped it in her mouth. "*España. Lo sabia.*" She pulled the rolled-up red cloth from her purse and held it in her left hand. The Jack seemed to give her confidence as she listened to the fighting that seemed to go on all around her, yet she saw nothing.

There were cracks of rifle fire from the rooftops. She saw shadows moving in the distance and heard heavy breathing approaching. She shoved her hand back in her purse. It was too dark to see inside it, but the shape of what she was looking for was unique. She found one and held it in her right hand. It was a dark red ceramic skull. It had a thick cork shoved into the top that she pulled out with her blackened teeth.

A huge, black bull trotted towards her and stopped within ten feet. It eyed her with sullen regard and blew thick snot out of its nostrils. It was Big Chief and at 900 kilograms was the biggest bull that Luisa had ever seen. It was breathing heavily and looked painted with black oily liquid. There were a few long quills hanging from the sides of his neck. She gave it no more interest than a neighborhood cat shitting in her garden. "*Vete! O te hare hamburguesa!*"

The bull dug his front hoof into the dry dirt and bellowed. It seemed to smell something nearby and tore off towards a more appropriate adversary. Luisa followed the sidewalk, muttering about the lying *Americano* and wondering what part of the mainland this was. *It must be in the south for all of these fucking bulls*, she thought. She stopped at the base of an olive tree and peered with disgust at a dying creature that to her, looked like a fat cockroach. "*Que asco! Que demonios es esto?*" She waved the Jack over it. Nothing. There was hardly any life-force left in it. She decided to spare her weapon and continue looking for Diano. She would make sure that nothing harmed him.

When she got to the driveway, there were several other creatures that had been killed by the goring of bulls and some that looked severed in two. While she peered over at one that still appeared to have a human face, two similar creatures approached her from behind. A dragging noise alerted her and she stood up, holding the small red skull at the ready. One creature, looking like a large cricket, dragged itself forward. It had somewhat of a human face or mask, but it was encircled by long, twitching quills. Something was walking behind it, upright like a human. It was skinny and angular. In the darkness, it looked like it was holding two long daggers from its hands. As it approached, it hissed towards the creature sliding along the ground as if it was giving it orders. She realized that they were not daggers or hands, but claws.

She dashed her right hand down, spraying the prone creature with powder from the skull, and then made the same motion towards the one following. The result was almost instantaneous. They both stopped as if switched off. She waved the jack towards both of them and could feel their energy—it was enormous. *Not nearly as much as what Diano possessed or as much as that bastard Rip*, she thought, but it still gave her chills. She approached the one on the ground and examined it. It appeared to be breathing—good. In a few moments the poison would sink into its central nervous system and bring on a nightmare from which it would never recover. Splendid. She walked over to the tall one and looked into its face. It looked like a face made out of an old paper sack. It was once skin, but had at one point separated and hung as a remnant. The rest of this creatures skin was hard and thick like the armor of a lobster. It began to twitch. *It's coming on now*, she thought. And she stepped back just before it dropped to the ground.

She intended to preserve her new pets and decided not to let it harm itself—victims from her devil's powder had the tendency to tear themselves up when the nightmares began. She fidgeted in her bag and pulled out a paper cone. She gently unwound the paper and pulled out a small dried up piece of fish that looked like a grayish-white raisin. She looked for the creature's mouth and found it just under the face-mask. She dropped it in and the movement ceased. She did the same for the one lying on the ground—its four legs began to kick and its body was shuddering. Soon after, the movement stopped. She saw some shapes retreating away from the onslaught of the bulls and heading over to the other side of the house. She waited for any sounds from Diano and held her skull tight.

Simon ran back into the living room with a syringe and IV bag. He knelt down next to Rip and tied his arm with a rubber strap. He massaged his arm until he could see a vein and expertly shoved the IV home. *I guess all that money for veterinary school paid off*, thought Rip. Simon attached the bag midway up a floor lamp and then pulled off the needle cover with his mouth. He injected a solution into the IV bag and then removed the rubber strap from Rip's arm. "Rip. This is going to dissolve the blood clot. It will thin out your blood and should take away any pain you are in. It's also going to make you very sleepy..." Rip was out cold and snoring.

Simon double checked Rip's right eye and still received no response. He loosened Rip's sweaty clothing and pulled a pillow from the couch and placed it under his head. He heard a shuffling noise near the outer door and spun around. An ugly black creature was coming through — it was listing sideways and was flat on one side. Sharp claws were moving towards him. Simon jumped up, ran into the doorframe and grabbed the top with both hands. He tried to fill out the frame as much as possible with his body, and then hardened. The creature slid into the house and approached Simon. Two stocky claws gripped his ankles and tightened. It shot a group of ten quills into Simon's midsection, but they just glanced off and clattered on the floor. The creature's claws can make short work of pine logs, but the creature began to feel sharp pains in its joints and released its grip. It used its fore-legs to climb up on Simon to see if it could dislodge if from the doorframe, but this stone-like man was jammed in place. It tried to maul the man's face and body but only managed to shear off some of his clothes. The man looked like a statue and without a single scratch.

The creature began to work at the wood frame and started excavating the plaster and mortar surrounding the man. It would dislodge him and kill the one lying on the floor. Only then could the creature receive what it craved most from its cruel masters. The creature felt something approaching from the left. It shifted sideways and saw an old man walking unsteadily towards it. He was extremely thin and wasted. He was wearing a hospital gown and was muttering something with a gravelly voice. The creature lurched to the floor in excruciating pain. The Drone was being pulled inside out from an unseen force. It's tissue separated from all sides its body and it blacked out in the relief of a quick death.

Filodraxes overcame a wave of dizziness from such a quick loss of energy. He shook his head, walked up to Simon and appraised him with a frown.

Simon's color returned and he released the doorframe and clutched at his shredded clothes. He gasped for the breath that he held during the short fight. "You—you should be in bed resting..."

Filodraxes looked past him at the shape of Rip lying on the floor. "Is that my servant Danhieras? Watch over him—I'll take care of the disturbance outside." With that, the old man shuffled to the side door and stepped outside. The air still irritated his lungs and he coughed and hacked. He saw a fat woman looking at him with a sour look. She was snapping at him in a language that he could not understand and shook a rolled up red cloth at him.

To Filodraxes, the object in her hand didn't appear to be anything that could be threatening, but just the same, he waved his hand in front of it, accelerating the age of the material by thousands of years in an instant. The red cloth disintegrated through her fingers, raining grey dust to the ground. A silvery coin clinked on the sidewalk between her dirty feet. He was in no mood or mind to be social—especially to an old woman who spoke to him without respect. He extended an arm to push her from his way. She jumped back swearing. When he walked past on his way to the drive, she bent down and picked up the coin. She gave it a kiss and put it in her bag.

The night was dark, but the old man willed himself to see the blackened sky as if it were day. The shadows that moved around became clear—beasts of different types were being fought by men and large, black Aurochs roamed the grounds—some driving tirelessly into the remaining beasts and some staggered drunkenly from what looked like long quills penetrating their skin. He saw Diano hurling beasts repeatedly into the rocky ground, only to see them roll over and continue to attack. "All ye that fall under my rule," croaked Filodraxes, "Get behind me now!" All of the men except Diano squinted to see who was yelling in origin.

Diano, breathing heavy from his energetic battle explained it simply, "It looks like the great Filodraxes is at last among the living!" The men rushed to his side while watching the beasts stalk towards them, slowly and ceaselessly. Diano walked to Filodraxes' side and noticed that the old man was glaring at him. He felt awkward at that outburst and lowered his head while bowing. "...Forgive me, m-Master."

Filodraxes lifted his left palm towards the advancing beasts and made a sharp *chiss* noise from his yellowed, stained teeth. Shearing away the darkness, a bright ring of light pierced the night sky. It pulsed and whirled slowly. A similar ring of light erupted from the soil and stretched itself outwards, encircling the beasts. Abruptly, they were all sucked downwards into the ring along with debris from the field in a loud rush of wind. The ring winked out with a loud crack. All eyes turned to the second moon in the sky, pulsing with even greater light. Small, blackened objects slowly fell towards the Earth from over two miles up. For good measure, their bodies were twisted and corrupted when they emerged from the second ring. *If the fractured transformation didn't already kill them, the impact will*, thought Filodraxes. He felt drained and began to sink to his knees. He felt two massive hands take hold of him. Before he fainted, he peered into the concerned eyes of Koriet Leigh. *It is good to finally have this one*, thought Filodraxes, before he slipped into unconsciousness.

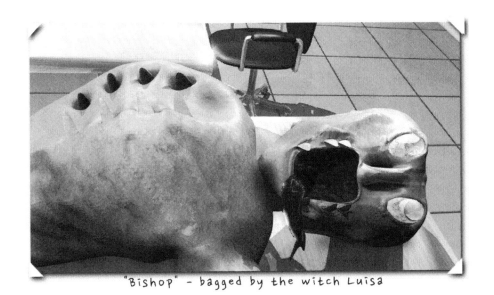

"Bishop" - bagged by the witch Luisa

Chapter Twenty Three:
Rip's Special Delivery

Filodraxes dreamt. When he was trapped in that miserable,
shriveled body, he did not dream. He lived in blackness, never ending
and unforgiving. For some short periods, he could hear his trusted
servant Danhieras speaking to him. At first, damning him for risking all
to attain immortality, then pleading to him for the strength to lead his
men. It was always hard to hear him—especially after the first few
generations when his eardrums hardened. He could yet feel him there,
chatting away as a young boy, measured discussion as an adult or
muttering and wheezing as a sage at the end of his years.

He recalled the good years, at the end of his reign in Babylon.
He was prosperous, commanded 11 of his fellow exiles and a human
army of over 200 thousand strong. He was standing on a massive
terrace amongst lush plants that cascaded over the walls. At last, life
held a sweet savor.

His eyelids fluttered and he was back in his bed in the infirmary.
Danhieras was watching him while sitting on a bed opposite. His shirt
was off and the young man that turned to stone was removing a wide,
black belt from his arm. He looked down and saw that Danhieras' left
hand was bent in a withered grip that disobeyed the owner. Filodraxes
tried to speak but felt his throat thick with mucus. He cleared his throat
and instinctively pulled out the plastic oxygen tubes from his nose just
before sitting up.

"Filodraxes, you should lie still until you regain your strength,"
said Rip. Although his face still felt somewhat numb, the left side of
his face was no longer paralyzed.

"Danhieras—don't you feel that I've lain long enough?"
wheezed Filodraxes. "Besides, it looks like you may need my help.
Would you mind telling me what our situation is?"

Rip briefed Filodraxes on recent events and introduced him to
the key members of the Lodge. He asked few questions and only
mildly questioned Rip's decision to blow himself up, hoping to take
Rothiel with him.

It was morning, and Kayanan helped both Rip and Filodraxes
ascend the stairs to the chow hall. There were several children of all

ages eating and talking amongst themselves. Rip shuffled to his usual chair at the end of the largest table, remembered who was behind him and offered the chair. "Please. Take this seat. You can better address them from here."

Rip sat in the seat next to him, while Filodraxes' eyes scanned the room, impressed by the smells of the food and efficiency of the kitchen. All of the children stopped eating and stared at the new arrival. Kayanan walked to the intercom, flipped a toggle switch and said simply, "Meeting. Chow Hall."

One by one, Rip's key team arrived and sat at the big table. Some looked worn out and before taking their seats, migrated to the coffee machine and filled up their mugs. Big Lee was the last one to arrive and had already shrunk back to his human-sized state. His stubby dog followed dutifully behind. He took the seat that no one occupied—the only chair in the room that could bear his weight.

Luisa walked in chatting loudly to Juani, still wearing the filthy clothes from the previous evening. Juani was trying to get her to be quiet and she directed the old woman to a separate table. Rip glowered at the woman and called Gellan over.

"Do me a favor son," whispered Rip in origin. "Go ahead and translate for Juani, but anything that may sound... sensitive, leave out. I don't want that old bitch sitting next to her to find out what's going on."

Rip spoke up in origin. "Lodge brothers and sisters. Last night the fortress was ambushed. I believe, that without a bit of intervention from our friends upstairs as well as the timely arrival of our leader here, we would be in a world of shit today. You've all learned about the master Filodraxes and have at one point or another seen him downstairs." He turned towards the old wrinkled man. "Do you wish to address them?"

Filodraxes nodded. He worked to clear his throat until he felt that his voice was strong enough to be heard. "I am impressed. I have never seen so many of you joined together before—this is indeed an achievement. Your origin has changed somewhat, but I am able to understand most everything that is said. Danhieras has done well leading you. I do not wish disrupt his fine teachings, so I shall allow his successor to remain in charge—I shall merely advise. I have discussed this with master Danhieras and he understands my reasons—the world has changed too much for me to understand at these final days of this life." He raised a hand towards the children's table. "I am even worse off than you. I have much more to learn of this strange world." He finished and looked at Danhieras. "What is *that* they are drinking?"

Danhieras looked at Kayanan. "Rick? Do you think his stomach can handle it?"

Kayanan stood up and walked to the coffee bar. "One cup shouldn't hurt. After all, he was bathed in this stuff just a few days ago." He put in two spoonfuls of sugar and some milk and set it down in front of Filodraxes. "Go slow, it's very hot."

Rip took this opportunity to brief the rest of the room. "I'm going to see Rothiel today. I intend to kill him. Unfortunately, this idea was set in motion years ago. If I had gone to Morocco prior to Rothiel's release we probably wouldn't have been attacked last night. Anyways, all players in this room as well as our east and west coast offices are to find me as soon as possible. I imagine that the hell I am going to stir up with my new parents will probably light up the press, so keep your eyes open."

Rip looked around the room and saw most nodding or whispering to each other. He glanced over at Gellan who was translating his speech to Juani. Her face shook in desperation as hot tears streamed down her face. *She couldn't possibly realize what humanity is up against*, thought Rip.

Rip stood and placed his hand on Filodraxes' shoulder. "Well, I'd best be on my way."

Simon stood up and walked with Rip upstairs to his room. Rip sat on his bed and tried to fidget with his shirt buttons. *Damn things are hard enough with two hands*, thought the old man as the fingers of his left hand dragged across his shirt without control or feeling. Simon bent down and undid the buttons of his shirt. When he opened the front, a deep purple stain was moving outward from Rip's heart. His body was already consuming the layers of fat under the skin.

"It doesn't hurt—it just itches." Mumbled Rip. "I need all these fats to bind their energy if I'm to blow up several houses. Most of my energy will be released in the fire—I'm fairly certain that I can take down a block of houses without too much damage to the surrounding areas."

Simon nodded and fetched a clean shirt. He helped push Rip's dead hand through the sleeve and then buttoned him up. He combed Rip's hair and then held up Rip's jacket with a questioning expression.

"Naw." Said Rip. "I'm already getting too darned warm. Besides, I really like that jacket--it would just be a waste. Remember to get my clothes dry-cleaned when I'm gone. Do you have your change of clothing?

Simon nodded. Gellan and Filthy appeared in the doorway.

"We're ready," said Filthy. "Do you want us to go ahead and start evacuating houses?"

Rip stood up and was steadied by Simon. "Yeah, why not. Wait until I walk into their building before you take out the first families. Once I go in, I'll wait to pop 15 minutes later. Not one minute later, do you understand?"

Simon reached down and handed the small duffel bag to Filthy. Filthy slung the bag over his shoulder and said a curt "Good luck."

Simon parked the green Seat car near the marina close to the lighthouse. Rip needed help getting out of the car from Simon and he leaned against the car while Simon locked the door and placed the keys in his pocket.

"Um. It's probably best that you leave the keys hidden under the tire or some place safe." Said Rip.

Simon remembered that Rip's heat would most certainly incinerate the keys in his pocket and promptly removed them. He placed them under the car, next to the tire where gypsies won't see them and then walked with Rip towards old town.

Rip had the feeling that they were being watched, but shrug off the danger. *After all, he was about to deliver death himself—what difference did it really make*, thought Rip. He tried to keep his thoughts on the game ahead and not think of the risk. *Simon can withstand anything so long as his oxygen level holds out. Gellan can swoop in and snatch him away if need be*, thought Rip.

They arrived at *calle central* and found that they were only three doors down from Rothiel's new residence. Rip caught sight of Filthy and Gellan, dressed in their *Salvagas* butane gas inspector clothing, going door to door with their clipboards. *All is ready.*

When Rip and Simon arrived at the door, Simon tried the knob. Locked. Rip nodded towards the door and Simon rapped sharply with his knuckles.

After a few seconds, a young man stepped up from behind them holding a shotgun. *"Que quieres?"* said the man. His irises were white and he was missing his fingernails. His pallor was ashen and areas of his skin were horribly dry and cracked. *Protraxis' work I imagine,* thought Rip.

Simon raised his arms in surrender and Rip merely looked away with indifference. The wooden door swung open and two more men stood looking at them with pistols tucked into their waistbands. They were in the same condition as the man with the shotgun.

Rip grunted and spat on the ground. "Take me to Valgiernas."

The three could not speak English but instantly recognized the name that the strange old man muttered. One of the men in the doorway stepped forward and frisked Rip and then Simon. When satisfied, he said, "Esta bien" and motioned for them to follow. They walked into the building and through the unkempt courtyard towards the back. Rip glanced down at his watch — 10:16.

When they arrived in the back, there was a secure, steel door with a numerical lock. There was a TV camera peering down at anyone outside the door and a monitor bolted to the wall that was dark. One of the two carefully hid the numbers with his torso and punched in the code. The door made a loud *clack* noise when the latch electrically opened and the guard passed through. Two minutes later the monitor glowed to life and filled with the grinning face of Valgiernas.

The speaker crackled to life with a slight german accent. "I see you survived our little party, old man!"

Rip grunted and looked at the two remaining men standing near him. "Why the two goons?"

"You really have to ask? Come now Danhieras, let's just call them a precaution. Besides, even *if* you were able to get past them, there's several more of them on our side of the door."

"I'm not here to discuss your crappy security, Val. I want to speak to *him*."

Valgiernas' smile receded a small amount, but his eyes displayed uncertainty. "Oh, I don't know about that," said Valgiernas, scratching his cheek. "He's a very, very busy man these days."

Rip glanced at his watch. *Got a few more minutes.*

"I'm sorry," said Rip. I thought your master was interested in a trade for Diano — I heard he was looking for him. If you're not interested, I guess we'll be on our way." Rip motioned for Simon that it was time to leave and they both turned from the monitor.

"Hold on boys—we just started talking! Maybe we can work something out, but you have to go through me."

"Val, if I don't see Rothiel's ugly face in two more minutes, the deal's off the table."

Valgiernas' face froze in anger and the smile drained from his face. He slowly nodded and got up from his chair, intentionally replacing the view of his face with his holstered hips. "Just hold your fucking horses."

After a short moment, a man appeared in the monitor and sat down. He stared into the camera and smiled. Although his face filled the monitor, he was not familiar to Rip. He wore a white sweatshirt and had dark hair and eyes. Rip and the man eyed each other for a moment. Neither had any recognition of each other. When Rip was getting ready to turn and leave, the speaker crackled and uttered in perfect origin, "Could this old, frail man be my brother Danhieras?"

Rip turned, astonished. He did not remember the features of Rothiel, but the voice he knew. It sent chills through his bones. "Rothiel?"

When he saw the recognition flow across Rip's face, Rothiel laughed hard. "Who else could I be? Listen to what you are hearing— these worthless cowards have forgotten our language. How did you manage to keep it intact?"

Rip's brow furrowed. "First things first-- my house. Why was it attacked?"

Rothiel waved a hand in dismissal and leaned back in his chair. "You own nothing, brother. Not even a house. I do, as I like. Remember who I am Danhieras—I own this world and that means everything on it-- you and your people as well." Rothiel drank in the anger that grew in the lines of Rip's face and wallowed in his satisfaction. "Think of it as my calling card. I have yet to exact punishment on the exiles that betrayed me. I'm glad you are here in any case. You may begin serving your punishment today."

Rip grinned and glanced at his watch. *It's go time.* "Punishment? Ha! First of all, your… *calling card* was defeated without a single casualty from our side. Secondly, we've been playing with the leftovers from your menagerie and we know what you and Protaxsis are cooking up. Here's my deal to you: You will agree to take your army of assholes somewhere else and give up any ideas on taking over this world. If you do not concur to a truce and peaceful co-existence, I will put a hurt on you so bad, you'll wish you were back in that fucking ball for all eternity!"

Rothiel shot to his feet and turned towards Valgiernas. "Do not kill them—take them alive!"

"You and what army," Rip chuckled and turned towards Simon. "Oh—Hey Simon? *Flagstone.*"

Valgiernas bellowed orders in Spanish to the guards in the lobby.

Simon acknowledged Rip's queue with a nod and then felt one of the guards roughly jerk his wrists behind his back and snap cold handcuffs in place.

Rip's clothes darkened as liquid ran from his pores all at once. He shut his eyes and felt the warm liquid cascade down over his eyes and mouth finally pouring onto his collar and shoulders. Wetness shot outwards, soaking his interior garments and saturating his shirt and trousers within a second. His shoes overflowed and a puddle expanded across the terrazzo floor. The guards that laid hands on him, recoiled from the cold touch and the strong vapor emanating from the liquid.

Simon's guard noticed the reaction to Rip's guards and grabbed a handful of Simon's hair in his hand and jerked his face towards his own. *"Que paso con ese!"* The guard's voice trailed off when he saw Simon's skin flash white and the soft hair held in his fist turned hard, as if made of stone. When Simon's irises faded from blue to white the guard muttered, *"Dios mio…"*

As Rip's skin became fully darkened he could feel the burning in the center of his body increase exponentially. *At a point, the energy will go wild and hunt on its own*, thought Rip. *I've got to go premature or the explosion will be too big.*

A man can spend his life building pyramids that fill the horizon or skyscrapers that coat the land in perpetual shade. He can convert lush forests into a naked, cauterized moonscape or punch yawning holes through mountains. Rip Damhorst let his accumulated life's energy go in a mere instant.

Rip felt as if he plummeted down a deep hole as his body was instantly consumed and collapsed to a size smaller than a speck of dust. His physical form disassembled but his mind continued to go along for the ride. *Not too much longer now.*

Rip's body winked out of sight. The transfer of Rip's 260-pound frame into the size of a bacterium sucked and tore asunder everything from the walls, including the men present in the room. Simon's rigid body resisted the crushing vacuum and careened around the room in the vortex, tearing large tracks of brick from the walls. The release of energy blew apart the large building and engulfed the interior in a massive fireball that rushed upward, churning everything in its path to carbon.

Gellan and Filthy had evacuated scores of women and children from the surrounding apartment buildings and herded them towards the lighthouse. Many were bickering that they couldn't smell any gas and why hadn't someone called the fire department? Filthy was tying up the loose ends of the crowd with his skills of persuasion until an enormous explosion rocked the old town. The women and children screamed as four massive buildings were consumed and brought down. A huge ball of fire ascended over the rubble and pulsed and shrieked as it sought sustenance. When the buildings fell, the fire burned itself out as it ran out of things to consume. Thick black smoke continued to course from the rubble.

Gellan rushed to the scene, carrying Simon's bag and just in case, a fire extinguisher. He found Simon lying naked in the rubble. Gellan pushed away the brick and charred beams and Simon's color returned. As he was helped to his feet, Simon brushed his hand through his softened hair and freed the charred remains of the henchman's fingertips. Simon cried out, bringing up his left wrist-- dangling the remains of the handcuff. Its twin was lost in the violent inferno. It was still blazing hot and Gellan quickly brought out a thermos from the bag and emptied ice water over Simon's wrist while Filthy used a ring of keys to release him from bondage. With the handcuff off, he wiped his soot-covered face with a damp towel and put on the sweatpants and shirt from the bag. Just before setting off for Gellan's car, he noticed the charred, black wire lying along the ground. It lay in the rubble, a stark contrast from the surrounding grey dust and red brick. It was the coaxial cable that ran to the monitor—it continued on the ground until it ran up the roof of an adjoining building, then over the street towards buildings in old town. The cable ran to a distant location where Rothiel sat, laughing at the static snow displayed on his monitor.

Chapter Twenty-Four:
Re-birth

Rip became bathed in an instant, overpowering flash of light that when it winked out, left Rip in total darkness. This moment of the transformation was not unpleasant. Rip felt serene — somehow this feeling tended to elude him while on Earth. He wasn't encumbered by the stress of managing the affairs of the Lodge or protecting the human race — after all, at this point he didn't really exist. He tended to place false hope that whatever it was that dragged him kicking and screaming into a new life would forget him — and just leave him floating in darkness, so that he could slowly dissolve and become part of nothingness itself.

This time, like the thousands of times before, he was not so lucky. The darkness that ran forever before him shuddered and glowed green. He felt a slight breeze on his cheek and gentle pressure under the soles of his feet. The green became brighter and separated into the thousands of leaves that he recognized as the willow tree. Light, dancing between the leaves of the tree, played a warm caress to his face and his ears filled with the noise of birds, music and loud cheering.

As he materialized, his eyes scanned the multitudes of smiling faces, loudly cheering his name. Then he saw her. She was the only one crying. She held a scarf — the one she stole from him in Copenhagen, clutched to her chest as her lips mouthed 'please', beseeching him to step away from the tree and remain with her forever. Her chest began to heave in sorrow when he did not step forward.

It could be so easy, he thought, as he drank in the sight of her. *Her lovely neck, the outline of her face.* He reflected that even in tragedy she's the most beautiful thing he's ever seen. *I've fought this guilt long enough. With Filodraxes back, I've done my part.* He could feel his knees quake. He knew that no matter what excuse he could dream up, he still had to make things right. He still had work to do — he had to bring his brothers home.

"I'm sorry," he choked out. He outstretched his hand to her and she did the same. "…But I must go back." The moment their fingertips touched, his fingers dissolved as cascading sand. He was again engulfed in a rushing darkness but this time there was no serenity. His soul cried out in anguish at the loss of Theo. The darkness tightened around him and pain racked his head. A final eruption of searing pain tore into his chest as the origin numeral one was branded anew into his small chest.

A few moments later he was out. Harsh, fluorescent light pounded his eyes and freezing air shook his diminutive body. A hard, rubber spout buried itself into his throat and sucked the warmth from his windpipe. The spout was yanked free and replaced by sour, freezing air. Before he could catch his breath, each nostril was equally ravaged and throbbed in pain. His ears were filled with the warbling sounds of beeping machines, and the voices of uniformed humans routinely preparing a newborn for the first day of its life. Rip always hated the first day for the massive headaches that he had to endure and being treated like a piece of meat. *At least they're speaking English*, thought the newly named Samuel Augustus Kaplan.

Great. A Jew. If this wasn't bad enough, I'm going to get snipped in a week, thought the newborn as he was brought to his new mother's breast.

Chapter Twenty-Five:
Saying Goodbye

Jim Smith wandered the streets of Rota following Rip's service at the Rota cemetery. He felt numb and confused. His suit was getting hot, so he took his jacket off and slung it over his shoulder. As he walked, he loosened his tie and tried to come to grips with how he felt. *How could he be dead? I can't believe I'll never see him again*, he thought. Elena was at Manoli's house and he decided it would be best to leave her there for now, walk home and try to get his emotions in order.

Jim thought about how he first heard of the explosion that took his friend's life. He had watched the base fire department rushing towards Rota and saw black smoke looming over old town. Butano bottles have blown up kitchens in the past, but not one that caused a chain reaction large enough to take down four buildings. He never knew why Rip was even there since he didn't even live in Rota.

He walked up the steps to his second floor apartment and fished out his keys. On the porch was a small package wrapped in brown paper. He bent down and picked it up. It said on the outside 'To brother Jim'. He turned the package over in a fruitless search for the return address.

He walked inside his apartment and sat down at the dining room table. He flopped his jacket down on an adjacent chair and began opening the package. On the top was a folded note. As soon as he opened the note he felt stunned. It was Rip's handwriting:

Jimmy,

For some time now, I haven't felt my best. I don't like to leave things unsaid, so if you are reading my note, I'm sure that at this moment you aren't feeling your best either.

As I'm writing this note, I have no idea how I ultimately die, but it's obviously happened. It's been my absolute pleasure being your friend and I didn't want to leave this shitty world without telling you that you've made this old man a better human being because of your influence.

Now, with all that sappy stuff aside, I also want you to know that all I've ever wanted was for you to join our lodge. Our Masonic lodge was not built upon rituals or secret handshakes, but by the bonds of true friendship.

If you honor me in your memories, you'll do me this small favor—inside this box you'll find a receipt for the $40.00 registration fee and my Masonic ring. Both are worthless, but mean the entire world to me. Please consider walking through the Lodge door not as a mere friend but as my brother. One of my lodge brethren will contact you when they have an appropriate date.

Very truly yours,

Lieutenant Roger Damhorst, US Navy Retired

P.S., if Gideon Blunt attempts to get money from you for the initiation, just show him the receipt and tell him to piss off.

Jim pulled the old ring out of the box and held it in his hand. The gold was a darker, copper color—the inside of the band read 10k. *Figures*, thought Jim. *Even if it was melted down, you couldn't get a dollar for it.* He tried to put it on his ring-finger but it was several sizes too large. He contemplated the man that once wore this ring with endless pride. He placed the ring and the receipt on his mantle and looked at them together. *Why didn't I do this while he was still alive?*

Jim sat on his couch and looked out his patio window at the blue ocean. As he watched the sunlight dance across the surface of the lazy swells, salty tears coursed down his face forming an infinitesimal bond between all the world's oceans—and a simple man who felt that his sorrow could replenish them several times over.

Chapter Twenty Six:
Symptoms

Jim Smith sat at his desk drawing a slow, black circle around today's date on his mil-spec desk calendar. Today was the six-month anniversary of Rip's death, but it still seemed like yesterday when the news slapped him across the face. The past few months seemed hollow and unsure without Rip's presence. Elena could now walk, and she's been learning a little English and a whole lot of Spanish. He reflected on what the Angel Clarence wrote to George Bailey in *It's a Wonderful Life*: 'A man who has friends is never a failure.'

Jim still had many friends, but the pool of buddies had tarnished with the loss of someone so brilliant. He checked his messages on his phone and heard Frank's message prodding him with a little less intensity — Frank knew how much Rip meant to him and was just letting him know that he feels his pain too.

Jim reached in his pocket and pulled out the letter he received the day before from someone named Gellan – apparently the reining Worshipful Master of Rip's Lodge. He thought about the invitation to join — he would be presenting himself at the lodge tonight. He missed his friend and intended to honor him with his last request. His reminiscing was shifted to annoyance when his phone rang. The ringer was always louder than expected and there was no way to stifle it. He had stuck band-aids on the bottom speaker, but it was still too noisy.

"Hello, DEA field office, Jim Smith speaking."

Chief Simmons was on the phone — he sounded out of breath. "Jim! I really need you to come over to medical — one of my AWOL guys just turned up and he's a real mess."

"You're at the base hospital?"

"Yes! Now get over here quick — you *gotta* see this. Jesus. Just come to the emergency room!"

Jim dropped the phone back in the cradle and walked the short distance to the base hospital. He wound his way through the hallways wrinkling his nose to the smell of antiseptic until he reached the emergency room and found his friend Deron sitting on the waiting bench holding a wad of cotton to his bleeding nose.

"What in hell..." said Jim, peering up at Deron's face. "Did this guy smack you or something?"

Deron opened his mouth and displayed his upper teeth, still coated with blood. His upper lip was swelling. "Well you know me, I always seem to get the weirdo's at my command. Murphy was missing for two days and he tended to hang out in gypsy bars. We've been trying to bust him on a urinalysis, but he's always come up clean."

Deron got up off the bench. "He's restrained in there," Deron said, pointing with his free elbow. "He's definitely on something, but no one knows what."

Jim pushed open the swinging doors and entered Emergency Room 1A.

Murphy was lying on a hospital bed with both his wrists and ankles shackled to the gurney by handcuffs. One Naval Security guard was lying in an adjacent bed getting stitches sewn into his scalp.

"The other cop," said Deron, while grimacing at the amount of blood in the wad of cotton. "Is in Xray getting his shoulder and neck scanned."

Jim walked over to Murphy to look at him. He had blood all over his lower face and shirt, but it didn't appear to come from him. He noticed that his skin was very white, almost ashen in color. His eyelids appeared closed and his lips dry, cracked and the color of pigeon shit. Murphy jerked forward, straining the cuffs and bed rails trying to get closer to Jim.

"Let me go *motherfucker*!"

Jim looked over at Deron and the other policeman. "No. That's not a very good idea—I'm still wearing my school clothes." Jim scanned the room and saw a box of latex gloves. He put on a pair.

Murphy groaned and strained against the cuffs. "I'm dying. I need... to get my medicine."

Jim thought he heard him slurring and he looked closer at Murphy's cracked mouth. He noticed that he was missing his teeth. "So, uh, what happened to his pearlies?"

"Deron nodded and sighed. "Good thing too, otherwise my nose and most of my ass would be inside his stomach." He grabbed a fresh wad of cotton off the examination desk and tilted his head back. "I say he's on angel dust—maybe he pulled his own teeth out days ago."

Jim lowered his head within a safe distance of Murphy's pillow. "Mr. Murphy—tell me about this medicine you've been taking."

"N-no. Fuck off. Take these cuffs off first."

The corpsman walked in carrying several printouts and a handful of empty blood vials. "How's the nose chief?"

"I think it's slowing down, " said Deron, examining the saturation of his wad of cotton. "No thanks to that prick. What did you find out with his blood test?"

The corpsman fanned out the litmus wicks on the table, alongside a reference manual identifying color swatches. "Well, preliminary tests show that he's clean—other than heavy amounts of protein in his urine. We won't know for sure until tomorrow morning when the complete urinalysis and blood tests come through. I'm going to need to take some more samples to check for blood markers."

"Jesus," said Jim, looking at Murphy's hands. "What happened to his finger nails?"

Deron shrugged. "Tap the skin on his hands if you want to see something even wilder."

Jim walked closer to the hospital bed and made sure the rails looked strong enough. He took one of Murphy's wrists into his own and gently rolled his hand over. The skin was darkened and tough. It looked the color of roast pork and appeared very hard, but not cracked. He tapped it several times and realized that it felt like thick coconut shell. The skin dividing the hand from the forearm had bubbled up with the same thick material, but the creases were hard but the seams flexible.

Jim couldn't believe what he was looking at. "He hit you with these?"

Deron was gently feeling his own teeth to make sure they weren't loose. "You better believe it—I felt like he was beating me with a hammer."

Murphy was wearing a bloodstained *Navy* sweatshirt and Jim gently pulled it up to expose his belly. The skin on his abdomen was the same. Any hair left on his skin looked like the trace amounts that are sometimes found on pork rinds. The skin felt hard and thick. Areas across his abdomen were split with flexible joints to allow movement. His breastbone was extruded and gave his chest an almost bird-like appearance. His chest looked more like a truck's snowplow than a man's chest.

"Just what the fuck is wrong with him?" Asked Deron, looking over Jim's shoulder. "Murphy—what have you been doing to yourself?"

Murphy began to squirm again and Jim moved away from the bed, fearful that he would shake the bed loose.

A portly doctor walked into the room wearing swim trunks and a damp t-shirt. "Why are there so many people in here—dear God—what in hell happened to him?"

The corpsman showed the Doctor the litmus tests and the state of Murphy's hands. The Doctor lifted Murphy's shirt with a frown. "Fire? Acid damage? How did he get like this?"

Deron walked in front of the Doctor. "Sir, he didn't look like this a week ago."

The Doctor put on latex gloves and ran fingers down his tissue. "Well these wounds aren't fresh—they must be at least six months old. I need all of you gents to leave so I can examine him."

The men left the room and walked back into the waiting room. Deron was the first to break the silence. "This is bullshit—he looked fine just a week ago. His eyes were turning white, but he wouldn't go to medical."

Jim was thinking about the thickness and feel of the skin. "Wait, what do you mean his eyes were turning white?"

"Human nature, really." Said Deron. "When you suspect someone is lying to you, you watch their eyes. He was being evasive, so I watched his eyes carefully. That's when I noticed that his irises had become white. I thought he was getting sick or something and had him sent over. He ran off once he got here."

"Where did you find him?"

"Benny's bar out in Rota. They called base security when they found him. He had broken in during the night and raided their kitchen. He was as quiet as a lamb when they put him in the truck. When they took him over to the brig, I guess he puked up some black goo, so they ran him straight over here."

Jim thought a long while. "I don't know about you, but I've never *heard* of anything like this before."

Doctor Goodman walked out of the room looking more worn from his encounter with Murphy than all day at the beach. "Chief Simmons? You're his department head?"

Deron stood up. "Yes sir. And, I'm telling you that a week ago he didn't look like that."

Doctor Goodman rubbed his hand through his unkempt hair. "I'm actually the duty obstetrician. The general practitioner is ill, so I was called in. I've been in medicine for almost thirty years and I don't know... what's wrong with that man."

Jim thought about the loss of color of the eyes as well as the thickening of skin. "Did he speak to you?"

"Well, he isn't making much sense. He keeps asking about his medicine—he calls it *Cambio*."

Chapter Twenty Seven:
Initiation

Jim called Frank as soon as he returned to his office. They spoke at length about what Jim saw and the destruction Murphy had caused. Frank brightened up and told him that he had a book to show him during lunch. Later at the Windjammer club, Frank brought along a large, red book called *Incredible Life*, by William Corliss.

He had Jim read the chapter on a man who frequently shed his old skin, leaving newborn-like skin underneath. Jim read the passage with a touch of skepticism and pointed out that in the examples, there was no mention of changing eye color.

"Phooey." Spat Frank. "Just details. You got a better explanation, Trixie-bell?"

Jim winced when he heard Frank loudly calling him cutesy, girlie-names when he felt challenged. Jim sighed. "Yes, matter of fact, I do have a possible explanation." Jim sat up straight in his chair and poured Frank another glass of Sangria. "This Murphy guy was taking some type of drug—he could have been taking anabolic steroids or anything that could kick-start some form of... Oh, I don't know, some weird type of psoriasis."

Frank belched out laughter and smacked the table hard. "Crap! Nothing but weak, crap!" He looked at Jim's empty glass. "What'sa matter lightweight? Aren't you going to have some?"

Jim shook his head. He wanted to remain clear-headed for his initiation that would start in an hour's time. "No. Tonight is my initiation."

A huge smile grew across Frank's face, but the meanness in his eyebrows stayed put. "You...have...got to be kidding me. You're joining the Masons? Why?"

Jim shifted in his chair. "It's something," he began. "Well, Rip had been bugging me for years and it was his last request—for me."

"Jim," Frank began with a more sympathetic tone. "No offense, but Freemasons aren't what you think they are. You're going to be sitting in a room with a bunch of old, bored retirees giving each other secret handshakes. Then the real truth of Masonry will be revealed to you; that they have no real power to change things and you will be roped into a pyramid scheme to generate money for some slick-willy at the top."

"Frank, I don't know what to expect. I just want to take this first step to see what Rip liked about it." Jim checked his watch and realized that it was probably time to head over.

Frank stood and grabbed Jim's arm. "Good luck *Nancy*." Frank looked dead straight into Jim's eyes. "Rip was a nice guy, but *you ain't gonna find him at that lodge*. He's gone—forever. I don't want to disappoint you, but if you are attempting to get closer to your friend you'll have to wait for the next life."

"...Thank you Frank. I have no *frigging* idea what you meant, but I'm glad you care. I'll call you tomorrow and tell you how many times they paddled me."

Jim turned, and walked towards the door. When he looked back Frank was sitting back down looking right at him with a sad look on his face. Jim stopped and wondered why Frank would look so dejected.

"Gretchen!" Frank screamed over the noise of the crowd. "If they harm one hair on your creamy, white ass with that paddle, they are going to hear from me!"

Embarrassed and with a reddening face, Jim hurried out of the club amid the crescendo of guffaws and whistles.

Jim pulled his green Seat up to the small, pre-fab building located near the drive-in movie theater. There were about eight cars, a large flatbed truck and a minibus already parked outside in the sand and an old man was standing outside waiting for him. As Jim locked the door of his green Seat, he noticed Rip's old yellow Renault. He walked to the back and looked at the license plate. It was his all right. Jim looked in through the window and noticed a child seat strapped to the back. *Figures*, thought Jim. *Rip hated kids. One of his lodge buddies must have kept it.*

Jim walked over to the lodge, towards the old man standing outside. The man had wispy white hair and was wearing an apron. In his left hand, he was holding a thin, decorative sword. "Hi, are you Jim Smith?"

The man took Jim's outstretched hand in his. "I'm Jess Lopez. Sorry about the sword—it's an old tradition—I'm playing the part of a Tyler."

Jess looked at Jim's light coat and tie. "You're a bit overdressed. We're going to begin in just a few minutes. Are you ready to get into your attire?"

Jim nodded politely and followed Jess into a forward area of the lodge building that was no bigger than a broom closet. The building was probably 20 years old and smelled twice as old. A crude sign on the wall read 'Preparation Room'. Jess rummaged through some dusty drawers and pulled out a torn t-shirt and equally ripped sweat pants. "Here. Put these on please. Oh-- Are you wearing any jewelry?"

"Um, no." said Jim as he pulled off his shoes. *Maybe Frank was right after all*, thought Jim. Through the thin walls, he could here the dull sounds of voices engaged in some type of ritual. He could hear the banging of a gavel and people stomping around the raised floor on the other side of the door.

When Jim had removed his clothes and put on the torn clothing, Jess pointed to his socks. "Those have to come off too, I'm afraid."

Jim pulled off his socks and felt relieved to have trimmed his nails just the night before. One of the sleeves was missing and was slit up to the neckline. He pulled it up so that at least most of his upper torso was covered.

Jess walked up behind him. "Wow, you're really tall. I'm going to put this blindfold on you. Nothing strange is going to happen during the ritual—it's just a formality. One thing though, if someone asks what you wish for most—ask for light." With that, Jess reached up behind him and tied a full-face blindfold behind his head. When it was in place, he felt the man gently pull a rope over his head.

Jess noticed that Jim jumped slightly when the noose rested against his neck. "Just another formality—it's a rope that goes over your neck and around your waist. It will be explained to you in a moment. There. Let's bring you over to the door... that's perfect."

Jim kept his eyes closed and tried to listen to his environment. His feet could feel areas of the old carpet that were worn through to the plywood floor.

Jess knocked on the door three times.

Jim thought he heard, "Hark! There is an alarm at the door of the Preparation Room!" Jim sniggered and his head bonked lightly against the door. *Jesus, the door's an inch from my nose*, he thought as he regained his composure. Someone on the other side of the door pounded on the door three times with such ferocity that the noise wracked Jim's hearing. At once, the door was yanked inwards and the vacuum nearly sucked Jim inside as well.

"WHO...GOES...THERE!" Yelled Hank, just centimeters from Jim's nose.

Jess looked at his index card. "Uh, a poor, lost candidate who um, --oh yeah, is in the dark, yet seeks the light."

Jim could hear snickers coming from the inside of the lodge. Someone near the back was muttering for quiet.

"Has he been duly prepared?"

Jess looked at his card, then flipped it over to the back. That answer was missing from his notes. "...I guess so?"

Hank leaned over and whispered, "Yes, he's been divested of all minerals, blah, blah."

Jess rose up on the balls of his feet when he remembered. "Of course, sorry. Yes! He's been divested of all minerals and metals."

There was a moment's silence as Hank looked at Jim's clothes. "...One of his tits needs to hang out Jess," he whispered.

Jim felt a big hand grip the top of the torn shirt and in one violent yank, ripped the shirt downwards to his waist.

A guffaw roared from the back of the room and was promptly muffled.

"The candidate is to wait," yelled Hank. "Until I inform the Worshipful Master!" With that, Hank took one step back and slammed the door with such force that the crash sent shockwaves through Jim's eardrums.

"You're doing fine, Jim," Said Jess, still gently holding the back of his arm. "Brother Hank is kind of a character."

Jim could hear more pounding of something hitting the floor and the same man's voice shrieking that there was "a candidate outside the preparation room." He heard a soft-spoken person ask questions and again more pounding on the floor, answered by someone's gavel beating on a table.

Jim could feel movement from the trailer's floor that someone was once more, approaching the preparation door. *Shit. Here we go again*, he thought.

Hank balled up his fist and again, slugged the door three massive times. The impact was so strong, that small bits of veneered wood cracked off and popped harmlessly against Jim's blindfold. Immediately following the last knock, the door was once again wrenched open and the vacuum gently rocked Jim and Jess forward. Jim felt three loud blows against the floor inches from his foot. The man was clearly beating a staff of some type against the floor.

Hank inhaled an enormous gulp of air prior to screaming at the top of his lungs, "The Worshipful Master invites the candidate inside!" In a more hushed tone, Hank whispered, "You can come in and sit down, Jess." Hank grabbed Jim by his other arm and guided him forward. In a soft voice, he steered him to the right and had him come to a stop. "Right there, perfect."

Jim felt three loud whacks of the staff on the floor followed by two short clacks of a gavel. The man next to him inhaled, then shrieked, "Junior Warden of the South, I have a candidate for your viewing!" Jim's ears began to ring.

Someone was giggling and had trouble composing himself. People were tittering on all sides of him. He also heard a soft sound like a water droplet or the sneeze of a mouse.

Finally composed, Filthy said gently, "Is the candidate truly prepared?"

Jim heard the inhale. "YEEESS!"

More laughter. Again Jim heard the short, high-pitched noise that sounded no louder than a drop of water.

"OK then," said Filthy, struggling to maintain his composure. "Convey the candidate to the Senior Warden in the West for his inspection."

There was one short clack of a gavel and Jim was once again yanked in the opposite direction towards what he assumed was the other side of the room.

His guide spoke softly to him as he was brought to the other side of the room with comments like, "Careful with your foot there—that's good. A little to your left—Ah, that's great."

Again, three huge whacks to the floor from the staff, followed by two short clacks from a gavel. Again, he heard his guide inhale his almost limitless lungs and scream, "Senior Warden of the West! There is a candidate for your viewiiing!"

Silence. Kayanan looked sullenly at Hank and mouthed a silent, *what the fuck?* He looked towards the East, nodded, and then whacked his gavel twice. "Is the candidate prepared?"

"SHIT YES!" Hollered Hank. Big Lee let out another tirade of booming laughter.

Kayanan rose to his feet, glaring at Hank the entire time. He approached the left side of Jim and whispered, "Is this of your own free will?"

Jim's ears were ringing, but he heard what was whispered. "Yes."

"Convey the candidate to the altar," said Kayanan. "To await inspection by the Worshipful Master."

Hank slammed the staff into the floor three times then gently spun Jim around towards the altar. The altar was a simple affair that looked more like a children's picnic table with padded seats and a marble top. On the surface, rested a fat King James edition bible and some lit candles. Hank brought Jim to the altar and helped him kneel on the padded bench.

Silence. Jim again heard the short, high-pitched cooing noise. His bare knees could feel cheap vinyl stretched over foam padding. *The altar top was cold—probably marble*, he thought.

"Who goes there?" Asked Gellan, sitting in the throne-like wooden chair. He wore a top hat on his head.

"A poor, blind candidate, Worshipful," said Hank, no longer yelling. "Who wishes to be brought from darkness to light."

Gellan stood from his throne and approached the altar. "Is he duly prepared?"

"He is, Worshipful," replied Hank, in the same reverent tone. "He is well qualified and comes under the tongue of good report."

Jim could feel this 'Worshipful' man whisper near his left ear: "Is this of your own free will?"

Jim detected a slight English accent from the man. "Yes."

"Very well," replied Gellan. He opened the large book lying in the center of the altar in front of Jim. "In front of you is a bible. I want you to bow your head and kiss the page, providing proof of your honest intent."

Jim bowed his head slowly until his nose picked up the smell of processed paper. His lips brushed against the pages, so he gave an audible smooch noise in case they felt he didn't go all the way. Then he heard it even more clearly—an 'ickoo' noise, soft yet high-pitched. It was the noise a german cuckoo clock would make if smothered in towels. This time, the noise came from directly across from him. *Obviously this 'Worshipful' fellow had a strange case of hiccups,* thought Jim.

"Very well," said Gellan. "You, being in a condition of darkness, what is it you most desire?"

Jim remembered what Jess had instructed. "...Light?"

Jim heard a soft inhale. "Verry well." The voice was high-pitched and sounded like a toddler. "Gib ow candle- candle-date... aw hell, gib him light."

Jim felt hands untie, then remove his blindfold. He blinked and looked into the darkness. Twin candles lighted the altar, one on each side of the opened bible. Opposite from him knelt a slim black man wearing a tuxedo and top hat. Jim looked around the room for the mysterious child's voice but only saw men wearing grins.

"Hi Jib!" The child's voice again came from right in front of him. Jim looked at the man kneeling across from him and saw movement just below his chest. He squinted in the dim light and rose higher on his knees to get a better look over the altar's surface. He saw a white baby strapped into a restraint attached to the man's chest. The child kicked in excitement and smiled. Jim noticed that he was wearing a yellow bib that was embroidered with *'Rippy'*.

Jim stood up from the altar in horror. Children that young should not be able to speak. The baby frighteningly looked like a chubby, infant version of Rip Damhorst. Jim felt his head swim as little flecks of light danced across his eyes and his knees buckled. He heard a man standing next to him yell "Whoa!" and was caught before he hit the floor. He was gently lowered to the carpet. Jim's eyes played around the room in fear. He looked back at the baby. *By God, it really looks like him,* he thought.

Gellan removed his hat and laid it on the altar and came around to inspect Jim. As the man knelt over Jim, the baby attached to his chest swung very close to his face and it now held a serious look—the same methodical frown that Rip constantly wore. "Hum," said the baby. "Sum buddy hit da lights pleeth."

Fluorescent lights hummed to life and bathed the small room in harsh, white light. Jim's feeling of dread compounded now that he could see greater detail—the baby was a spitting image of Rip, albeit young.

The baby wiped a face-full of drool from his chin using the bib. "Jeezuh-- Sorry Jib. I'b only god foh teeth, an id makes me droowel—are you ogay Jib?"

"Perhaps," said Gellan. "It would be better if I explained things." Gellan helped Jim up to a sitting position and unbuckled Rip from his Baby Belly carrier and set him on the floor between them. "Mr. Smith? My name is Gellan." He hooked a thumb at the baby seated on the floor, hiccupping every few seconds. "Rip Damhorst, I believe you already know."

Chapter Twenty Eight:
Forget What You Know

Jim knelt near the toddler and examined him close up with a perplexed look. "His cheek mole, same damned expression — everything."

"I tol ya. Idz mee, Jib." The baby yawned wide, and almost toppled backwards. He began to rub his ears.

"Aw shit," said Big Lee. "His ears. He's gonna pop if you don't get his ass outside now."

Rip went back to squeezing his toes through his yellow footie pajamas as a steady stream of drool ran off his chin. "Id's nutting — I jus tired das all."

Gellan went back to explaining Rip's condition to Jim. "...As exiles, we die and come straight back — Rip was born just after he died... with most of his memories intact." He unzipped Rip's pajamas slightly and opened the shirt near the collar. "Look here — his birthmark — the origin number one."

Jim examined his birthmark more closely. "It looks like a hatchet or something. Why a number one?"

"Rip was the first of us to figure it out. When we were first exiled on Earth, we were each branded with the number thirteen. Rip believed that we were to atone for what he had done through servitude to man. He began a movement — this organization, to help humankind. After a few hundred years, he was born with the number twelve."

Rip and Big Lee continued to verbally jab each other. Gellan felt he was having trouble getting his point across to Jim. "Will you guys please give it a break?"

"Idz himmm," said Rip. "I'b a lit'l tired, bud he needz do bag the fug off!"

Big Lee jumped up from his cement chair. "Bullshit, dog! Look at him! He's playing with his ears! If he doesn't get a bottle and get put to sleep, he's going to burn this bitch down!"

Gellan looked over at Kayanan. "You smell anything?"

Kayanan squatted down next to Rip. "Not sure — he may just have a wet diaper." He slid his hand down the back of his pj's and fished a finger into the back of his diaper to check. "Hmm. He could use a change—I think we should wrap this up and get him home just in case."

"I'b fiiine," whined Rip. "Dis guy iz pithing me off an I need..."

"See?" Yelled out Big Lee, pointing to Rip's face with a fat forefinger. "Now he's cryin'. He's gonna spin himself up just like last night..."

Kayanan wrinkled up his nose. "He's got a point, I can smell it now."

Gellen pointed at Big Lee. "Corey—get him outside, now. We'll change him out in the truck and give him some electrolyte water. He should pipe down when we get him into his car seat."

Corey's big palms closed around Rip's small chest just as his face flashed red and he began to howl at the ceiling. Flames erupted underneath Rip's clothing and everyone standing nearby got out of Big Lee's way as he trotted his flaming package outside. Kayanan stamped out the small fire that erupted in the carpet where Rip was sitting.

Jim sat stunned. Some of the older men in the lodge that Gellan said weren't origin, were enjoying the show—but weren't entirely shocked at what happened. *This is all becoming too much to believe*, he thought. *First, that most of the men in this building aren't human and that Rip is back from the dead. Then he goes up in flames and no one bats an eye.*

Gellan noticed that Jim was as white as a sheet. "I apologize. Rip has some special abilities—namely, the means to create violent, pyrochemical compounds with his body. Very powerful, but unstable—especially when he loses self-control."

Jim stood up and touched his hand to his temple. His head hurt. "Are you saying he's OK?"

"Right as rain. Cory Lee can't be hurt by fire either—that's why he's the one that usually carries him around. Can't say the same for Rip's biological mother though—she suffered some third-degree burns when he was just a newborn—we didn't get there in time to snatch him away before he did damage. Oh, don't worry about her—we picked up her medical costs and even purchased her a new home. She doesn't even remember having him, thanks to Mr. Blunt."

"Yeah," said Jim, looking at Gellan sideways. "I'm pretty sure I know what his speciality is."

"Tell you what," said Gellan, "Let's get your clothes back on and we'll give you a tour of the Fortress—I'll explain the rest on the way."

"We're not monsters." Gellan drove the yellow Renault towards Puerto with Rip strapped into the rear child seat, snoring softly. He had a diaper change and now wore blue pj's with a bib that said '*Li'l Shit*'. Jim sat in the passenger side and listened to Gellan explain the history of the Exiles and a brief mention of someone named Rothiel. Jim kept turning around to look at Rip's sleeping form. Buckled into the seat next to him was a fat, red fire extinguisher. "Are you sure he won't come around—you know, and start burning up the car?"

Gellan looked at Rip in the rearview mirror. "Double-dose of Children's Tylenol. I don't like to do it, but we need him calm. If he does set the car on fire, the extinguisher is for us. He can sit there until the car is turned to ashes and he won't suffer any harm."

The Renault pulled up to the gate and Gellan punched in a numerical code. A young girl's voice crackled to life over a small speaker and said: "Charlie, 3, 3, 4."

Gellan counted off numbers from his fingertips while his lips mumbled silently. "Um, Cavalier, 1734."

The gate in front of them began to swing inwards the voice said, "Correct. Thanks Gellan. I hope everything went well with the conduit."

"Thanks Trudy. You'll get to meet him in a moment."

With that, he put the Renault in gear and drove into the ranch. The other vehicles followed through the gate. "The guys somehow make sure I'm the first one at the gate," said Gellan laughing. "The code to get into the gate changes every hour and I'm able to calculate it faster than they can. Big Lee takes forever and Filthy—I mean, Gideon-- isn't even *allowed* to access the gate by himself."

"What did she mean by *conduit*?"

"I think it'll be better if we explain that later."

Jim sat in the living room of the Fortress sipping his coffee as Gellan carried Rip to his room, changed him into a fresh diaper and placed him in his crib. A few men walked into the living room and sat down on the big, leather couches. A few children walked past and stole glances towards the stranger and whispered excitedly towards each

other. A tall, fat man walked into the room and extended a burly hand
—Jim recognized him as the man that was antagonizing Rip.

"Corey Lee—everyone 'round here calls me Big Lee." To Jim,
his hand was so large that it felt like he was shaking hands with a
catcher's mitt filled with lead. Although chubby, his hand felt like
stone. "It's gotta be some kind of shock, seeing all of this at once." He
walked over to the far wall and plopped down on a huge gray chair—
one that didn't give when he sat down.

Jim noticed that he was wearing some kind of strange sandals—
the bottom rubber looked like the thick tread of a car tire.

"Sorry about the wait," said Gellan, walking back into the room.
"I see you've met Big Lee. "The rest should be here shortly—we'll go
into more detail of what we're about and where you come in."

A short, stout dog trotted in and started wagging his tail when he
saw Big Lee. He stopped and looked over at Jim.

"Tha's my dog, Enano." Said Big Lee. "You don't want to pick
him up though."

The dog sniffed Jim's pant leg, snorted, and then trotted over to
Big Lee's chair. He licked Big Lee's foot a couple of times, then
flopped over on his side and laid still.

"Cute dog," said Jim.

"He shits twice as much as he eats, but at least he goes outside."
The man was standing near the back of the room, but Jim didn't notice
him until his outburst. "I'm Ricardo Kayanan—Rip always spoke very
highly of you."

Jim shook his hand and became aware of how slim he was, but
his hand was knotted with muscle. He was built solid. "Thanks. –I
remember you from dart's night—Rip—I mean, when he was older-- he
introduced us then."

Gellan took a seat across from Jim and nodded. "Precisely. You
see Rip has known you for years because he sought you out. We have a
man downstairs by the name of Seth. He is able to look into something
like a crystal ball and find out where to find certain people. Every now
and again 'specials' are brought into the world that have certain talents.
A couple of years ago, Seth found just such a person—you, in El Paso
Texas. As luck would have it, you were working for a government
agency that we just so happen to have a *unique relationship* with. Rip
put in for your transfer and brought you here."

Gellan opened a green folder and began leafing through some of the entries. "You were always good at things that you didn't practice with. You were as good or better as the best man in your high school football team. You were the same with all sports. Math came easy to you, yet you never studied. Your handwriting always changed styles— sometimes flowery and delicate, sometimes stark and angular—haven't you ever wondered why?

There was the time, however that you sat for an exam and hardly got any of the answers correct. You always wondered why you did so well in the classroom but did so horribly in exams or at home. The answer is; you channel off the energies of others near you. The exam in question was a makeup test that you took after being sick. The only other person in the room was your P.E. coach. The energy wasn't there and you didn't understand the content in front of you."

Jim shifted uncomfortably in his seat.

"Still, we had to make sure ourselves." Gellan continued. "You may not have realized it, but you have been tested to check your skills, speed and self-control—by interacting with us. I helped you with your run a while back, Ricardo assisted in your darts game and Gideon over there..." Gellan pointed to Filthy sitting sheepishly in an easy chair. "Tried to throw a whammy on you just like he does to everyone else, but this time, you were able to feed it right back to him—no one's ever been able to do that!"

There was some sniggering around the room and Filthy seemed to turn red.

"The ability you possess is loosely called 'conduit'. You are able to mimic and sometimes surpass the abilities of anyone if you concentrate hard enough. What we would like to do is help coax your abilities to become stronger and more manageable. To tell the truth, we are going to be confronted with something formidable and we are going to need your help."

Jim sat quietly on the couch, saying nothing but turning things over in his mind. *It all sounds so far-fetched*, he thought. "I'm no one special," he blurted out. "I've seen a lot here that I don't know if I can really believe-- but I'd do it for Rip. How can I help?"

Gellan fished out a government form, already filled in. "This is a TAD request form—all it requires is your signature. Starting tomorrow, you'll begin your training, here at the fortress."

"...What kind of training?"

"All kinds," said Kayanan, reaching behind him. He pulled out something metal and shiny. It was the size of a small ashtray, but appeared to be very sharp by the way he handled it with such care. He held it up so that Jim could get a good look. It was thin and similar to the shape of a butterfly. He held it by his index finger and thumb. As Jim looked at it, he somehow knew its heft and knew that it was dangerous. Kayanan flipped it onto the top of his hand and let it roll across his knuckles until it reached his little finger. Then he rotated his hand and let it roll across the palm. He repeated it faster until it was just a blur—fingers jerking and hand rotating. The butterfly spun in an almost fluid motion as if it hovered just above his skin. At once, Kayanan backhanded the air and the butterfly accelerated towards a beam in the ceiling over the fireplace. The impact made a dull thud as the butterfly became buried in the dark wood. When Jim looked back at Kayanan, he was holding out another butterfly towards him. "Careful," said Kayanan. The edges of the wings are razor sharp."

Jim reached out and took the butterfly from him the same way he held it. He held it for a moment trying to remember how he flipped it onto the back of his knuckles—*it's mostly all sharp edges*, thought Jim. *How the hell can you juggle this if it slices your hands to ribbons?* He thought more on how Ricardo was able to juggle it until it somehow just popped to the top of his hand. The bottom of the butterfly was now resting on his index finger—he thought if he could just get it to hop head to tail across his knuckles, the blades wouldn't touch him. Before he could finish that thought, the butterfly was already at his little finger.

"Damn!" Blurted out Big Lee. "He learns fast!"

Jim realized that Big Lee's laughing voice was the same laughing at him during the lodge. By the time he looked down, the butterfly was effortlessly spinning across the top and bottom of his hand just like Ricardo. He felt perfectly in control. He kicked up the speed and the blade began to whine as it arced across his hand. He looked up at the beam and felt the familiar spider strand pull towards the butterfly's half-buried twin. He backhanded the blade towards the beam and it cracked into the old wood just a centimeter above the first butterfly.

Wow! Thought Jim. *Did I actually do that?* He looked down at his hand and saw two thin lines weeping droplets of blood from the tops of his fingers.

"You need to slow down a bit, Jim." Said Kayanan. "They're just scratches-- I'll get you some bandages."

"You'll be killing monsters in no time, Jimbo!" Laughed Big Lee.

"Speaking of which," said Gellan. "Ricardo, why don't you invite Diano in to meet Mr. Smith?"

Chapter Twenty Nine:
This Is War

Jim arrived back at his apartment just after 11:30 at night. He regretted being so late and had told Manoli that he would be back before 10:00. He opened the door and Manoli woke up on the couch.

"I'm so sorry. –It took longer than I thought."

She got up and smiled. *"No te preocupes.* It's nothing. She went asleep at nine."

Jim fished out a five mil note and handed it to her. "Thank you for this—I'm sorry I was late."

They both heard Elena moving around in her crib. A soft yawn, followed by a sneeze.

Manoli hushed to a whisper. *"Calla—*she's waking up." She waved and walked out of the door, closing it softly.

"Papa. Hola, Hola?" Said Elena.

"Shhh. Go back to sleep sweetie." Jim was too wired from what he saw to go to sleep. He sat in the easy chair and turned on the TV with the volume low. It was the news, but all he could think about was this evening's events. *Diano. What on Earth was it? It was so big it came in hunched over—almost on its hands and knees. One of his horns kept scraping the ceiling of the hallway. I wouldn't have been more shocked if it was Satan that came into that living room,* he thought.

It could speak Spanish, but by God that thing's voice! As it moved around the room I felt threatened the entire time.

He remembered what Ricardo whispered in his ear—*"Can you feel it? Where would you strike if you were fighting it?"* Somehow he knew that the claws were deadly—as were it's powerful jaws and sharp teeth. He knew he had to get behind it and attack the neck or lower spinal cord. He found in all of his fear, concentrating on the ligaments behind his legs, the soft tissue at the elbow and the jugular. He didn't know if he was in Ricardo's mind or if he was in his.

"Hola? Papa?"

"Sleep darling. Daddy's gotta think."

Gellan spent ten minutes entering in the events of the evening in his database. His fingers were a blur across the keyboard as paragraph begat paragraph at lightning speed. He wore his headphones and listened to *Tangerine Dream*—only when played loud could you hear the subtle changes in the song's mood.

His door flung open. Seth was standing in the doorway yelling at him with his blindfold on. When Gellan pulled off his headphones he heard Seth's loud voice.

"Get everyone now! Why aren't you answering the damn phone?"

Gellan ran up to him. "I'm sorry—had my headphones on—what's going on?"

"The kid was here. Cesar. He said that Rothiel knows about the conduit and he's going to kill him and his daughter tonight—*now!*"

Gellan flew to the intercom and hit the red button. "All seniors to the main living room now! Be dressed and ready to go!"

The big diesel trundled into Rota with Filthy lead-footing the entire way. They stopped halfway between Jim's apartment and Virgen De Los Dolores, where Manoli lived. The men weren't sure if Elena was spending the night there, so it was best to send a team. Big Lee trotted down to the beach, outside the harsh glare of the streetlights and expanded himself. He could unfold in less than three seconds and with his full size would make short work of the beach route to Jim's apartment. It was too risky to bring Diano out of the fortress, so he remained there with Gellan and Filodraxes to protect their headquarters.

Hank and Gideon walked briskly with Enano towards Manoli's house. They didn't know what to say, but they had to make sure everyone was safe, and then get Jim and Elena back to the fortress. The dog began to howl.

Kayanan sped down the sidewalk with Simon in tow. They were careful to make sure they weren't headed into an ambush. Kayanan smelled the air for the tell tale signs of Valgiernas.

It was dark and Manoli walked briskly towards her home. The dim, yellow streetlights played tricks on the mind, bushes and palm trees cast shadows of things reaching for her—she just shut them out and increased her pace. When she got home, she heard rustling at the end of her street. There was something coming towards her. Normally she wouldn't be concerned about gypsies walking down the road, but this time she felt the fear in her bones. She fished out her keys and opened the door. She quickly went inside and locked the door. The door had a deadbolt and gypsy bars on the windows kept predators out, but this time she still worried. There was clunking around upstairs. "Oscar! What are you doing? You'll wake your grandmother!"

"It's not me—it's my toys!"

The front door rattled. Manoli ran up and put both hands on the door in a vain attempt to keep the door from being kicked inwards. Something large and sharp pushed its way through the door, splintering wood in its path. It grazed Manoli's arm and she shrieked in pain. Another black claw tore into the door and began pulling it outwards into the street. Loud cracking noises exploded from the door as it was torn from its hinges. A dark shape slowly crept into the house towards the woman as she backed away from the door crying. Two quills shot out of the creature and buried themselves into her ankles. She dropped to the floor.

"*Dejara mi Madre!*" Screamed Oscar, standing at the bottom of the steps, terrified at the sight of his mother in pain. In each hand, were the two hefty statues, fiercely wriggling their arms and legs. Their violent movements spun them free from the boy's grip and they both fell, clattering to the stone floor. Once free, they doubled their speed, beating their balled fists into the terrazzo floor, sending shards of stone flying as they clanked towards the black creature. The drone didn't know what to make of the two statues—it hesitated and then shot a quill towards the bronze one—it merely deflected off. The iron statue arrived at the drone first and leaped upwards, wrapping it's legs around its arm near the shoulder. It immediately began raining fists down upon its head, knocking it down. The power of each strike was enormous and crushed areas of the drone's armor with each impact. The bronze one finally got in range, jumped and began a hail of strikes on the creature's left side.

"*Matalo!*" yelled Oscar as he gripped his mother in fear. His toys punished the creature with terrific speed. The drone rolled out of the house and tried to fend off the two statues as two more creatures approached, another drone and a bishop. They both watched the first drone rolling on the ground in agony, then slow as death began to overcome it. A long growl erupted behind them.

"Oh, fuck, there's two of them!" moaned Filthy. Enano was dragging them both down the sidewalk and growling.

Filthy saw the hideous faces of the creatures and instinctively tried to slow the dog down. "Hank, they're coming this way!" He fumbled with his pump shotgun, but Enano kept yanking him off-balance.

"They're not going anywhere." Hank inhaled and both creatures halted. The Bishop looked in all directions for the invisible force pushing him down to the sidewalk. Cracks appeared in the walls of the houses that lined the street as their combined weight was rapidly transferred to the two remaining creatures. Their joints buckled as the weight increased exponentially. They were both brought face down on the cement.

Hank was holding the chain with Filthy and trying to slow the dog down. "It's alright—let him go. Go, Enano, change! Aw shit, his collar is still on—wait a minute, damn!"

The collar split as the dog began to unfold. Loud popping noises echoed from inside the dog as his flesh and bones began to free themselves. Wet, matted hair emerged from the dog as he doubled, then quadrupled in size. The bigger the dog got, the faster he began to run at the black creatures. The dog shivered and reached his full size. He was larger than a polar bear and ten times as nasty. He ran up to the bishop and rent it in two with just a few shakes of his powerful jaws. The drone next to it was pumping quills towards the dog, but most just fell away. Some had become buried in the dog's nose, which made him bellow in pain, then charge. The drone was torn to pieces in seconds.

"Well," said Filthy with a relieved smile on his face. "That wasn't so bad, huh?"

Enano howled and ran off into the night.

"Shit!" Cried Hank. "Now where the fuck is he going?"

Jim sat in his easy chair staring at the television. The late night news was simply a blur—his mind still buzzed from this evening's events. His entire understanding of the world and its history had come to a confused end. He glanced up momentarily at the curtain as the wind blew it gently inside the apartment. He thought he heard a whisper or hissing. He looked at his bandaged fingertips and mimicked the rolling motion of the butterfly. He imagined the shining blade dancing across his fingers. He winced and stopped after a few seconds as his healing skin began to sting.

He reached down to scratch his shin and felt two hard needle-like quills extending outwards. He touched the area that it entered his shin and it felt like dead meat—no feeling.

He tried to lean forward to get a closer look at his leg and only managed to move his head slightly. His body felt like strength was running out of his wrists and feet. Fear began to creep through him when he realized that he was paralyzed. He made a silent prayer that whatever had attacked him will not discover Elena.

He glanced up at the curtain and it no longer swayed in a fluid motion. It was jerking and the TV images were shifting rapidly. Jim realized that part of his paralysis was like being in slow motion.

His head slowly lost its fight against gravity and slid back into the chair. He tried to shout for help—nothing came out but a weak, throttled moan. His eyes scanned the room and he saw nothing. He saw a thick black sickle gripping the curtain as if frozen in time. He stared in dull curiosity until he realized that it wasn't a sickle but a claw. It stayed there for a few seconds, just long enough for him to blink his eyes. The curtain was now pulled wide open—something black was holding the curtain open—and approaching him.

Jim felt dread overcome him—he couldn't believe what he was seeing. A distorted dark creature entered the room, wearing a long dark cloak. It was wearing Cordón's greasy hat and his leathery face. The face, upon closer examination, was severed from its former owner was now draped over something more sinister. The ragged skin looked like a mummified mask, complete with twisted smile. Jim tried not to blink, but it was no use. When his languid eyelids opened it was standing over him. The creature stood there for several minutes, regarding the frozen man. It shivered and shook as if laughing, but only a low hissing sound emerged.

Jim's mouth was wide open in a silent scream. He begged whatever force had paralyzed him to let him scream for help.

The creature's claws pulled open the cloak so that Jim could get a better look. The body was the same as the arms, leathery and hard. Instead of a rounded chest lined with ribs, bleached white horns emerged from its hide, encompassing the hollow of its chest cavity giving the impression of a yawning dragon's mouth.

"Papa? Hola?"

Tears streamed down from Jim's cheeks both in frustration and dread, as the creature listened to his daughter's soft voice. The creature made a low throat clearing noise like the grunts of pleasure from a perverted old man. The creature removed the hat from its bald head, letting it fall to the floor and then pulled the cloak all of the way off. Last to come off was the face mask. Like the body, it was completely devoid of hair and of hardened, rawhide-like material. There were bulging eyes, unblinking and yellowish-pink. A large mouth remained open in a yawning O. Surrounding the mouth were six claw-like teeth. The creature's body was slim and angular. The blade-like claws were not uniform and some were more developed than the others.

The creature regarded Jim's state with obvious pleasure.

"Papa? Oye?"

The creature hissed a long note that ended with several clicks. A beast dragging itself on its belly slid past the curtain. Across the front and along the top were hundreds of quills. Its face was misshapen and flattened against its body. Thick, lobster claws helped drag it towards Jim's immovable form. It reached out for one of Jim's legs and Bishop hissed for it to stop. The drone obeyed instantly and folded its powerful claws against its belly like a cat settling in for a nap.

The Bishop reached out and dragged a claw lightly across Jim's forehead and watched as a thin line of blood began to trickle back into his hair. The creature brought up his claw to its yawning mouth and the quivering teeth reached out expectantly. A thick, coiling tongue shot out and danced along the edge of the claw. Jim became more frantic and tried to scream again. The creature shook anew with hissing laughter.

In another blink it was gone, walking towards the back of the apartment, where Elena stood, gently bouncing up and down on her crib's mattress.

The doorbell rang.

Please, please, God help me! Help her! Jim's thoughts were running wild as he desperately tried to regain control of his body. He felt like he was staring out of a hole and the weight and strength of the world was on top of him. *Please, whoever's at the door help me!* Prayed Jim. His mind flashed to the times that he saw his daughter cry and it always broke his heart. There were moments like her first day in daycare, the way she cried with her arms outstretched. He felt as if he was betraying her.

"Papa? No?"

Jim's eyes went to the closet nearest the door. Boardman's assault rifle! He willed himself to try to get up. Nothing moved but his eyes. The doorbell rang again.

"Mr. Smith!" It was Ricardo's voice. "Mr Smith-- Jim! Are you in there?"

The doorknob was being rattled. The door was locked and the deadbolt thrown. The windows in the kitchen were secured with gypsy bars—there would be no entry for the calvary.

He heard Elena whimper and drop down to her mattress. When she was frightened, she would dive under a blanket and shiver. Jim could imagine her shaking and silently begged that this creature take him and not her.

Jim heard someone beating a shoulder against the door. *Please hurry*.

A hard crashing noise stopped Jim's heart momentarily. Elena shrieked and began a loud quavering cry. Her cries rose and fell as the creature toyed with her. Abruptly, she made a piercing scream over and over until it sounded as if she was being drowned. Jim's wet eyes scanned the room for any sign of help. Although Elena's screams stopped he could hear the rending of fabric and splitting of wood coming from the bedroom. Someone was attacking the front door and yelling something about not being able to break down the door.

The creature walked back into the living room and stood in front of Jim. It was drenched in fresh blood. It's tongue, like a thick tentacle, was extended out of its mouth and working the blood off the head and from around the neck. The creature hissed in laughter. Jim's eyes were wide in horror.

More voices were heard outside the door and the creature continued to groom the blood from its quivering head. A long howl was heard from the outside and some men were calling something called Enano. The creature stopped and shot a look towards the front door. It hissed instructions to the drone on the floor and then rushed out of the terrace, leaving streaks of fresh blood upon the curtains.

The drone pulled itself towards Jim and used its claws to clamber up towards Jim's face. The dead, leering face was pulled to the side and Jim saw multiple rows of stubby, conical teeth lining a huge mouth. The claws grabbed Jim's shoulders and began to draw his slackened body towards the gnashing teeth.

Jim felt the crash as the door imploded and saw shards of mortar and wood fly past his head. An animal like a massive bear rushed into the room, gripped the creature in its powerful jaws and yanked it away from Jim. The huge animal's pelt was a blur as it shook its prey violently in the center of the living room. Pieces of the creature flew off, bathing the walls and ceiling in black liquid.

Jim's chair was pulled backwards and spun around. He saw Ricardo's concerned face and the man named Simon rummaging through a black doctor's bag. Ricardo seemed calm, but alert and was handed a syringe. He buried it into Jim's leg nearest the quills and when expended, threw it to the floor. He pulled Jim from the chair and laid him on the carpet. "Relax Jim—everything's going to be fine."

Simon walked to the back bedroom and saw red lights dancing around the room. When he stepped through the door, he saw the shambles that was once a pink crib torn to pieces. The creature must have tore Elena from the crib and performed all it's vile work in the middle of the bed. Nothing was recognizable. He saw what appeared to be half her ribcage; bright red and lying near bloodied matted hair. Her blood was everywhere and spattered across a swinging Chinese lantern shade, causing the sea-sickening red illumination around the room.

Simon turned around and went back to Ricardo's side. He looked into the depths of Jim's eyes and saw madness. *He must have heard everything*, he thought. He didn't dwell on it, but he knew what must be done. He knelt by Jim's horror-stricken face and placed his hands on both sides of his face.

Ricardo gripped Simon's arm gently, "Don't."

Simon's mind started to pull. As much as he could move physical objects from remote locations with a hex, he could also pull emotions, memories and personalities—and hold on to them for some time. It stood out like a lighthouse on a clear night—Jim's shock, his horror, his greatest of fears. The human mind is a fragile instrument. When it becomes overloaded with anguish, it can temporarily shut down in order to reestablish a semi-clean start. Jim's brain was all too happy to rid itself of this ghastly strain. When the memories flooded in, Simon was sent sprawling backwards, his face flashed pale, contorting in sadness, desperation and panic. His hands shook like he was trying to keep invisible wasps away from his face. The thousands of years of watching humans die will ultimately desensitize exiles to mortals dying. This was different—with the horrific atrocity against Elena, came all of Jim's feelings of love for his daughter.

Kayanan grabbed him by his shoulders. "Simon—Look at me. Are you okay?"

Simon ignored Ricardo's question and broke into tears. His lower lip trembled and his nose began to run. Unintelligible moans and screams came out of his mouth.

Enano had finished with the Drone and his panting was beginning to subside. He looked at Simon with concern—it had never seen Simon emotional before. It loped over and brought its huge muzzle near his hair and sniffed. It gave a short whine, then crouched down and put its muzzle on the floor near Simon's leg.

Hank ran through the door with Gideon following a minute later, hyperventilating. "Jesus! What in hell happened here?" Hank saw Simon draw his knees near his face and erupt into soft wails. "Simon?" He looked down and saw that Jim Smith was lying on the floor with a blank look on his face. Four blackened quills protruded out of his right knee. He saw Kayanan flashing a penlight into Jim's eyes. "Shit. He got hit huh?"

Kayanan looked up. "Yes. The good news is that he'll recover —Simon, however took his memories of what happened. Why don't you see if he'll be all right?"

Hank knelt near Simon and murmured in Origin, "Buddy—you gonna be okay?"

Simon looked up with bloodshot blue eyes. "I... I'm having a bad time with this one! His...his--- no! I don't know how I'll be able to bear this!"

Hank was surprised to hear him speak. He couldn't remember the last time he heard his voice. "Shit, easy decision—let go. Let him work out his own emotions, man."

Simon gripped his face in his hands while his body trembled. "You know I can't! We need him. If... if I let go, he will *kill* himself."

The creature once known as *El Cordón* jumped off the second story balcony landing firmly on the courtyard below. It cocked its head toward the man's apartment and chuckled to itself. The Drone will make short work of that *cabrón* Smith. It trotted towards the sea wall licking the remainder of the girl's blood from his neck and claws.

Although it lost most of its humanity from the transformation, it enjoyed the feeling of power and remembered in full clarity, those that it reviled. Its master would understand that he had to kill him to prevent the others from having him. He would allow it more of the blessed drug, which gave it so much strength and would allow it to feed on the people that he rounded up during nightly raids around the town.

As it leaped over the sea wall to the sand below a massive hand snatched it out of the air. "Where the fuck you go'in?" The creature was working its claws into Big Lee's skin, to no avail. The claws couldn't penetrate. It tried kicking and rasping its way into his skin with the sharp teeth surrounding its mouth. It wasn't even a tickle to the giant.

"What the fuck? What are you covered in? Is that blood?" Big Lee walked closer to a lamp near the courtyard. "You disgustin'... bitch! You better not have *touched* one of my friends!" Big Lee climbed over the wall into the courtyard to examine his new toy.

The creature hissed louder and louder, desperate for any reinforcements.

"You somethin' kinda *ugly* too!" Big Lee grimaced at the creature as it desperately tried to kick itself free. "Lemme see if I can make you pretty again!"

Big Lee took one of the creature's claws in his left hand and tore it off. "You just tell me to stop if I'm hurtin' you!" One by one, the claws were torn free. The creature writhed in his hand and hissed louder and louder. "We're getting there! You're looking better already! Hmmm. Look at these ribs. Y'know, I love some ribs, but these are just too ugly to eat. Let's get these off you." Big Lee peeled the ribs backwards and it split the creature's breastbone. Organs piled out of the cavity. The creature wheezed and began to lilt. "Aw. My little buddy doesn't want to play anymore." Big Lee drove the creature into the courtyard wall and crushed it to just a few inches thick. "Yuck!" Big Lee stepped down from the courtyard, walked to the shore and washed the black liquid from his hands. He heard Enano howl—it came from the apartment building.

Hank surveyed the destruction in Elena's bedroom. He tried to imagine the horror going on in his buddy's head and just couldn't conceive of what he was feeling. He hoped that he could cope with it and recover.

"Yo *dog*, what happened here?" Big Lee's head was poking above the rail of the balcony.

"Oh man, did we fuck up." Hank pulled the window curtain wider so that Big Lee could see. "Jim survived—barely. This mess is what's left of his daughter."

"Well, I got me the nasty thing that did it. I made it good and slow if that's any consolation. Everyone else all right?"

Hank looked towards the living room. He could still make out Simon's shoulder, sitting agains the wall weeping. "Not really—Simon did something stupid—he took this guy's emotions. Now, *he's* a mess. Your dog got a few quills too. Ricky's taking care of it."

Big Lee snorted. "Well, lets not make any more mistakes." Big Lee surveyed the darkened houses nearby with a look of disgust. "Let's get back home—I think these fuckas *own* this town."

Chapter Thirty:
The Fountain

Cesar and his friend Aaron were tired of riding the boats around the lake. Margaret wasn't there to taunt, so they went for ice cream and sat on the grass watching the birds float in the air. They told each other jokes and giggled even though they weren't very funny. They even laughed at the jokes they told each other the previous day.

Cesar's patch glowed and rang a melody of bells. He pulled it from his back pocket and unfolded it.

Aaron looked over at his shoulder. "What'cha doing?"

Cesar saw an image of the willow tree shimmering. "C'mon— we gotta hurry!"

As the two boys ran past the pavilion towards the tree, Cesar explained in excited breaths, "This has come in real handy! Bob said that someone was gaining access to the tree that wasn't supposed to—I guess one of the exiles. I set up the patch with something called a 'trigger' so that it would watch the tree and alert me if anything happened that was strange."

Aaron was a bit shorter than Cesar, but kept up the pace with no difficulty. "What do you mean by strange?"

"I don't know…" said Cesar. "I know that either nothing happens there, or people show up there that have died. I figure that this exile probably didn't die, but you still have to get here either through the tree or through the stadium—and nothing has happened there since like, forever."

"Well, what did the patch show you?"

"Nothing really—it just looks like it's shining."

They ran to the base of the tree, but remained on the sidewalk. Light was shimmering near the trunk of the tree. Although hard to see, it looked ungainly and pulsed around. It looked like it had difficulty getting up.

"What is that?" asked Aaron.

"Heck, I don't know." Cesar looked at the image in the patch. It looked the same. "Patch? Can you change the picture so we can see it better?"

The image on the patch grew and then shifted in colors and hues as it cycled through different filters. Suddenly, a black and white image showed almost perfect detail. It was a big man, strong and hulking, with a huge beer belly. He was drunk.

He pushed himself to his knees and looked around. He seemed very disoriented. He looked over and saw the boys looking at him and froze.

"Mister?" said Cesar. "Who are you?"

He pretended that he was invisible and didn't move. After a few moments his eyes crept back towards the boys—they were still watching him. "Uh, go away."

He tried to get to his feet again and stumbled. He made it to the sidewalk and tried to stand up straight. His tight t-shirt had rode up over his belly. He instinctively pulled it down and began his unsteady walk towards the temple.

Aaron looked at Cesar, bewildered. "What should we do?"

"I don't want to scare him away—let's see if we can find out who he is. If we need to catch him I can always call Tieran or Bob."

The boys walked behind the shimmering apparition and kept consulting the patch's filtered image to make sure they weren't getting too close.

The ghost turned around. "G'wan. Git. Yuh gonna git me in trouble." He waved a fat hand towards them and it just passed through Cesar's chest. He felt nothing.

"Mister? What's your name?"

"Git I said!"

Cesar shook his head. Patch? Please identify this person."

The patch showed a picture of a tall black man in a speedo bathingsuit, rippling with muscles. "*Abraham Kennedy. Born in 1960 in Spotsylvania Virginia. Origin name is Naius Athum. Former Origin occupation was master cook to games and circus. He is classified as an exile with no remaining memory of the Expulsion or of his circumstances. He is one of the 16 unaccounted exiles not belonging to the Lodge or followers of Rothiel.*"

The big man stopped. Hearing his name seemed to spark a memory. "Naius—wuz that my name..." He turned around unsteadily. "Naius Athum. I memem—I remember that—that... that's my name." He stood for a few seconds lost in thought, weaving from side to side, then slowly turned and began climbing the steps to the Temple. He continued walking to the door until he passed right through it.

"Crap!" said Cesar. "I didn't think that he'd make it through the door!"

Both boys ran up the steps and the doors opened inwards when Cesar approached. He looked at the patch and the apparition was making its way to the fountain. It walked through the guardrail, hesitated for a moment and then fell in. The fountain's bluish-white light darkened for a moment, then returned to its former splendor.

Aaron looked into the fountain. "Where did he go?"

"I'm about to find out. Patch? Where is Abra—Naius Athum now?"

The fountain glowed and showed a darkened room with the big man strapped to a chair. The bonds around his wrists were so tight that his hands were swollen. They had gone without circulation for so long that they were biologically dead. His clothes were a mess and his t-shirt was torn open. His chest and belly were slick with alcohol. There were empty whiskey bottles littering the floor. Valgiernas stood over the man firing questions at him as his eyes rolled in his sockets. "What did you see! Did you get the word?"

"P-p-please—no more..." Valgiernas forced the bottle into the man's mouth, snapping one of his front teeth in half. The man's eyes lolled then his head fell forward as he passed out.

Valgiernas cracked him across the face with the back of his hand to wake him.

"It's no use. He can't go back in if he's had too much." The voice came from the back of the room. It was Rothiel. "We'll wait a few hours and try again. We've already gotten a treasure of information."

Valgiernas made a slight bow to the man sitting in the back of the room. "Lord, I just wanted to make sure."

"Has your team left to take care of Danhieras' conduit?"

"Yes, lord. They've just left."

"Excellent. I want him dead or in our custody tonight."

Cesar looked at Aaron's face with a slackened jaw. "Oh no! I think they're going to try to take Jim Smith!" He began tapping on the screen of the patch.

Aaron looked away from the fountain and glanced at Cesar's patch. "Who's he?"

"Patch—get Theo." Cesar turned to Aaron as the Patch made the connection. "He's a human—a special one. He was going to help Danhieras against Rothiel."

Theo's face appeared on the screen. "Hi sweetheart!"

"Theo—they're going after Jim Smith! I just saw it at the fountain!"

"Theo's smile fell. "Are you sure Cesar? Are you certain?"

"Yes—Aaron and I just saw Rothiel order it—we've got to do something!"

"I'll have to discuss this with Bob. We may not be able to do anything since he isn't one of the Exiles. When we get an answer, I'll call you." Theo's face faded back to her still image.

Cesar and Aaron both watched scattered images flowing through the fountain.

Aaron watched as each image fluctuated while Cesar pointed at various ones for more information. "What do we do now?"

"Theo said to wait. I don't like this."

Aaron looked at the image of Naius Athnum stooped in the chair with droplets of blood dripping from his mouth. "Shouldn't we tell someone about him?"

Cesar looked at the picture and thought about what they would do to Jim Smith, or anyone else that got in his way. "Seth. Show me Seth."

An image of Seth appeared in his room as he read from a book. "Aaron—I need a favor. Please don't tell Theo or Bob what I'm going to do."

Aaron looked at Cesar perplexed. "What—are you going to do?"

Cesar put his finger up this lip for a short moment and then pointed to the fountain.

Seth sat in his chair reading an ancient tome on healing dead skin. He was preoccupied that Filodraxes' extremities were dying off and soon the lack of circulation in his body would kill him. His fingers were already turning either black or the color of a rawhide chew toy. Some of his toes had already dropped off.

"Seth? We need to talk." Cesar stood near the far wall of his room. He was in spirit form so only Seth and some of the resident spooks could see him. A short, stumpy duck-like spook made a wary departure from that side of the room.

Seth put the book down and stood up. "It's good to see you again-- is something wrong?"

"Afraid so." Said Cesar. He looked back towards someone that Seth couldn't see. "We saw something—Rothiel has a man—he's a prisoner and he's similar to you. His human name is Abraham Kennedy —his origin name is Naius Athum. He can see things up here, but he shows up at the willow tree like some kind of ghost. Rothiel is keeping him tied up and drunk—somehow he's able to show up here and snoop around."

Seth buried his face in his palms as he thought about it. "Does he suffer like I do when he's there?"

"Not that I could tell-- Aaron? No?" Cesar turned from his invisible friend and shook his head. "I think... I think that he has to be drunk or halfway asleep for it to work—it kind of seemed like he was drunk when he was up here."

"I'll let the guys know. Was there anything else?"

"Yes. Rothiel ordered some kind of team to go out and get Jim Smith. They must know about him."

Seth grabbed for the phone nearest his bed—it was spray painted flat black so that it would not reflect light. "Damn! Gellan's not answering his phone. I'm going to alert the guys. Thank you Cesar."

Seth retrieved the blind that he kept in his pocket and placed it over his eyes. He opened the door to the hallway and hurriedly felt his way down to Gellan's room.

Cesar climbed down to the floor and continued to watch the images flow past.

"Aren't you afraid of getting into trouble?" asked Aaron.

Cesar looked at his friend. "Yeah. Sure. I don't want to be kicked off the team, but on certain things I *know* I'm right. For some reason, the Creator wanted me as part of this team. I don't really know anything, but I figure he wants me to be *me*—I just had to warn them."

"But didn't you just disobey Theo? She told you to wait."

Cesar looked exasperated. "I know! Gosh Aaron, I'm not proud of doing that, but she said she wasn't sure. I've been watching everyone involved. Jim Smith is a good man. I like him. I don't want to see him or his daughter hurt."

Aaron went over to the stone bench and sat down. His feet didn't reach the ground, so he swung them back and forth while he looked at the images course past.

Cesar went over and sat next to him. "Hey, don't be mad at me. I'm not trying to cover anything up-- if they ask if I did something, I'll tell 'em."

Aaron nudged Cesar's arm. "I ain't mad at ya. I just don't want you to get in trouble. There's the kite competition that we haven't even started yet and that canoe race that's next week. I told Margaret that we were going to *slaughter* her and Amy. You can't do either if you're grounded."

A chime issued out of the Patch.

Aaron looked over at the image on the screen. It was Jim Smith's picture. "What's that, another trigger?"

"Yeah…" said Cesar with unease. "Patch, identify."

It showed two creatures walking from the beach up to Jim Smith's courtyard and three more heading toward's Manoli's house. "Oh no… They're already at his house!" Cesar's finger hovered over Theo's image, but he stopped. *She may not be able to do anything,* he thought. He looked at the icon holding Tieran's image. *No. He won't be able to help no matter how I ask.*

"Patch? How do I prevent someone from dying?" The display glowed an image of the fountain and the willow tree.

"The deceased are channeled through the fountain as a final record is made of their life's knowledge. Their souls then pass to the Tree as they begin their new life here. Humans are either kept alive on Earth or their mind is kept in stasis without the final record being entered. If their bodies are repaired, their souls and knowledge may be returned and their lifespans will continue."

"Um. Okay. How do I keep their minds in—uh, stasis?"

"As knowledge is energy kept in a logical form, energy is required to hold it in place. By using a low-energy container, the knowledge and soul can be held indefinitely." A demonstration video displayed someone pointing to areas within the fountain and pulling it out. The knowledge was automatically encased in a translucent bubble. *"Once removed from the fountain, the energy may be re-released into*

*the host on Earth if the body is viable, or re-introduced into the
fountain for ultimate delivery to the Tree."*

"What are you planning now?" asked Aaron with skepticism.

"I don't know yet." Cesar looked at the map on his patch for the
location of Rip's men. They were just now pulling into Rota in the big
truck, but two creatures were already standing on Jim's balcony. He
selected the image of Jim sitting in his chair watching television. He
looked very troubled. One of the creatures, a Drone, lined itself up
behind the fluttering curtain. The Bishop pulled the curtain away for
just an instant and Cesar watched as a group of quills shot out of the
front of the Drone and became lodged just below Jim's kneecap.

"Look at that! He didn't even feel it!" shouted Cesar.

The boys watched in horror as the beast walked into the living
room and taunted Jim. Both boys were scared and had unconsciously
picked up their feet from the floor and watched in silence. As the
Bishop disrobed, showing it's ugliness, the boys looked at running
visual commentary about the creature as well as the purpose of the
venom coursing through Jim's veins. The Bishop only scratched Jim--
it just seemed to want to gloat over him. It began its walk to Elena's
room.

Elena saw a shadow moving towards the hallway and became
excited to see her father's face. She saw a stark, bony beast walking
towards her with an enormous gaping hole for a mouth. The tongue
shot out in excitement and the claws danced with anticipation.

Elena stopped bouncing and felt cold fear creep into her heart.
She dove down to the mattress and made an unsuccessful attempt to
cover herself with her blanket.

The creature stood over the crib hissing in excitement, then tore
off the side rail with a single swipe of its primary claw. The wood burst
apart in a loud crash and Elena shivered in fear. The creature tore off
the blanket and jerked the toddler from her mattress and brought her to
its face. She squeezed her eyes shut and screamed in horror. The
creature walked towards the bed with its new prize and with one
downward movement, hacked off her pink pajamas and threw her to the
bed. Elena, screaming, cocked her head towards the door hoping her
brave father would dash in and save her. He remained frozen to his
chair. Only his hearing was in perfect order.

The creature moved its longest claw towards Elena's shivering abdomen and poked slightly. Her skin yielded instantly and a sliver of blood ran down her small belly. To the creature, it was immaculate. Nothing could be more perfect. It would rip her to shreds and devour her. He should have dragged the *Yanqui* into the room to witness this banquet. The creature heard a doorbell. *It's too late for them* the creature thought as it chuckled and turned its attention back to his victim. Elena shrieked in pain over and over in a dreadful crescendo as it shoved the claw deeper into her body inch by inch.

Cesar dashed off the bench, letting his Patch fall to the floor as he ran to the rail. He kicked a leg over and fell to the other side, knocking the wind out of him. He grimaced in pain and his face betrayed the horror of Elena's situation. He gritted his teeth, jumped to his feet and jammed his hand into Elena's moving image, tearing it free from the fountain. He staggered backwards trying to breathe amongst the pain in his ribs and looked at the object in his hand. No bigger than a goose's egg, the shining ball showed a picture of Elena at peace and asleep. He looked towards Aaron.

He looked horrified. "Cesar! What have you done! Bob is going to lose his mind over this!"

Cesar tried to kick his leg over the rail but the pain was too great. "Ugh. I'm fine. Thanks for asking. Don't worry about Bob— help *me* get back over so I can think about what to do."

The creature saw the girl howling in pain, mouth filling with blood suddenly stop, sighed then collapsed. *She died too fast*, it thought as it dragged its tongue all over the gore. It crossed its mind that she may have passed out, so he held her by her feet, upside down. Nothing. It drove a smaller claw through the bottom of one of her feet. Not even a flinch. It chuckled in amusement and continued with its violent spree of destruction by tearing her into pieces.

The boys walked back to the bench, staring at Cesar's new possession. Cesar looked up at the fountain and grimaced when he saw the Bishop gorge itself on Elena's body. It finished in mere seconds and walked back out to show the anguished father it's sinister work. It appeared to be startled from the commotion outside and fled, leaving the drone to finish off Jim.

They both cheered when Rip's men burst into the door behind Enano and came to Jim's aid. "That's one big dog," said Aaron with Cesar nodding his head and clutching Elena's soul tightly. Aaron looked down at the ball. "So... what are you going to do with that?"

Cesar moved a free hand towards his sore ribs. Where he touched made him suck in air in sharp pain. "Why all the questions! If I knew, I wouldn't be sitting here like an idiot wondering what made me jump over that rail in the first place. I... I don't know. I can't tell any of the adults—they'll kill me. I just want to figure a few things out. I couldn't let her suffer like that. I'd like to see if there's a way to bring her back."

Aaron pointed to the image showing the bedroom soaked in blood. "She's not coming back—there's, like, nothing left. You could pop her back into the fountain."

"I... No. I want to make sure there's no way I can't help her. –I still haven't met the Creator yet. I'll ask him for help. If he says no, then I'll put her back in the fountain."

Cesar's Patch chimed. It was Theo. "Cesar—it's me. Bob says we cannot interfere with the human. We're watching it now—Rip's men are taking him back to the Fortress. Apparently, his daughter didn't make it. You didn't watch any of this did you?

Cesar looked at Aaron. "No, uh, we didn't." Why?"

"It was just very violent. The girl didn't suffer too much—she died right away."

Cesar was pushing the ball into his trouser pocket. "That, uh, that's too bad."

"My patch didn't show her appear at the Willow Tree."

Cesar swallowed. He could feel Aaron staring at him.

"...So, she was probably reincarnated immediately," said Theo. "By the way, we're having dinner in less than an hour, will you and your friend join us?" Cesar heard Bob shushing her on that last part.

"I guess so—Aaron?"

Aaron shook his head. "No. I'm supposed to help my Grandmother today. She's making Jelly. She says it never turns out right unless I'm there to help stir."

Theo nodded with a smile. "All right, we'll see you there, Cesar. Bye."

Both boys left the temple. Cesar, with a not-so-conspicuous bulge protruding from his pocket. They both looked nervous. Aaron looked at Cesar. "How's your side?"

"Still sore. It hurts a lot when I breathe in."

"Where are you going now?" said Aaron, looking at the bulge in Cesar's pocket.

"I'm going to hide her in my room until I can figure this out. Please don't tell anyone."

The boys gave each other the funny handshake that the men in Rip's Lodge used. Both boys snickered and said in unison, "So mote it be."

Chapter Thirty One:
Training

"It's just a temporary bout of paralysis." Said Gellan, while changing Rip's diaper. He zipped up Rip's pajamas and sat him up up so that they could continue the conversation. "...And I'm going to need you to stay calm about something." Gellan eyed the red fire extinguisher hanging on the wall three feet away.

Rip had his complete attention. He rocked back and forth slightly and wiped the drool from his mouth. "Wha izit? Juss dell me whad habbend."

Gellan sighed and shook his head. "Jim's daughter was killed before we could get there."

Rip's brow betrayed shifts between pain and anger. His mouth quivered and his nostrils flared. While contemplating the situation, he grabbed his footies and began playing with his toes. "How. Howz Jib's mood?"

Gellan exhaled in relief that Rip didn't lose control of his emotions. "Well, not bad. Simon took his memories—Ricardo tried to stop him."

Rip began rocking again as he thought about Simon. "Howz Zimon? Dis may hode him back too?"

Gellan mopped the drool from Rip's mouth. "I'll be honest with you--Simon took it really hard. I told him to take tomorrow off. Lucas is staying in his room with him—I don't mean to imply that he'll harm himself, but he's definitely fragile right now. I think he'll be okay, but he's got to relax and get past the emotional pain."

"Yeah. Good, dat's good," nodded Rip. He looked up at Gellan with sad eyes. "I lubbed Elena. Dat's bad—bad fo' Jib. Bad fo' all uv us."

While Gellan was putting away the baby wipes, Rip grabbed ahold of his sleeve. "One more ting. Rota izzn't safe any moe. I want all ow brudders back hewe—to leab dere homes an' come to the fo'tress.

Gellan nodded. "I'll get the truck ready. I'll tell their families to only bring a suitcase each." He remembered how Juani didn't want her family to know what she did for a living. "What do I do about Juani's family?"

"Bwing 'em all."

"What do I do if she doesn't want her family to know—you know, about us?"

"Take Filtee."

Jim sat on the edge of the bed in his new room looking at the walls. Something was missing. He knew Elena was dead. He knew that she was killed in his apartment, but he could barely remember who she was. It seemed that he barely knew her—he couldn't really picture what she looked like. He wanted to feel sad, but he found that he was unable to consider it. *I don't get it—she was my daughter, but I feel nothing for her*, he thought.

He heard a knock on his door. "Um, Come in?"

Kayanan opened the door and brought a set of sheets, a blanket and a fresh pillow. "Forgot to give you these. Are you hungry or anything?"

Jim stood and took the bedding. "No—no thank you, Ricardo. I think tonight was enough for me to swallow for one evening. The girl —Elena. She was my daughter—right?"

Kayanan fumbled with what to say and scratched his cheek. "Yeah man, she was yours. Don't worry—it's just been a traumatic evening. Everything will be fine in a couple of days. ...What do you remember?

Jim looked at the ceiling. "I, uh, remember the lodge, then coming here to get briefed by you guys. I remember the butterfly too. I came home and paid Manoli for babysitting. I think I remember something dark, standing in my livingroom. That's it, really."

"How's your knee?"

Jim tapped lightly on his bandaged knee. "Feel's just a bit sore, but pretty good. I can't believe that I was incapacitated just a couple of hours ago."

Kayanan nodded his head. "Powerful stuff really, but just a temporary nerve agent. We were lucky to get our hands on some of this stuff a few months back and we were able to produce antibodies for it. You'll notice a few side-affects such as a blue tinge in your vision and cold sweating. Those will both go away in 24 hours." He pointed to the phone on the nightstand. "There's a list of phone numbers on the wall—if you need anything, just dial 519—that's me. Don't call Rip though—he's real cranky if he's woken in the middle of the night.

We'll wake you up at 7:30 for breakfast and we'll begin training right afterwards."

"Sounds good," said Jim. "I just hope I don't disappoint anyone."

Kayanan patted him on the shoulder. "Not a chance bud. Get a good night's sleep—you'll need it."

Kayanan turned to go and Jim stood up from the bed. "Those… *things*. What are they?"

Kayanan pressed his forehead into the cool edge of the door. "They're people. That's what makes this so hard to deal with." He turned to look at Jim and saw him perplexed. "They can't get in here though. They've already tried and we sent 'em packing. You're safe here."

Jim sat back down on the bed. "I don't feel afraid. I guess I'm lacking the ability to have fear. …I honestly don't know why considering tonight's events. I feel tired, but I don't know how I'll be able to get to sleep."

"Would you like me to have Gideon stop by and help you out? He can make anyone fall asleep either with his talent or just by discussing some of his whacked-out theories."

"That guy everyone calls 'Filthy'? I'd rather try it the old-fashioned way."

Kayanan gave him a nod and then walked out of the room, closing the door behind him.

The silence in the room made Jim's ears rush. He tried to think about the girl again. He could think of amazing detail, her name, age, everything but what she looked like and how he felt about her. He rose up off the mattress, feeling the twinge in his knee, and began making his bed. *Maybe I'll remember after I've rested*, he thought.

He awoke with his phone ringing. He picked up the handset—it was Ricardo. "How'd you sleep?"

Jim cleared his throat and scratched his head. "-Yawn-. Fine—I think. I felt like I just closed my eyes for a short moment."

"Well, slip on the clothes that I've placed outside your door and head down the hallway to the elevator. Push 'C' for the chow hall—there's a commissary and barbershop at that level too. We'll be waiting for you."

Jim hung up the phone stood up from the bed. His knee was stiff, but didn't hurt anymore. He turned on the lights and opened his door. On the floor, was a set of gray sweats, a new pair of tennis shoes and packages of new socks and underwear.

Jim walked into the elevator and saw two panels of buttons, one higher up with buttons related to the four levels of the fortress and another similar panel lower to the floor with bright, candy-colored buttons. He pushed the 'C' button for the chow hall and heard the sound of pots clanking and dozens of people chatting as the door opened. The smell of cooked eggs & bacon filled his nostrils. He walked into wide dining area and was surprised to see so many children. There were four behind the serving line asking if he wanted eggs & pancakes and at least twenty other children of different ages eating at the other tables. Ricardo walked up to him wearing identical sweats. "'Morning, Jim. We're over at the far table—get plenty to eat-- but none of that sausage—it'll give you the shits."

Jim walked to Ricardo's table with a tray overloaded with eggs, bacon and toast. Already at the table sat Big Lee, Hank, Gideon, Gellan and Rip, sitting in a yellow highchair. Everyone was cheerful. While they ate, they talked about things from the past. Jim wondered why nothing was mentioned from yesterday. "Hey, where's that other guy— Simon? Is he coming for breakfast?"

The table fell silent. Gellan shook his head. "You just missed him. I think he came early because he was going to do some research on Filodraxes."

Jim remembered that name. "He's the really old guy? The one that's having problems with his fingers and stuff?"

Gellan smiled. "The very same—we'll introduce you this afternoon."

Jim ate until he was full and enjoyed the cheerful banter between all of the men at the table. His guilt continued to poke him in the back of his mind. His daughter had died not twelve hours ago and it meant almost nothing to him. To Jim, Gellan seemed to be the man with all of the answers. "Gellan? What attacked me last night?"

Again, all of the men seemed to stop with the revelry. Gellan put down his coffee cup and said in a low voice. Why don't we discuss what's going on in more detail in the training room? Some of it needs to stay out of these children's ears."

Jim nodded and following Big Lee's queue picked up his breakfast tray and carried it to the scullery. The men filed out of the chow hall and took a flight of stairs down one level to the training room —a massive room with some home-made obstacles, exercise equipment and what looked like various oriental weapons. It was the width of three racquetball courts stuck together and another nine in length. There were numerous scuff marks along the walls.

"We've got observers," said Kayanan, pointing towards the observation windows near the ceiling. "The old guy sitting next to Simon is Filodraxes." Jim raised a hand and waved to them. Filodraxes sat looking impassively at Jim and Simon looked haggard. Simon hesitated and gave a short wave back to Jim.

Gellan was placing Rip down on the floor in one of the far corners. He was crouching down listening to the toddler's instructions, nodded his head and then walked back towards Jim. "We're going to start with me. As you know, we all specialize in certain areas that we're comfortable with. Our hope is to have you tie them all together. My best quality is speed. All you need to do in these exercises it try to keep up."

Gellan walked over to a set of bleachers and stood at the base of the lowest seat. Jim walked up and stood next to him the same way. Gellan lifted one foot up off the floor and placed it on top of the bleacher's seat. He then lifted off and placed his other foot next to the first, now standing on the bottom-most seat. He continued looking towards Jim. Then he lowered his right foot back to the floor, followed by his left. "See? Nothing to it. We're going to start off slow and see how quick we can get."

Jim followed suit—these were the same exercises that he had to endure as a teenager for high school wrestling. They both went in unison, up down, up down at a fairly leisurely pace.

"We gonna see something," bellowed Big Lee. "Or are you two just dancin'?"

Gellan turned to look at his feet and immediately doubled his pace. His feet turned into a blur as his feet drummed against the floor and the bleacher. Jim instinctively did the same and the noise was synchronized. Gellan gave a smile and nod of approval. Their feet pounded at the exact same time and level.

Rip began to smile and rock back & forth excitedly.

"That ain't shit, Gel—c'mon," hollered Big Lee, with his arms folded in front of him. "Move yo' ass! Show this white boy who's boss!"

Gellan nodded to Jim, who nodded right back and then both began to pick up steam. The hammering on the wood bleacher filled the gymnasium like rolling thunder. The pounding continued to increase in speed and then it began to get erratic. Gellan would put on bursts of speed, only to be matched by Jim. Both were now drenched in sweat but both looked equal. Gellan closed his eyes and began to accelerate to his fastest pace. Jim felt like he was approaching the top of a hill with his speed. He began to pour on more and more velocity until it felt as if it was getting easier. Gellan's ears picked up the difference first— and realized that it wasn't him. He looked over at Jim and saw that his legs were pumping almost twice as fast than his own. He couldn't believe it—for thousands of years no other human could go as fast as he could. Gellan slowed down and hopped down to the floor. His leg muscles felt like jelly. Jim stayed where he was, torso in perfect balance as his legs pounded the floor and bleachers in a flurry of movement. His arms pumped at a dizzying pace and finally he too slowed to a complete stop. The thunder had ended and everyone's hearing felt hollow, as their eardrums began recovering from the tremendous noise.

Kayanan walked up and brought a stethoscope to Jim's chest. "Hmm. You're barely over 130 beats per minute." He looked at Gellan with concern. "How are you doing?"

Gellan was breathing heavy and gave him a salute. He finally started to get his breathing under control. "Damn. That's really... really fast man."

Kayanan pulled the stethoscope around his neck. "Yup. Too bad we don't have a way to see just how fast. Let's take a five-minute break. I'll brief Jim on last night's adversary while you both cool off."

Jim turned and sat down on the bleacher while Kayanan walked to the far end of the gymnasium and began pulling over a hospital gurney with a sheet over it. When the gurney was close, he pulled off the sheet.

It came back a little. Jim could almost remember the face, or what was left of it. Large, bulging eyes and a massive mouth encircled with six chisel-like teeth. Jim stood up from the bench. "Is it dead?"

"Quite," said Kayanan tapping the creature's chest. "When they're cut off from their... nourishment, they cannot survive. This one literally ate itself from the inside out."

Jim looked at it and noticed that it resembled a human form. "Where do these things come from?"

Kayanan placed his hands on the creature's ribcage horns like he was holding the bars of a prison cell. "We bagged this one during an evening raid in Rota a few days ago. It was gathering up people from their homes. The compound responsible has all the qualities of an addictive drug, intermingled with a manufactured virus — there's a few of them actually." He nodded towards Hank and Big Lee.

The both stepped forward, picked up the dead creature in their arms and walked it over to a far wall. They shackled it up in a standing position against the wall. When they stepped aside, it was lurched at an angle, with the head lying against it's pronounced shoulder.

Kayanan walked to the center of the room holding a pistol. "You may want to cover your ears for a moment." Everyone held their ears tight while he took aim and fired off three rounds. Two of the bullets ricocheted off the creature's chest and became buried in the ceiling. The third round entered the creature's eye pit, knocking the head violently backwards, until it lolled back against its shoulder. "Hmm. Lucky shot, I guess." Kayanan walked over to the gurney and set the gun down. "The drug is called *Cambio*. The Spanish believe it's called that because it's so cheap. You lay down a 100-peseta coin and get change back. As you can see, the only change you get is what it does to you physically.

"So guns don't work," said Jim examining the creature's chest.

"No, not very effective," said Kayanan. "The drones are even harder to kill — that's why they're sent in first. But, that's why I introduced you to these lethal babies here." He held up a butterfly. "Why don't you try it out?"

Jim walked over and took the butterfly from his hand. The moment it was between his fingers, he could feel the spider strand. He didn't even have to look. He knew it was running between himself and the creature. He turned around, extended his arm backwards and flung the butterfly towards the creature's head. It arced to the right halfway, then curved back to the left in an increasingly sharper turn, slicing through the creature's head and burying itself into the concrete wall.

Filthy whistled. "Hey Ricky, he even copied your little hand-flick there."

Gellan looked over at Rip, who was jabbing his finger skyward. He understood the next test. He walked over to the phone on the wall and dialed the observation room. "How're you holding up? I want you to think about Smith—just for a few minutes. All right—thanks."

He hung up the phone, looking back towards Kayanan and nodded.

"This test may seem funny to you," said Kayanan, picking up a handful of golf balls from a bag off the floor. "We're going to test a certain knack that Simon has in defending himself. Kayanan tossed a ball underhanded towards Jim's head.

Jim caught the ball in his right hand. "What's this supposed to test—my reflexes?"

"No. Don't catch them. You'll see."

Kayanan let another fly and it popped off the top of Jim's head. "Ow! Shit!"

"Not sooo haard Wicky!" Yelled Rip from the back of the room.

"My apologies Jim," said Kayanan. "I'll aim for something that won't hurt so bad. Hold up the back of your hand."

He let loose another ball, but it only traveled a few feet into the air. It came down and whacked the knuckles on his hand. Jim looked at Kayanan incredulously, then shook the sting from his hand.

Kayanan gave an apologetic shrug, then motioned with another ball. Jim held out his hand and saw the ball rise up into the air.

His hand flashed white and the ball ricocheted off his hand with a loud clack. It immediately returned to its natural color. "I'll be damned," said Jim. "I didn't feel it at all."

Kayanan let another fly, and another and just before the ball struck, Jim's hand flashed white and deflected the balls as if made from solid marble. He continued to lob the balls higher and migrated them higher up on his arms and shoulders. Jim could now feel the sensation of willing his body to harden. It was the sensation of pushing his skin outwards and felt almost natural.

Kayanan showed Jim the final ball in his hand and lobbed it gently skyward towards the top of Jim's head. Jim knew where it was going to fall and hardened his head. His vision clouded and he could feel numbness rush from the top of his head down to his chin.

Kayanan snatched the handgun from the table and cooked off three rounds directly into Jim's forehead, kicking Jim's head backwards. The force of the bullets hitting his head made Jim react by hardening his whole body. He clattered to the floor, frozen as the golfball gently bonked against his neck and rolled away off the floor.

The men around the room gasped from Kayanan's unexpected gunplay. Rip shivered in shock as he sat on the floor, voiding his bladder into his diaper.

Jim's color returned and he got up from the floor unsteadily. "You could have killed me!"

Kayanan placed the expended gun back on the table. "Not a chance. When Simon hardens, *nothing* is strong enough to penetrate his body. I wanted to test your reaction time."

"You couldn't warn me first?" Asked Jim, feeling his forehead.

Big Lee, grinning, began to pull his shirt off, revealing the winding scars running around his body. "I'm next! If Jimbo can do this, then I'll be *real* impressed!"

Chapter Thirty Two:
Circus

Cesar went into his room and found the perfect hiding place for
Elena's soul. It was an old wooden cigar box—the same brand that his
uncle smoked. He opened the lid and took out the pictures of his family
to make room. "Don't worry *niña*," he said as he placed Elena's soul
carefully into the wooden box. "I'll figure something out."

He looked up at his clock—he had a few minutes before lunch.
He decided to head to the armory to get Tieran. He was worried about
the sword. He wanted to make sure that it was impossible for someone
like Naius Athum to steal it. He walked out of his room and headed out
of the building, across the green lawns to the armory. He liked to run
up the steps, but his side hurt too bad. He took them one at a time.

He walked into the simulation room and saw Tieran limping
over to the wall while winding up thin cables. He was sporting a huge
smile and was singing an old Chinese song. Behind him on the floor
was the remains of a freshly killed Jantu worm, blood still oozed from
it's fatty hide, contrasting dark fluids against it's glistening white skin.
"Ah! What do you think of my latest kill, young warrior?"

Cesar remembered the fear he felt when he saw Tieran torn apart
from the last one, so he kept his distance. "Um. Looks like he got you
—your leg is bleeding."

Tieran looked down, still smiling and kept winding his cable.
"Naw—my fault, that one. I was a little too premature with one of my
butterflies—it dug into my armor and cut into my leg." Tieran placed
the silver coil on the wall and walked over to the healing portal. He
passed through the thin doorway and was completely healed and
wearing Origin armor when he emerged through the other side. "Much
better. I'm quite pleased with myself—this was the first time that I was
able to defeat one of these creatures and walk away." He began to
remove his armor and place it on the wall rack. "Now tell me how you
hurt your side."

Cesar felt a cold chill run down his back. "My side—it's fine.
Are we going to lunch?"

"I could tell right away—you're favoring your left side—your
ribs must hurt to stand straight. When I heard you speak, it was
confirmed. Your voice isn't as loud and it's a bit wheezy. You also

aren't breathing as deeply as you normally would. What happened to you Cesar?"

Cesar tried to straighten his posture, but felt the sharp stitch in his side. "Um. Nothing—I was climbing a tree—you know, that big Oak near the lake—I slipped and fell on the ground—knocked the wind out of me. I'm fine—really."

Tieran walked over, still smiling. "We'll see." He bent over and grabbed the hem of Cesar's shirt. Cesar looked at him warily, and then moved his arm to the side so that he could get a better look. "Whoa. Cesar, this is really serious! One or more of your ribs could be cracked."

Cesar shook his head, but he looked down himself and saw deep purple and black bruising radiating outwards from his ribs. "Gosh—I didn't realize that it was that bad!"

Tieran clucked his tongue and walked Cesar over the healing portal. "In you go boy—I think you needed this more than I did." Cesar walked into the doorway and saw the room on the other side bend and shimmer. He stepped through and felt a soft breeze blow on his size, a slight tingle and all the pain was gone. He lifted his shirt and saw perfect skin.

Tieran chuckled. "Better? I'm starving and you're always hungry—so let's get out of here!" They walked out of the armory and continued to the pavilion. Cesar told Tieran about the attack on Jim Smith's daughter and that she was killed. Tieran listened patiently to everything he said, but his joviality was gone. His jaw was firm and he looked concerned.

When they arrived at the pavilion, Theo and Bob hadn't arrived. They sat at their usual table and drank Chinese tea. Cesar watched Tieran's gaze and wondered why his mood turned dark. "Hey Tieran, you should have seen Big Lee's dog."

Tieran looked at Cesar. He put down his cup. "Things are happening faster than I thought Cesar—I don't know what's on the horizon next, but I think it involves Ikorsom."

"Isn't it safe?" Asked Cesar. "I mean, who else knows the word to unlock it?"

"Only two—the creator and myself. So you saw Naius Athum here—tell me what you saw."

"Not much to tell," said Cesar. "He looked really drunk and walked from the tree to the temple. He made it to the fountain and fell in. I looked to see where he ended up and Rothiel is holding him prisoner. He's in really bad shape."

"Sorry we're late!" Bob and Theo sat down at the table. Bob was sporting a famished smile and snapped his fingers for service. Theo kissed the top of Cesar's head and sat next to him. Bob noticed Tieran's less than glowing smile. "What's up sourpuss?"

"I'm just a bit concerned," said Tieran. "This business with Smith and these visits from Naius. Doesn't it seem a bit odd that things are happening more quickly?"

Bob nodded to the waiter for the coffee and then looked Tieran in the eye. "Well, to be honest, we've noticed increased activity from Rothiel's camp. He's been performing nightly raids on Rota and by our estimates, has already taken about 40% of the town."

"Raids? Tell me," said Tieran leaning forward. "What's he doing with all the people?"

Bob grimaced and then turned to the waiter, "I'll have the Carbonara." He put his menu down and looked back at Tieran. "He's building an army. That's probably around 10% of the people he's already taken. The rest is simply to feed them. Let's talk about something else."

"Bob, tell the creator that Rothiel needs to go."

"I've tried. Why don't you tell him?"

Tieran impatiently flicked the edge of his Chinese cup, making a soft clink. "I've been trying. I've been telling him that this is precisely what he would do *before* he was freed from his cell. He told me to stop asking. And now with Naius walking around—I'm worried that he could get access to the armory."

Bob leaned back in his chair with a snide look on his face. "Now, that's a stretch."

"In all seriousness, I think all angles need to be considered at this point. What about Rip's men—what are they up to?"

Theo poured some tea. "Quite a bit—mostly training. Now that Rip is small and can't watch over the men like he did, Ricardo Kayanan has been sneaking into Rota at night and reconnoitering the old town. I think he's trying to pinpoint Rothiel's lair. They've also begun training the conduit—so far he's matched every one of their abilities."

"How would Rothiel take control of Ikorsom?" asked Cesar. "Wouldn't he have to come here to get it?"

Everyone stopped to consider Cesar's outburst. Bob tapped a pen on the table while thinking. "Either the tree or the Circus," he said at last. "That is, unless you bring it to Earth with you."

Tieran shook his head. "I'm leaving it in the vault. If God gave me the go-ahead, I still wouldn't use it—I can defeat him without it."

Theo was looking through her patch-glasses. "Rothiel has the number thirteen—he's not coming through the tree. Can he get through the Circus?"

Tieran shook his head. "As I recall, the last time it was used was to judge and subsequently exile Rothiel and the traitors right after the rebellion. It was sealed thereafter."

Cesar sat in his chair, deep in thought. He was using his fingertip to draw pictures in the condensation on his water glass. "How does it work? –The Circus, I mean. Can someone like Rothiel travel through it?"

Bob sat back in his chair and shook his head.

Tieran turned the thought through his head. "No one in a mortal state has the power to project himself through it. You see, it was used in the old days as an arena to watch games. Epic battles were fought there between Origin, humans, animals—almost anything. Humans on Earth didn't travel to it, it sort of bridges the two worlds so that we can observe. If you are Origin, you have sufficient power to just step through, back and forth. None of the mortals have that kind of power."

Cesar noticed that he had drawn the word 'Filo' on the side of the glass. "Bob, you said before that Filodraxes could hex entire armies—couldn't he hex through the Circus?"

Bob shook his head again. "No. I don't think so. It would require much more power than what he has."

"But what if they work together?"

"What? Simon and Filodraxes?" Bob laughed and sipped his coffee. "Simon can barely manage a portal for just one!"

"No," said Cesar. "What if Filodraxes and Rothiel combine forces?"

Bob looked perplexed. "What?" He sat up in his chair and fidgeted with his watch chain.

Theo saw that he was concerned. "Bob. What is it?"

I thought I remember hearing about something," said Bob, wrinkling his brow as he searched his patch. "It was called 'honor sacrifice'. It had something to do with a loophole in preventing Exiles from killing themselves and not being reincarnated." Bob found what he was looking for and narrowed his eyes. "Hmm. Here it is. Apparently, if the Exiles have the ability to teleport themselves to a permeable plane, they can either kill themselves or each other or not come back. Reincarnation depends on them dying on the Earth plane."

Theo folded her hands on the table. "Let me guess, the Circus is a permeable plane."

Bob nodded his head. "The two of them definitely have the power to get there—if I know anything about Rothiel, he's probably aware of it."

"But it doesn't make sense," said Cesar. "If they go there and fight, they may die—for good."

Bob closed his patch and took a deep breath. "Time to go see the old man again. I think that Rothiel will plan on going there, if only under the belief that he can break through to this world."

Chapter Thirty Three:
Romper Room

Jim Smith now understood why Big Lee was given that
moniker. He also realized why he weighed so much. The thing that
now stood over him was massive. After Big Lee 'grew' by snapping,
popping and pulling itself outward, he towered over Jim Smith,
shivering. It had the same face, but had a single, mean-looking horn
towering over it. His voice was much deeper, but his loud demeanor
was still the same.

"C'mon boy! Don't just stand there—show me whatcha got!"

Big Lee gave a sidelong glance toward Kayanan, who winked
back at him. Big Lee wound up and hurled a massive punch towards
Jim's head. Jim flashed white and windmilled across the room, coming
to rest in a sheared pile of splintered wood and metal frame. Rip was
angry. Those bleachers cost real money and were hand-made. He was
too busy enjoying the show to yell at Big Lee. He would wait until it
was over.

Jim stood up from the ruined bleachers and noticed the Bishop
hanging from the wall only a foot away. He leaped towards the carcass
and grabbed at the butterfly, sending it spinning towards Big Lee's
kneecap. It deflected off without making the slightest scratch. Big Lee
whooped and ran at Jim, cocking a hand backwards like he was holding
an invisible bowling ball. Jim put up both hands in a vain attempt to
block the strike and flashed white. Big Lee slapped Jim's diminutive
body upwards, driving him into the massive steel I-beams running
along the ceiling. A loud crunch echoed through the gym as he buckled
the steel beam and sent surrounding cement and plaster flying. His
body fell to the floor and cartwheeled twice before clattering to a stop.

"Shit—shit!" yelped Rip as he rocked in anger on the blanketed
floor where he was sitting. He popped a pacifier in his mouth and
glared at Big Lee. Big Lee looked up at the damaged ceiling and then
towards the baby. He shrugged his shoulders and mouthed, 'sorry'.

Jim got up from the floor and looked at his body for damage.
He was missing both tennis shoes and his sweats were mutilated. *I
don't know how long I can keep this up*, he thought. He looked at the
grinning giant and suddenly felt his skin tremble. He looked at his left
hand and saw the skin swim across his hand. He imagined making it

larger like Big Lee's and felt a slight twinge in pain. His hand expanded in waves. It nearly doubled in size. Big Lee stopped and stared at his adversary's large hand.

Jim somehow understood that his body could expand as well as contract. He could almost visualize the atoms moving apart by a small amount, making his body grow exponentially. He was lost in thought when he saw Big Lee's massive hand sweeping towards him and he again, flashed white. Jim's hardened body struck a wall and bounced back, clattering across the floor. Jim rolled over on his stomach and placed his palms on the floor. He pushed his atoms apart. He could feel the cement floor seemingly contracting under his hands and the remaining tatters of his sweats bursting at the seams. He got up on all fours and saw Gellan staring back in shock. The top of his head throbbed and itched. He stood up and at that moment realized just how tall he was. He stood easily a full head and shoulders higher than Big Lee. He raised his hand to scratch his forehead and was greeted by a crown of horns. Short, but sharp, they grew in all directions.

He looked down and saw that he was naked. He instinctively dropped both hands over his crotch. "I'm relieved," said Jim, smiling. "At least everything grew by the same amount."

Big Lee hesitated for a moment, shrugged and said, "Let's see!" and after slapping Jim's modest hands aside, grabbed a handful of crotch. Jim's ability to harden was immediate. Big Lee hoisted Jim from the floor and shook him around. "Yo guys—he's the same weight! A lot of good gett'in big is going to help if he's still around 200 pounds. Shit...I could blow him away."

Jim could hear his opponent laughing and could feel the slight movement of being yanked around by his manhood. He unfroze his head to take a look. Big Lee was holding him over his head like rigid umbrella. He unfroze his arms and folded them. "Um, when did you first discover that you like to hold cocks?"

Big Lee swung and uppercut towards Jim's face just after it flashed white again. "You call this a cock?"

Jim unfroze everything except his crotch and swung his legs around Big Lee's torso. In the same quick movement, he locked both arms firmly around Big Lee's neck and flashed white.

Big Lee let go of Jim's crotch and tried to pull him off. He began to hammer against his body with his hands—nothing worked.

Jim had squeezed Big Lee's neck hard enough so that it was getting difficult to breath. His vision began to grey out. He fell down to one knee, still tugging on Jim's body trying to dislodge it. "Fuck. All right, I give. Lemme go!"

Jim unfroze and jumped off Big Lee, narrowly avoiding his fist when he swung it towards his head. Big Lee was too winded to get up from the floor so he sat down, glowering at Jim's naked form. "Now I need to wash my hands, you dirty bastard."

"That's... simply amazing," said Kayanan, clapping his hands. "The fact that you were able to enlarge yourself and choke off Corey is really something."

"It ain't gonna happen again!" hollered Big Lee getting up from the floor. "Next time I'll wait until he runs out of air and he has to unfreeze. Then he gets an ass-whipping!"

"Actually," said Jim, feeling his horns again with his hand. "I could breathe the entire time. I think just my exterior was frozen."

Kayanan nodded. Well, let's see if Hank can do something about your weight."

Hank walked towards Jim and eyed the free weights lying on racks towards the far wall of the room. "We're going to start off gently —I'll begin with 200 pounds." He inhaled and set his jaw firm while he concentrated.

Jim felt his body weight bearing down on him. It was heavy. He stood his ground. Hank kicked it up a notch by adding double the weight. This time, Jim's knees almost buckled and he felt his body begin to shake. He could feel the weight moving about his body like heavy eels swimming through his veins. He tried to fight against the onslaught but was failing. He looked into Hank's eyes and for a moment, felt that he was able to displace weight from nearby objects. Somehow the free weights were temporarily emptying their combined weight into Jim's body. Jim could feel the eels moving around inside his body, more and more of them, driving him down. He concentrated on moving the eels out of his body and felt them struggle. In an instant, he forced the eels out and towards the rack of iron weights.

Hank was surprised that with all of his concentration, the weight was being forced away from Jim and back towards the rack. "No fucking way you are going to best me."

He directed all of the weight towards Jim and he could feel it approach. He blocked it with his mind and the swarming mass of weight hovered just before him. It was unseen, but he could feel it there. Hank's brow was contorted in concentration. He gritted his teeth and clenched and unclenched both hands. It was no use—the mass would not budge.

Slowly, Jim moved the mass towards Hank. If he didn't give up, he would see how Hank could deal with all the weight. Hank began to shuffle backwards and hyperventilate. The mass continued on its journey towards him and he could not make it stop.

"Now what the fuck are you two doing?" asked Big Lee. "You gonna drop this guy or what, Hank?"

Hank let go and the weight rushed towards him. Jim was surprised at the loss of Hank's control and stopped it at the last minute by sending it all into Big Lee.

"Ugh!" Exhaled Big Lee when the mass entered his body, making his body as responsive as a rag doll. His knees were the first to impact the floor. He put his hands out to prevent his upper body from making contact, but it made no difference—his chest, followed by his face, slammed into the deck.

Jim immediately released the mass and it swarmed back into the free weights. Big Lee rolled over on his back and took a deep breath. "Oh *fuck*. Guys? Are we done here?"

Chapter Thirty Four:
The Worth of Naius

Rothiel stood over the table and looked at his notes. Naius'
drunken ramblings had yielded a table full. He glanced up at the clock.
"Valgiernas? Where is your team?"

"My lord, they should have been back by now—I've dispatched
two more teams to investigate. We should hear something within the
hour."

Rothiel stared at Valgiernas for a few more silent moments. He
watched him swallow and knew the point had been made. He looked
over at Abraham Kennedy's sleeping form. His breathing was shallow.
He would probably not live much longer. "He said his name was *Naius
Athum*. Do you remember someone of that name?

"No my lord. He was probably one of Rip's men—over the
centuries he probably forgot who he was."

Rothiel picked up a piece of paper with the origin word of *cook*
scrawled next to *circus*. "I believe I remember him," he began.
"During the many circuses we enjoyed plentiful food. And do you
remember what else there was?"

Rothiel lowered his eyes and shook his head. "I'm sorry my
lord, I remember nothing of the circus."

"Pity. It was the best place to plan rebellion."

Rothiel walked over to the sleeping man's form. His belly was
slick with sour booze and infection began to form around the wire
holding his wrists and ankles. "Ah, Naius how I enjoyed your crafts of
those days! ...It may have been your very concoctions that gave me the
will and vision I needed to become a God."

He placed a hand on his sleeping shoulder and reflected on the
past. He spun towards Valgiernas. "We need to prepare Naius for one
more journey. I believe he can bring back something extremely
valuable."

"Something that can defeat Rip's men?"

Rothiel smiled. "Almost—at least something that will enslave
the strongest of them."

Chapter Thirty Five:
Night Ops

Jim walked into the living room wearing the black nomex suit that Kayanan handed him. It fit easily, since he shrunk down to his normal size. His many horns also disappeared when he returned to normal. His boots looked like something out of the military, but had thick plastic plates covering the tops and ankles. Kayanan said they were made out of Kevlar. On the large living room table, were maps of the old town of Rota. Kayanan was pointing different things out on the map and drawing something with a marker.

"Hey guys, did I miss anything?" Jim noticed that only Gellan was wearing a similar suit.

Gellan was making final preparations with a video camera. "How do you feel—you've had quite a workout this afternoon?"

Jim noticed Big Lee sulking near the fireplace. "Just fine. Aren't we all going?"

Kayanan motioned Jim over to the table. "Nope. It's going to be just you and Gellan. Hank and I will be supporting from a short distance. Simon's not feeling well enough yet, but he's coming along for moral support. Kayanan opened a silver case, pulled out a handgun and slid it across the table towards Gellan. Gellan picked it up, checked the clip and pushed it into a holster under his armpit.

"A gun?" asked Jim. "I thought they were useless."

Kayanan looked at Jim. "Nothing to worry about. He's not going to be hunting any of those creatures—he may need it for something else." He opened a black rucksack and pulled out a nylon fanny-pack. He opened it and showed Jim the plastic cylinders. "Cyalume light sticks. You'll be carrying these."

Jim looked at Gellan's pistol and then to the light sticks held in Kayanan's hand. "Excuse me for saying, but it doesn't seem fair."

Kayanan laughed. "You're the one with all the abilities! I would give you some butterflies and cobra cable, but I don't want anything to slow you down. Come over and take a look."

Jim looked at the map of Rota on the table and saw two routes drawn in red and black.

"The red one's you," said Kayanan, pointing to the beginning of the line near the lighthouse. "You are going in first. You have an...

unexpected ability—to solidify parts of your body. Simon can do all or nothing. He also cannot breathe when he does it. You seem to be able to freeze areas on demand—that is going to come in real handy." He pointed to the lighthouse. "You'll start here, approximately thirty seconds before Gellan begins here, at the entrance of Rota beach. You're going to run towards this wall—it's shared by two homes—don't worry, the occupants have been gone now for weeks."

"A wall? You mean a solid, brick wall? Right?"

"Don't worry—we calculate, that if you get your speed up to around thirty three to forty miles per hour, solidify at the right moment, you'll sail right through it. The problem is, you are going to have to maintain that speed the entire time as you'll be penetrating other walls throughout this path." Kayanan zipped up the cyalume sticks in Jim's fanny-pack and snapped it around Jim's waist. "One other thing—Gellan will be coming through thirty seconds later—you are going to have to drop these sticks in every other room—Gellan's camera is low light, but his eyesight isn't—this will help him navigate through the rooms where he'll be taking high-speed video."

Jim looked at the camera with distrust. How will he be able to tape everything—is he going to spin it around?

Gellan turned the camera sidways so Jim could get a better look. There were lenses on each end. "Both are fish-eye lenses. That way it has an infinite depth of view—no need to focus and the software that Mr. Plak has coded will translate the image flat so we can see the rooms perfectly."

"What are you hoping to capture with that thing?"

Gellan looked at Kayanan. "Well, we need an accurate count of how many people Rothiel's stolen. We'd like to see what his new army looks like."

"We're also looking for Rothiel's prison," added Kayanan. "When he was first released we saw some writings carved in the inside. Rothiel was able to stay almost perfectly preserved during his multiple-millennia stay inside—it may provide answers on how to get Filodraxes back in shape."

"Ahem." Luisa was standing in the foyer with her daughters on either side. "Is this the *man* that's going to help you fight Rothiel?"

Kayanan muttered under his breath in English, "Just ignore her."

Luisa glared at Kayanan. "Does he understand Spanish, pineapple?"

Gellan grabbed Kayanan's forearm. "Rick, don't let her piss you off. We need to stay clear."

"*Si, señora*, I speak Spanish," said Jim with a slight smile. "How may I help you?"

"*Por fin*, someone with some manners!" said the witch. She clutched her jack close to the small of her back and felt it surge with energy. *God-damn, is this one strong*, she thought. "I brought something that will protect you tonight."

She motioned her dark-haired daughter forward. "It will not allow anything to harm you—very magical!" The girl was carrying a bead necklace that had a small leather pouch dangling from the center. She placed it around his neck and then turned around to join her sister. "*Por favor*, keep it with you." She took her eyes off Jim and looked around the room at the others-- her perpetual scowl returned. "*Suerte eh?*" She turned on her heel and left with her daughters in tow.

"Who—the"

Jim was cut off from Kayanan. "Don't. We'll talk when we get to the truck."

The men walked out to the truck and climbed in. Gellan gently removed the necklace from Jim's neck, turned and dashed into the night towards the bullpens. He was back in a few seconds, climbing into the cab.

Kayanan was smiling. "Which one?"

"Oh, uh—I put it on Marfil. It woke him up—he'll be pissed off and running around for hours!"

Luisa sat staring into the small copper pot filled with water. She watched the paisley oils in the surface of the water swirl from the warmth of the candle's flame as it licked the bottom of the pot. She could only see flashes of the surrounding area, not the full view that the long-dead sheep's eye projected while nestled in the leather bag that she placed around Jim's neck. She could make out a dark animal— something rubbing its head against a tree. Running towards a fence. Watching a big, white truck drive off with men inside. *Maldición*, thought the witch, chewing the side of her cheek in anger.

Jim stood between the lighthouse and the white truck. He looked over at Simon who was listening intently to the truck radio for a signal from Kayanan. With Kayanan roughly a mile away, he could still feel him—or better yet, the way he constantly measured the things around him for battle. He felt his skin flutter—Big Lee was back at the ranch, a good 40 minutes drive from here—he could change if he wanted. *Better not*, thought Jim. *I'd ruin these clothes and be too big to perforate these walls cleanly.* He drummed his fingertips against his leg and heard the pitch change when he hardened just the fingertips.

Simon nodded.

Jim tore off from a standstill and accelerated beyond thirty. He was easily doing fifty miles per hour. He bucked 90 degrees to the right towards the old wall running parallel to the sea. He hardened and burst through the wall with an enormous crash and before he knew it, went through two additional walls without slowing down. He remembered the light sticks. "Shit!" He spun around, dove a hand behind him into his fanny pack and pulled out a stick. He snapped the inner chamber, gave a quick shake and dropped it into the first room. He turned and continued into the massive holes that he punched through previously. He accelerated to a more manageable thirty miles per hour and punched through another wall. He found himself in the middle of an outdoor courtyard, where he grabbed another light stick, snap-shake and dumped it on the move. *Wall ahead*, he thought as he hardened the front of his body. This one had a steel door blocking what looked like a garage. He slammed through it easily but it came with him, wrapped around him like a cardboard box. He slid to a stop, with his knees riding the misshapen door and threw it aside. He dropped another cyalume and shot to thirty within a few feet of the next wall.

Kayanan whistled when he saw the dust and brick shards rise above some of the courtyards that Jim was penetrating. "You seeing this Hank?"

Hank stood closer to the buildings and answered back over his radio—"He's making a huge racket—it's sure to bring 'em this way!"

Kayanan thought about it—checked his watch, it had only been fifteen seconds. "Go ahead and send in Gellan."

Gellen saluted Hank, pushed the red record button the camera and took off. He banked 90 degrees west and entered the hole that Jim made. *He must have been flying by the look of this destruction*, he thought. He saw bricks and dust everywhere; plumbing sprayed water from upstairs pipes and in the second room the upstairs floor had buckled downwards. *Good boy*, thought Gellan, as he saw the first of the light sticks lighting the way.

Jim broke through more and more walls, sometimes slowing him down so that he felt like the walls were trying to pull him back in like vines. He kicked up the pace, making the bricks explode off him. He was tossing light sticks at a rapid pace and twice he had to stop, turn back and pick them up to break and re-shake them. *Calm down—we're doing fine*, he thought. He burst through an alley way and saw the sign, Calvario. *Whoops! Turn north here and enter the fourth house*, he thought to himself. He knew this was the longest run, which in all probability would take him through the center of Rothiel's camp. He burst through the front wall of the house, snagging his right arm on the gypsy bars. He flung them aside and dropped another light stick. He went through at least eight walls until he burst through a large room that was illuminated.

He knew to ignore what was in the room, but his eyes showed people shrieking and groaning in large, wooden crates. He dropped a light stick and from the left saw a man level a shotgun towards him. He turned directly towards him, hopped up in the air and hardened. He heard the shotgun boom, and then felt himself stop against the wall. He unfroze and saw the dead man, crushed beneath him. He dropped a fresh light stick into his open mouth and continued through three more walls. Most of the rooms were lit, as there were open fires in the middle of the rooms with black logs protruding out of the flames. He passed more closely and to his shock, found that they were some of Protraxis' creations slowly rotating in the fire. Some were groggily getting up after hearing Jim's commotions as he burst through the walls.

Halfway there, he thought—*gotta look for a well*. After he broke through two more walls, a loud shriek cried up somewhere behind him. *Damn—that must be their alarm. 'Bout time, too*. He hit a wall that almost stopped him completely—there was a stone spiral staircase behind it. *Fuck! That, I felt*. He saw the well, turned 90 degrees and bashed through the next wall. He kicked up the speed and went through another nine walls. All the same, fires, bugs and people in crates. *These all look dead*, he thought as he took a second to glance at the people stuffed in boxes. At the tenth wall, he burst through, saw the big red arrow that Kayanan painted on the wall and hooked south. *There's the big X on the wall-- time to head back to the lighthouse*. He hardened and passed through, dropping a light stick after he passed. He smashed through more and more walls, sometimes contemplating whether this was damaging his brain-- all the while fishing out light sticks, breaking the inner chambers, shaking and dropping with the skill of a mobile Rosie the Riveter. He was back in the big illuminated rooms and saw the glowing green of his previous work. He saw something dark shooting through his previous doorway, so he cocked a hardened fist. Instead of one of Rothiel's creatures, he saw Gellan, legs pumping furiously while holding the camera perfectly still. He unfroze his fist and held up his palm, making a loud crack as the two passed each other in a loud high-five.

Gellan shook the pain from his hand thinking, *Now that was stupid—especially at this speed.* He felt energized that everything was going to plan. He could feel the whirring of the highspeed camera and knew that he was halfway finished. He began to doubt that they would find the casing that held Rothiel until he emerged into the next room and saw it. It had yellow stickies stuck to the inside. He held the camera to make sure it got a good shot, then ran up, swiped off all the yellow squares of paper, and then stood back to make a clean shot. He heard someone behind him snore.

Startled, Gellan spun around and found a large black man asleep in a chair. The chair was solid wood; similar to something you would electrocute a death row inmate with. His ankles and wrists were tied tightly to the chair with thick wire. The man stunk from alcohol. His shirt was torn open, displaying the origin number thirteen over his left breast. Gellan looked at the huge oak table next to him and it was covered with papers. He stuffed a handful inside his Nomex shirt, pulled out the pistol and shot the sleeping man twice through the heart and once in the head. Gellan didn't know if he struck something or fatigue from his running, but he felt a sharp pain in his calves. He glanced down and saw three black quills hanging out. He looked towards the door and saw a drone slowly climbing towards him. He shot out of the room and tried to reach his maximum speed out Jim's exit path. He had everything they were looking for—no need to hang around. Automatic rifle fire opened up somewhere behind him, but he was out of the room and following the little green dots showing the way out. The pain in his legs began to fade and so did his speed. The strength in his legs was dropping off rapidly. He tried to move at a slow run, but his legs felt like jelly. He knew that the faster he ran, the quicker the black bile would run through his body. His tongue began to thicken inside his mouth and his breathing was difficult. He began to search for a place to toss the camera, in the event that he wouldn't make it.

"Gellan! Man, are you hit?" Jim shot up behind him and grabbed him around the waist. "I heard some gunfire and came back—can you walk?"

"Just take the camera, man—I'm finished. Get it to Rick—tha's all that... matters."

"You just hang on—I'll get us out!" Jim flipped the camera strap over his head and then put Gellan's arm around his neck. Gellan tried to lift his legs but they were now unresponsive. They just kicked and dragged as Jim tore through the passages. They emerged on the street and saw a mass of black creatures blocking the path to the lighthouse. They were hissing and advancing towards them. Jim knew that Hank and Kayanan were on the opposite side of Rota and that they needed to get to the truck first. Jim ran at full speed towards the black army and sliding Gellan onto his back, passed both of their combined weight into the first line of drones in front. Jim kicked off from the ground and both rose into the night air. Jim hardened just in time, as hundreds of black quills rained against him, deflecting off his skin and falling harmlessly below.

After they passed over the army underneath them, Jim noticed that their path was taking them over some nearby rooftops. He let a little more weight creep in and they both came down on top of the *Los Arcos Bar* roof. He noticed that the black army below was turning around with ungainly clumsiness and getting gridlocked in the narrow passageway leading to the lighthouse. Jim looked at Gellan's face and saw him shivering. His eyelids were fluttering as he succumbed to the poison coursing through his central nervous system. He jumped down and carried Gellan to the back of the truck. Simon had already started up the big diesel engine when he saw Jim land on a nearby rooftop. When he saw both men enter the back, he drove the truck towards the *Playa de Costilla* road to double around and pick up the other two. Jim pulled Gellan towards the cab and rummaged through a black bag that Kayanan prepared. He found a clear syringe with a red label and knocked on the rear window of the truck. Simon turned around to look.

"Is this the right one? Gellan was hit with quills!"

Simon looked at the syringe and nodded. He mouthed the word, leg.

Jim pulled off the cap with his teeth and buried the needle into Gellan's leg and pushed the plunger down. He tossed the used syringe into the back of the truck and looked back at Simon. "Just one?" Simon nodded, then turned around and continued to drive towards the pickup point. Gellan continued to shiver, so Jim grabbed a blue tarp lying in the back and wrapped him in it. He looked over at the camera and hoped it was all worth it.

Chapter Thirty Six:
Inventory

Rothiel looked at the scattered documents on the floor as several stage-II addicts worked to clean up the mess. Two were cutting the wire bonds on Naius Athum's wrists and ankles, finally sliding his dead body to the floor. "He was almost dead anyway. Besides, we have what we wanted. Do we know what documents were stolen?"

"I'm not sure my lord," began Valgiernas. I believe that they are my notes on the carnival arena. He may have also taken the notes describing the location of the armory and the temple, as they're missing."

Valgiernas thought about the missing documents. "It's good. I want them to know about the arena—ultimately it is our destiny, our salvation. The location of the armory is meaningless to them. When I have the ultimate weapon in my hands I will use it on a scale never seen since the moment of creation."

"My lord—I have stationed a dozen drones at each entry and a bishop at each to control them. They won't be coming back through those areas."

Rothiel scowled at Valgiernas. "Are you blind?" He waved his arms around at the visible destruction in the room. "Should I have Protaxsis create a new set of eyes for you? What makes you believe that they couldn't make their own way in like they did this evening?" Rothiel struck out his right arm and dug his fingernail into Valgiernas' forehead. Valgiernas felt worms coursing through his skull devouring flesh and bone as they coiled through his neck and into his chest. His scream was muffled with bloody froth as the worms multiplied exponentially and shredded his lungs in a thick, coiling mass.

Valgiernas dropped to his knees as blood poured from his face and chest. He tried to beg but the pain was too great as the worms corkscrewed into his bones. He could feel the crunching and popping as they hungrily devoured marrow and cartilage. His eyes greyed out and he slipped into darkness.

He awoke on the floor—his face lay in a pool of vomit. The only blood he found was weeping from his forehead. There was no pain. He got up on his feet unsteadily and looked into the face of his master. "My lord—it wasn't real?"

327

"Oh it will be. It most certainly will. The moment you fail me again, those worms will return—and they will take days to kill you. The pain you felt was but a small sample of what you will truly feel. Do you understand me, servant?"

Valgiernas didn't want to look him in the eye—he knew that through the briefest of eye contact he could get inside if he wanted. His head swum. "Yes my lord. I'll—I'll never fail you again."

Jim sat back in the chair nursing a cold root beer. Filthy was excitedly scanning through the video. "This is fucking gold! Come on mama, show me what you got... Oh yes! Oh yes! Jesus, you can make everything out!"

"Does any of this help," asked Jim, growing impatient with Filthy's delight. "This wasn't easy you know—Gellan got hit bad."

"Actually he's coming around nicely, said Kayanan, entering the room. He doesn't even remember getting hit with quills. How's it look Gid?"

Filthy was bouncing up and down on his roll around chair. "Oh man, perfect detail! You can make out all the carvings. I'm having trouble deciphering some of the characters—we need Gellan for this. But look at the detail—there's something here about names—I'm there, so are you! I think we're all in there. It must be his hate list!"

Kayanan stifled a laugh. "Great news, I'm sure. After I left Gellan I checked on Rip—he's sound asleep in his crib. I say we let him sleep until morning." Kayanan looked over at Jim. "You did a great job tonight—especially saving Gellan like you did."

Jim removed the root beer bottle from his temple. "I'm feeling really beat—it must be the energy hangover you described. One thing I saw lots of—people stuffed in wooden crates. That and a bunch of those bugs were crawling around in fire. What gives?"

Kayanan sat down at the table and fished out a Coke from the cooler. He contemplated Jim's question with a frown. "I think that the people are for two things. To make more of their menagerie...or to feed them. From what we know about these creatures' thick skins, they appear to thicken up based on threats from their environment. They probably use fire to invoke a reaction so that their hides will harden for protection."

Filthy rewound the video to look for the crates. He found them in the chamber before Rothiel's cell. He zoomed in closer to observe the cells and panned over to each one.

Jim was horrified by what he saw. He saw Manoli's sons, Oscar and Pablo, pale and listless, hanging onto the slats of the crates and crying for help. He had stood only feet from their box. His root beer bottle crashed to the floor as he shot to his feet. "I've got to get them out of there!"

Kayanan leapt out of his chair and grabbed Jim by his shoulders. "You can't—none of us can. Listen! By now they've got all of their freaks surrounding that place. They won't allow us to get back in there. The best thing we can do is analyze the data we've got and try to put a stop to them before they get harmed."

Jim couldn't pull his eyes away from the screen. He was shivering and brought a nervous hand up to his mouth. "Look at them! They're dying! I've got to do something!"

The phone rang. The answering machine instantly came to life with Juani's voice, announcing the business hours for the fictitious bull ranch. Valgiernas' voice crackled over the tinny speaker. "Gentlemen —please pick up. We wish to declare a truce. Come on—pick up the phone."

Filthy walked over to the phone and looked at Kayanan. Kayanan looked perplexed. He nodded for him to answer it. "Um Hello?"

"...No...I'm Gideon. Yes, you too. Ah. I'll have to check. Please wait."

Gideon covered the mouth piece with his hand. "He wants to talk to Corey."

Kayanan sat back in his chair mulling over the request with a sullen expression. He raised his eyebrows and looked at Jim. "...I'll get him."

He jumped out of his chair and pushed Jim down into his. "Wait here! There may be a solution!" He ran out of the room and down the hallway.

With a fresh smile, Gideon returned the handset back to his face, "He's coming, one second please. –Rather exciting night eh?"

He was answered in silence.

329

Kayanan and Big Lee stood outside the gate, alongside the road that ran in front of the fortress. Kayanan gazed intently into Big Lee's eyes. "Do you remember what to do? It's important that you do not accept anything from them—I don't care if it's an olive out of a can or a piece of paper with the world's greatest cookie recipe—nothing of theirs can come back here."

"Man, back off." Said Corey, looking towards the night sky in aggravation. "I remember. I'll git you what you want. There's nothing that he can hurt me with—they just want to talk, tha's all."

Kayanan tapped Big Lee's chest. "They want Diano—you know this. Try to stay flexible—we won't ever give him up, but they don't need to know that."

They both heard a truck lumbering down the road in the distance. Big Lee looked down at Kayanan's face. "Dude—tha's probably them. If he's in that cab I *know* you two are going to go at it. Why don't you go ahead and git back to the house?"

Kayanan felt for the close-quarters fighting knife in its sheath at the small of his back. "Valgiernas won't have the balls to come near this place again. Good luck."

Kayanan looked back towards the approaching headlights and walked backwards past the gate. Kayanan raised his handheld radio to his mouth and nodded at Big Lee. "Close it and alarm." The ranch doors swung shut and Kayanan melted into the shadows.

An old, flatbed truck trundled up next to Big Lee. The window rolled down to show the face of a grade-II addict—an older man in his fifties. "*Es usted, el...Beeg Lee?*"

Big Lee walked to the back of the truck, slung up a fat leg and hoisted himself onto the bed. The springs of the truck bottomed out, shaking the driver roughly while Big Lee settled into a sitting position. "Le's go, man. *Vamanos.*"

"Koriet—I haven't seen you in ages," said Valgiernas, as Big Lee stepped off the truck. "Welcome to our humble abode!"

"Actually Val, I saw you in Missouri back in the 1800's. We weren't friends then, as I recall."

Valgiernas noticed that Big Lee was staring at his holstered guns. He began to unbuckle them. "Sorry old man. You don't know who to trust these days—I mean look at what your friends did to my home?"

Big Lee looked at the rubble from the operation, then back to Valgiernas' guns. "Keep them on—they don't do nuthin' anyways."

Valgiernas tut-tutted him and offered a gloved hand. Big Lee looked at it with indifference.

"Sorry about the truck—it's the only thing we have that can handle a guest such as yourself—thirsty?"

Big Lee stood motionless. "I'm used to it, and no. I'm fine. ... What is it you want to discuss?"

"Not me, Koriet—our leader wishes to talk to you. Follow me please."

Big Lee followed Valgiernas through the smashed walls and into a living room area. He saw a large table with fruit stacked on it, large wine glasses and a big pitcher sparkling with condensation. Behind the table stood Rothiel. He looked relaxed and was smiling. "Welcome, brother."

As Big Lee approached the table, his nose felt something. It was a slight tickle—familiar, but he couldn't place it. It was a smell—something like a delicate spice—fruity, heady. He almost forgot that he could be in danger. "Wha's up, Rothiel?"

Rothiel motioned to a chair, especially built for him. It was made of recently welded steel, still unpainted with scorch marks where the welds burnt the original painted surface. He shuffled sideways and sat down.

"My, Koriet you are still as imposing as ever. So—you have allied yourself with Danhieras. By the way, have you found him yet?"

Big Lee didn't look at Rothiel. He kept his eyes on the fruit. He felt impatient. "What do you want Rothiel? Vengeance? Redemption? I can't help you. I don't know if you remember, but I didn't betray you—none of us did."

Rothiel chuckled and picked up the pitcher. "We'll get to that. For now, I merely want you to remember. To give you a small *taste* of the past." He picked up the clay pitcher and poured the red liquid into the goblet closest to Big Lee.

That familiar smell again. Endlessly sweet but with sourness that wakes the senses. He locked eyes with Rothiel. "I'm not... what is it—is that wine? I'm not thirsty."

My dear Koriet—this is something far greater than treasure. You have walked this miserable place for the better part of ten thousand years yearning for this liquid and now it sits before you! Are you going to let it waste away?"

Big Lee's eyes grew. He remembered a wine drunk at the circus that could fill his mind with stars with just the slightest sip. It satisfied the senses so completely that love and honor were just forgotten, unimportant concepts—they were mere whisps of feeling that fell from existence when this wine was sampled.

Rothiel poured himself a hearty portion, raised his goblet and took a gulp. He barely had time to place the goblet back on the table when his head was flung back in passion. His breathing increased in gasps and a small groan issued from his lips as his body betrayed his unlimited pleasure. He leaned back in his chair as his shoulders drooped and his head lolled downwards. He sat there for over a minute as as his breathing calmed. His head rose from his chest with a dreamy smile. "It's inconceivable that you can resist—do you remember this wine? It was called *Cassius Essence*. Naius was the only one that could make it—and now it sits before you."

Big Lee picked up the goblet and breathed in the endless vapors. It could drive someone mad, to be able to hold it but not drink. He felt tightness in his chest and dimmed vision. He felt as an old priest battling the urge to touch youthful beauty. So profane, so beckoning. He didn't feel the cool touch of the goblet to his lips-- only the red liquid that broached itself into his mouth. He felt the dust of thousands of years wash away from his throat. Flavors exploded across his tongue as a blind man's eyes would behold the whole of the Earth's beauty in an instant. There was no more want. Nothing else mattered.

The bliss seemed felt like it would last for days. His cheeks ached from the smiling. "How... how were you able to get this?"

"I had it made for you. Luckily for all of us, I wrote down the recipe before your men could assassinate Naius. That's him under the sheet."

Big Lee's gaze followed Rothiel's outstretched finger towards a body lying on the floor under a bloody sheet. Even in the midst of bliss, Big Lee became uncertain. "Why would they want someone like him dead—unless he is a threat to them?"

Rothiel smiled and tilted his head to the side. "Naius was no more a threat than a spring shower. I'm sure Danhieras—or whomever leads your people these days, wanted him dead because Naius and I can offer you things that they could not." Rothiel raised his goblet.

"Happiness for example. I get the feeling that he insists on forcing you to live like animals—like humans."

Big Lee shook his head in doubt. "I can't believe that they wanted him dead—I've never even heard his name before." He looked his goblet and saw a reflection of Rothiel's smiling face. "Why did you ask me to come anyway?"

"I've come to claim my birthright—starting with this world. I want to return to the ways of the past. Danhieras and a few others oppose me. We were made for greatness—not to suffer under the rule of primates."

"What about my son? What will you do with him?"

Rothiel kept his eyes on Big Lee's face. He noticed his furrowed brow and flare of his nostrils. "Nothing. From what I gather he was already banished from the face of the Earth." Rothiel laughed. "I ask you, is this the will of a benevolent creator? Ha!"

Rothiel leaned towards Big Lee to make his point. "He betrayed me—do you want to know why? He's half human. I can't blame him —he's a slave of his very blood. What I want from him is to stay hidden. When I assert control, I will slay those that oppose me. I only expect a few obstacles."

Big Lee sat up in his chair. "What do you have in mind for me?"

Rothiel smiled wide. "Simple. Do not get involved when I come for Danhieras and the few loyal to him. Do not get in the way. I want you to go back and tell those that will listen that I will bring back the greatness, the games, the gardens and I will bring back our former selves. But first, I intend to take my rightful place in heaven."

"You had tremendous power before," said Big Lee looking at the floor. "You were defeated easily."

Rothiel continued to smile, but the gleam was lost. "Why do you think he left me alive? The answer is, of course-- I cannot be killed. Being trapped inside the Earth gave me time to contemplate. A *long* time to contemplate. I know how to defeat him. Previously, I did not have the resources to take control. Now I have it—so close I can almost grasp it. The day I come for Danhieras and his loyals, I will be able to use it." Rothiel looked at Big Lee's goblet. "Join me in another drink to my success."

Kayanan and Jim sat on opposite couches brooding. They passed the time flicking butterflies back and forth at each other with perfect precision. Jim noticed that the dawn sun was peeking through the windows so he glanced at the clock. "Shit. It's nearly six — where the hell is Big Lee?"

Kayanan slipped the polished steel blade back inside his vest and rubbed the back of his neck. "I don't know how long this may take. He would be really hard to bring down, plus if things got too hot he'd break out of there."

The intercom crackled. It was Big Lee. "Yo — go ahead and open the gate — I'm too tired to figure out the frigg'in code!" There was the sound of wood breaking.

Kayanan peered into the monitor on the security panel and saw Big Lee, tearing open two crates just outside the gate. Kayanan scanned the other monitors for anything suspicious, then hit the green button.

Jim noticed the grin on Kayanan's face. "What is it — did he make it back okay?"

Kayanan was hurrying towards the door. "Better than okay — c'mon — he's got something to show you."

Jim stepped out and saw Big Lee walking up the drive with a content smile on his face. He was holding the hand of a disheveled-looking boy walking next to him and a younger, chubbier boy was tucked under the big man's arm like a football. It was Oscar and Pablo. Pablo was squealing in fright. The moment he saw Jim he stopped screaming and blew a big snot-bubble that covered half his face. "Mama..."

Jim picked him up from Big Lee's arms and gave both boys a hug. Oscar remained silent and didn't want to let go of Jim's hand. Jim looked at the two of them and other than scratches and bruises, both looked OK. Jim knew that Nino and Manoli were probably dead and only hoped that the boys weren't there to witness it. It took a good five minutes for Pablo to finally calm down and when he did, Jim whispered, "I know, I know. You're safe now. Are you hungry?" He already knew Pablo's answer.

Chapter Thirty Seven:
Status Report

"He said no." Bob closed the door behind him and shook his head towards the three sitting at the table in his conference room. Cesar sat in the middle and looked watched Theo and Tieran's reaction to Bob's news.

Although Bob's hair was flecked with grey, he still came from redheaded stock—so his anger was easily visible when his face turned flush. "I told him about the Circus, Naius—everything—he still refuses to shut Rothiel down."

"Did you tell him about his new army-- or the people he's taking from the town?" asked Tieran.

Bob nodded his head and seemed to turn more flush. "I told him in my most strongest terms that Rothiel is unleashing a veritable disaster on mankind. He just said, '*thank you*, but no military action is required.' Then he asked me to leave."

Theo held her face in her hands. Tieran was tapping a pen onto the surface of the desk in impatience.

"I found out some interesting things," began Cesar, just to break the uncomfortable mood. "Koriet Lee had a meeting with Rothiel early this morning."

"When?" Echoed the three adults in shock.

"Well—not long after Rip's men made it back to the fortress. They were reviewing video of the break-in and Valgiernas called them on their phone."

As if on queue, the three broke out their patches and were skimming backwards to see what happened during the meeting.

Bob was the first of the three to see the wine. "I'll be damned. That's *Cassius* wine that he's got there. How the hell did he get it?"

Cesar suddenly felt important, already knowing the answer. "Naius Athum gave him the recipe. Remember? He was the cook for games and circus. He was the only one who know how to make it out of things grown on Earth."

Bob was perplexed. "Well… yes, but I'm sure he would have forgotten it after all this time."

"That's just it," began Cesar with excitement. "He could sneak back here by getting drunk on Earth. I think Rothiel was making him return here to get information from the fountain."

Bob went back to digging through his patch. "Here, it says that he fell into the fountain in order to return to Earth—he was only inside it for a second or two."

"Maybe a few seconds was all that was needed," said Cesar, spinning his patch around so that Bob could see the display. "Look. Just before he died, he traveled here no less than nine times yesterday."

Theo blinked. "He died yesterday?"

"You didn't see it? Gellan *blew his brains out!*" said Cesar with youthful delight. "Oh. Sorry. Um, while you were watching Jim Smith run through the old town, I watched Gellan videotape some of the areas in Rothiel's stronghold. He found Naius and shot him."

Bob looked up at Tieran and shook his head. "This is of course, your fault. You and your weapons!"

Tieran folded his hands and looked towards the ceiling with a pious smile.

Bob's attention returned to his patch. Just as Big Lee sat down at the table the conversation died out under a garbled static.

"What the hell? What happened?"

Cesar was smiling again. "Same thing happened to me. If you pan the image back, you'll see an old, skinny man hissing at some children in boxes. See that? Somehow, that boy and girl go into some kind of... fit and whatever is going on in their minds is causing interference with the sound."

"It sounds like scratching or whispering," said Theo. "It sounds terrible."

"Don't turn it up," said Cesar wagging a finger. It's sounds terrifying if you turn it louder. It's from a poem by Rudyard Kipling called *Boots*. The children are repeating it inside their minds and it sounds like they're going crazy."

"Rothiel can defeat our monitoring?" Tieran was back to tapping the pen on the table with irritation. He looked up at Cesar. "Were you able to make out anything?"

"Not from their conversation." Cesar savoured the moment that all eyes were on him. "Here's something really weird though. After Big Lee left with Nino & Manoli's sons, Rothiel retired to his rooms.

His walls are laced with something that doesn't allow a patch to see through, but his bathroom doesn't. Watch this."

Cesar spun his patch around for the others to see. Rothiel's image was fuzzy and indistinct until it passed into the bathroom, becoming clear. He was sweating. He hunched down near the toilet and started heaving.

"Looks like he can't hold his liquor!" laughed Bob, grinning.

Tieran joined in while watching Rothiel's back arch. "Well, he's been on the wagon for ten thousand years—he's out of practice!"

Cesar grinned in anticipation.

Big jets of red liquid erupted out of his mouth and into the toilet. Bob and Tieran hoorayed. He continued regurgitating until something pale and slippery began to emerge from his mouth. Rothiel's eyes bugged out as he choked on the object in his mouth. He gripped it and began to pull. Inch after inch of the glistening tube came out of his mouth until a large mass as big as a man's fist came out and plopped into the toilet. Rothiel was so out of breath that he collapsed next to it and lay there, gasping.

"What the bung is that damn thing?" said Bob. "It looks like his stomach, but it's the wrong color. Patch, identify."

The patch's soft voice answered, "An acrylic-latex compound, possibly used to protect the stomach lining."

Bob thought about the wine. "Protect it from what?"

Rip sat in his high chair, still stained from his attempts to eat his broccoli-cheese baby food without spilling. "I can't tawk for shit. Gewan?"

The cafeteria was filled to standing room-only with exiles and humans. They were there to hear the news from the past two days.

Gellan stood and read off the paper that Rip prepared for him. It took Rip a long time to type it out, but he felt it was better that his instructions were understood.

"Um. Good morning. A big congratulations to Jim Smith for rescuing me last night." Gellan grinned sheepishly as Big Lee laughed and others cheered.

"I am very, very grateful by the way! Okay, back to the list... Hank, Gideon and Mr. Plak are to drive to Madrid immediately to pick up the terra cotta warriors. Brother Qin has generously obtained thirteen of them, originally for the Madrid museum of history. You gents are to fly them back as fast as possible—what's this say Rip—it's got food on it."

Rip looked at the paper. "Steal a ayoplane. A *caago* plane. Dey can get one fwom Towe—Towoho..."

Gellan continued. "He means Torrejón. You guys are to load up the statues onto a cargo plane from Torrejón and fly it back here."

Hank raised his hand, but interrupted with his loud voice anyway. "We got a problem here. Gellan is the one with the pilot's license. Who's going to fly the fucking plane?"

Rip shot back, beating on the food tray of his high chair, "Why do you tink I am fuck- sending Plak? He wull fly da plane! Jezis!"

Gellan whispered to Rip's ear, "Rip—take it down a notch. Don't get pissed off in here."

Rip stopped his anger-induced rocking and looked down at the pacifier lying on the tray. He ignored it for now.

"Where were we," began Gellan looking back at the list. "Statues... ah. Filodraxes. We have found a solution to Filodraxes decay from Rothiel's engravings in his former cell. Quite simple really and it worked just great. We entered it into the library if you're curious on seeing it. We were able to recover all of his numb fingers and the toes that hadn't dropped off yet. He's actually regained all feeling in his hands."

"It had something to do with his piss didn't it?" said Big Lee. He was beside himself in gaiety.

Gellan looked at Rip, then continued with the list while Big Lee laughed even harder. "Myself and Ricky will reconnoiter Rota Air Base, as we've found a document estimating the amounts of weapons the marines have. It also had a rough diagram of where the base's major communications are located. We think that if Rothiel attacks, he'll hit the base first. And lastly, a big welcome to our two newest members, Oscar and Pablo. Two brothers from Rota. They are currently with some of ours that are the same age to help them overcome a very traumatizing event-- try to make them feel welcome."

Frank liked being in charge. He enjoyed life when he knew what was flying his way and anticipated each move with confidence. He likened the swordplay strategy of knowing your opponent was going to strike downwards at you with full force. He would stand there — fully confident without moving. At the last moment, he would side step, slide his katana out and sever his opponent's sword hand. Then, at his absolute leisure, savor his enemy's doom.

He didn't anticipate today's events. Captain Taylor was on the phone — angry, paranoid and fully in charge of Frank Gutierrez. *Damn.* Frank knew something was screwy when two of his men didn't show for work on Monday. *Probably had a long weekend drunk going on,* he thought. *I'll chew their ass on Tuesday.* Tuesday came with the same results — no men. He sent out a trusty on Monday night to check on them. Surprise, they didn't make it Tuesday morning either. *Fuck... me.*

"Yes Captain, I understand. I'll begin emergency recall and inventory of light weapons. ...Yes sir, I'll remain on base. If you don't mind me saying sir, between the *guardias* and Spanish MP's, your company F marines will be behind the gate... Yes sir. My men will be there."

Captain Taylor insisted right before he hung up, "Get all of your fucking men, locked and loaded behind the gate now!"

Ruth was standing in the doorway, holding the swinging door open while she dragged on her cigarette with a look of worry on her face. Frank knew she was worried because she hadn't insulted him all day. "Can I get you something Frank?"

"Naw. Just a noose and a short stool — I'll take it from there."

"Is this about your missing men?"

Frank leaned back in his chair and rubbed his bald scalp with his palm. "Shit. Yes — maybe. It looks like a good percentage of people that live out in Rota have come up missing. The base CO is certain that the communists or terrorists — he doesn't have a fucking clue — are holding them hostage. There are rumors going around that something out in town is going to attack. Good thing you live in Puerto eh?"

"What does he want you to do?"

"He wants all my guys to muster, pass out weapons and then help defend the front gate. Why don't you send Boardman in here—he needs to get the ball rolling."

When Ruth left his office, Frank opened the bottom drawer of his desk and removed a walnut box. He raised the polished lid and saw what he was looking for. An Italian reproduction of an 1852 Colt Navy black powder revolver. He began wiping it down with his oil cloth and would soon begin the lengthy task of loading it. It only held six shots, but the balls were .44 calibre in size. When it went off, it deafened the battlefield. He would take aim carefully. *Only the maggots that managed to break through. The sting of the damn shot would be intense* he thought. *After all, the powder is still burning when the balls hit you.* He didn't feel himself to be a weak man—just prepared. The last slug in this Colt was for him. It was the express lane of resigning his commission by squirting his brains out of the other side of his head. *Either way, I hope I get an open casket funeral*, he chuckled to himself as he cleaned.

Ruth looks worried, Jared thought to himself as he stormed down the hallway. *I'll see what that impatient fucker wants this time.* Boardman pushed his way through the Commander's doors prepared to ask Frank by first name, what in hell he wanted. When he saw the gun, it came out differently. "Uh, *Sir?* Ruth said you wanted me?"

Frank smiled and laid the gun on the table as carefully as a Fabergé egg. "New plans for today. Please re-do the muster chit this morning to reflect an accurate count. List the assholes that didn't make it in as UA. Drop it off at building 100 and then get back to your room, pick up your beautiful girl and get her ass off this base as fast as you can. Make sure you take the Puerto gate and tell her to stay away from the township of Rota and stay gone until everything's back to normal."

Jared stared slack-jawed. "Is this about the rumors of monsters in Rota?"

Frank spun the gun so that the barrel pointed towards Boardman. "Scoot. Get back here as soon as you drop her off."

Chapter Thirty Eight:
Clay Veterans

Hank drove the truck through the busy streets of Madrid, cursing Filthy for getting him lost and getting the only truck 'without a goddamn hydraulic lift in the back'.

Lou Plak sat in the middle, mumbling interesting strings of numbers from the license plates that he saw. Hank pointed out a truck from Sevilla with a license plate beginning with *SEX*. Lou didn't understand what was so funny.

"Cortez Street! Take a right!" Gideon sat back with a smug look on his face. "Follow this straight and it will take us right by the museum. Remember to park in the back."

Hank swore and jackhammered the horn when a driver cut him off. "I don't know—*fuck*! I don't know how we'll get 13 of those clay statues in the back without crushing them—this is a damned small truck."

"Relax," said Filthy, folding up the map. "They're *Chinese*. They're like, half as small as us white guys."

The truck pulled into the rear of the museum, ignoring the *no entrada* sign and backed up to the loading ramp. Standing at the dock was Qin, visibly nervous and shaking, despite wearing a heavy winter jacket. "Where were you guys? People are wondering why I'm hanging out here!"

Hank hopped up on the loading ramp and opened the rear doors. "Good to see you too, Qin. We're late, because every frigging time we need to go somewhere, Filthy just has to navigate." He pointed to Plak. "I would have had him show me where to go, if he wasn't such a retard."

Qin shook his head while Lou Plak pretended not to notice. It was more interesting to count the knots in the wooden cargo floor of the truck. Hank pointed at Plak. "Stay here. We'll be right back."

Qin, Filthy and Hank walked through the shipping area of the museum towards four large, plywood crates with Chinese characters painted on the outside. "That's them."

"Are you sure?" asked Hank looking at the outside of the box for any type of image. "Rip's going to have my ass if there's nothing but happy-meal toys inside."

Qin warmed his hands by blowing on them. "You crazy? I know what's in this box! Rip said he want thirteen terra cotta warrior wiss weapon—that's what's inside!"

Hank was making calming gestures with his hands. "Chill, brother Qin—I had to ask. When you get irritated, your English suffers. You're sure the weapons are inside, yes?"

"Goddamn, yes!"

"Okay, that's good enough for me," said Filthy. "Got a forklift around here?"

Qin frowned. "First, you help me—talk to boss and make clean —you know? Thass why you are here."

Filthy nodded and followed Qin to the curator's office.

Qin knocked on Sr. Fernandez's office door. *"Si?"*

When Filthy walked in, he turned on the charm. *"Buenos dias.* I'm sorry but there's been a dreadful mistake."

Señor Fernandez stood. *"Como?* What mistake?"

"Well, these clay warriors must go back to China. We've discovered that they're recent copies—probably made in '74, and we're taking them back. Sorry for the confusion—sign here please."

Without hesitation, Señor Fernandez retrieved his pen and took the paper, apologizing for the confusion. Realizing the paper was blank, he looked at Filthy in surprise. "Oh, I'm sorry," said Filthy snatching the paper away. "The writing's on the other side." He handed it back to him the same way, but this time the form looked official with a flourished Chinese state logo on the top. Filthy and Qin saw nothing on the paper, but Señor Fernandez signed the blank area at the bottom and handed it back to them.

"Pardoname—do I get a copy?"

Filthy smiled at Qin. *"Claro*—of course. Here's your copy. He handed him nothing but air. Señor Fernandez smiled at the beautiful characters and the soviet-bloc design of masculine women holding the Chinese flag. *"Gracias."* He opened his desk drawer and filed it away.

After Qin finished loading the four crates into the truck he thanked Filthy. "Gideon, I don't know how you do that, but it's great magic. Good luck on your way back... and for what lie ahead."

Hank pulled the truck onto the national highway that led to Torrejón airbase. He'd let Filthy do the talking when they approached the gate.

It was close to noon when Boardman made it back. Frank was dressed in black fatigues with a navy-issue .45 holstered on his hip and his black-powder revolver in a long holster just under his left armpit. He was mucking with a field radio, trying to tune to the correct channel. "Ah! Just in time! I'd look weak if I had to drive myself there. Hurry up and get changed so you can drive me over."

Boardman contemplated Frank's battle dress. "Are we going to war?"

"You'd better believe it!" Frank rolled up his left sleeve and showed Boardman the inside of his forearm. "See anything special?"

Boardman smirked, "Just another part of your body that doesn't work worth a shit—what am I supposed to be seeing?"

Frank stared at Boardman with his jaw set firm. After two eternal seconds, he pointed to the cluster of arteries at his wrist. "Like clockwork. When I wake up in the morning, I examine the veins on my wrists. Sometimes they stick out and sometimes they don't."

Frank rolled down his sleeve and buttoned the cuffs. "This morning, all of the visible veins were sticking out and some were actually throbbing. They've done this very few times in my life—just before I got my 'dear John letter' from my *whore* wife while on deployment, once when I was almost killed in a car accident in Bahrain and when I almost croaked from food poisoning in Thailand."

"Is it both wrists or just the one?"

"Both—and more strongly than I've ever seen it—why?"

"No, it's nothing." Said Boardman. "If it was the one wrist, I'd say it was just you, playing with yourself."

"Ha. Enough bullshit. If you don't want to hear my gospel, go get yourself ready. Make sure you're packing heat too."

Frank went out and sat in his Jeep. The sky was overcast and breezy. He had a feeling of dread but didn't know how to enunciate it to anyone. If he was willing to bet on it, he'd sink his savings on the fact that he was going to be dead shortly. He thought about his past lives and wondered if some clairvoyant woman in the future would tell her client about the glorious battle that he would soon endure. By the time he finished his second cigarette, Boardman had walked out to the

Jeep with two of his gas-powered assault rifles and a case of bronze pellets.

"We're not going target shooting moron," said Frank sitting up straight in the Jeep. "You brought the other one for me?"

"Of course," said Boardman, dropping the gear into the back and then jumping into the driver's seat. "My older brothers were bullies just like you. If I wanted to enjoy ice cream, I'd have to make sure they had theirs or mine would be taken away. By the way—these babies penetrate a whole lot better at close range than those AR-15's."

"Just remember," said Frank, nodding his head in satisfaction. "It's us bullies that get to write history."

Chapter Thirty Nine:
Flight

"Vehicle pass and ID please." Said the air force security guard into Hank's open window.

"One sec," said Hank. Turning to Filthy, "You're up—go ahead —tell him."

Filthy dismissed the guard with his left hand. "These are not the droids you're looking for."

"What? What'd you just say?" asked the guard.

"These are not the droids you are looking for. Let them through."

"I *love* Star Wars." Said Lou, softly.

Hank scowled at the both of them. "I'm tired. Just do your thing so we can get the fuck back home."

"Sir, I need you to turn off the ignition and step out of the vehicle. Now." The guard had his hand resting on his pistol grip.

"Blow it out, zoomie!" Hank turned back to Filthy, hooking a thumb towards the angry security guard. "Bend this guy's brain and fast—I want to get back!"

The guard yanked his pistol out and aimed it with both hands at Hank's face. "Out! Exit the vehicle now and keep your hands where I can see 'em!"

The guard couldn't remember hearing the portly man on the far side of the truck speak. He barely remembered returning his gun to its holster and then pulling out his wallet, handing it over to the driver and then raising the barrier. He remembered how full of pride he felt, standing tall to attention and giving the most crisp and professional salute possible.

He walked back into the guard shack, relieved and still full of pride.

The airman that watched the spectacle was mere seconds from calling in reinforcements when his partner pulled his weapon. When he saw him re-holster, he put the receiver back down. "What in hell happened? You gave them your wallet?"

"Didn't you see? It was president Richard Nixon."

Hank drove the truck towards the flight line and looked for a likely plane that could carry them. "What kind should I be looking for —that big one maybe?"

"We won't need one that damned big—let's look for something that won't wake up the city when we take off."

Hank saw smaller, propeller-driven planes near a large hanger. "What kind are those?"

Lou Plak only glanced at the planes for a second. "C-130 Hercules. Rear cargo ramp and short take-off and landing. You should take the one nearest that fuel truck."

Hank was impressed. "How much do you know about aircraft?"

Lou gave a blank expression and shrugged. "Nothing."

Hank pulled up to the back of the plane and got out of the truck. "Looks closed. –Where's goofy going?"

Lou walked to the front of the aircraft and plugged in a heavy electrical socket from a yellow gear truck to the chin of the airplane. He then walked to the side, pushed in the slide handle and dropped open the cockpit door. He pulled himself in, sat down in the right seat and began flipping switches.

The rear door began to lower with a loud mechanical groan. The cockpit window slid opened and Lou called out. "There's a forklift inside the hangar."

Hank shook his wrists to loosen them up. "Filthy—help me with these." He laid his hands on the crate and sucked almost all of the weight out. Between the two of them, they gently picked up each crate and carried them out of the truck and into the Hercules.

Lou checked the fuel dials and instantly knew the answer— more than enough fuel for the downhill run to Jerez airport. All switches to the motor magnetos were green. One at a time, he hit the starter switches and let the turboprops run up to speed. He stepped out of the cockpit and pulled the power source cable from the nose of the plane and closed the latch. He walked to the back of the plane and saw all of the crates nestled into the back. Hank and Filthy were tying down the crates with heavy nylon straps. "If one of you pulls the chocks, we can take off."

Hank looked up at Lou with tiredness on his face. "So you've never flown a plane before—right?"

Lou looked puzzled. "No."

"*Fuck it.* I'll get the chocks—this life was shitty anyway."
With that, Hank shooed Lou back to the cockpit and after getting the
signal, pulled the front chock. He jogged to the back and walked up the
ramp. With immaculate timing, Lou raised the cargo door and switched
on the running lights. He taxied the Hercules away from the hangar and
requested permission from the tower to take off.

"Roger Lima-214—uh, wait... you are not, I repeat *not* cleared
for take-off. Your flight plan is filed for a take-off at 1900 hours. Please
remain at taxiway 2L."

Lou pulled off his headset and yelled towards the back. "Gideon
—you're needed up front!"

After the briefest of chats from Filthy to the control tower, the
C-130 sailed into the frigid sky and turned south, settling into smooth
climb to cruising altitude. Lou was all business, punching buttons in
the flight computer and making minute adjustments in RPM between
the four engines to trim out vibration.

Hank was curled up asleep on the cargo floor in a makeshift nest
of blankets, snoring slightly less noisily than the engines. Filthy sat in
the copilot seat and watched Lou expertly handle the controls. "Piece
of cake. When we get close, let's radio the fortress and let them know
we're almost there."

Lou remained silent, checking and rechecking the route he drew
with a grease pencil on the map. In his mind, he was calculating fuel
burn rates, airspeeds and lateral drift more accurately than the flight
computer.

"It's getting dark. Damn." Frank squinted into the fading light
of the sunset and then looked back to the front gate. He was filled with
apprehension.

One of his men jogged to his position from the front of the base.
It was Romero—light on his feet and full of energy. "Sir! There's
something moving up ahead—we're not sure what it is, but it appears to
be a crowd moving towards the base."

Boardman tickled the steering wheel with his nervous fingers.

"Are you guys using the radio?" asked Frank, shaking it near his
head.

Romero peered over at the front. "Switch to channel two, sir."

Frank exhaled. "All right. No need to waste ammo. Let the *Guads* take the first shot and if they get overrun, let the Spanish Navy take over. Since the jarheads will probably be shooting by then, I want you to watch the flanks—they never do. If you see penetration of the base gate, open up the .50 cal. This isn't rocket science, but just the same, save the small arms until... well, if they get past."

The Seal smirked. "Not a chance." He ran back to his position and hunkered down, passing on Frank's instructions.

In front of the base gate stood six Guardia Civil. They were the paramilitary police that the townspeople still respected since Franco gave them Torquemada-like power during the civil war. They wore the shiny, stiff-leather hats that were flattened in the front and flowing green capes. Each were wearing 9mm Uzi sub-machine guns and all six had clicked off their safeties and placed index fingers over their triggers. The *Guardias* had reason to be jittery—they were a detachment from Puerto that arrived earlier to investigate the abrupt silence from their station in Rota. The inside of the station was demolished with copius amounts of blood on all surfaces. They saw spent cartridges littering the floor and no sign of their compatriots. They radioed in for reinforcements, but were assigned to guard the base. The base sat between both towns and would be the logical crossing point for anything on its way to attack Puerto.

"*Que?* Are those dogs?" Asked the sergeant.

His corporal squinted in the looming darkness to try to identify the black mass shuffling towards them. "*No se.* There's people in front —I think."

Several hundred drones were shuffling slowly towards the gate. Their claws were tucked underneath and only displayed their black, rugged bodies as they lumbered steadily forward. In front were dozens of children, bound with ropes wrapped around their shoulders, with cloth gags stuffed into their mouths. They were prodded and pushed towards the base.

The corporal saw them first. "*Son niños*! I think they're held hostage!"

The six lowered their muzzles to the ground. They could make out all of the children crying and taking jerking steps forward. To their horror, they saw that the children were being held around the throat with a noose that prevented them from falling down. They all had visible rope abrasions around their necks.

The sergeant raised a bullhorn. "Attention! Release the children and you will not be harmed. If you do not let them free, we will begin firing towards you!"

The drones continued shuffling forward.

"I can't tell what they are wearing," said the sergeant. "The things in black—are they people wearing some kind of costume?"

They looked like huge, twisted walnut shells that were painted shiny black. Some of them had what looked like misshapen human heads hanging sideways. Every now and again the head would protrude from the shell, look around and slide back inside. The closer they came, the Guardia Civil could tell that they were not costumes. With feelings of trepidation, they knew the rumors of monsters were coming true.

"Try to not hit any of the children," said the sergeant, raising his weapon. "If you can't get a clear shot, try to prevent the child from dying slowly."

The sergeant took aim and fired a cluster of three shots towards the closest creature in black. The impact from the bullets appeared to have caused little damage. The creature reacted by jerking the nine-year old girl smartly upwards and between itself and the six men. "The girl's eyes bulged and her airway became strangled from the rope.

The sergeant was shocked. He brought up the gun sight to his right eye and attempted to sever the girl's rope with his next burst. The fifth bullet tore the rope in half and the girl fell. The sergeant's last view of her was her head rising from the asphalt in momentary relief as a terrible, teeth-lined mouth emerged under the creature and devoured her within seconds.

Frank heard short bursts of automatic gunfire at the front. Frank had heard gunshots during his entire 22-year military career—especially during his last two years commanding Seal Team Six. His sinking feeling was compounded when the first shot rang out. Frank brought up the field radio and noticed the slight shake. "Yo guys, what's going on? Gimme a status, over." Suddenly, the gunfire became frantic, with long bursts and shouting. Louder, sharper *cracks* were echoing from the Spanish navy using high-power rifles.

Frank turned up the volume knob and at last heard Romero's voice. "—people. I repeat, these are not people!"

Frank's brow knitted. He was getting ready to hit the push-to-talk button when he heard the .50 caliber open up with the slow, rhythmic, *TUM-TUM-TUM.*

"Romero! Have they passed the gate? Answer! Over!"

The radio crackled, "Sir." A burst of static and then Romero's voice ended. Frank's eyes were locked on the gate just over 800 meters away. He only heard the small arms and the continuing discharging of the .50 caliber. Romero came on again, speaking rapidly, "Sir, they're shooting something—arrows or spines—some of our guys are hit!"

Frank saw something fat and black leap onto the top of the barbed-wire gate. It became stuck, but was attempting to clamber over until the .50 caliber began chewing it up. Another, then two more black shapes leaped to the top of the fence and began leaping down. Frank noticed that marines were sprawled over the pavement and trying to shoot at the oncoming creatures with their assault rifles.

Frank elbowed Boardman. "Get this damned thing closer!"

Boardman fired up the Jeep and pulled ahead. Boardman turned on the headlights and saw what he thought were black knitting needles laying on the ground. The Jeep's tires made a dry crunching noise as it drove over them. Up ahead, Frank saw men laying on the ground with wide eyes lolling in their heads. Many were entirely incapacitated. The 50. caliber went silent and to his right, saw three of his men walking backwards and shooting towards the enemy. One of the men had Romero over his shoulder. A long, black quill was sticking out of his cheek. "Get him in the back!" yelled Boardman, jumping out of the driver's seat to help. Frank saw two lumbering beasts approaching with claws scuttling forward. He pulled his .45 and shot three rounds directly into the front. It slowed and tucked what looked like a distorted face underneath as the bullets struck, then continued forward without any visible damage at all. He saw something bristle in the front and then felt a slight sting in his right shin. He glanced down and saw two quills sticking out. He felt a cold sensation flowing from his injured leg and staggered backwards to his door of the Jeep.

Frank dragged himself back into his seat and pulled out the quills with his right hand. They snapped off, leaving two short stubs hanging out. "Aw, fuck." He noticed black juice running out of the broken ends of the quills in his hand. He threw the quills down and looked back at his adversary. It had closed the distance between them and was only ten feet away. It was scuttling even faster now that it was closer. Frank's ears were ringing and he could hear Boardman yelling something. He picked up his .45 and went to raise it towards the squat creature. It took monumental effort, but he managed to lift it towards the oncoming creature. He shot off two rounds, but the weight of the gun became too much for him and his arm dropped. The gun slowly slid out of his grip.

Frank slowly turned his head towards the driver's seat to tell Boardman to hit the gas. He noticed the seat was empty. Something passed in front of the headlights. It was Boardman holding his air rifle. Frank saw the rapid vapor blasts leave the end of the barrel and saw the blackened creature unfold in a mixture of colors. It seemed to have opened up from the middle and split apart. The rifle was sawing through it like a chainsaw. Boardman walked forward and sheared apart two more that were close by, then turned and ran back to the Jeep. He put it in reverse and barked the tires with the pedal down. The Jeep's transmission whined in complaint that they were going too fast. The steering was erratic, but Boardman had a strong grip on Frank's shoulder. He was shouting in his ear, asking if he was still with him.

Boardman slowed the Jeep, put it in first gear and turned around to go back to the armory. *At least*, he thought, *it's damned hard to get into.*

The Jeep passed the Pizza Villa on its way to the main intersection and Jared felt his heart sink. Hundreds of the black crawling things were swarming the roads and coming from both sides. He tried to think quickly on where to go, but he wouldn't be able to drive anywhere without hitting some of them. He thought about getting one of the uninjured Seals in the back to drive while he manned his air rifle. He saw something dark flash out of the woods at incredible speed. It looked like a man running. The running figure was zig-zagging around the creatures and some would get flung over on their backs, other's seemed to get sliced in two. The running figure burst towards them at the same terrific speed and Boardman raised his rifle. He pulled the trigger and released a dozen bronze balls towards it, striking it across the chest and face. It leaped away from the front of the Jeep and stopped suddenly next to Boardman.

"Knock it off, Jared. It's me, Jim."

Boardman had tried to hide his face with his elbow. He lowered his arm and swallowed. "How...?" Jim was wearing a black Nomex suit and had loops of thin cable attached to his hips and glimmering metal objects connected to the front of a black, nylon vest. Other than the fresh holes is his clothing from his air rifle, he didn't have a scratch on him.

"I'll explain later—Jesus, is that Frank? How 'bout you guys? Your friend is hit too?" Jim looked around at the moving hordes and pointed towards the North. "Head towards the chow hall. I'll clear a path for you. Get yourself inside and I'll be back with medicine." Jim pulled the black balaclava down over his face and shot off towards the intersection. He stopped, looked back and waved his arm for them to follow. He ran towards a creature that had turned and sprayed quills at Jim. Jim let them ricochet from his skin and ran towards it. He pulled out one of his butterflies and threw it at the drone, letting it's thin, steel guide-wire zip between his hardened fingertips. When it passed under the creature's low abdomen, Jim yanked it back, allowing it to project upwards as it spun underneath, hacking through it's tough shell and spilling its organs. He ran past as he re-spooled the cable and continued hunting drones as he made his way North.

The Jeep pulled into the parking lot of the chow hall and Boardman, Allison and Lee began pulling the injured men out and dragging them towards the front of the building. Boardman looked back to get another glimpse of Jim, but he was gone. Allison pulled out his pistol and shot out the window to the door. "We're surrounded by glass windows. There's no way we can hold them off from in here."

"Yeah," said Boardman, grunting while dragging Frank by his armpits through the doorway. "Except that guy that told us to come here has been the only one able to do some real damage out there. Did you see how many of those things he killed to get us here?"

Allison laid Romero on the carpet and looked out of the window for any of the creatures. "Shh. Somebody's coming."

Jim popped through the doorway holding up his hand. "Don't shoot—it's only us." He was followed through the door by a smaller asian man, dressed the same way. He saw the two injured lying on the floor and began rummaging through a small fanny-pack. He pulled out two syringes and popped the plastic caps off. He buried both into the men's thighs and bottomed out the pistons quickly. He withdrew them and tossed them aside. He was looking around the room at the windows, no longer concerned about his patients.

Allison walked up and pointed at the syringes. "What's that stuff—are they going to be okay?"

"Antiserum," said Kayanan looking down at Romero. "This one took a shot in the cheek. The quills are difficult to remove from bone and may get infected. He'll be up and around by tomorrow."

"Thanks. He's my friend."

"What I'm most concerned about," said Kayanan looking around the room. "Is that we're hiding inside a building with glass walls. What were you thinking, Jim?"

Allison nodded. "I felt the same way as you."

Jim rolled his eyes. "Sorry—okay? Don't worry, I'll keep them away from the building."

Kayanan walked over and grabbed the phone. He dialed the fortress.

The recording of Juani came on. "Gellan, pick up, it's me."

The recording stopped when Gellan answered. "Ricky—have they made it through the base yet?

"Yeah, you could say that. Wait a minute--how'd you know that?"

"The kid, Cesar—he came and visited Seth again. You guys had already left before I could tell you."

Kayanan looked around him at the last remaining survivors of the assault on the base gate. "They pretty much met with very little resistance. I'd say that the base lost around sixty to seventy men at the front gate."

"Damn. Even with weapons?"

Kayanan scanned the windows while he spoke. "Assault rifles were useless. Someone was using a large, belt-driven gun—maybe a . 50 caliber. It was able to penetrate, but it was overwhelmed."

Jim walked up to Kayanan. "Tell him about Jared's gun."

"Oh yeah—a guy named Jared has a custom air-type rifle that fires brass..."

"Bronze." Said Boardman, sliding a seat cushion under Frank's head. "I use bronze ones."

Jim took one out of Boardman's feed-clip and handed it to Kayanan.

"My mistake." Said Kayanan to Jared. "They're made of bronze—kinda heavy. The edges are rough—machined. Anyways, the things tear right through them. I think we may have a use for ordnance like this."

"Make sure you bring some back. I can't extract you yet— Simon's on his way to Jerez airport to pick up the boys and the statues."

Kayanan scratched his head. "We may have trouble getting out of here—the base is swarming with them. Can't you redirect them to the flight line here for a pickup?"

"Hell. I don't know why I didn't think of that. I'll get them on the radio now and ask them to land at the base. Head over to the airstrip and keep an eye out."

"Gotcha. Don't forget to radio Simon and tell him they'll be a bit late."

Kayanan hung up. "Change of plans. We're going to catch a plane."

"Lou, this is Gellan, change of plans, over."

Filthy picked up his headset. "What's going on Gellan?"

"The base has been overrun. We need you to fly straight there. Jim and Ricky are already there and they will meet you on the flight line."

Lou had already flipped the pages and looked for the GCI frequency for the airstrip at Rota. He redirected the trip computer for the extra 44 miles and switched off his landing lights.

Filthy pressed the PTT switch, "Roger Gellan. ...I guess if things get hairy we can always just open the boxes."

"Don't worry—Jim and Ricardo will clear the area. Good luck."

Filthy got out of his chair and patted Lou on the back. "I'll go wake up Hank. "Great job flying—I just hope your landing skills are equally as good."

Lou kept his eyes locked on the instruments.

Jared maneuvered the jeep through the dark streets, slowly passing by dead drones left quivering in the street. Kayanan was busy taking out streetlights and Jim had dashed ahead to pick off any drones that got too close. He pulled the jeep into the VQ-2 squadron's gate and saw Jim and Kayanan waving from the far end of the big hangar. He drove up and shut off the engine.

"Errr. Where...are we?" Frank felt groggy as he looked around. "Jim? Wha...what are you doing here? ...What am I doing here?"

Jim grinned. "You're going to be fine, Frank. Just relax — you've been poisoned."

Frank looked at Jim through hooded eyes for a moment, then his head slowly retreated back towards the seat. He began to snore.

"There it is!" Kayanan was pointing to a light in the sky. "It must be them. We wait until it lands and turns around. Then we'll drive out and get onboard."

As the plane descended from the sky, Kayanan was staring at the end of the runway. "Do you see something, Jim? Over there — towards the right?"

Jim squinted in the darkness. "I don't know — could be just be grass blowing in the wind-- oh, shit. I see something. I think they're drones!"

"Stay here. There's too many of them. Hopefully Plak can see them and he won't touch down."

They both watched as three trailers were being pulled onto the runway. Jim was blinking his eyes and trying to see more clearly what they were. "Rick — I can't be sure, but it looks like there's metal cylinders in the back of those things — it could be anything, like welding gas — or oxygen. What do we do?"

Kayanan grabbed one of the Seal's assault rifles and aimed it towards the distant end of the runway. "I just hope they can see the muzzle flash, just in case I can't hit any of the cylinders." He sprayed gunfire towards the trailers, but ran out of ammunition after just a few bursts. The cylinders didn't explode. Kayanan ran back to the jeep and slapped in another clip when the jeep and hanger became bathed in white light.

Lou guided the Hercules downward towards the Rota base. The runway marker lights were off, so Lou switched on the landing lights and made out the strip. It appeared to be clear of all aircraft, so he eased off power from the engines and lowered the flaps. Airspeed was still around 60 miles per hour too fast, so he deployed one degree of spoiler. The extra wind resistance was sufficient to slow the plane to the proper speed, so he backed off the spoiler and began to level off.

He saw small flashes up ahead like someone welding in the distance. Or it could be someone shooting. He brought the nose gently up as the Hercules settled in the air cushion and abruptly felt the plane lurch when it struck something on the ground. The massive explosion tore the wings and tail off the plane and the fuselage nosed downward towards the oncoming pavement. What little of avionics Lou Plak knew, he was certain that this was a landing that he would never walk away from. The nose of the plane struck first, collapsing the cockpit like a crushed beer can. Lou was killed instantly. The fuselage slammed flat on its belly and slid sideways, tearing off huge sheets of aluminum as friction and heat claimed their spoils of destruction.

Hank grabbed Filthy around the waist and dropped all of their combined weight into the surrounding metal. The walls buckled and separated, hurling the two of them outward into the field. Secondary explosions of the fuel tanks blew them like tumbleweeds outwards, away from the fire. As they slowed, Hank released the weight in small increments and they both settled to the ground. Filthy was coughing like his lungs were on fire and Hank's hands were burned. Both of their ears were ringing. Hank saw Jim run up to them shouting, but he couldn't hear a word. He mouthed that he was fine. Jim looked around for Lou and Hank pointed to the fire. Jim frowned and began trying to herd them away from the fire when he noticed them. Moving masses were coming towards them. *There must be hundreds of them*, he thought.

Filthy and Hank began staggering away with Jim covering them. Jim knew that the speed they were going, they wouldn't get out in time. The horde was moving much faster now that they were close.

An arrow shot out of the night sky and buried itself deep into the first drone. It rolled around on the ground in pain and two more arrows dove into its thick skin. Jim looked and saw a man walking towards the drones, pulling arrows out of a quiver around his waist and then sending the arrows flying from a long bow. Jim saw two more men running from the wreckage of the plane with swords drawn. *They look real*, thought Jim, as he watched the two engage and slaughter the drones that turned to attack them. More and more warriors emerged from the plane. Some were still on fire as they stepped out of the wreckage and didn't appear the least bit bothered by the flames. The archer that killed the first drone walked up to it and turned its quiver towards the dead beast. The arrows dissolved from the drone and reappeared inside the quiver. It didn't glance at the three men for even a moment, turning on its heel and continuing to hunt down more drones, just like it's other brethren.

"I'll be dipped in shit," said Filthy, shaking his head in amazement.

Gellan was worried that no one had checked in yet. It had been over three hours. He called Simon and asked if he saw the plane. Simon hadn't.

Gellan tried to radio the plane and no one answered the call. The phone rang. Before Juani's taped voice could come on, he snatched the handset from the cradle. "Rick?"

"Yeah, it's me. We're still at the base."

"What happened? Is everyone all right?"

"We lost Lou — and the plane." Kayanan looked out of the maintenance officer's window towards the morning's peach sky. The runway was littered with the black carcasses of drones. The Terracotta warriors were lying nearby their final victims, still and serene with alert expressions. Some were blackened by the crash, but it didn't stop them from attacking the drones with deadly ferocity. They fought tirelessly throughout the night until the few remaining drones crawled away in retreat.

"We need someone to pick us up."

"Any other casualties?"

"Most of the US forces are gone, but Jim was able to save five of them — two are wounded. Nine of the terra cotta warriors survived the crash. They pretty much destroyed Rothiel's army."

Simon drove the truck to the Puerto gate and saw the demolished guard shack strewn across the gravel near the road. Jim Smith was standing at the gate with a young sailor behind the wheel of a white jeep. Jim waved and the jeep pulled into the base with Simon following. As they drove across the base, Simon saw the dead bodies of soldiers and eventually the body of a drone. When they made it halfway across, there were dead drones everywhere. As he passed in front of the barracks, he noticed that all of the front doors to the rooms were forced inward. The truck had problems navigating around some of the drone carcasses as they approached the flight line. Two more sailors were carefully carrying the clay soldiers towards the building and Hank was getting his hands bandaged by Kayanan. Filthy was trying to get candy bars from a stubborn vending machine. His face lit up when he saw the truck. "Hey Simon—did you bring any food?"

Simon was relieved that his two friends survived. He shook his head.

"Give it a rest, Filthy!" shouted Hank.

"Sit still," admonished Kayanan. "I can't get this bandage on right with you jerking around."

"It pisses me off, that's all. I get my hands burned and he comes out hungry."

Frank was limping around holding his head. "Now what do we do? Jim—d'you think those things will come back?"

Jim looked at the dead drones. "Certainly. I think you should all come back with us. What do you think, Rick?"

Kayanan nodded. "No sense staying here. There's nothing worth protecting at this point—I'm betting everyone's dead... or worse."

The men loaded the statues into the back of the truck and Frank limped over to a dead body lying next to an Alfa Romeo convertible. "I'll be damned! This is Tony—he's VQ-2's Operations Officer! He paid a fortune getting this car restored-- it'd be a waste if I left it here." He rummaged through the corpse's pockets and found the keys.

Boardman saw the white truck pulling out of the parking lot. Jim was looking at them and honking the horn. Boardman waved back. "For shit's sake, Frank—the man's dead."

"...And he won't be needing his little red convertible like me. What'sa matter? Haven't you ever seen any of those 70's end of the world movies? I'm in Heston-mode-- just making the best of a situation."

He opened the door and winced when he bent his leg to get it inside. His grimace turned to pleasure when he fired up the Italian engine and he gave it a few good revs. He looked up at Boardman getting behind the wheel of the jeep. "Finder's keepers!" He put it in gear and tore off after the truck. As he drove, he looked at the insides of his wrists. The veins still stood out. *I'm still here*, he thought. *Am I here because I didn't accomplish anything in battle?* He saw a pair of Ray Ban's sitting on the passenger seat and put them on. *Well what do you know? Just my size.*

Chapter Forty:
Phone-tag

Rip was fed, given a nice bath and a diaper dusted with talcum powder just before the men arrived at the fortress. He was concerned that some of the warriors were destroyed and that they were now without a savant. He reflected that they made good use of Mr. Plak's talents while at the fortress. Besides helping transcribe Rothiel's cell he single-handedly formulated Filodraxes' medicine to recover his dried-up fingers. *Those guys only show up once every few hundred years*, he thought as he flipped through pages of his journal. *Pythagoras was amazing before he went nuts — Newton was fun just to watch since he was so quirky.* He wished he had gotten to know Lou Plak better.

Ricky and Jim walked through the door first, both looking very run down and dirty. Rick's demeanor was always the same. He had visited death so often throughout his lives that they might as well have been a routine case of hiccups. Jim looked burned-out. He lost track of the amount of drones that he had killed trying to save their victims. He found that when he carried his wounded to a safe location, they ended up missing when he came back to check on them. He found that most were devoured on the spot by the small bits of remains that were left on the grass. He had a bagful of antiserum and had run out during the first hour. When he found Frank, he ran back to get more from Kayanan. He hadn't used a single one. Kayanan knew by experience, that there was no way to save the wounded from an army that large.

Kayanan briefed Rip on the night's events and pointed out the five sailors that were saved from the night's events.

Rip sneaked a peek towards the men discussing their options on the far side of the living room. "Doze ahh da only suvievos fwom last night? Juss fibe?"

"Two were wounded. They're fine, but one needs some more work done on his cheek. I'll take care of him before I get some sleep."

"Jib — taig me oudside — I wanna see da clay sowjers."

Jim yawned. "You're not going to set me on fire are you?"

Rip smiled, showing his two lower baby teeth. "No. I'm in cundroll now."

Jim picked him up and as any parent would, instinctively propping him on his left hip and strolled outside. Big Lee was deftly carrying the warriors from the truck and standing them up on the patio. Jim walked Rip near them to get a better look. Rip wanted to see their backs. He shook his head with the first one and Jim walked over to the next one.

"Dare! Dare's my mark! My naaame. I made dis one. See? See dese figgerpints? Dose are mine." Rip giggled and then sighed. He remembered Emperor Shi Huangdi and the hell they went through to defeat the black hordes.

Jim sat down on the steps of the porch and placed Rip on his knee. He spent the better part of an hour telling him his versions of the battle. Rip was most interested in the warriors. He couldn't remember that the archer's arrows reconstituted themselves from their victims. "Dis is good! Whad abboud his bow? Qin said dat day didn't fix dare weppins—dats very ineresting."

Jim saw the longbow lying on the ground next to the soldier in the kneeling position. "I don't know about you, but this string looks new. Twisted horsehair maybe?" Jim felt Rip shiver and decided to take him back inside the house. "Feeling cold?"

"No, I'b fine."

When they walked into the house, Gellan was standing just inside the foyer with his chin in his hand. He was looking into the living room, slowly shaking his head. Filodraxes was standing over the phone and alternately speaking into the mouthpiece and then bringing the earpiece to his head to listen. Jim concentrated on what the old man was saying but could pick out few words. He watched Rip's face while he listened to what the old man was saying. The sound seemed to break apart and become organized into Jim's mind until he at last, heard the clear speech.

"Then it is settled," said Filodraxes. "Tonight we end *this*. Your followers will keep your distance—yes, as the laws of circus. Whoever is victorious shall not engage the opposite side in warfare—you have my word. No contact is to be made until we reach the plane. I will bring three witnesses... and you? Then the arrangement is made. Until tonight." Filodraxes passed the handset to Gellan who promptly hung it up, letting go of it as if it was burning his hand.

"Whaz going on, Gewwan? Fiwo?"

Gellan was nervous. "Just so you know, I advised him not to speak to him."

"Who? Whaz id Valgurnis agin?"

"No, said Gellan, rubbing his brow. "It was Rothiel. He challenged Filodraxes to a duel."

Rip's face turned flush. He started jabbering with such fury that no one could understand him. The fact that they couldn't understand him made him all the angrier.

Filodraxes gave a gentle smile, walked over to the coffee table and picked up one of the cognac snifters and handed it to Gellan. "Water."

"Wouldn't you like a clean glass?"

Filodraxes looked at Gellan as if he were mad. "It's not for me —it's for him."

All Rip could get out clearly was, "*No no no!*" He was crying in frustration, but his face was pure anger.

Filodraxes touched his finger to the side of the glass and then touched his finger to his own ear. He then held the glass out for Rip to touch. When Rip's hand brushed against the glass, Rip's matured, deep voice rang out of the glass in perfect diction. Rip was astonished. Filodraxes sat down on the big leather chair and slid the glass to the other side of the table and pointed to Rip.

On queue, Jim carried Rip to the other side and sat down on the couch. Jim picked up the glass and looked inside. It was silent. Rip was stretching his hand out to touch it again, so Jim obliged and moved it closer. Rip's booming voice echoed again out of the glass. "...You mustn't do this! Rothiel's had the benefit of not dying for over ten thousand years!" The surface of the water rippled fiercely with each tone.

"It's simple really," began Filodraxes, making himself comfortable in his chair. "I had not died as much as you gentlemen. You are impressed with that trick of sound and water, but it's mere child's-play. A large portion of my memories are still intact. My accumulated knowledge is either in my head or written down in our library. Rothiel only had his cell—you might say that he'd run out of writing space."

The water shot to life again. "But we're winning! We've defeated his army on the battlefield this morning, don't you see? This is only out of desperation!"

"Do you recall," began Filodraxes leaning forward. "Where the cure for my dying tissue came from?"

"From Rothiel's cell. What of it?"

"It worked fast didn't it? I felt as new just after a few hours."

Rip tried to think about where this line of conversation was heading. "Yes, lord, it did work quickly."

"What do you think Rothiel and his minions are doing now — they are most likely reviving that army of his. Your men left Rothiel's fallen on the battlefield, didn't you."

"That's just it, they're dead! There's nothing to revive!"

Jim began to feel sick to his stomach.

Kayanan stormed out of the front door. He was connecting his web belt again and running over to the garage.

Jim set Rip down on the top of the coffee table and ran out after him.

Kayanan was wheeling out a black BMW motorcycle and firing up the engine.

Jim shouted over the noise of the motor. "Where are you going?"

"What does it look like? I'm going to see if they really are dead."

He pushed a green button on his handlebars and the gates opened by three feet. Kayanan gunned the engine, hopped aboard and tore off across the gravel, spinning the rear wheel all the way to the pavement. He was off like a shot, slamming gears as fast as he could get them.

The gates swung shut through the cloud of dust kicked up from the motorcycle. Jim listened to the whining rise and fall of the motorcycle's engine fade into the distance.

Kayanan had been able to get from Puerto Real to the Rota base gate in 34 minutes in the past. This time, he was reckless and worse-- seething in anger. He blasted past the abandoned Guardia Civil guard post in no less than 19 minutes from leaving the fortress. He kept the revs high so that the integrated turbo gorged the engine on boosted intake. Hank would kill him if he knew how he had punished his handiwork.

He passed through the base gate coasting and knew right away that something was wrong. The drones that had once littered the streets were gone. There were a few here and there, but they were the ones that were the most mutilated. He stopped the bike near one and bent down. The unmistakable smell of bacteria and nitrocellulose hung in the air over the corpse. It was the same smell of the chemical used to restore Filodraxes. He tore off down to the middle of the base and saw at the most, a dozen unrecoverable drones. *Why didn't we torch the bodies*, he thought as he passed slowly around the base.

He turned south towards the main gate in the town of Rota and smelled it. *The stink of their blood. They must have been restored and dragged themselves home.* He looked around the sky. No birds. He had this feeling before. The animals knew. He smoked the rear tire and turned back towards the Puerto gate. He tore past the guard post at over 190 kilometers per hour, heading back to the fortress. *Maybe Filodraxes is right.*

Chapter Forty One:
Duel

"We want to help," Luisa was standing in the doorway of the living room flanked by both of her daughters.

Rip's still sat on the coffee table, clutching the snifter. The glass came to life, booming his old voice from the rippled water. "What makes you think that we need your help, *Señora*?"

"I have been watching. There is something evil in Rota. All of us can feel it. I can put a stop to it."

The water rippled. "Hmmpf. Doubtful."

Luisa scowled. "You are going to meet with it. You know what it is—it is lies. It is death. If you think for one moment that it will let you leave, then you will pay dearly."

Rip knew that she and her daughters were capable of strange powers. He didn't have Filodraxes' faith that he would prevail. "What do you propose?"

"Simple." Luisa walked over and sat lady-like on the sofa nearest the glass and peered in. Rip protectively pulled it closer to him. "Relax, *pequeño*, I don't want your glass. We will escort you safely into Rota and stay on the outside of where the evil lives. No matter the outcome, when you leave, we will make sure that you get out safely."

"How," asked the glass in Rip's bored tone. "What can you do?"

With a smug look, she placed her hand in her bag. She looked around the room and then settled on the fireplace. She began growling. "Ay! Aya!"

Mortar spit from around the centermost brick in the fireplace until it was wrenched free from unseen hands. It shot towards the old woman and stopped in a hover over her outstretched hand. Rip noticed her left hand was still in her bag. She hissed and the brick crumbled into fine, reddish dust into her palm. She dropped the dust on the coffee table and removed her hand from her bag. "We can do this with any rock or brick. Their army cannot stand against us!"

"What's in the bag?"

Luisa looked at the baby with hooded eyes. "Tell me this mystery of your voice then."

"Forget it." Rip contemplated the brick dust on the table. "Tell you what. Do that to Corey's cement chair, and you've got a de…"

Luisa snapped her fingers and the chair burst apart from the center, scattering rusty iron reinforcement bars on the floor and filling the floor with rubble and the air with thick dust.

Rip coughed and hacked from the dusty air while he tried to cover the top of the glass with his small hand. The voice boomed from the glass just the same. "…You're in."

Filodraxes left the library muttering to himself. He reviewed the notes that he took in the past in preparation for the final battle with Rothiel. He walked down the hallway towards the chow hall where the men awaited. They were all prepared for battle and wanted to hear the final briefing from the one that would change everything.

"The fabric between the two worlds is powerful. There is a way to break through, although temporarily." Filodraxes walked to the blank wall and motioned for Gellan to turn down the lights. He drew an imaginary circle on the wall with his finger. After a few seconds the line became visible and began to glow with further intensity. "One can create a hex strong enough to threaten the fabric. The fabric resists by changing time. If another person creates a second hex over the same plane, the fabric will again react. It changes back to original time and dilates. We can enter the Origin plane, but our Earthly energies continue to keep us bound to this one."

Filodraxes moved away from the wall and tapped at his temple. "I have a theory—that the moment we pass through, we are initally mortal. None of our powers will be at our disposal. The duel will probably not commence until after the twin hexes stabilize—then our powers should return. This should only take a few seconds."

He walked back to the wall and tapped on the illuminated circle with his knuckles. "If the two of us engage in battle and one or both are killed, there will be no reincarnation. Simply put, there is no place for the soul to go. The energy of the fallen is released and the hex collapses."

Gellan cleared his throat, "My lord, what is wrong with our current plan of attack? That we continue to route his army and weaken him?"

Filodraxes waved his arm over the wall and the hex disappeared. In its place was a flowing image of a terracotta warrior. "Danhieras had hundreds of these when he fought Protraxis' hordes. We have but nine. We may be able to produce more, but we have no victims of their violence this time. They are either taking their victims back to their strongholds or devouring them on the spot. Even if we were to build more somehow—Rothiel can re-animate his fallen soldiers in a matter of minutes. You see, no matter the losses that he suffers, it is simply temporary—for us, it is a different matter."

"What have you got in mind, master?" asked Kayanan.

"That we go in and establish the hex right away. I want no posturing or threatening displays. When we go in, I want you to act as though everything Rothiel has is invisible. I will surround Rothiel and his three witnesses inside my hex, alongside Simon, Danhieras and Koriet. When one of us dies, the hex will be released and we will return amongst the rest of you. We will begin an orderly exit from his house and return here."

Gellan licked his lips in nervousness. "M'lord, what if it is you that is killed?"

"No difference. Return to the fortress."

Gellan shook his head. "With you out of the way, he will surely attack the rest of us."

Filodraxes was impassive. "I am not weak of the mind. Before we leave this building, I will hex the remaining terracotta warriors just overhead of our position at Rothiel's stronghold. If I am killed, the warriors will slip from my hex and come to rest on the rooftop. You only need to open the roof in order to get them into play."

While Filodraxes spoke, Kayanan translated for Luisa and her daughters, while Jim translated for the sailors.

Luisa became indignant when he failed to mention her role. "*Que*? And what about us, what are we supposed to do?"

Filodraxes' eyes narrowed. He was not accustomed to being addressed with such disrespect. "The *witches* will guard the escape route nearest the sea. The surviving sailors will be used to extract you from the West—Diano will go with them." Diano, head stooped, walked into the living room and sat down on his haunches.

The five sailors jumped back when they saw the size of the beast. Jim tried to keep them calm by acting nonchalant about his size. Big Lee stormed forward. "No! Diano stays here!"

Diano glared at Big Lee and growled, "I can take care of myself!"

"I saw what Rothiel does to others. I know, deep in my heart that he would change you into one of them, given the chance."

Filodraxes raised his hand for silence. "Diano remains in the shadows unless required. He knows what is expected of him. If our position becomes uncertain and his safety is threatened, he is to depart immediately, never to return."

Big Lee looked over at his son. Diano lowered his head. "Depart for where?"

Filodraxes answered for him, "That is between him and I only. It is far better than no one in this room knows where he may go—for his safety, you understand."

When the final translations were made, there was silence. Filodraxes noted the grim mood and smiled. "Well, if we're ready, let us all assemble outside."

They all filed outside into the chilly night air. The sky was overcast, but dull light shone weakly through overhead. Filodraxes looked around and whispered for Diano. "Do me a favor first,"

Diano nodded.

Filodraxes bent down and picked up a dry leaf. He held it aloft and let go. There was no wind, but the leaf tore away from his fingers and tumbled away rapidly. "Follow this leaf and then kill the spy that it lands on."

Diano dashed towards the compound's fence and jumped over in mad pursuit of his prey. A short scream was heard off in the distance in the woods across from the street. Diano trotted back and hopped over the fence, landing on the other side in silent grace. He tossed a bloodied pair of binoculars and field radio on the ground. "He is dead —he didn't have time to use it."

"Then let us begin." He motioned for Diano and the five sailors to get closer together. The tallest of them, Allison only came up to Diano's armpit. They couldn't help but stare at his bovine features.

Jim put his hand on Frank's shoulder. "All ready buddy?"

Frank was holding one of Boardman's air-powered assault rifles. "As ready as I'll ever be." He glanced up at Diano's face. "By the way, how do I speak to the big guy?"

Jim laughed. "Very politely!"

A bright circle of light flashed around their perimeter. Jim stepped back and watched the light pulse in intensity. Frank looked at the dazzling light show just at his feet. He bent down to take a closer look just as the light exploded in all directions and he found himself standing next to an old fountain in old town Rota. There was the dim afterglow of light in his eyes while he tried to get adjusted to the darkness. He eased the safety off his rifle and motioned for the other four to do the same. Boardman whispered, "How are we going to get through that wall if we need to save them?"

Frank looked over at Diano. He had his muzzle against the wall, sniffing in earnest. "I don't think we're going to have a problem, seeing how we've got Angus over there." Off in the distance towards the seafront there was another crackle of light. "Must be the ladies auxiliary arriving on station. I'm guessing that the rest of them should be inside any moment." Boardman pointed to the big rooftop to the East and floating just above the tiles were the nine soldiers, rotating slowly in a lazy circle.

Filo hexed the rest of them directly into Rothiel's central courtyard, where just twelve hours prior, they agreed to have their duel. Filodraxes stood at the head of the column and was flanked by Simon and Big Lee. Rip was strapped onto Big Lee's chest.

Behind them were Jim, Kayanan, Filthy, Hank and Gellan. All around them were creatures of all shapes and sizes. They were growling and shrieking at the invaders. Some would rush forward to provoke them, but never making contact. Rothiel stood opposite Filodraxes, flanked by Prestor, Hale and Protaxsis. Prestor was grinning at Filthy and making soft popping noises from his mouth. Hale had evidently been modified from his human form. His huge, scarred arms were now replete with bony stumps that had metal blades affixed with screws. Protaxsis was untouched but old. The last months' work had taken quite a bit out of him. He was jittery and pale.

Rothiel removed his robe and dropped it to the floor. He was only wearing white linen trousers. "I hail!"

Filodraxes raised a hand. "I hail!"

Rothiel pointed to the floor. "At last. Let us begin. Circus!"

A white ring began to glow around the eight men. The glow intensified exponentially. Rothiel twisted his face in concentration.

Filodraxes waited until the ring throbbed in resistance to the fabric protecting the worlds. He too, pointed to the floor and said, "Circus."

The nine soldiers stopped rotating and sunk slowly to the rooftop. "I guess they're in," said Boardman. He looked over at Diano to see if he too noticed the settling of the warriors. The beast grunted, gave the men a baleful look and then began to slowly stretch his shoulder and arm muscles.

Jim watched the circle of men rise up towards the ceiling, passing through a semi-opaque layer when their images became frozen. He could see their images facing each other, but all movement stopped. "What's going on?"

Kayanan leaned forward and whispered, "Their time is different from ours. They may be fighting right this moment, but to us, they appear frozen."

Jim nodded and looked around the room at his adversaries. He could feel multiple spider webs connecting to the creatures gnashing teeth and brandishing claws from the sides of the massive courtyard. Something in his head told him that Kayanan was worried. "Is there something that you're not telling me?"

Kayanan leaned forward, "Valgiernas. I don't see him anywhere."

Jim knew from Kayanan's teachings that Valgiernas preferred long distance weapons—during the past hundred years he had adopted the gun. Jim began to uncoil a segment of wire and snapped it to a connector on a light, 100-gram butterfly. He scanned the room and tried to imagine where a shooter would take his aim. His eyes flitted around the room but he kept coming up empty. He spun around the courtyard, as did Kayanan, looking wildly for the shooter, knowing that the cruel Valgiernas would take his time and enjoy killing his adversary —something he had never been able to do.

Gellan, Hank and Filthy were likewise looking around for the missing danger. "What if he's not here," said Filthy in a nervous tone. "Maybe he's one of these damn things?"

"Keep looking!" shouted Kayanan. "He wouldn't miss this for anything!"

It dawned on Jim that he was able to master anyone's skill—so long as that person was nearby. He had always been a poor shot—with everything except a BB gun. His grandfather presented his grandson with a spring-loaded Daisy that looked like a lever-action Remington. It was the only thing that he could shoot that would allow him expert aim. He closed his eyes and tried to imagine pulling the trigger on a rifle that would blow his Filipino's head clean off. *No, not Valgiernas' style*, thought Jim. *He'd want him to suffer. Perhaps his abdomen or legs.*

There were rafters holding up the roof that ran the perimeter of the courtyard. *Too easy—Kayanan would have seen him by now.* He looked to his right, there were Protraxis' creatures only a few feet away. *He wouldn't shoot from there*, he thought. *They would get in the way and spoil his shot.* He glanced briefly to his left and noticed that the creatures there were further back—almost by fifty feet. Some of the creatures were alternately growling at them and then glancing down towards the dirt floor between themselves and Kayanan.

Jim stepped sideways, scooping Kayanan behind him while flashing the front of his body to maximum hardness. Just before his eyes glazed over, he saw dust kick up off the floor and felt his body rock from taking the high-power slugs from Valgiernas' rifle.

Gellan saw the dust shift over the trap door and at the last minute, grabbed ahold of Hank and Filthy, accelerating them backwards behind one of the fat columns holding up the second story.

Kayanan was surprised by Jim's action and ducked behind him at the last second. One of Valgiernas' bullets whizzed by his temple just before he was able to shield himself with Jim's shoulder. He let his momentum carry him toward's Jim's right side and hurled a butterfly before he emerged on the other side.

In the dim light of the courtyard, Valgiernas saw a small sliver of light flash and then winced as his left elbow was sheared off. The pain arrived in an instant. His left arm dropped to his side as he gritted his teeth and continued firing the three-round bursts toward his enemy.

Jim didn't know if he was successful in saving his friend, so he spun around and hardened his back. Kayanan's face was right in front of his. Bullets slammed into the back of Jim's head, making his voice vibrate as he spoke. "R-Rickkk! Arrre you...hit?"

Kayanan was relieved that Jim hardened in time. "Just stand still for a second—I'm sure I wounded him! Wait a minute—can you walk backwards?"

Jim went to answer and felt three more rounds pound against his head. "Yeah—you tell...*fuck*! You tell me where to go!"

Kayanan pushed Jim backwards while watching where the slugs were hitting and took quick glances to try to see where the muzzle flashes were coming from. *He's close now.*

"Freeze all the way!"

Jim stopped and froze.

Kayanan threw another butterfly linked to a steel cable over Jim's shoulder and then yanked backwards. The butterfly jerked downwards and returned underneath Jim's armpit. Kayanan waited until the butterfly sailed past and then pulled with all his might to have it go back under and then over Jim's shoulder. Kayanan pulled Jim's standing body to the left, toppling him into the dirt with himself following and redirecting the slinging action of the cable towards the shooter's chest.

Valgiernas saw another glint of steel and knew the consequence. He jumped to the right to avoid its path, but his paralyzed left arm lingered too long. The butterfly sliced through it like a helicopter blade through wet toilet paper. The arm dropped into the dirt and the butterfly continued it's meteoric path behind him.

Kayanan tugged the wire sharply, reversing the butterfly into a careening path sideways, reconnecting with Valgiernas as it cut through his skin and wrapped the slender cable around his upper body with three deep passes.

The assault rifle was now silent, lying in the dirt next to a collection of mangled fingers. Valgiernas was held tight inside the steel cable and the butterfly, now unmoving, was nestled deep inside his right buttock. The cable had lain in the new trenches dug by the spinning blade. Any movement was excruciating.

Jim unfroze his head and looked up just as Kayanan stepped over him. He fished out a knife from the small of his back. "I've looked forward to this."

Valgiernas spit on the ground. "You bastards won't win. Rothiel promised me that you would be my slave for all..."

Kayanan spun the blade upside down and fed it inside Valgiernas' mouth. His eyes bulged when the tip of the blade pierced the back of his throat and cleaved through the back of his head. When the hilt came to a stop against his lips, Kayanan jerked the knife upwards, splitting the top of his skull in two.

"Ugh. You really didn't like that guy, did you?" Jim was brushing off the dust from his trousers and examining the holes that were torn through his chest and back. "Look what that dick did to my shirt!" Jim turned and saw Gellan, Hank and Filthy walking back to the center from behind the pillar. "You guys okay?"

Filthy gave a wavering thumbs-up while Gellan's face soured at the sight of Kayanan's opponent.

Kayanan grasped onto the cable with one hand and picked up the assault rifle in the other. He dragged Valgiernas' body towards the center where the two groups departed and dumped the body in the middle. He pulled out the clip, cleared the chamber, and then dropped the expended weapon on top of the body. He walked back up to Jim's side, dusting off his hands and then looked around the room. The growling had subsided and the creatures were looking around the room in confusion.

Filthy whistled. "I think at last they know what they're up against."

Gellan looked back towards the hex. It was fluctuating in flashes of light and darkness. "We're not out of the woods yet."

Theo and Cesar both caught a glimpse of Bob running out of the temple and down the sidewalks towards the pavilion where they sat, sharing ice cream. Bob's suit jacket flapped in the wind behind him while he kept his left hand clasped over his vest pocket to keep his pocket watch from bouncing out. His right arm pumped furiously as he ran—somehow, even while running he did it with exquisite style.

Cesar found this view hilarious, as he had never seen a man in his fifties running and especially one trying to look dapper while doing it.

Theo knew something was wrong. Bob wouldn't be this anxious if it wasn't important. "Bob! What's wrong?"

Bob came to a stop inside the pavilion and grasped one of the rails for support. He ran a finger around the inside of his collar while he tried to get his breathing under control. "God…He…Rothiel's going to the circus!"

"What? Now?" Theo grabbed Cesar by his wrist and pulled him along towards the circus. "What did he say to you?"

Bob walked briskly alongside Theo and gave an irritated glance down at Cesar's laughing face. "The bulletin is going out as we speak. He's announcing the battle in the circus—to everyone!"

Cesar's smile disappeared. "Is this between Filodraxes and Rothiel? Is God going to be there?"

Bob growled, "Yes and yes! Hurry along!"

Cesar tore his arm free from Theo. "I've got to get something first!" He tore off back down the path towards the temple as fast as his legs could pump.

Bob looked at Theo incredulously. "Where in tarnation is that brat off to now?" He shouted over Theo's admonitions, "You'd better get your ass over there fast!"

Cesar tried to run up the steps two at a time like Tieran usually does, but fumbled on the first pair. He ran up the steps and pushed open the door to his room. He jumped onto his bed and grabbed the wooden cigar box and flung open the top. Nestled in some soft red cloth was Elena's soul. He picked it up and marveled at her beauty. He carefully slid it in his pocket and ran out the door. He found Aaron sitting at the bottom of the steps. "Aaron! Did you hear the news?"

Aaron got up and nodded excitedly. "Just did! I looked at my grandmother's patch and saw that you came here. Do you want to go together?"

Cesar ran down the steps and grabbed Aaron's hand. "We gotta hurry! Bob's already mad at me for coming back here."

The boys ran towards the circus and Aaron looked down at the lump in Cesar's pocket. "Is that what I think it is?"

"Sshh! Yes. Bob said that God is going to be at the circus. I want to ask him if he can help bring her back."

"Do you know what he looks like?"

Cesar shook his head. "Bob said he's an old man. --Kind of on the thin side. I'll ask Theo to point him out."

Cesar thought about something and laughed.

"What's so funny?"

"Nothing. When I was alive, I thought that God was younger, with long hair and a beard. He was covered in blood and stuck to some lumber!"

"That's grim!"

"Yeah. Well, I'm from Mexico."

The boys arrived at the steps and saw throngs of people climbing the stairs and passing through massive doors that had stood sealed for thousands of years. They passed through the packed passageway, weaving themselves between the excited adults and emerged on the upper fringe of a massive amphitheater. The steps and floor were carved from the purest white marble. The seats were cast in ornate gold with deep red cloth on the seats that shone with tiny gold specks. It was like peering into a red universe. Massive pillars surrounded the outer fringes and they in turn, held up massive gables that stretched out to cover the seating areas with a deep blue roof. The center of the Amphitheater was a shining floor in a checkerboard pattern of white marble and deep black onyx. There was a constant flow of people, filling the seats and singing.

Aaron tugged at Cesar's shirt, "There's Mr. White and Theo!" Theo was waving the boys over and Bob was raving into his patch and shaking his head. The boys worked their way through the clusters of people with Cesar being extra careful with his precious cargo.

"Hello Aaron," Theo ran her fingers through his hair and he smiled up at her. "We're sitting near the front. Care to join us?"

Cesar was thrilled. "We're in front? C'mon Aaron—you've got to sit with us!"

"If you don't mind..."

Theo glanced at Bob out of the corner of her eye and watched him stiffen. "Why, of course you can!"

They all proceeded towards the front of the arena where there was a private box. It was big enough to hold at least fifty people. There was a fat man sitting by himself in the box. "Bob cut short his animated discussion with his patch and looked at the man. "Hey pal, are you lost? This is *our* box."

The man looked up at Bob with a sour look on his face. "I don't see your name on it."

Bob clenched his right fist. "C.S.B. Bob White. Git your fat ass out of that box."

The man seemed to recognize the name and changed his tune. "No problem,—I'm moving...I'm moving." The man reached down, picked up a fat, overstuffed bag and sidestepped past them. He moved up four rows and sat down. His eyes stayed on Bob.

"The nerve!" Bob saw Aaron looking up at him. He stepped back and opened his arm towards the interior of the box. "After you kids... Go ahead and sit where you want." He waited until the boys ran to the front and peeked over the rail before he brought up the patch. "Sorry, Tieran. ...Naw, some total ass was sitting in our booth. He took one look at my biceps and ran off. ...Well you'd better hurry up— I think they're already in position. ...Yeah, good luck to you, too." He closed his patch by snapping the pocket watch shut and looked at the heart engraved on the front. He imagined for a moment on Rothiel's hordes bulldozing through his neighborhood in Alexandria. He could almost picture his wife and daughters screaming in terror. Bob saw a brilliant flash of light rocketing towards them and he called out to the boys, "Look who's here!"

Tieran blasted upwards with his translucent wings swept back. The crowd cheered. He flew in a lazy circle, looking at the edges of the amphitheater to make sure there wasn't anything strange. He had his patch held out, sniffing electromagnetic waves from the surfaces. Everything appeared normal. He snapped his wings and accelerated towards the private box. He stopped in mid-air. The wings were fully extended and vibrating. "Bob! Everything reads normal! Be on the lookout!" Cesar instinctively looked at his side for the sword of Ikorsom. It wasn't there. Tieran tilted over and fell downwards, building up speed and then gently landed on the perimeter of the floor, his mechanical wings folding in immaculate precision behind him. He waved his hand towards the energy gate and passed through. The hum of the gate returned, preventing anyone from exiting the circus.

Tieran checked his men one last time. Eleven of his best men stood at the ready. "Be on your toes. I'm certain that Rothiel is not here for a duel—he's here to create rebellion."

Cesar looked over and saw a massive box on the opposite end of the stadium with massive blue curtains covering the seating area. The curtains slowly parted showing the booth to be empty. "Who sits there —is that for God?"

Theo looked over Cesar's shoulder and smiled. "Sure is. Keep your eyes peeled—I'm sure you'll see him today."

Cesar thought about Rothiel's coming. *He tried to defeat God before*, he thought looking around at the multitudes of people. He tried to convince himself that it would be impossible for him to do it again. *He couldn't break through the security of the circus—after all, he's trapped in a human body*. He thought about what Bob said—only

Origin can come and go between the worlds—that the exiles weren't strong enough. Cesar glanced back at the thin man sitting his his bag on his lap. *What if he had help on this side?*

A long horn blew over the circus and the buzzing crowd grew silent. Cesar looked at his palms and they were sweaty. He kept thinking about Naius Athum, the sword and Rothiel's eagerness to destroy himself at the circus—*he wouldn't take risks like this*, he thought to himself. *He just wouldn't.*

He wanted to deliver Elena's soul to God and ask for his help. *Sheesh, it would take half a day to get across to the other side*, he thought. *I'd ask Aaron to do it for me, but I can't get him in trouble.* The back of his mind tickled with the image of the sword.

Cesar shot to his feet.

"What's wrong?" asked Aaron, looking at the uncertainty of his friend's face.

"Um... I don't know—I can't explain. I have to check on something. I gotta go."

Aaron noticed that Cesar's complexion looked pale. "I'll go with you."

"No—it's okay. I'm sure you don't want to miss this—I'll be back soon enough."

Cesar started walking briskly out of the box and Aaron stayed right on his heels.

"Now, where the hell is he going?" asked Bob watching the two of them negotiating their way through the thick crowds.

"Don't get sassy, Robert White." She smiled at the way they were soldiering around people with such purpose. "Besides, he's in good hands."

Rip hung from Big Lee's chest harness as he felt the hex take control or their physical bodies. He felt his legs pull downward and the tightness of the harness increase as they rose upward. The walls of Rothiel's courtyard dimmed and then begin to course with sharp light. The blinding light overhead crackled and Big Lee exhaled sharply. He began to double over. "Lee?"

Big Lee gasped and his body shook. Rip tried to turn his head around to get a better look and saw that his eyes were big and watery. *He's in some horrendous pain by the looks of it*, thought Rip as his stress grew.

The walls exploded away and melted into the walls of the circus. The majestic beauty of the circus was breathtaking. For several seconds, Rip completely forgot about Big Lee's pain. Big Lee must have been mesmerized as well, as he paused his contortions when he saw the view.

Big Lee groaned and bit his lower lip. Rip reached up and grabbed Lee by his chin. "Lee? Wha's rong? Dell me!"

"Uggh. I.." He exhaled sharply. "Pain—in my belly. Tremendous pain."

Simon grabbed ahold of Big Lee's arm and tried to steady him. He was looking into his eyes for any sign of narcotic.

Rothiel's upper lip curled in satisfaction as he watched Big Lee contort from the pain and fall to one knee.

The arena was packed with untold thousands all cheering the appearance of exiles. More out of curiosity, people wanted to see Rothiel—the one that masterminded the great rebellion.

For the exiles standing on the black and white tiled floor, there was no sound. The field separating them from heaven only allowed a view of paradise. Rip was tempted to scan the crowd for his beloved Theo, but he had other concerns at the moment—Big Lee was wounded —either by the hex or by Rothiel's trickery. Filodraxes had Rothiel locked in his vision. He would not be misdirected nor lead astray. He knew that this was the last, best way to finally rid the worlds of Rothiel's evil.

Rothiel turned in all directions with his arms spread wide. He looked towards the side and saw what he was looking for. He began walking purposely towards the side of the arena towards Bob and Theo's private booth.

Filodraxes watched him strut away and raised his right hand. He drummed his fingers into the air repeatedly until a loud cracking noise emanated from between his fingertips. Electrical arcs discharged between his fingers as he prepared to release his bolt toward Rothiel.

Prestor and Hale jumped between Rothiel and Filodraxes. Protraxis skulked over and got behind them. His strength seemed to have left him entirely. He hung onto Hale and let his head droop downwards.

"Gentlemen! I believe that there will be no duel." Filodraxes turned to the three and pointed back at Rothiel's witnesses. "Those vermin are almost dead as it is. It's clear that they are to sacrifice themselves so that Rothiel is free to accomplish his mission."

"Oof! What do we do man?" Big Lee's eyes leaked tears as he tried to cope with the pain.

"We collapse the hex and get out of here. You lot prepare yourselves—we may have to fight our way out when we get back."

Filodraxes raised both his arms and sucked the energy from his hex back inside. Nothing happened. They were still there.

Filodraxes looked back towards Rothiel. He was laughing. He again turned and continued his walk towards the side of the arena.

Filodraxes blew out air from his clenched jaw and massaged his knuckles. "Well, at least now, we know."

"Whaz goi'n on Filo?" Rip was getting agitated. Nothing was going as planned.

"It takes two to open a connection between the two worlds. Apparently, it only takes one to maintain it."

The multitudes were booing and hissing when Rothiel began to strut around the arena floor. Theo looked past him towards the four representing the Lodge. Her heart skipped a beat when she saw him. Goose pimples coursed across her arms when she saw his little arms and legs moving. Danhieras was here.

Rothiel walked steadily towards Bob and Theo's side of the arena. His face stared upwards at them, a confident smile on his face.

"Theo?" asked Bob in a low voice. "Any thoughts on why that rat-bastard is walking this way?"

Theo shook her head and slowly unfolded her patch. She was knocked lightly against Bob as the fat man barreled past them towards the edge of the arena.

"Stop him!" Bob lurched forward to grab the man's arm but only managed to grab air. He saw that the man had unzipped the large bag and hurled the contents forward over the guardrail. A beige plume of dust scattered outwards, falling by inverted peaks towards the arena floor. When it came into contact with the protective field, the particles sparkled with white and blue electricity.

Theo shouted into her patch, "Identify that dust!"

The patch echoed back instantly, "Seventy-eight percent sodium chloride, fifteen percent calcium and seven percent trace organic matter."

She looked at the electrical firestorm scattering over the protective field. "Bob—it's mostly salt."

Rothiel watched his servant hurl the salt over the balcony directly over where he was standing. *Salt from the Dead Sea*, he thought with satisfaction. *How appropriate that something of that name will initiate death to so many of my enemies. This should decay the field at least for a few moments. Long enough for just one word.*

He heard a heavy rush of noise, at first a rumble, then the cacophony of an excited crowd. The noise tumbled from the widening hole as the salt gobbled up heavy ions from the field and brought them to the floor. Rothiel noticed two people standing at the rail in alarm. One, the old man, had grabbed his servant by his collar and flattened him to the floor with a single punch. The young woman was holding something in her hands and shouting loudly. She then pointed the silver object in her hands towards Rothiel. A thin length of chain leaped out of the device and curled itself rapidly towards him. The chain wrapped itself around his torso and tightened. Then another dashed out, followed by more and more until hundreds were spewing towards him. The chains dashed around his head and arms until he was completely covered in a matter of seconds.

A red light began to form in the center of the mass of chains wrapped around Rothiel's head. The light grew in intensity and spread across the all of the chains.

"Bob! This isn't going to hold him for very long!"

The chains burst apart from their links and exploded off of Rothiel's body. He wore a maniacal leer on his face as he inhaled deeply and with all of his strength, screamed out, *"Shanica dorum Triel-Ikorsom!"*

He looked down at his right hand and saw the soft blue glow that covers the caller of the Universe's most terrible weapon. "Vengeance!"

Cesar and Aaron bounded up the stairs to the armory and ran through the front door. The hallways were deserted—everyone had gone to the circus to see Rothiel. A resonating boom sound echoed down the hallway and froze Cesar in his tracks. "Oh no! That's the vault door!" He reached down for his patch, but he had left it at the circus. "C'mon, we gotta hurry!"

Aaron was breathing fast and heavy, but he kept up behind Cesar's furious legs. Cesar swallowed to overcome the nausea of what lied ahead and ran into the doorway that glowed 'Tieran' in soft green light. The vault door had almost swung completely open. The astronomical wall was already dividing and began to dilate, showing the sword of Ikorsom levitating from the statue's outstretched arms. Cesar looked around the vault's doors for any means to close them, when he noticed the sword's point rotated outwards and began gliding swiftly through the air to reach the hand of it's new owner.

Cesar gritted his teeth and jumped in front of it. He felt a gentle knock on his abdomen and a cold rush that coiled through the lower half of his body. He tried to exhale and screamed. The pain was sharp and burning. He fell to his knees and writhed on the floor from the pain. The sword stopped moving. It began to pull backwards and Cesar panicked and grabbed the hilt with both hands. "No! You'll kill me!" The sword instantly obeyed and ceased all movement.

Aaron knelt next to his wounded friend and felt the warm blood soak into his pant legs. "Cesar—talk to me... what should I do?"

'Just... just don't touch the sword..." He cried. Each inhale sent shockwaves of pain through his body. "I...I left my patch at the circus—you've got to go get help. Go back and get Bob or Theo—they'll know what to do."

Aaron softly patted his friend's shoulder and dashed out of the room. Over his involuntary sobs, Cesar tried to listen to Aaron's footfalls, but he began to get dizzy and could feel his heartbeat through his ears.

Bob was frantically searching through his patch for a way to restore the shield while Theo threw barrages of intense heat and light towards Rothiel. Nothing seemed to affect him. "The aperture—it may have restored some of his power!"

"Well, there's one thing we haven't tried," said Bob, wrenching the serving table off the ground and deftly hurled it towards Rothiel. "Good 'ol fashioned brute force!"

Rothiel brought up his hand to block the table and it wracked against his wrist, sending a streak of pain through his arm. He looked down in surprise. The blue glow was gone. *"Shanica dorum Triel-Ikorsom!"* The blue glow did not return. The sound of the crowd began to fade. The aperture was closing as the salt became saturated and the field equalized. "Nooo!"

Bob at last found what he was searching for within his patch. He could redirect the field's energy to disrupt the hex. "C.S.B. Bob White-- I order a full flux-shift of the protective field to any active hexes inside the arena!"

The floor of the arena shuddered and each one-meter tile of the floor vibrated, then rotated on its axis.

Rip was trying to coax Big Lee into taking longer breaths, when he looked up and saw the image of the circus vaporize. He felt relief that Rothiel's second attempt at rebellion was quashed. He knew that his problems were just beginning.

Cesar lost the fight against the blood loss and slid gently onto his side and saw the walls of Tieran's room spin. He closed his eyes shut and began to sing his grandmother's nightly song to himself. *"… nos vamos a dormir…"*

He thought he heard a voice and then felt a hand grab him. His half-lidded eyes slowly opened and he saw Tieran and Bob carefully carrying him into the simulations room.

"I've got him," said Tieran as he held Cesar in his left arm and grabbed the handle with his right hand. "Steady now."

In one quick motion, He yanked out the sword and hurled Cesar through the regeneration doorway in the middle of the room. Cesar awoke sliding to a stop on the floor. He didn't feel any pain and felt wide-awake. He sat up and saw Aaron standing in front of him. "That was close, Cesar."

He turned his head to the side and saw Tieran holding the sword of Ikorsom. Tieran was speaking to Aaron. "If you'll excuse me my Lord, I'll just put this back." He turned and ran back to the vault. Tieran had never hated this sword as much as now. He was glad however, that he ordered it to never harm Cesar or he would have been lost forever.

Aaron called over to him, "Make sure you change the password —he still has the ability to come back."

Cesar felt confused. Aaron no longer seemed young. That, and Tieran called him 'Lord'. He got up off the floor and looked up at Bob. Bob gave him a slight shake of the head to remain silent.

Bob turned to the white-haired boy and gave a slight bow. "What would you like us to do, Lord?"

Aaron looked up at Bob. "You and Tieran shall depart for Rothiel's stronghold immediately and place him into custody. I want all of his followers eliminated." He handed Bob a small piece of paper.

Bob read some of the writing. "You want me to read this out to Rothiel?"

"In origin of course. Rothiel cannot speak English."

Bob poked the paper into his suit pocket and dropped his hands in frustration. "Excuse me for being so blunt my Lord, but why can't we just get rid of him? I mean, look at all the evil that he's done!"

Aaron looked at Bob impassively. "You have all done well. As I expected you would. Rothiel has merely acted in a way that we all knew he would. The real purpose of this test was to see how everyone else would react to his presence."

Bob stood with his jaw set firm. He wanted to add that it was senseless for so many to have paid a price.

"This is my will, Robert White."

Bob bowed and walked out of the room with Tieran. Tieran had already suited up for battle in his Origin armor and had slapped his wings into place.

Cesar stood for the longest time looking at the blank wall. He was afraid. During all of this time, his best friend had turned out to be God. The "Great Architect of the Universe" as Bob sometimes called him. He didn't know what to say.

"I'm still Aaron."

Cesar turned and looked at his friend's face. "But you've seen me do bad things."

"Wonderful things. Glorious things! Don't you see? An adult would not have made your decisions or taken your risks. An adult would try as Bob and Theo tried—to take on Rothiel directly. Ultimately they would have failed. They didn't see that his only real power was to steal this sword."

Cesar felt the lump in his pocket. He might as well have been naked—he could feel Aaron's eyes on it. "I've stolen Elena's soul from the fountain."

Aaron laughed. "Wasn't I your accomplice? Merely borrowed it, as far as I'm concerned. ...but let's not get into the habit of doing that frequently, mind you."

Cesar felt relieved. He broke a small smile as well. "Are you going to tell Bob or Theo?"

Aaron laughed. "Why should you mind? You are an equal member of the team. You are also completely entwined to each other."

Cesar thought about what he said but didn't understand. "How so?"

Aaron looked down and noticed that he was still covered in Cesar's blood. "Whoops—I'd better get cleaned up before my grandmother sees me."

Cesar blinked. "You mean, you really have a grandmother?"

"Well, not like you'd think. She was one of the sweetest ladies I've ever made, but since she's arrived here, she's missed contact with her grandson terribly. I merely spend time with her as her grandson until he arrives. –Think of it as a 'part time job'."

He walked calmly through the regeneration doorway and came out with fresh, clean clothes. "Where was I? Oh yes, it was Bob that delivered the infected mosquito to you while you slept. You died two days later. Theo killed your father while he was beating your mother in a drunken rage. She was four months pregnant with you. You may not have recognized her, but three hundred years ago, Theo was the *Virgen Protegedor de niños*—she's the image of the virgin on the arch that you helped save."

Cesar brought his hand to the side of his head. "That's where I knew her from! How could I have been so stupid... What? She killed my father?"

Aaron folded his hands behind him. "It needed to be done. He wouldn't have allowed you to live."

Cesar felt confused, but still a bit relieved. He nodded for a moment. "So, um, what happens with Elena?"

Aaron grinned. "A friend of mine once told me that he wanted her to live. I think that Rota has lost much too many great people. Follow me."

Aaron and Cesar walked together out of the armory and along the path leading to the temple. Cesar felt liberated. Aaron socked him in the shoulder and giggled. Cesar socked him in return, but not clearly as hard—*he was God after all,* he thought. Cesar barely knew Elena, but knew that she was key to Jim Smith's life and his sanity. He didn't want to push his luck on asking for details, but he hoped that God would return her to her former life and not send her to a different one.

They walked toward the inner chamber holding the fountain. When Aaron approached the door it did not open. "I forgot—you better lead."

Cesar stepped forward and touched his finger to the bronze knob. The characteristic wooden *thunk* sounded as the lock was released for C.S.B. Rivas and the massive door swung inwards.

The boys strolled inside towards the fountain. Cesar never tired of seeing the beauty of the glowing fountain. He could feel the rush of information all around him. His mind began to tickle about the future of Elena. He knew from before that introducing her to the fountain would complete her death. The moment that she is slipped back in, she will either arrive at the willow tree or be reborn as someone else. He hoped for neither. "Aaron? I didn't think that we would be taking her back to the fountain."

Aaron looked at him and grinned. "Is that what you thought? I just want to make a slight change. Aaron held up his hand and violent images of a fight displayed across the rushing waters of of the fountain.

"Is that them fighting below?" asked Cesar. "It looks like they're losing."

Aaron watched the display with mild interest. "They most certainly are."

Cesar furrowed his brow. "But—you told Tieran and Bob to fight them! I don't see any of them yet!"

"In due time."

Cesar watched the melee in frustration and confusion. Members of Rip's team were falling with each passing second.

Aaron nodded and raised his head. "Tieran, you may begin."

A second window on the fountain displayed Tieran and his men morphing into Earth armor and diving with furious speed into a portal taking them to Rota.

Aaron then raised his hand and the fountain stopped. The column had gone deathly quiet. A slight gurgle and trickle of liquids was all that was heard. Lying at the bottom of the still pool was thousands of glowing balls, bunched together like multi-colored fish eggs.

"I'm surprised at you Cesar. You've spent absolute *days* here gazing into the fountain and you didn't see these?"

Cesar was amazed. *Thousands of faces*, thought Cesar. *Thousands of people, all held here on the bottom of the pool.* "Who are they?"

Aaron pointed to Cesar's bulging pocket. "Give her to me and I'll show you."

Chapter Forty Two:
The Return

Rip swung around violently from the nylon harnass attached to Big Lee's chest. His little neck didn't have the strength to counter against the forces working against his large head. He glimpsed flashes of Filodraxes generating massive flashes of energy around them as he tried to reestablish his hex to get them out of Rothiel's domain. When the field suddenly collapsed, Big Lee ended up on his back, groaning and wretching. Filodraxes had hit the ground with such impact that his pelvis was crushed and his shoulder separated. Simon had hardened just before impact and had perforated the hard clay floor of the courtyard with the top of his head. He came to immediately and rushed to Filodraxes side.

Rothiel screamed in rage. Jim ran over to Big Lee and couldn't believe the difference in his color. His usual light-brown skin was now ashen. His tongue was thick and almost white. Jim tried to get him to stand up. Big Lee was able to move to his side and get his feet back under him. He rose up from the ground weakly and began to stagger towards the back, behind Kayanan. Hank lessened Big Lee's weight by half and it allowed him to walk easier.

Kayanan ran forward and gripped Filodraxes' coat with his left hand. "We move out now!" Simon and Kayanan began to drag Filodraxes backwards as the old man gritted his teeth and moaned against the pain.

Rothiel stormed forward and glared at Valgiernas' body on the floor. He tightened his fists, growled and kicked his split head with such force that flesh and bone spattered around the retreating group. He shook in rage, opened his mouth and screamed.

Filodraxes' lower torso began to disintegrate like meat rotting with lightning speed. His hips, ribcage, and legs coursed outwards with blackness. The blackened areas of his flesh collapsed rapidly until it caved inwards, slipping off the bone. The rapid decay caused intense heat killing the old man instantly. Kayanan let go of his leader's shoulder and pushed Simon behind him. He reached back to throw a butterfly into Rothiel but froze when he felt multiple cactus needles prick his skin. The cold feeling rushing through his spine told him what had struck him from behind. He turned towards Simon. Simon had a two dark quills hanging out of his throat.

Jim exploded outward, doubling in size every half-second until he arrived at his full height. He smashed the drones out of the way with a single sweep of his hand and when other shot quills at him, he deflected them with ease. Even with his massive size, he used Gellan's speed to take out the drones surrounding them on all sides. Dozens of bishops leaped on him and attacked him at all angles with their claws. They didn't even hurt, just barely a tickle on his impervious skin. He smashed the bishops against walls and ripped them apart. He drove the horns poking out of his head into two of the bishops, spilling their internals on the clay floor. He began to wade his way towards Rothiel, in an attempt to stop him once and for all. Hale, Prestor and Protraxis tried to get in his way and he flung them against the heavy beams of the roof, killing them upon impact. Their bodies exploded in a blackened dust. Jim held his breath, but it made his nostrils and eyes burn. He examined their bodies and saw that they were merely crude puppets formed out of molted human skin. He looked around the room and saw creatures swarming out of the walls.

Hank yelled for Jim's attention. "We gotta get out of here! We're cut off from behind!" Jim raised his head towards the ceiling and inhaled deeply. He roared so loud that the skin along his neck and face rippled and shook the roof tiles. "DIANOOOO!"

Frank thought he could hear some commotion coming from the center of town but couldn't place it. It sounded like men shouting. This was different from the racket of the single assault rifle they heard before. He looked over the rooftops and saw a dull, pink tinge in the sky. Morning was on its way. Somehow he felt comfort, knowing the sun was on its way. The loud scream from Jim almost stopped his heart. The booming voice echoed around the town's ancient walls. Diano leaped from a crouch and barreled headfirst through the wall, sending brick and dust everywhere. The beast continued on its mad dash to bring the calvary to the desperate exiles.

Frank switched off his safety and nodded at Allison. "Ye'r the point man—don't waste ammo either. I'll be right behind you. Boardman? You bring up the rear."

Allison lifted a leg to scramble over the broken brick wall and made his way through the dust-clouded interior of the buildings. Frank could barely make out Lee's black uniform in front of him. He knew the heat was on when he heard the gas escaping from Allison's assault rifle and the clack of the bronze pellets leaving the barrel. Frank squinted into the darkness and saw movement everywhere.

He sidled up next to Allison and pulled his trigger. The drones that were converging into the newly built tunnel made by Diano were exploding from the impact of the heavy ammunition. To his left, he saw Romero open fire towards advancing bogies that were hugging the walls at their flank. Frank chuckled to himself. *There ain't a chance in hell that we're going to survive this*, he thought as he exhausted his first clip, slapped in a second and let fly with the continuing barrage. *But if we do, I'm going to slap so many medals on their chests that they'll get hernias just trying to walk.*

He and Allison were making headway into the cavity that Diano disappeared into. "Alright! Allison—get through that hole! Let's go!"

When the men passed through the hole they were immediately awestruck at the spectacle of Diano rending the black creatures apart under the shadow of a much larger giant. The men could feel each stomp and crushing blow from the giant as he rained destruction upon advancing beasts.

Hank sent tons of weight from the surrounding buildings, coiling and coursing towards the roof. The roof began to buckle and then imploded, bringing down thick wooden beams, clay roofing tiles and the nine Chinese warriors. They tumbled through the roof, rigid and frozen, but loosened up and twisted into position to land gracefully on the clay floor below. The first to land was the longbowman, who landed on his feet, descending to one knee in the same movement and loosed two arrows before his brothers touched the floor. The swordsmen landed with their swords already drawn and began hacking with dizzying speed into the crowds of drones and bishops.

Rothiel watched as the statues obliterated his creatures in untiring fashion. One swordsman hacked past Rothiel without giving him any regard. It was only interested in the black army. Rothiel reached out and touched the back of its clay head with his index finger. It became rigid and collapsed into tinkling shards. He bent down to examine the contents of the soldiers and saw soot and ash. *Very similar to his witnesses at the circus*, he thought with a sneer. He picked up a handful of the ash and whispered, "...curse the ash, offend the dead and deny the enemy." He blew the ash from his hand and the remaining eight soldiers froze and toppled over, breaking into shards.

Hank picked up a brick and hurled it at Rothiel. Just before it impacted, he increased the mass of the brick to over a thousand pounds. Rothiel raised his hand to deflect the brick and it snapped his arm backwards, crushed his collarbone and separated his shoulder. Rothiel rolled to a sitting position and commanded his body to heal. His flesh and bone restored itself in a mere moment and he shot back to his feet. He willed tremendous weight to converge into Hank's body.

Jim could feel the enormous bands of weight passing by him and entering Hank's body, so he reached out to move him out of the way. Hank's eyes bulged and he fell over. Jim instinctively grabbed his body and felt the enormous pull dragging Hank's body down. He tried to keep him from impacting the floor and felt Hank's bones rupture and his body pull itself apart like wet algae running between his fingers.

"Jim! Git behind me!"

Jim looked back and saw that Big Lee was on his knees, unable to walk. He was disconnecting Rip from his harness. Rip was covered in wetness and his face was turning purple.

Jim ran past Big Lee and looked at the remaining men. Kayanan was gone. White foam leaked from his mouth. He had dropped his bag of antiserum syringes on the ground and a smaller, warped creature was busily popping off the plastic caps and sticking them one at a time into Kayanan's lifeless body. The creature looked up at the giant for a moment as if uninterested and went back to its freakish hobby. Jim dashed it against the wall with his palm. Gellan was torn in half near the pillar and two drones were fighting over his remains. Filthy was riddled with quills and staggered in a slow circle. A long, clear icicle of drool hung from his lower lip. Simon was sitting against the wall holding something near his abdomen that was glowing pink. His face was pale and he was sweating. He couldn't speak, but his mouthed writhed with 'I'm so sorry…"

"Time to kiss the baby you mutha-fuck'in *bitch*!" Big Lee drew Rip backwards and then flung him directly at Rothiel.

Jim hardened.

The room flashed white as the fireball consumed everything from the center of the room. Fire swirled around the pillars putting Filthy out of his misery and consuming the creatures dining on Gellan. The fireball burned itself out and Jim's hardness ceased. It wasn't voluntary. He began to shrink. He looked over at Big Lee and saw that his skin looked like streaked marble. He was shivering.

Diano rushed into the room and began attacking the reinforcement army that was surging through holes in the ground and walls. Rothiel stood in the center of the room without so much as a scratch or singe.

Big Lee's vision swam. He could feel death approaching. It was unmistakeable. "Diano! You got to git out of here now! It's a trap! Go!"

Diano was furious and ripping apart the creatures nearest him. He looked down and saw the charred form of Kayanan, with molten blobs of syringes sticking out of his body. He began to snort in fear and anger. He looked down at Jim.

Jim nodded. "Quick—to the East. We're done for."

Rothiel placed his hands together and red smoke began to seep out from between his palms. It took massive concentration and Rothiel laughed when he saw that his smoke began to take form and take control. He directed the thin sliver of red smoke toward Diano. *Just one touch to his skin and he'll be mine forever*, he conspired. *From him I'll make a creature that will destroy all mankind.*

Frank opened up his assault rifle on Rothiel and watched as the bronze balls ripped massive holes out of his body and tore his face to ribbons.

Diano looked about him and shrieked in grief. He turned and blasted through the East wall.

The red smoke dissipated, leaving Rothiel on the floor as a bloodied heap. His body lurched and then sat up, without as much as a drop of blood on his face. He hissed something and nearby brick walls plummeted to the ground, revealing hundreds more creatures. Some were drones and bishops but there were others- some so twisted and misshapen that they were horrifying to look at. Some were massive. They all trundled forward to kill the sailors. Two centipede-like creatures fell upon Allison and Romero from the ceiling beams. Frank looked up and saw dozens climbing along the beams. He opened up with his rifle alongside Boardman and dropped them, dead on the floor. By the time he looked back at the rest of his men, only Boardman remained. He tried to say something witty to his young friend but nothing came to mind. He shrugged, turned and blasted at more of the advancing creatures and finally expended his final clip. He looked back at Boardman. He was gone.

Frank pulled his Colt. He had swapped out his lead balls with Boardman's bronze ones. He pulled the hammer back and pulled the heavy trigger. Although the shot felt like it split his eardrums, the effect was extraordinary. It tore through several creatures and stopped them in their tracks. He let more and more fly, keeping count of the remaining bullets. The creatures were no longer advancing. The combination of the extreme power of the Colt and the enormous racket of each black-powder explosion was spooking the nearby creatures. He had one more shot. *The money shot. This baby is all for me.* He could leave this battle without pain. *Well, maybe a little at first*, thought Frank as he pondered how much brain is required to actually feel pain.

A hulking creature stalked towards Frank and the other smaller creatures got out of its way. It was similar to a huge human shape, except the oversized fingers ended in claws. The lower torso didn't end in two legs, but six of them. The legs were short and stocky. From the torso on down, it was a reddish, bubbled armor like that of a crab. The creature had a human face, but one half was displaced slightly downwards like it was made of wax and had melted that way. Frank realized that everything on this creature wasn't proportionate. One arm was much larger than the other and it stomped on some legs, while it dragged others behind. The creature flexed its claws in anticipation of using them on Frank.

Frank peered into the remaining cylinder of his Colt. "Well, this isn't the first time I've done something stupid." He pointed the barrel towards the creature's head and pulled the trigger. The head burst open like a rotten melon, peeling back skull from the bottom of its nose and opening in a gruesome yawn. It dumped to the ground like an old geezer in a broken porch swing. As Frank was taken to the ground by several other creatures, Frank's final memory was the satisfaction of blowing that brute's head clean off. *Sayonara, Dickhead.*

The witch, Luisa and her daughters heard the horrific commotion nearby and stood their ground. The daughters were visibly afraid but Luisa stood in front of them with her thick arms crossed. She only looked annoyed. Her lips were pursed and the more violence that she heard, the more her eyes squinted. "Hmmpf. I just hope that some of them survive."

The brunette, Alexandra leaned forward and pleaded with her mother. "Mama, why are we even here? I can feel death here—it's everywhere."

"Simple," said Luisa chewing the inside of her cheek in anticipation. "We wait until these *cabrónes* are much too weak to fight against us. Then we take control—when we have them all under our power, the world will be ours."

"I thought," said Maria, with a frown, "that we were going to help these people fight against Rothiel."

Luisa dared not look back at her daughter in anger. She kept her eyes towards the sounds of fighting. "Pse. Don't be *estupida*. Can't you see they're all the same? These people are worth more than diamonds."

An explosion of brick and dust blew outwards from the walls behind Diano's accelerating shape. He bounded over the cobblestone road in one leap and crashed through the wall leading to the beach. He hit the cool sand running at full speed, tears streaming across his angry face. He bellowed and hit the surf, blowing foam high into the air and forming a bulge under the water. He continued deeper and deeper under the dark water until the surface returned to calm.

Luisa stood looking through the rubble of the wall in hatred. "*Me caga en la leche...*"

She stalked back towards her daughters, being careful not to twist her ankles on the loose rock. "*No importa!* It seems to me his *nigger* father was much stronger! We'll make do with him!" She peered into the darkness to see if it was time to enter and lay claim to the exiles. She saw blackened creatures swarming towards her. She raised her head in defiance and stepped back. She retrieved another red skull from her purse, pulled the cork with her teeth and sent a cloud of the white powder into the hole. The drones that touched the powder came to a stop. Others simply pushed them aside and continued towards their prey.

"*Una... mierda!*" Shouted Luisa as she quickly walked back to her daughters. She turned and growled an incantation. She began to hiss words through her lips and the surrounding buildings caved in on the creatures trying to exit the wall. "We wait."

Alexandra heard a scuffling noise behind her and saw the road was choked with them. They were slowly marching towards them. She crouched down and placed both hands on the cobble street. The stones underneath the approaching drones began to rattle and jump, throwing the drones in disarray. She was the best at moving several stones at a time, but couldn't raise them very high. Luisa and Maria used her stalling tactic at their advantage to raise single blocks from the road and send them flying into the disabled creatures. The rocks flew in repeating passes back and forth across the road, battering the creatures into submission.

Alexandra heard a hissing noise over head and saw a bishop leap off the roof and land on Luisa, slamming her to the street underneath him. As he worked his claws into her, she continued to glare at it with a foul expression. She finally turned to her daughters and said in a weakening voice, "...*niñas*...get out of here."

The two girls were shrieking in horror. The strongest force they've ever known was being devoured alive. Alexandra had lost her control on the stones and Maria had dropped to her knees, praying.

Alexandra knew that their best hope was to combine their strengths, like they did as little girls. Alexandra knelt next to her younger sister and picked up her hands in hers. She interlocked her fingers in hers and began to say the singing game they played when they made dust devils out of sand on the beach. Maria, through tears began to repeat the words with her sister as the creatures marched in determined speed towards them.

Again, the cobblestones began to jump out of their sockets and fly in circles around the women. They closed their eyes and concentrated the energy so that the stones whipped around in a powerful whirlwind, taking out anything nearby. The stones racked against the buildings next to them, bashing their walls apart and creating more material for the strengthening vortex. The advancing creatures were getting torn to pieces as they edged closer to the funnel cloud of rock. A steady column of bishops leapt into the vortex from the rooftops and was instantly crushed by the speeding debris. More and more jumped in and were caught before they could reach the ground. A heavily built centipede-like creature lumbered to the edge of the roof and dangled the front of its segmented body over. Several of its legs kicked in the air as it continued over the side. It teetered over and fell into the vortex. It reached the bottom and crushed both women on impact, sending a concentrated burst of energy into the vortex as it tightened the funnel and then released the stones outwards, decimating everything in its path. All traces of the young women were gone.

Luisa's half-eaten body lay in the street in silence with a sour frown spanning her face.

Rothiel picked up a fallen chair and sat down to watch the waning battle before him. *The great Koriet Leigh—killed by poison*, he thought, laughing to himself. *It wouldn't have ever affected him if he didn't become mortal during the entry to the circus.*

He watched as the final member of Rip's team battled against his forces. *He easily defeated my regulars*, he thought. *Now that his teammates can no longer offer their talents, we'll see how he can handle my special menagerie.*

Jim picked up one of the Chinese warrior's swords and began to hack at the various creatures that were attempting to surround him. He could harden himself for only a second or two, but he felt like Simon was slipping further away. He deflected more quills and then looked back at the two remaining men. Big Lee wasn't moving. His skin separated at the seams by a few centimeters but that was all. He must be dead, he thought. He glanced over at Simon. He was still holding the glowing pink light. It was growing even stronger and was now poking through his clenched fingers. His head was bowed down and his breathing shallow.

Jim was brought back to the battle by something slamming into the right side of his body. A massive creature similar to what he saw Frank Gutierrez kill had struck him with a wooden club. It bowled him over onto the floor and another creature lashed out with its claws raking his back. Jim rolled away and jumped up from the floor before the club could finish him off. He hacked with the sword and only scratched the tough chitin that covered the creature's fat legs. The creature bellowed in hideous laughter and brought the club down. Jim raised his arm in defense and hardened. It deflected most of the impact, but his ability to remain hard was failing quickly. He found himself on the ground with aching shoulders and fresh scrapes along his arm.

Simon's breathing began to falter and his heart skipped a few beats. The memories of Elena finally slipped from Simon as he passed away and returned to its former owner.

Jim relived Elena's life and violent death in all but a few short moments as the memories flowed into his mind. His inability to scream when she was being killed didn't prevent him from doing so this time around. He fell to his knees shrieking hysterically as hot tears flashed down his cheeks. He buried his head in his hands and grieved loudly until his vocal chords cracked in futility.

He forgot entirely about the massive creature that was preparing the final blow with the club. It paused when his quarry became overcome by his emotions and it raised a shrill laugh across the room at the weakness of its victim. The surrounding creatures shook in glee at the spectacle and moved in ever closer to begin feasting on the last survivor.

Tieran and his twelve soldiers flew in tight formation through the tunnel between Heaven and Earth at dizzying speed. As they sped downward, Tieran barked his final instructions, "No one is to confront Rothiel. Protect any survivors, but you leave him to me."

As Tieran exited the tunnel, he saw Jim Smith about to be executed by the massive creature. He punched the rapid release fitting on his chest and hurled his wings towards Jim Smith with his remaining momentum. The wings remained folded backwards for minimum wind resistance and only popped open when it reached the screaming man crouched on the floor. The wings snapped around him, forming a protective ball just as the creature delivered his final downward blow. The club impacted the golden-feathered ball deforming the shape slightly and rustling the feathers in a loud shearing noise. The ball returned to its shape and the feathers re-adjusted themselves to better protect the frail man inside. The giant pouted when he saw that his victim had disappeared inside the gleaming ball, so he tried to bash it open with the club. The ball was knocked around the clay floor with each impact and ended the lives of two other creatures as he swung wildly trying to open it. Other drones and bishops hacked at the ball with the same lack of success.

While the creatures were concentrating on the feathered ball, Tieran's men took up their positions. "Up!" shouted Tieran. The wings split apart, flapping upwards, dragging Jim upwards to the rafters. The wings grabbed hold of the rafters for support and tucked Jim inside itself, forming a ball again. Several quills struck the feathers and bounced off harmlessly. Tieran stepped over to the drone that fired the quills, pulled his sword and sliced it in two. He turned back to the wings, "Get him out of here—keep him safe."

The wings rattled, let go of the rafters and flew out of the hole in the ceiling that the Chinese warriors fell through. Jim was held tight by the leather straps under the wings as it flapped furiously into the morning's yellow sunlight. It carried him over rooftops and headed towards a nearby apartment building. It gently set him down on the rooftop and then bustled backwards and perched itself higher up on the top of the maintenance shed. It sat silently, dangling its wings below it. Although it had no visible eyes, it appeared to watch him with great interest.

Jim lay on his stomach for a moment, damning himself for not being killed by the beast's club. He rose to his knees and let the tears wash the blood from his face. He couldn't take the emotional pain. It was just too great. He stood up and saw the end of the roof, just a few feet away. "Don't worry baby," said Jim in a shaking voice. "Daddy's coming." With drooped shoulders, he shuffled towards the roof's edge, crying hoarsely.

The wings stirred. When Jim neared the edge, they shot away from the shed and wrapped themselves around him. He kicked and screamed at the wings, but their hold was too strong. The wings opened up and gently glided alongside the beach. It found a likely stretch of unmarked sand with few rocks and again, gently set the man down. It flew upwards and soared over him, floating in the shore breeze.

"Damn you! God...damn...you!" Jim rose up on his knees and wailed in resignation.

The wings jerked suddenly in the wind and made a low pass to check on Jim. Satisfied, it flapped furiously to gain altitude and headed back to the old town.

"Let me guess," said Rothiel in a sarcastic tone. "You and your pathetic army are here to kill me."

Tieran slid his sword back in his back-mounted scabbard and stepped forward. "Not just yet. I still have time to play."

The big creature with the club shuffled directly in front of Rothiel and growled menacingly. Tieran's men stood behind their leader with their faces firm.

Tieran pulled out a butterfly and clicked it to his spool of cable. He swung it in a long, lazy arc near Rothiel, who only regarded it with disinterest. The big creature snatched it out of the air with its clawed hand, after the butterfly wrapped the cable twice around its wrist. The creature laughed it's shrill cry of victory until Tieran sent up a cutting brace that rode the cable all the way to the creature's arm, tightening against the skin. The creature regarded the brace in alarm, just before Tieran pulled the cable taught, popping off the hand with a clean cut. The creature howled in sharp pain up until another loop of cable dropped over his head. It abruptly stopped when it felt another brace slide along the cable to his neck. It gave a short grunt of fear moments before Tieran clipped off it's head. Tieran's men were grinning ear-to-ear from the spectacle.

Rothiel clapped slowly in mock enjoyment. "Well, it's not Ikorsom, but let's see how you perform against something a bit more... *formidable.*"

Tieran looped his cable and smiled. "What do you have in mind?"

Rothiel got up from his chair and kicked it to the side. "A wager. You and your army are obviously here to engage me. I say that you fight me as an incarnation of my choice. We face each other with no use of Origin armor—only materials found on Earth. If I lose, you may do what you wish. If I win, you let me continue to live here on Earth."

"Oh, fuck him." Bob White stepped out of the shadows dragging behind him the fat man from the circus. The man's arms and ankles were shackled. Bob dumped his squirming package on the floor, then fished out a handkerchief and dried off the perspiration from his forehead. "Don't waste any time with this bastard, Tieran. Let's get this over with."

Tieran smiled. "Don't worry. This guy's a push-over."
Tieran looked around the room at the hundreds of creatures swarming over each other in the courtyard. "Can you perhaps, ask your slaves to make some room?"

Rothiel glared silently, seething in anger. He hissed a command and the creatures began exiting towards available windows, doorways and holes in walls. Other than the dead carcasses of the fallen, Rothiel stood as the only opposing threat in the room. "Let me introduce your opponent," said Rothiel, walking to the back of the room. He walked over to a large tapestry hanging from the wall. He grabbed the corner and yanked it down. The tapestry fell to the floor uncovering a massive iron cell, containing a glistening white Jantu worm.

Tieran had practiced daily against them, but they were just simulations. There's no telling what improvements he may have made in them, he thought while fingering his spool of cable. "So you plan to use a Jantu worm then?"

"Well, at least you have your memory," said Rothiel, raising the gate by pulling down on a steel chain. "Remember, no origin weapons or armor. –Make your self ready as I'll be out in a moment." Rothiel only raised the gate a few feet. He ducked underneath it and approached the worm. It began to shake. "Wake up, worm. It's time to feed."

A long, spine from the Jantu rushed out of one of its barnacle-like holes and buried itself into Rothiel's chest. Rothiel seemed to enjoy the feeling as he tipped his head back in a show of ecstasy. The worm retracted the spine and Rothiel's body stayed connected for the ride. When his body slammed into the Jantu's glistening white flesh, he dissolved into it. The Jantu began to squirm around and flash in different colors as Rothiel took over its mind.

Tieran walked over to the center of the courtyard, pulled off his helmet and tossed it to one of his lieutenants. "Grigoy-- Take up a post near Mr. White and ensure no harm comes to him. I'll be done with this in short order."

The Jantu tore the gate off the wall as it charged towards its opponent. Tieran looked up and saw his wings shoot through the hole in the roof and dashed to his aid. He felt the leather straps engage past his ribs just in time and the wings threw him skyward before the worm could run him down. As the wings pumped him over the head of the worm, Tieran connected a butterfly and hurled it towards the worm's head, catching it on the corner of its vertical mouth.

Tieran snatched his starboard reel, connected a like butterfly and threw it downwards towards the worm's belly. It buried itself deep and the worm shrieked its disapproval. It began to roll over the cable to take it out of commission.

Bad move Rothiel, thought Tieran as he linked the two cables and then sent the brace flying towards the intersection to lock them in place. The horizontal roll began to reel up the head, bending the worm in the middle.

Tieran flew down to secure a cable to the floor and two spines shot out, narrowly missing him. He rolled out of the way and the left wing kicked his body out of the way when the third and fourth spines careened towards him. Safely out of distance, Tieran watched in satisfaction how the mouth gnashed at the cable with it's multiple rows of teeth. "Temper temper!"

Rothiel stormed forward in a jerking manner as the slicing cable restricted the Jantu's legs. It turned slightly towards the side and expressed more of it's holes. Tieran saw two that were ejecting small amounts of mucous and knew which ones would be used. He threw a third butterfly towards the middle of the two holes and then ran past the front of the jaws holding the cables tight. The two spines rocketed out and dashed against the floor. Tieran passed the cable through butterfly's eye connected to the thrashing jaws and pulled tight. The pressure angled the worm's body towards where the two spines ejected out. With its body bent, it could not retract them. It began to eject more and more spines out of its opposite side in frustration. The spines crashed into the floor and ceiling, tearing out chunks of brick and tile.

Tieran stood next to the u-bend of the creature in complete safety. It could not eject any spines without hitting itself and could not roll back over since its ejected spines couldn't retract. Tieran pulled out his sword and walked up to the side, just inches where the first of its many hearts pumped. He slipped the sword between the first layer of fat and its external, acid-filled stomach and sliced the beating heart in two. The creature shuddered and shrieked. Red blood ran swiftly out of the hole and Tieran took two steps to the right. He laid his hand upon the gyrating bag of fat and felt. "Now I'm not an expert," said Tieran, guiding the sword between the fat and stomach gland. "But I'm fairly certain, ticker number two is right...about...here!" When he severed the second heart the head turned grey. "I can keep this up all day, Rothiel. Do you want me to pop number three now?"

The worm went still. Tieran could tell that the remaining four hearts had stopped. The flesh near the feet began to putrify and fall apart. It decomposed outwards, leaving a large, oozing cavity. Rothiel sat in the center, groaning and wiping muck from his face. Tieran reached in and grabbed Rothiel by his neck and pulled him out of the carcass. Rothiel tried to speak but Tieran's grip tightened. Tieran pulled him along by his neck and threw him at Bob's feet.

Rothiel coughed and gasped. He turned his face to Bob and tried to speak.

"Save it." Bob fished out the letter that Aaron gave him and he began to read. "Ahem. Rothiel Astasiora, you—again, have been found guilty of rebellion. You are to be held in confinement..."

Rothiel shrieked and tried to grab for Bob's ankles.

Bob pushed his slimy head backwards with a short kick of his shoe. "...Asshole...shit! Gitoff!"

Rothiel covered his head with his hands and begged for clemency.

Bob frowned in distaste and continued reading, "for no less than ten thousand revolutions around the sun, in this..." Bob looked around for a moment in confusion and then back at Tieran. Tieran shrugged.

The middle of the courtyard slowly ruptured pushing large chunks of foundation and clay out of the fissure. Slowly, a large stone ball began to push its way out and came to a stop. A flash of light separated the ball and it began to rotate open, showing a hollow, polished interior.

"Thank you Lord! Right on time too!" Bob continued reading with renewed enthusiasm, "Let's see...ten thou—you know of course this means ten thousand years, right Rothiel? Just checking. Anyways, you are to spend this semi-eternal time with this piece of trash lying behind me. That's right, you will have a guest this time." Bob looked at Tieran and pointed the man on the floor with nod. "Mark Grier. You, like this other worthless sack of shit have been found guilty of rebellion and so on and so forth. Get him outta here."

Two of Tieran's soldiers walked behind Bob and picked up the panicking man and slung him into the ball. Tieran reached down, grabbed Rothiel by his neck and likewise, hurled him inside. The ball closed tight in seconds and began to descend back into the ground. Bob could hear voices screaming inside as it disappeared out of sight. The fissure closed leaving the room entirely silent.

Bob shrugged. "Is that it? Are we done here?"

Tieran chuckled. "That's not what the paper said!"

"It was close enough. Besides, I died to enjoy the afterlife. I've never been through so much stress in my entire existence."

Tieran surveyed the creatures pacing in the shadows. "Well go on and head back—we've got a bit of mopping up left to do."

"You mean the rest of his zoo? Are you going to destroy them all?"

"They're so juiced up on Rothiel's reanimation sauce that it will take them decades to die properly. We're going to hex them into dust and get rid of the remains of the others. We don't want the rest of the planet to think that the Martians have arrived."

Aaron and Cesar walked past the fountain towards the far wall. There was a doorway by itself. "I don't remember a door here," said Cesar. "In fact, there used to be a row of chairs here." He looked over at Aaron and knew who was responsible.

"Last minute decision. No one used those seats anyway." Aaron opened the door and sunshine poured in, making Cesar squint. "C'mon."

The boys walked down the white staircase that overlooked the Atlantic Ocean. Cesar looked behind him and saw that the doorway hung in the sky over the water. The staircase was tall, descending down into the calm morning sea with the brilliant white steps leading to the sandy beach. They walked down to the last step and Aaron sat down and pulled off his shoes. Cesar did likewise and the boys stepped onto the cool beach with naked feet.

"This feels wonderful," said Cesar as he walked next to his friend. "What are we doing here?"

"Us? Nothing!" Aaron laughed. He turned back towards the steps. "They're the ones doing all the work!"

Cesar looked back at the doorway and saw thousands of copies of Aaron bustling down the staircase, each holding one of the small translucent spheres in their small hands. The crowd of Aaron clones continued to swarm past the two boys and head towards the open areas of the beach. The ones that were furthest away dropped to their knees and began dig at the sand.

Aaron pointed to a dark shape further away. "Look who's over there!"

Cesar squinted and saw that it was Jim Smith, on his knees howling at the rising sun. The two boys ran towards him, past all of the Aarons, busily moving the sand into individual heaps. Aaron took the sphere from his pocket and trotted off to an area a few feet from Jim Smith's back. Cesar walked gingerly in front of the softly raving man and looked into his face. He found the look disturbing. He saw complete anguish—it pulled at his heart. "He can't see me, can he?"

Aaron answered from his knees as he worked the sand. "Him? No, we're still invisible."

Cesar stepped around to see what his friend was working on. He was busily sculpting something lying in the sand. Cesar bent down to take a closer look. "Oh wow! That's Elena—it's a perfect copy of her!"

Aaron grinned and bent down over her face. He puckered his lips and blew softly over her nose. A thin layer of sand blew off, revealing the skin of the young girl underneath. The single blow coursed across her entire body blowing away the sand and making her nose wrinkle and her eyelids flutter. She sat up right away and yawned. She saw two boys kneeling on the sand looking at her with bright smiles on their faces.

"She's so beautiful!" said Cesar laughing.

Aaron laughed and dusted the sand off his hands. "Yes, she sure is!"

Elena looked towards the sea and saw a wretched man next to her crying and beating the shore with his fists. "Hola? Hola?"

Jim jerked around in shock and saw hundreds of naked people sitting up on the beach and wiping sand off their bodies. Some were laughing, many more were crying. Many of them began to pray. Sitting in the sand just behind him sat Elena beaming a perfect smile. He didn't waste a single moment--he gathered her in his arms and hugged her, crying swift tears down her back. "Thank you..." was all he could choke out for several minutes.

He eventually realized that she was not going away and that she was truly real. He sat with her on the beach and giggled with her at the thousands that walked the beach looking for their family and friends. Some were modestly trying to cover up their bodies and some just didn't care. Jim knew exactly how they felt. Life was so precious that needless shame just didn't seem to matter.

"Jim! Oh, Jesus Jim!" Jim turned and saw Frank Gutierrez, walking across the sand, holding a discarded sea shell over his crotch. Two rather chubby women were hanging on each arm trying to convince him to get rid of it. "We made it! I don't know how in hell this happened—look at my arm!"

Jim looked at it in a daze and then looked back at Frank. "It looks fine..."

"The tattoo's gone! My U.S.M.C. tattoo is gone!" Frank remembered the girls. "Jim you remember Roberta and Milly—the girls from the Windjammer? We woke up together!"

"Jaime?"

Jim looked up and saw Manoli and Nino, both looked distressed. Manoli stood modestly behind her husband and fought back difficult tears.

"Have you seen our children?"

Jim jumped up and perched Elena on his hip. It was the greatest feeling in the world to have her back again. He didn't know if he'd ever put her down again.

"Yes, they're fine," said Jim nodding. Manoli burst out in tears and hugged Nino, who was also crying. "They're with some friends of mine, keeping them safe."

"*Es un milagro*." Said Manoli. She held out an arm and tickled Elena's belly. "I think that God has touched all of us."

Jim started looking at men's faces to see if he could find anyone from the lodge. He saw a slim young man heading straight towards him. He looked to be in his early twenties and flashed a brilliant smile. "Hiya Jimmy!"

Jim couldn't believe his eyes. "Rip? What does this mean?"

Rip looked down at his body laughing. "I don't know! It sure beats crapping in a diaper though."

"Excuse me gentlemen," both men turned to the see a young woman speaking to them. Besides Jim Smith, she was the only other person on the beach wearing clothes. She was blonde with wavy hair and bright blue eyes. She wore a silver pendant on her neck that was engraved with the sun and moon.

"Theo..." said Rip almost breathlessly.

He grabbed her in his arms for a long kiss.

When he came back for air, she took the scarf off her neck. "See? I brought you something to wear. She placed the scarf around his neck and he began to laugh.

"He looked into her eyes and sighed. "Please tell me that you can stay?"

"She smiled and raised her face to the sky. The sunlight felt wonderful on her skin. "For this lifetime, at least."

Jim at last remembered that he lived only two blocks away. "Hey! Why don't we go to my apartment and get breakfast and something to wear?"

Frank's beefy girlfriends were giggling at Frank's reddening face, as they were able to take his shell away. "Sounds like a great idea," said Frank trying to act natural and deflect interest away from his crotch.

Aaron and Cesar walked back towards the staircase watching the carnival-like atmosphere around them. There wasn't a dry eye or lack of a smile anywhere. They stood upon the white steps and took in one last look of the miracle on Rota beach. Children frolicked near the shore while their parents hugged laughed and cried.

"It was what she most desired," said Aaron, waving to Theo. "I think one more lifetime with her is all Danhieras will be able to stand." He looked at Cesar. "He's a powerful man—I doubt if all his strength will keep him away from her for eternity."

Theo returned the wave to the two boys and returned her head to her lover's shoulder as the two walked towards Jim's apartment.

"Hard to tell," said Cesar. "He isn't just one man, he's part of the lodge. The lodge seems to shore up the weaknesses of some of the men and enhance the greatness in all of them."

Aaron smiled and nodded. As they ascended the staircase towards the floating doorway, the bottom steps began to fade. "Say, isn't today the kite contest?"

Cesar snapped his fingers "Darn! I don't have anything ready!"

"We still have time," said Aaron looking at the height of the sun. "If we get started right away."

"Race you!" Said Cesar dashing up the steps in front of Aaron. "And no cheating!"

Francis Grier moaned in fear as the sphere plummeted through the crust of the Earth to begin their ten-millennia sentence. He felt rough fingers entering his mouth in the pitch-black darkness.

"Stop moving," said Rothiel. "Your teeth are just a small sacrifice for the knowledge that they'll write."

COMING SOON

WICKEDER

Mick Lang

The Foot of Evil

"Ohmigod! You've got to get out before me 'usband comes back!" shrieked Melanoma, jerking herself upwards in bed. She winced, holding her huge pregnant stomach and then blinked around the room.

"Ah." Said her husband Freeks, tying his cravat in front of the mirror. "I see you have awaken." He sighed and went back to tucking the fabric around his fat neck, just under his bushy beard. He was a minister for the Bunionist Church, which leads the land in just another absurd belief that people took hook, line and sinker—usually out of sheer boredom. He shined amongst other clergy—he was gifted with large, swollen bunions on both feet—instrumental in decyphering the will and might of the Unshod God. "There is evil afoot!" remarked Freeks, looking down and wiggling his toes.

"Don't say such 'orrible things on the day yer son is to be born!" yawned Melanoma, sliding her fat bottom off the edge of the bed. She pulled up the bottom fringe of her nightgown around her thighs and squatted over the chamber pot. Her first piss of the day rang out as loud as a horse doing the same over a flat rock. She gratefully busted wind, gripping onto the footboard for support. Something skittered away from her onslaught underneath the bed, which she first thought was another field rat, making itself at home. She peered under the bed and let her eyes get accustomed to the darkness.

"I don't mean in this house," said Freeks as he hitched on his codpiece and checked his profile in the reflection. "My prophetic bunions are never wrong—something bad approacheth." He watched his young wife flop down in front of the bureau and retrieve the silver key from between her hefty bosom. "Why are you writing in your diary before breakfast?" He asked, grabbing his cane by the doorway.

She noticed him watching and kept it locked. "I... can tell that this is the day our son arrives, so I want to write about how I feel this morning—that's all." She smiled and giggled, then reached for a quill and dipped it into the ink well.

He pondered what she said. "Well... if you think you'll have the baby today, I can delay my ministering—"

She dropped her diary and shot to her feet, knocking over the lava lamp on the side of the table with her belly. "Nonsense!" She bellowed.

She trudged over and gave Freeks a peck on the cheek before spinning him around and shoving him to the front door. "People are sinners! They need your divine guidance!"

He was halfway manhandled out the front door, trying to hold on to the doorframe. "But, you haven't made me breakfast yet!"

She launched him out the door with her thick foot buried in his backside. He landed spread-eagle in the dirt with his bare feet raised in the air. When he rolled over, looking at her with consternation, she tossed two granola bars onto his belly and slammed the door shut. She bolted the door and yelled through the mail slot, "In my delicate state? I must rest, my darling. Go forth and save the world!"

Freeks stood and stuffed both bars in his jacket pocket. She was right. His job was to enlighten the masses against evil and treachery. The Unshod God would watch over his chaste woman. He struck both bunions with his hard cane to start the pulsing pain of providence and down the lane he strode towards the bustling town of Trash Pickings.

Melanoma, smiling, sashayed back to the bureau and flopped back down on the wood chair. She opened her diary to the first page, labeled in bold script, '*All The Men I've Fucked*' and sighed. There were about twenty different dates on each page, followed by a unique name. She then flipped through dozens of pages until she arrived at the entry with the name Freekspoor Throp. His name was just below William Clinton's and just above O.J. Simpson's. She had waited a full three days following her wedding before moving on to O.J. She picked up the pen and began flipping pages so she could make a new entry. She was surprised by the amount of pages that had been completed, as she steadily worked her way to the back of the diary. *Bullocks*, she thought. *Only one page left—I'm going to need a new book.* She cleared her throat and asked, "So what's yer name then love?"

From under the bed, a timid voice spoke, "Is he gone fer good then?"

"Oh don't mind him," she said giggling. "He's off to save the world from the usual evils—you know, for'ners, 'omo sexuals and chimney sweeps."

"My name's Burton Sod."

Melanoma retrieved the quill from the inkpot and drew his name in her flowery script. "Occupation dear?"

"Um. Chimney sweep."

She had long since stopped adding codes such as B.T.F., which stood for 'Bigger Than Freeks'. They all were.

She would give the chimney sweep another hard flogging before she had her breakfast, but then her mind wandered about the baby. She began to think about dear Tranny — what was the song she would sing about babies?

Born early morning;
Struck o'er the head, the baby will begin snoring;
Born just around noon;
Bastard kid will be hungry soon (better hit it again to make sure);
Born late at night;
Tripping over wine bottles/higher than a kite;
Born at 1:00 a.m.;
Nothing but shit on TV, amen!

The Cock of the Time Dragon

Freeks' mind spun with worry about Melanoma's condition. His feet padded over the dirt trail as he marched towards the sinners of Trash Pickings, all the while preoccupied with the impending birth of his first son.

He saw a wooden sign swinging from a hut near the Swillwater river that read, "L.J. Silvers, Fishmonger" and tapped his cane on the wood door.

A grimy man opened the door with a scowl, wiping fish guts from his hands into his soiled apron. "Whad'ye want?"

Freeks stood straight and announced in his superior voice, "I am Reverend Freekspoor—just down the road from you and my wife is pregnant..."

The fishmonger's face was struck with horror. "It ain't mine, mate!"

"You mis-understand my good man. She is ready to deliver any moment and duties of the Unshod God call me away." For good measure, Freeks motioned with his nose towards his feet. He wiggled his toes in his lordly way when the fishmonger took notice. "Would you perhaps have a goodly woman who may watch over her?"

The fishmonger looked relieved, although rivulets of sweat continued to appear on his forehead.

"Me wife and 'er mother will look in on 'er," said the fishmonger backing into his hut. "Wife! Wake your mother and go over to the preacher's 'ouse—yer to 'elp 'er crap out 'er brat!"

Freeks nodded in appreciation and turned back towards Trash Pickings. He felt relieved, knowing that his wife was in good hands.

He walked until he was in an isolated area, with no prying eyes to see. He sat upon an old stump and opened the large pocket of his jacket, pulling out a copy of *Altar Boys Monthly*. The cover displayed an altar boy lighting a candle with a coy look on his face and adorned in frilly lace. Inside the cover was a letter, written by his cousin, Reverend Mike Jackson:

Brother Freekspoor, I hope you like the latest edition of ABM...I don't know, there's just something about the lighting and soft lens that Guccione used...

I digress. I write about something of grave importance. The Cock of the Time Dragon. The Cock itself is mounted on a massive self-propelled wagon. There are an abundance of cocks to be seen in these parts, but this cock is so tall that it casts a shadow over all Tush Margarine. On the head, sits a mechanical dragon with metallic scaly skin and large leathery wings.

Freeks thought about how ghastly an enormous cock would be. He wondered how his parishioners would react by seeing such a foul thing advancing towards them.

The Dragon began to move and pointed his wing at a shy and retiring man named Grime who sported a black postage stamp-sized moustache. The crowd became hushed. Then the other wing pointed to the widow, Lotta and her Goth daughter, all dressed in black with matching combat boots. The crowd gasped. The mouth of the Cock opened and a stream of bubbles flew out of it while a small door opened at the base. A sock puppet appeared in the doorway with a crudely sewn felt mustache.
A woman in the crowd gasped, "It's him!" and fainted on the spot. Men fell upon Grime and killed him in a frenzy, as they were so struck by the technical wizardry in front of them. The sock puppet stopped, as if thrown off from its act and the door promptly closed. Another door opened near the first and two puppets, a tall yellow one with an angry expression and the other orange with a more rounder countenance, were bickering about who left cookie crumbs in Burt's bed. "It's them!" shrieked another in the crowd and the crowd equally slaughtered the widow and her daughter. Can you imagine such horrors, O brother Freeks? This Cock of the Time Dragon must be a creation of the devil... or at least by the PBS. You must remain vigilant!

Freeks knew that his parishioners were the superstitious sort who would believe any ravings from fortunetellers, chicken bones thrown into the dirt or the internet. He would reassure his congregation not to fall into the trap of mechanical imagery and to let faith triumph over technology. He delicately folded the letter into the pages of his smut magazine and stuck it back into his pocket with a final pat of reassurance. He had sinners to see to. He redoubled his pace towards

Trash Pickings and to confront his destiny; to give that huge Cock a taste of his own medicine.

The Wirth of a Bitch

It was early evening by the time the storm arrived in Trash Pickings. That storm was named Freeks and was full of destructive energy. He stood in the town square, red-faced and scowling at passers-by.

Polly, the flower girl, curtsied and said, "Good evening to you, kind pastor."

Freeks responded in kind. Good evening to you, you... you dirty little pandering WHORE! Did it ever occur to you that flowers that you peddle are the crotches of the plant world?"

Polly looked horrified. Tears began to well up in her eyes and Freeks pushed past her looking for more people to rile up in religious fervor. "You there! Fishermen! Did you catch anything today?"

The fishermen, who were mending their nets from a sore day's work, shook their heads in disappointment.

"It's because the fish were frightened!" said Freeks hautily.

Hampie, looked up from his net in curiosity. "Frightened? Of what, may I ask?"

Freeks made a circle between his thumb and forefinger and used the index finger of his other hand to drive home his point on each syllable. "From dir-ty bug-ger-ing sail-ors like your-selves! Your thoughts of sodomy, your feelings of breech loading your partner over there—don't look offended, you were thinking it! My God—you didn't use your nets at all did you—you went *pole* fishing instead, didn't you?"

Before Hampie could get up off the dock and lunge at Freeks, the preacher had wisely spun and began working his talents on infirm beggars and old widows lining up to buy day-old bread. "Devil worshippers! Whores of Babylon! Scientologists!"

Eventually, a crowd formed, angrily denouncing Freeks ravings. Freeks composed himself and stood, gripping his lapels. "You all don't like what you've just heard, do you?"

The crowd simmered in its anger as Freeks began to pace.

"In just a bit more time, the truly righteous will be calling you by those *proper* names, for temptation comes!"

"What are ye on about then?" asked Pollup, the caretaker of the local orphanage, whom Freeks had just moments ago called 'an anus fingerer on steroids'. "What temptation?"

Freeks pointed to the black sky behind him and shrieked, "Why, the Cock of the Time Dragon!"

The crowd gasped and began to murmur amongst themselves.

"Ye mean it's coming here," said Pollup, nervously fingering his collar. "Tonight?"

"As we speak!" grinned Freeks in a diabolical way, which he believed was mimicry of the inner souls before him. "...And if ye don't repent now, that enormous Cock will set upon you all!"

A deep rumbling sound was heard approaching Trash Pickings.

Old women with lust painted on their faces, darted past Freeks shoulder-to-shoulder on their way to get a glimpse of the approaching tower of ardor. Children ran into the square horrified. "It's coming! It's coming!"

"GAWK! GAWK! GAWK!" thundered through the sky, freezing people in their tracks. The noise was ear splitting.

"GAWK! GAWK! GAWK! BAA-GUUUCK!" Over the square's torch lights an enormous mechanical rooster head loomed over the town with its beak moving up and down. "BAA-GUUUCK!"

Freeks was speechless. It dawned on him that all this fear about an approaching sex organ on its way to defile his flock was just a bit over-stated. He had to think quickly on his feet. He would discount this bizarre mechanical chicken as mere technical hooey and try to display it as a pale imitation of the true power of faith.

The rooster's wagon lumbered to the town square without aid of horse or beast of burden. It came to a stop and steam hissed out from valves underneath. The beak opened one last time and a final siren scream of "BAA-GUUUCK!" echoed across Trash Pickings. The Cock had arrived.

The animatronic Cock stood at least sixty feet high. White synthetic feathers rippled in the gentle breeze all the way down to the massive cart underneath. If it had feet, they were tucked underneath, as if it was resting. The beak was closed and the eyelids ceased opening and closing. There was a noise of gears whirring and pistons moving about from somewhere in the inside. In the front of the cart was a small stage, ringed with chrome levers and rows upon rows of candy-colored buttons and dials of all sizes. There was a long mechanical groan coming from the back and the tail feathers began to rise up. A hatch opened with a loud hydraulic hum under the bird's anus and a dwarf stepped out, dressed in a white laboratory coat with black boots and wearing black gloves. He had red hair that was parted on the side and wore large black-framed spectacles. There were yellow signs on the inside of the room warning of radiation exposure and a flashing yellow beacon spun just over a sign that read, 'No Admittance. This means YOU Dee Dee!' He walked to the front of the Cock and bowed low to the crowd.

Freeks seized his opportunity and jumped onto the front stage of the cart. "This mechanical bird isn't anything divine! Why, 'tis nothing but decoration!"

"Hey! Jou!" Shouted the dwarf with a thick Germanic accent. "Jou get down from there! Jou haff no idea vat you are do-ink!"

"Haw!" Chortled Freeks, at the dwarf. "You don't want these people to see what this really is-- nothing but smoke and mirrors. You want to frighten them. You want them to cower—" Freeks pulled one of the levers.

A chrome gatling gun emerged from the front of the cart and began to spin.

TUM-TUM-TUM-TUM-TUM-TUM-TUM!

The people standing closest in front of the stage were churned to hamburger. Others nearby were spattered with blood and flecks of human tissue. Freeks let go of the lever as if it were an animal that bit his hand. The gun slowed to a stop, spilling acrid smoke upwards into the black sky. He pointed a shaky finger at the dwarf. "S-s-see what this short bastard's evil did to those poor people?"

The crowd surged forward and pulled Freeks down from the stage. He was thrown to the muddy ground and was kicked and stomped on.

"Peepull!" Shouted the dwarf taking center stage. "Jou must shtaaap wis der kicking und pounching already!"

The crowd turned and watched the little man step over the control panel. Freeks took his queue to retrieve his exposed smut magazine and crawl away to safety. He hid behind some smelly crab traps and massaged his aching belly.

"I am Dexturr! I haff come hierr to show jou zum tings dat zat religuss nut did not vant jou to see. Hierr is der eggshample uf der teach-inks uf his Unshott Gott!"

Dexturr pushed a green button and a window slid open at the base of the Cock. Filling the doorway was a round, opaque sheet of glass. It began to glow. An image of a purple dinosaur filled the screen dancing among children. It began to sing:

"I love you, you love me..."

The crowd's cries were hysterical and desperate. They clamped their hands firmly to the sides of their heads and wailed at the insanity tickling their eardrums and shut fast their eyes from the visual perversion that emanated from the doorway.

My God, Thought Freeks, peering from behind the crab traps. *That thing is evil of the highest order.*

Dexturr was shocked by the crowd's reaction and was fearful that he'd end up with a mass murder on his gloved hands. He rotated a dial and changed the video to a 70's commercial of a blonde woman in her living room rubbing a rose on her cheek.

"...Mammothdrill Douches come in two delightful fragrances. Rose Petal," She began to work the flower into her face in a most orgasmic way and then let it drop to the floor. She picked up a silver platter loaded with dark food. *"...And our always-popular, liver and onions."* She picked up a handful of the meat and veg and began to rub it sloppily down her neck and cleavage with eyes spilling over with desire.

The crowd was unnerved by what they saw and they rubbed their arms to recover from the cold feeling that produced an epidemic of goose pimples. "What did all that mean?" asked Pollup as discomfort washed over him.

Dexturr cleared his throat. "Zat... um... represented zum of die pahlicies uf die relijuss esdablishhment. Iff jou follow die nincompoops like der priest, jou vill ent up mit leaders sudge ass her!" He grimaced and in exasperation raised his fists into the air. "She vill break all your inventshuns unt make jour lives horreeebil."

The crowd stood still with blank looks on their faces.

10

Dexturr shifted uncomfortably on the stage. "Zo, maybe jou shult go und, I don't know, burning down hiss haus?"

The crowd's war cry was instantaneous. They fanned out and grabbed anything that they could wield to cave in Freeks' skull and snapped up the torches from the town square. Freeks stifled a yelp, slid a filthy crab trap over his head and stood still.

Back in Freekspoor manor, Melanoma was politely asking the fishmonger's wife if childbirth was as painful as they say.

"Keep on chewing up those BinLaden leaves my dearie," said the fishmonger's wife, as her drunken Grandmother crept up behind the headboard with a log behind her back. "You'll be out in no time." Grandmother got in position and raised the log over her head.

Melanoma kept chewing the bitter-tasting leaves. "So, (yuck), this will make me fall asleep?"

The fishmonger's wife nodded and said, "No, but it will reduce the swelling—Now!"

Her grandmother swung the log down onto Melanoma's forehead, belting her skull backwards into the pillow. Her eyes were crossed and half of the green BinLadin leaves were spattered on her chest along with one of her molars.

"It's not true," said the grandmother, tossing the log back into the fireplace. "All it does is make you dream of 70 virgins, sodomit'in other men in caves and all that."

They both leaped into coordinated action, tearing the cabin apart looking for valuables and fine linens. "It's just not fair," said the grandmother, stuffing her pockets with cutlery. "We're stuck with her and we can't even get a glimpse of the gigantic Cock they say is coming to town."

The door burst open and Polly the flower-pimp ran inside. "Quick! You must get out of here before the crowd arrives!"

The fishmonger's wife was piling several hats on top of her head and asked, "What are ye on about then? What's so urgent that we hafta leave?"

Polly was shocked to see the sleeping form of Melanoma.

Melanoma mumbled weakly, "Must...kill...Jews."

"BinLadin leaves?" Asked Polly.

The grandmother nodded and slid perfume bottles into a burlap sack.

"Good," said Polly. "She's probably just halfway through explosives preparation or small arms training." Then Polly remembered why she came. "Listen! The town—they're all in a ruckus because of that Cock and now they want to burn down the preacher's house!"

"We're done!" said the fishmonger's wife with a jewelry box under one arm and armload of fine clothes in the other. "Let's get out of here then."

"You can't just... leave her!" said Polly protesting. "I may end up going to hell for what I've done to those poor flowers, but I'm not going to let her go up in flames!" She ran outside and pushed up a cart half-filled with dried-up ears of corn. "We'll stick her in here and wheel her out to the forest!"

The grandmother, fishmonger's wife and the flower girl shoved the corn cart down the rough road towards Trash Pickings. They hoped to sneak into Farmer Clinton's barn and deliver Melanoma's baby in safety. Grandmother also hoped to score some of the farmer's choice *Rebel Yell* marijuana that would knock you on your ass and make your puke taste like angel food cake.

Polly heard an angry crowd approaching from up ahead. "Quick! Let's push her into the Rankin Bass graveyard!" The public, for fear of forced syndication, never visited that particular graveyard. The women passed by headstones marked, 'Little Drummer Boy', a sinister-looking one owned by 'Berger Meister, Meister Berger' and various toy-maker elves, one of which was a dentist. They passed by Yukon Cornelius' gravestone, upon which was etched,

Yukon 'Red' Cornelius

Here lies 'ol Yukon,
A man of glory, grit and grace.
He pulled the teeth of Bumbles
and spent a lot of time attached to its face.

In the mist ahead was the outline of a massive Rooster sitting upon a cart, slumbering. They continued forward apprehensively until they realized that no one was there. It was silent, with no sign of Dexturr anywhere. The back hatch was closed. There was a red light blinking softly.

Polly walked up and looked at the door. A woman's voice chimed out of a small speaker. "Please give the correct password, sir." Polly tried to remember what the dwarf said when she saw him enter the Cock after the townspeople left. She approached the door and cleared her throat. "Um. My sister's a bitch?"

"Welcome back, Dexturr." Said the voice, pleasantly. The door hissed outwards and lights began to blink to life inside the massive recess.

The women dragged Melanoma's corn-infested body inside and slid her onto a medical bed that was located underneath a massive probe suspended from the ceiling. The tip of the probe was a foot away from her belly and fanned out to a massive structure that took up most of the ceiling.

Grandmother was walking around gazing at the knobs and buttons, looking for something valuable to steal.

"Better not to touch anything," groaned the fishmonger's wife. "I don't like the look of this hocus-pocusy stuff."

"I'm just looking fer the kitchen's all." Said grandmother. She saw a button that she thought would produce ham. It was called 'Gamma Shot'. She pushed the button.

The lights began to dim and machinery began to whine. The women banded together nervously. Polly shouted over the din, "What have you done!"

Grandmother kept pushing the button to turn it off. "Hell, I don't know — it says Gammon or something. I don't know what in tarnation it's up to!" The women were oblivious to the white target of light that was illuminating Melanoma's stomach.

The whine of machinery grew louder until the women were holding their hands to their heads. An arc of light began to sputter from the probe until a steady lighting bolt shot from the tip, directly into Melanoma's belly. The women's horrified faces were illuminated from the intense light as the plasma shook and pulsated. White kernels of popped corn sputtered out of Melanoma's filthy nightgown.

Melanoma was shrieking loudly, "ALLAHU AKBAR! ALLAHU AKBAR!"

The beam cut off after a few seconds and the lights of the laboratory came back on. The women nervously approached Melanoma, crunching popcorn under their shoes. Their faces were stained with apprehension whether Melanoma was still alive. Polly opened the front of her nightgown, and saw that her belly was bright pink.

Melanoma's eyes shifted under her eyelids in keeping with a bad dream. "By Allah... I must have pork...maybe the men... won't see me if a sneak a little into my tent..." Her face grimaced momentarily in strain and her butt jerked upwards in one quick heave followed by a loud squishing noise. Between her legs a newborn baby glistened under the fluorescent lights.

Polly reached down and gently picked her up. "It's a girl!"

The baby was breathing, but kept her eyes closed from the harsh light. She began to suckle her thumb. Grandmother sneered. "It ain't right! All bastards need to cry some when they come into this cruel world. Why should she enjoy an easy ride? Give her to me then."

Polly gently handed the baby over to grandmother. "Be careful, we still need to tie off her umbilical."

"All in good time. Welcome to Mudskinland, girlie. Let's hear you howl some!" Grandmother rolled the baby over her forearm and gave her a solid whack on her bottom.

The baby's face contorted in pain and she screwed up her eyebrows in anger.

Grandmother looked confused. "Maybe she's a mute." She gave her another stiff whack.

The baby began to shake and her skin rippled. Her pallor began to shift in color from a healthy pink to a sour green. "AAAARRRRGH!" shrieked the baby and spun around in grandmother's arms. The baby's soft, chubby body hardened to thick muscle and her tiny hands reached for grandmother's throat. She tried to get purchase on the woman's turkey neck but her hands were too small, so she whipped her own umbilical around the woman's neck and began to strangle her while stomping on her abdomen. "AAAARRGH!"

Polly was terrified. She tried to coax the bright green baby away from grandmother, who in turn was turning a soft hue of blue. "Look at the pretty flower! Here! Want to hold the pretty flower?"

The baby snatched away the flower, bit off the rose's bloom and began striking at Polly with the thorny stem. "GA! GA! GAAAAA!"

Polly shrieked with each stinging stroke of the stem. The baby was gripping onto Polly's dress with a strong fist and whipping her with the other.

Grandmother at least could breathe again. She pulled off the umbilical and began crawling steadily for the door.

The fishmonger's wife pulled out her trusty fillet knife and held it with the blade pointing downward. She lunged at the baby and rammed it hard between the baby's shoulder blades. The blade snapped off on impact.

The two of them froze. The baby slowly turned to look at the fishmonger's wife and then down to the broken blade lying on the computer floor. Pure rage set in.

Outside in the graveyard's morning sun, the massive Cock bucked back and forth as pandemonium ensued from the inside. The newborn was spinning the fishmonger's wife around the lab by her ankles and letting her go at bulky machinery in her trajectory. The baby hurled monitors, power supplies and miles of cable at the hysterical women who cowered near the door.

"How do we get this fucking door open?" said Grandmother out of her swollen mouth as she looked at Polly through her remaining good eye.

Her question was answered when the baby tore a red girder out of the ceiling and charged the women with a makeshift battering ram. The heavy hatch was freed from its hinges as if made from tissue paper and the three women exploded outwards into the graveyard.

They helped each other get up from the moist ground and limp back to their homes.

The baby stood, growling in the doorway while gripping her girder. She dropped it and yawned. She began to tire and her muscles began to return to their normal size. With the last of her strength, she crawled up on the bed and to her mother's breast and began to suckle. Her skin remained green.

"Achmed…" murmured Melanoma in her fitful sleep. "I see… how you look at me. I want… you to polish my… Kalashnikov."

.   .   .

In the early 1970's my grandfather, R. W. Smith walked up to see what I was looking at.

I was crouched down on his sidewalk, watching ants as they marched their purposeful way, one behind the other.

"Mickey, what're you looking at?"

"Ants. Lots of 'em. Why aren't they scared of me?"

He crouched down next to me and watched for a while. "They can't see us."

He brought a finger down and gently touched one. It reacted explosively, scurrying about in a frantic way. Other ants nearby the first began acting in a similar fashion.

Although now apparently terrified, they continued running amok around my feet.

"I think they still can't see me. I'm huge compared to them."

My grandfather laughed and pointed towards the sky. "Imagine what huge, scary things are just up there that we cannot see."

Mick Lang

Made in the USA
Charleston, SC
01 February 2013